WISH ME LUCK
AS YOU WAVE ME
GOODBYE

ALSO BY MARIUS GABRIEL

The Original Sin
The Mask of Time
A House of Many Rooms
The Seventh Moon
The Testament of Marcellus
Gabon

WISH ME LUCK AS YOU WAVE ME GOODBYE

MARIUS GABRIEL

LAKE UNION
PUBLISHING

Text copyright © 2015 Marius Gabriel

Published by Lake Union Publishing, Seattle

www.apub.com

Amazon, the Amazon logo, and Lake Union Publishing are trademarks of Amazon. com, Inc., or its affiliates.

ISBN-13: 9781503945227
ISBN-10: 1503945227

Cover design by Lisa Horton

Printed in the United States of America

For Mervat

1.
FELICITY

Spain, Winter, 1936

'You're not listening to a word I say.' Isobel was standing at the front window of the little cottage, her arms folded on her breast. She looked, as Felicity so often thought her eldest sister looked, like Napoleon contemplating invisible armies.

'I am listening, darling,' Felicity replied.

'You're barely nineteen. You haven't even started to live. My God! Look at you! You're so bright, so fresh and young! Why do you want to throw these precious gifts away?'

'I don't intend to throw any of my gifts away.'

'You'll bestow them on the claws of a bunch of dried-up old harpies, which is the same thing. You weren't born to waste your days in some dreary convent. You were born to live life!'

'When I look around me, I don't see very encouraging examples of what life has to offer.'

Isobel frowned. 'How can you say such a thing to me?'

'Oh, my dear,' Felicity said remorsefully, 'forgive me. I didn't mean it like that.'

'You're so maddeningly smug. You don't know what it is to lose a child. To lose your home. To have your husband run away. How could you? You know nothing about anything.' Isobel opened the shutters of the window and leaned out. The sullen boom of artillery rolled across the valley to them. 'The fighting's getting closer. And we're trapped here. Sooner or later they're going to drop a shell on our roof and that'll be the end of us both.' She shook her head, talking almost to herself. 'I stayed here too long. I should have gone to Germany when Paul died. It would have been better than staying on here like a ghost, trying to pretend I still had anything to live for. And now I'm saddled with you.' She turned to Felicity. 'What on earth did you come here for?'

'To say goodbye, dearest. I'm going into the convent next month. And to discuss my property. When I enter the priory, I have to make over everything I own to the Order.'

'Oh, yes, of course,' Isobel said dryly. 'Your dowry. How clever of them to insist on that.'

'However,' Felicity pressed on, before Isobel could say anything inflammatory, 'I want you to have Mummy's jewellery. The emeralds, in particular. As the oldest sister, you should have had them in any case.'

'I don't want the damned things.'

'If you like, you can share them with Chiara.'

'Chiara's quite comfortable enough. She's got her flat in Mayfair, her nice little job, her happy little life.'

'Then you have them.' A particularly loud explosion made everything in the room rattle. 'Come away from the window, darling.' She reached out her hands to Isobel as her sister came forward. 'I haven't brought them with me, of course. I've put them in a safe deposit at Harrods in London. I've left the key—'

'Oh, damn the jewels. Stop talking about them. What do I care for them? I only care for you. I won't stop trying to talk you out of this.'

'I'll listen. Only, don't abuse God.'

'You might ask God to stop abusing me.'

'I will ask him. Let's close the shutters, I'm nervous.' The sisters closed the heavy wooden shutters, restoring the room to its semi-darkness.

The cottage was simple, with whitewashed stone walls and a clay-tile floor. Bunches of herbs and two dead rabbits hung from the exposed oak beams. The few sticks of furniture were home-made and painted in the brown which results from mixing the leftovers of several tins. Against one wall was a tiny cottage piano, its lid open, its yellowed keys like uneven teeth. A battered copper bath had been pulled up in front of the fire, where a cauldron was heating.

The sisters were not superficially alike. Isobel, now twenty-five, had the full figure, dark eyes and olive skin of their mother, who had been one of the great society beauties of the 1920s. Anyone looking at her felt that here was a woman of the world. Isobel had done so much – politics (she was a journalist who had written dozens of articles praising Fascism), marriage (though her wealthy Falangist husband had turned out to be a rotter), and motherhood (though her only child had tragically died at a year old).

Felicity, by contrast, seemed to be a woman very much *not* of the world. With her long legs, high waist and almost imperceptible breasts, Felicity was like a medieval angel, her face glowing, her blonde hair cascading over one shoulder like a sheaf of ripe wheat. Her feelings of love for her God were more intense than Isobel – who had already embarked on Life in a big way, as her sister had not – could readily accept.

Felicity was six years younger than Isobel. She had worshipped Isobel from infancy, this powerful, darkly beautiful, dominant sister of hers; and in many ways she worshipped her still. Isobel was brimful with emotions. She burned like a dark flame, her appetite for life insatiable. She devoured everything that came her way, misery and joy, with the same avidity. Beside her, Felicity had always felt insubstantial.

There was a third sister, Chiara, who came between them in age. Chiara was the only balanced one, the perfect combination of action and repose, the middle child, insulated by an elder and a younger sister from the double tragedy of their parents' deaths, one following three short years after the other.

3

Regarded as the only sane Redcliffe girl, Chiara was not given to extremes of any kind. When she was around, the three of them were in balance. Felicity missed her now, missed the good humour and practical wisdom that she brought. With Chiara, there was always release in laughter. But she was now in London, immersed in the whirl of one of the gayest seasons since the end of the Great War.

Felicity said, 'I wish Chiara were here. She always stops us from fighting.'

'You mean she always takes your side.'

'She's the most sensible of all of us. I would so love us to be all together one last time.'

'One last time?' Isobel repeated. 'Can't we even visit you once you're incarcerated?'

'The mistress of novices explained to me—'

'*The mistress of novices,*' Isobel cut in mockingly. 'What a very evocative title.'

'She explained to me that family visits can be counterproductive, especially during the first three years. A novice has to shut off from her mind everything external so that she can apprehend God in the very centre of her soul.'

'What rubbish.' Isobel's temper, as well as her voice, was rising. 'I can't bear to see you burying yourself in a graveyard for mouldering virgins. You don't care for anything except your own superstitions.'

'I care for you and Chiara more than anything in the world,' she said. 'But I don't want to be in the world. I want to dedicate my life to God.' She held out her hand to Isobel. 'You know as little about God as I do about Life. *You're* the one full of superstitions. You've never even set foot in a convent. It's not a graveyard where virgins go to moulder, but a place of light and peace and joy—'

'Rubbish!' Isobel grasped Felicity's fingers and twisted them cruelly. For a moment they grappled, as they had done in the nursery;

then, as always, Felicity yielded with a cry of pain, her face crumpling. Isobel was never content with winning a battle of words – and as a journalist, she had an unfair advantage – she also had the ability to reduce all arguments to a physical trial of strength which she almost always won. Isobel fitted a cigarette into her ebony holder and lit up, exhaling a blue cloud into the rafters. 'Impertinent insect.'

Felicity nursed her fingers. 'You belong in England, among your own people.'

'That vapid generation of bores and weaklings? No, thank you. If I went anywhere, I'd go to Berlin, to Hitler. He's the only decent man left in the world.'

'We're not all bores and weaklings. Come home with me.'

Angrily, Isobel brushed away the tears that had suddenly appeared on her eyelashes. 'Losing Paul killed me, Fee.'

'Please don't say that!'

'It's true. I will never get him back. I'll never be the person I was. It's all hollow, now.' Compassionately, Felicity put her arms around Isobel. 'Even if I wanted to go back to London,' Isobel said, enduring the embrace impatiently, 'how do you suggest I get there? Has it escaped your attention that we're surrounded by the Reds?'

'We could ask them to let us through their lines. I'm sure they would do that.'

'After they'd all taken turns raping us.'

'They wouldn't.'

'They bloody well would. You don't know Communists like I do. And if they found out who I was, they'd put me up against a wall. You shouldn't have come here. All you've done is give me something else to worry about. I just hope Franco breaks through their lines and liberates us without blowing us all to buggery. We're stuck here for the time being. At least it's keeping you out of your nunnery.'

In the past few moments, they had become aware of a commotion outside the cottage. Now they heard Manuela's voice raised in anger, and then the heart-stopping sound of a shot. Both women froze.

The door burst open. Felicity stifled a scream as a soldier in uniform came into the room, dipping his head under the low door lintel. Behind him marched Manuela, Isobel's maid-of-all-work, holding a shotgun at his back.

'He came all the way from America to steal our vegetables!' Manuela's fat face was florid with anger and triumph. 'Two of them, bold as brass! Pulling up our cabbages!'

'Where's the other one? You haven't killed him, have you?' Isobel asked.

'He ran like a rabbit. But he's got all our vegetables in a sack.'

'Tell her to put the damned gun down,' the soldier growled.

'You deserve to be shot,' Isobel said crisply. 'You're a thief.'

'We thought the place was abandoned,' he said sullenly. 'The windows are all boarded up.'

'The windows are boarded up because we don't care to have our throats cut by Anarchists.'

'I'm not an Anarchist.' Though his face was blackened with firing and spattered with mud, Felicity could see that he was in his twenties, obviously one of the hundreds of idealistic young men from all over the globe who had answered the Spanish Republic's plea for help against Franco. 'Tell her to put the shotgun down.'

'So you can rape us?'

'I don't want to rape you.'

'We must really have lost our bloom, Felicity,' Isobel said dryly.

The soldier looked uncomfortable. 'I didn't mean—' Groping for words, he found none.

Isobel took the shotgun from Manuela and walked around the soldier, studying him from head to toe as though he were some strange new animal. 'Name and rank?'

'Lieutenant William Willoughby.'

'Fill the bath for Lieutenant Willoughby, Manuela.'

Manuela began pouring buckets of steaming water into the copper hip-bath. 'Are you planning on drowning me?' the soldier asked ironically.

'Perhaps. I take it from your freedom with other people's property that you are a Communist.'

The man's eyes followed Isobel as she prowled around him with the gun. 'I'm not very political.'

'There is a hammer and sickle on your uniform.'

'That's the insignia of my brigade.'

'You crawled out of some Bowery slum, I presume?'

'As a matter of fact I was a teacher in Massachusetts.'

'A teacher of what?'

'Of English literature.'

'What possessed you to volunteer for someone else's war? Were you so eager to lose your life?'

'Somebody has to stop the Fascists,' he replied evenly.

Isobel's eyes narrowed. 'Do they, indeed? And so you left your wife and children weeping in Massachusetts.'

'I'm not married.'

'Ah. An excellent reason to seek death. You're a model of human folly, Lieutenant Willoughby. Allow me to introduce you to my sister, Felicity, who is another. You should get along like a house on fire.'

The man glanced at Felicity. 'Your sister is crazy.'

'I know,' Felicity said.

Isobel smiled thinly. 'Lieutenant Willoughby, undress.'

'What?'

'Undress quickly.'

'Isobel,' Felicity said quietly, 'don't be absurd.'

'I am not being absurd. You wanted to see what a Communist looks like. Do as I say, Lieutenant.'

'I refuse.'

'Do you think I would hesitate to shoot you?'

He met her eyes and saw something in them that made him begin, with great reluctance, to take off his uniform. 'If this is your idea of a game, I've heard funnier ones.'

'Hurry up.'

He unbuckled his belt and unbuttoned his tunic. 'Not the underclothes.'

'The underclothes, especially.'

He hesitated, but the twin muzzles of Isobel's shotgun did not waver. He stripped naked, revealing a wiry, athletic body with a runnel of black hair, stark against his white skin from his chest down to his loins. There were several dark bruises on the pale skin. He made no attempt to cover his sex, but looked Isobel in the eye. Feeling hot all over, Felicity turned away. 'Isobel, this is beyond a joke.'

Isobel was examining him with frank interest. 'At least he's not the usual undernourished slum-bred specimen. And it stops us from scratching each other's eyes out for an hour. Get in the bath. Manuela, see what you can do with the uniform.'

Grinning, Manuela carted off his uniform to the kitchen. Seeing his clothes removed from the scene, Willoughby lowered himself into the steaming bath.

Isobel put the shotgun down at last and took the tin jug from the shelf. She poured hot water over the soldier's head.

'Why are you doing this?' he spluttered.

'For the same reason that I would bath a puppy that had been rolling in dirt.'

'I hope you're amusing yourself.'

'So far you're only a distraction. You haven't reached the level of an amusement. Felicity, the soap.'

Felicity passed Isobel the soap and watched as her sister began to lather the man's head, neck and muscular shoulders. Even by

8

Isobel's standards, this was a freakish prank. But somehow, she found herself laughing at the sheer madness of it.

'Tell us about her,' Isobel commanded.

'Who?' the soldier replied.

'Who do you think? The woman who wouldn't marry you and who has sent you to your death.'

He wiped soap out of his eyes. 'She didn't send me. I came of my own free will.'

'Nonsense. If she was a Red Indian she would have taken your scalp. As it is, she'll wear a dainty black ribbon when she hears you've been blown to pieces. She'll cry for a whole hour and eligible bachelors will crowd round her with boxes of chocolate.'

'Where did you learn to be so cruel?' he asked.

'Unlike you, I am married.' She showed him the gold wedding ring on her left hand. 'It's a good school for cruelty. You don't suppose I would be scrubbing your back if I were single?'

'I don't see how your being married makes it any more decent.'

'Then you must have a very low opinion of women's fidelity.'

'Where is your husband?'

She scrubbed his broad back vigorously enough to make him wince. 'I have not the faintest idea.'

'Is he fighting?'

'Nothing less likely in the world, I should say.'

'He hasn't hightailed it, has he?'

'What does that mean?'

'Decamped, absconded, run off.'

'I like 'hightailed.' That's very much my husband's style.'

The grime had lifted from the soldier's face, showing him to be a handsome man of around twenty-three or twenty-four. His eyes, in particular, struck Felicity as very fine, grey-blue like her own, with a level and intelligent gaze which was now fixed on Isobel. 'Where is he?'

'I like to think of him in Biarritz or Monte Carlo, at the card tables.'

'He ought to be shot.'

'I would rather he lived happily ever after.'

He snorted in disgust. 'You're very forgiving.'

'You love a woman who doesn't love you,' she said. 'Why shouldn't I love my husband?'

'He'll realize his mistake and come crawling back to you one day.'

'Ah, is that your plan? You'll go back to Massachusetts covered with glory and medals – and Maisie will beg to be the hero's bride?'

'Her name is not Maisie.'

'You poor idiot. She'll be married to some fat haberdasher long before you're buried under a tin cross, or if you're less lucky, sent home in a basket. She won't even look at you as they wheel you to the poorhouse.'

'Isobel!' Felicity cut in sharply, upset by her sister's cruelty.

Isobel shrugged. 'I can't bear banalities. He should know the truth of his folly.'

He squinted through the lather at her. 'I didn't come for a woman. I came for Spain.'

'So, because you love Spain so much, you've come here to kill Spaniards?'

'I haven't killed a single Spaniard so far,' he retorted. 'We were fighting Moroccans three months ago. Now we're fighting Nazis with tanks and dive-bombers. It'll be Mussolini's legions next, fresh from massacring the Abyssinians. Franco's invited every Fascist nation on earth into his war. *That's* why we volunteered.'

Not liking this answer, Isobel tossed the bar of soap into his lap. 'You can do the rest yourself, Lieutenant.'

The soldier picked up the soap and began to wash the rest of his body. 'Well, I can see why your husband lit out,' he drawled, but his eyes followed Isobel as she walked out of the room. Not until she was gone did he glance at Felicity. 'Your sister is quite a piece of work. I guess she doesn't believe in causes.'

'She has causes of her own,' Felicity replied. 'Where are the rest of your men?'

'We're billeted in a big old house, kind of a castle, up the road a mile or two.'

Felicity winced. She knew that 'big old house, kind of a castle' very well indeed. Until a few days ago, it had been her sister's home; and the only reason they'd been forced to cram themselves hastily into the cottage had been to hide from unsympathetic soldiers exactly like this one. God alone knew what state the grand old place would be in by now. 'And the Fascists?' she asked. 'How far are their lines?'

'What are you, a war journalist?' Now that Isobel had gone, he was finally appraising her with his clear grey-blue eyes. His nakedness did not seem to embarrass him much, although the water in the tub was by no means deep enough to offer complete modesty. She had been left in charge of this dangerous animal, a Republican soldier, and she could not abandon her post.

'I'd just like to know whether we're in imminent danger of being blown to pieces,' she said.

'You could have chosen a better location, that's for sure. What the hell are you doing here, anyway?'

'We were on a motoring holiday and took the wrong direction,' Felicity said, lying with a smoothness which surprised her. 'Our car was requisitioned by some soldiers – that's a military word for "stolen", I believe – and we ended up here. Now we can't get out of Córdoba.'

'There is a way out. But you'd have to know it. I could even get one of my men to drive you if I could get the gasoline.'

'As a matter of fact, we've been avoiding contact with any soldiers. We've heard – stories. We'd rather stay where we are, out of the way, until the danger passes. But thank you so much,' she added politely, as though declining an unwelcome dance partner at a ball.

'The danger isn't going to pass anytime soon. And getting out of Córdoba would only be the start. Spain is in chaos.' He was watching her with that same steady gaze; but if he suspected she were not telling the truth, he did not pursue the subject. 'How come she called you a model of human folly?'

'I believe that was *you*,' Felicity pointed out.

'She called us both fools, if it comes to that.'

'We're having a family argument.'

'About what?'

'Now who's the inquisitive one?'

'Are you planning to marry some fellow whose blood is less than blue?'

'As a matter of fact, rather the reverse. I intend to enter a closed Order.'

'To become a nun?'

'Yes.'

He grinned. 'That *would* be a terrible waste. You're sure of what you're doing? In your immortal soul?'

'Yes. Are you a Catholic?' she asked.

'A lapsed one. What do your parents say?'

'They're both dead. The rest of the family tell me I'm throwing my life away. A few merely think it's irrelevant in the face of looming world conflict.' Felicity turned her head slightly so that she could observe him from the corner of her eye. She had never seen a man fully naked until now, unless you counted the antique casts gallery in the Victoria and Albert Museum, where she and her sisters had received drawing lessons from a private lady tutor. This creature was not constructed on such marmoreal lines, but was far more intriguing, an intricate arrangement of sinews, muscles and bones that was in ceaseless motion. Nor was he uniformly pale grey like the casts; his face and arms were tanned while his torso was creamy, with a runnel of black hair, as though one of the young ladies had spilled her ink. She recognized the exotic geometry of the male organs from the plaster casts but had not anticipated their mobile heaviness in the water. It was disturbing.

'You should give it a try,' he said.

'What?'

'The convent. Give it a try.' His tone was indifferent. He was no longer interested in her, but was staring at the doorway, looking for Isobel.

Unaccountably irritated by this dismissive advice, Felicity gave up staring at the wall. 'Thank you so much,' she said dryly. 'Is there really a Maisie in Massachusetts?'

'Something like that. Have you got a towel?' he asked. 'I'm done.' He rose, streaming, from the water, looking rather like Michelangelo's David in the casts gallery. Felicity turned and fled.

❧

They stood in the doorway of the cottage together, watching Willoughby walk down to the lane. He had left an olive green motorcycle parked there. His uniform was literally steaming in the cold air. As he straddled the machine and kicked it into life, a second soldier appeared from the dry brush where he had been concealed and hopped on the pillion.

'There he is!' Manuela exclaimed furiously, pointing at the sack he carried. 'With our cabbages!'

Willoughby pulled on goggles and gauntlets, and with a wave to them, roared away. His companion grinned impudently over his shoulder at the women as they departed. The sound of the motorcycle faded down the lane, leaving only the muttering of the guns beyond the mountains.

'You are mad, Isobel,' Felicity said. 'I thought the whole idea was to remain inconspicuous!'

'Pity he wasn't from the other side,' Isobel said. 'What did you make of your first Communist?'

'He said he wasn't a Communist. And he didn't have horns or a tail.'

'He had other things, though.'

'What?'

'Didn't you notice, darling?' Felicity became aware that Isobel and Manuela were smirking at her slyly.

'What are you grinning at?' Felicity retorted. 'I'm not a child. You may think you were very humorous in making him take his clothes off, but what if he comes back with twenty friends to get his revenge?'

Isobel seemed unperturbed. 'They won't last long against Franco. He told me they barely have enough ammunition or petrol to defend their positions. They'll be gone in a week.'

'You were still very imprudent,' Felicity sniffed.

'I did it in the interest of your deficient education,' Isobel said airily. 'At least now you've seen a naked man. It will give you something to remember in your seclusion.'

Manuela smirked and made a remark in Spanish which Felicity was luckily unable to understand. 'I don't have your dirty mind,' she replied tartly.

'As a matter of fact, I thought he was quite a fine figure of a man,' Isobel said, turning to go back into the cottage.

'Very handsome,' Manuela agreed. 'He had nice eyes.'

'And he was confident. I like a confident man.'

'Yes. Very manly.'

Irritated by their sniggering, Felicity went to the piano, where her sprained fingers soon reminded her of her grappling match with Isobel earlier that afternoon. Fortunately, however, Isobel seemed to have spent all her aggression for one day, or at least alleviated her boredom, and did not renew her attack on Felicity. But a prolonged barrage from the Nationalist guns began, shaking the ground, extending well into the night and lighting up the sky with angry red flares.

❧

Manuela skinned and cooked one of the two rabbits which the gamekeeper had brought them (it was his cottage which they had requisitioned, he and his family having moved to a neighbouring farm). They ate it in a stew by the light of an oil lamp. The guns did not stop firing until almost midnight, when the temperature had dropped to freezing and a dense fog had settled around the cottage.

They slept in the single bedroom, huddled in the same bed for warmth. It was a far cry, Felicity thought, from the lovely house in Gloucestershire where they had grown up. As so often when she was melancholy, she lulled herself to sleep with memories of that life at Adlestrop, of days at the beach at Weston-Super-Mare when their parents were still alive, and the garden filled with the flowers of an English summer, of the high-ceilinged bright rooms filled with Chiara's laughter.

When she got back to London, she was going to see Chiara to say goodbye to her, too. It was hard to imagine a life without Chiara. Harder, if the truth be told, than imagining a life without Isobel. Again, she wished Chiara could be with them now – Chiara, always bright and happy, ready to amuse and be amused, the golden girl who had so often been a buffer between her and Isobel. The two of them had been so close, Felicity laughing at Chiara's pranks, hiding behind her when Isobel was stormy. Who would stick up for her now?

The guns woke them again early the next morning. The mist was not lifting, but clung heavily round the place. A hard frost had also taken hold, whitening the sparse grass so that it crunched underfoot. They were starting to run short of firewood and it was Felicity's turn to split logs while Isobel and Manuela walked over to the farm to beg the gamekeeper – who was Manuela's cousin – for whatever scraps of food he could spare. The loss of their last few vegetables had been a serious blow. All they had left was the scrawny corpse of their second rabbit. As she swung the ponderous axe in swiftly blistering hands, Felicity found herself cursing William Willoughby and his grinning partner in crime. They had sentenced the three women to hardship and hunger.

Half an hour after the other women had left, Felicity heard the rumble of the motorcycle approaching through the whiteness. She leaned, panting, on the axe handle. Willoughby dismounted and peered at her through mud-spattered goggles. He had a rucksack on his back.

'There's nothing left for you to steal,' she said grimly, by way of greeting.

'Where's your sister?'

'Out, looking for food. You'll have to make do with me.'

'You'll do, Sister Felicity.' He walked into the cottage. She followed him, wishing she were not alone.

He dumped the rucksack on the kitchen table and unfastened the straps. Felicity watched as he opened it and began to take out cans.

'Bully beef,' she said in awe.

'From comrades in Argentina.' He had brought a dozen of the precious tins and, incredibly, a lump of Manchego cheese and three bottles of red wine. 'I'm sorry about your cabbages. They've all been eaten. I stole these from our mess. Not very exciting, I know, but full of protein.'

'I think that's the most exciting thing I've clapped eyes on in a long time.' She ranged the tins along the kitchen shelf, gloating. She was seeing him in a new light, suddenly. 'I don't know how to thank you.'

'I saw a piano in there. Do you play?'

Ruefully, she showed him her hands, with their torn and weeping blisters. 'I'm somewhat out of action.'

He took her wrists in his hands and inspected her palms, clicking his tongue disapprovingly. 'From the axe?'

'I'm afraid so.'

'It's too heavy for you.' He filled a bowl from the pump in the sink and shook a teaspoon of salt into it.

'No!' she exclaimed when she divined his intention, swiftly hiding her hands behind her back.

'Come on. I'm just going to clean them. If there's one thing a soldier knows about, it's blisters. You'll get an infection in this filthy place, and then you'll probably have to have your hands chopped off.'

She didn't know whether he was teasing her, but she reluctantly presented her hands. He bathed them in the salt water. He was surprisingly gentle with her, but the salt stung the raw places mercilessly and she could not stop the tears from rolling down her cheeks, or her long nose from running unattractively. She bit her plump lower lip hard.

'Do you have any brothers?' he asked.

'Just one other sister. And you?'

'I have two sisters.'

'How do they feel about you volunteering for this war?'

'They say the kind of things Isobel says.' He smiled. 'Sisters are alike all over the world, I guess. You're the baby of the family?'

'I'm the youngest,' she said, trying to find dignity in her snivelling.

'Do you have a first-aid kit?'

'No.'

'A sewing kit, then?'

She told him where to find it. He used a needle to pop the largest of the blisters and the scissors to trim the skin from the blisters that had torn open. Surprisingly, his ministrations were comforting, rather than the reverse. She sniffed back her tears and studied the head that was bent over her wounded palms. Its hair was very black, thick and wavy. His lashes were dense and long for a man's. The mouth was decisive, but not insensitive, and richly coloured against the blue stubble of his beard. Isobel and Manuela had been right. He was a very nice-looking man. In a London drawing room, he might be considered quite a catch. She half-closed her eyes and tried to envisage him with a shave and a haircut, his cheeks shining with cologne, clad in an evening jacket instead of rough khaki. The picture was a very attractive one.

He looked up at her. 'Am I hurting you?'

'It's all right,' she said. 'Don't mind me blubbing.' She looked into his eyes, losing herself in their clear depths, as in a lake. Were there lakes in Massachusetts? She must ask him. She watched him cut simple bandages and bind up the worst of her wounds.

'There,' he said, putting the things away with a woman's neatness. 'You'll have to keep them clean, and wash with salt water at least twice a day. And no more splitting wood.'

'We have to have a fire. But thank you for tending to my stupid hands. They've never been very strong. Even as a child, I couldn't catch a ball or swing a bat the way my sisters could. I'd always sprain my wrist or hurt my fingers.'

He lounged against the old wood-fired range, a large khaki figure, observing her with a faintly amused expression. 'I hope they won't make you chop firewood in this convent of yours.'

Her eyes brightened. 'It's so beautiful. There's a garden that was planted in the fifteenth century, with knots of herbs and – you'll never guess: a real olive tree from Jerusalem!'

'Really?'

'It even makes fruit, and the sisters press the oil for the priest to bless. There are cloisters to walk in. And there's a magnificent Renaissance church, with a dome that echoes wonderfully. The altar is pink marble, and light pours down onto it from the stained-glass windows. And do you know the most amazing thing of all?'

He had been watching her attentively, his eyes moving from her rapt face to the white column of her throat and the graceful movements of her bandaged hands. 'No, what is the most amazing thing of all?' he asked gently.

'The floor is white marble. And it's so highly polished, that you can see a perfect reflection of everything in it. It's as if there are two churches, one upside-down to the other.'

'You make it sound very attractive.'

'It will be like living in heaven. I can't wait to be there.'

His eyes were no longer cool, but warm and kind, and somehow almost sad. She had seen that look in the eyes of others in whom she had confided. 'I hope you'll be very happy there,' he said.

'I know I will be. Why *did* you volunteer?' she asked him, emboldened by the slight intimacy that had grown between them. The words tumbled out of her. 'Did your girl really drop you? Do you really have any interest in politics? Isobel's frightfully political as you can see, she thinks—' She stopped herself in time. It would be folly to confide in this stranger, even if he was handsome and kind. 'Can you tell me anything?' she finished, looking up into his face.

He was silent for a while, his slight smile fading slowly. 'Why, yes,' he said at last, 'there was a girl and she did drop me. I thought I was broken-hearted. I suppose I was hurt, at least. And I do love Spain. It's a country of the heart. The Spain of Goya and Velasquez and Cervantes. Especially Cervantes,' he added wryly. 'I'm a kind of Don Quixote myself, charging at windmills and living in dreams.'

'Reality is unbearable at times,' she said softly.

'That's true. But probably the main reason I came was that I wanted an adventure. A real adventure. I didn't want to spend the rest of my life in a classroom. I wanted to do something, something big. To be alive. And I hate Fascism – it stinks. I felt Spain calling me and I answered.'

'And – ?'

'And what?'

'Has it been worth it?'

'Oh yes. I've done things and seen things that I would never have known otherwise. Some of them terrible things, some of them wonderful. I don't know what I'll be at the end of it. But I'll know that I've been alive.'

'That's very inspiring.'

'I'm just a restless fellow,' he said, smiling.

'I think I could play a little now,' she said, flexing her fingers experimentally. She wanted to reward him – and show him that she had some accomplishments.

'Sure. If it won't hurt you too much,' he said.

They went into the main room. He stretched out his legs by the last embers of the fire as she sat at the piano, and bent his head to listen.

With the first notes she played, she realized she had made an awful mistake. Stretching her fingers hurt terribly. Too proud to give up, she launched into Schumann's *Träumerei*, the shortest piece she could think of on the spur of the moment. The pain was excruciating, and to her own ears she played execrably, but she gritted her teeth and soldiered on, half-blinded by new tears.

Halfway through the piece, she almost faltered to a stop, but pushed herself to pursue her labour of love despite the burning of her raw blisters. However, before she could play the final, plaintive phrases, she was interrupted by the arrival of Isobel and Manuela back from their excursion.

'What's that awful racket?' Isobel demanded, coming through the door with a blast of cold air. 'You're playing abominably, Fee. Are you trying to punish Lieutenant Willoughby?'

Willoughby had risen to his feet. 'As a matter of fact, I came to make atonement,' he said.

'Did you, indeed?' Isobel shrugged off her heavy green loden coat and hung it on the back of the door. She was in a very bad mood. 'It seems you can't stay away from the place.'

'Lieutenant Willoughby has brought us some tins of bully beef,' Felicity said.

'I detest the stuff,' Isobel replied, unimpressed. But Manuela hurried to the kitchen, where she could be heard exclaiming in delight. Felicity noticed some spots of her own blood on the piano keys, and wiped them off. She had ceased to exist for Willoughby. He had eyes only for Isobel – who was, indeed, a magnet for male eyes. The cold had flushed her face with colour and made her dark eyes brilliant. 'We got lost in the bloody fog and walked around in circles, like Scott of the bloody Antarctic. I'm frozen.'

Willoughby quickly put some fresh wood on the fire and stirred up a blaze.

'He brought wine,' Manuela said, coming from the kitchen. 'Three bottles of *Ribera del Duero*.'

'There was a cellarful in the castle where we're billeted,' Willoughby said. 'It's almost finished now. The Comrades are carrying it off. I never knew Marxists had such a taste for fine wine. I grabbed the last few bottles.'

Isobel raised one eyebrow ironically at Felicity but made no comment. Manuela patted Willoughby's cheek. 'You're a good boy,' she said.

'I'll try and bring some more food tomorrow,' he promised. 'But I don't know what I'll be able to find. We're running out ourselves. Uncle Joe Stalin keeps promising to send us supplies, but they never get here.'

'Next time, choose a master who keeps his promises.'

'I don't regard Stalin as my master.'

'Then you're a fool,' Isobel rejoined. She stooped by the fire and combed out her rich, chestnut hair, which was clammy with the fog. 'Ugh. I hate the cold and damp.'

'It will be baking in the summer.' Willoughby watched her movements as a cat watches a bird.

21

'By which time I hope I'm far away,' Isobel said, 'and you're in jail, where you belong.'

'Very kind of you.'

'It's all you Bolsheviks deserve.'

Willoughby smiled. 'I'm not a Bolshevik.'

'You say that with a hammer and sickle on your arm?'

'When we've won the war, we'll get rid of the Communists, too.'

'Really, you belong in a Museum of Stupidity. I hope you get a bullet in the leg and are sent home before you realize what a fool you've made of yourself.'

'A bullet in the leg is usually fatal,' Willoughby said mildly. 'They don't bother trying to remove it. They just amputate, right away.'

'American ingenuity will provide you with a mechanical one in Massachusetts.'

Willoughby prepared to leave, seeing that the atmosphere was not very friendly. 'Thank you for the Schumann,' he said to Felicity. 'My mother used to play that piece.'

Felicity brightened. 'I'm glad I chose it, then.'

'I'll bring more food, if I can.'

'How very kind,' Isobel said ironically, and turned her back on him. They heard his motorcycle fire up and rumble away into the silence. From the kitchen came the smell of Manuela frying bully beef for their lunch.

'You're horrible to him,' Felicity said.

'What do you want me to do? Kiss him and tell him how clever he is?'

'Be kind, at least.'

'I'm not kind. You know that. You shouldn't encourage him.'

'I haven't done anything to encourage him.'

'Liar. Sitting there like a mooncalf, playing him *Träumerei*!'

Felicity's pale cheeks flushed. 'I was merely thanking him for bringing us food.'

'Yes, wasn't he generous!' Isobel said bitterly. 'That's Marxism for you. They take away everything you have. Then they give you back a tin of bully beef and put a pistol to your head and demand thanks.'

'He didn't have a pistol to our heads. He was just trying to apologize for taking our vegetables.'

'Well, drop to your knees, darling, and pray for his immortal soul. He's likely to be dead in a week.'

'You can be so callous,' Felicity said. But she went to her sister and took the hairbrush from her and began brushing the thick waves of Isobel's hair. Isobel sat on the little stool by the fireside. Felicity's gentle brushing seemed to soothe Isobel, and she sighed at last.

'I've come to hate this place so much.'

'I know.' Felicity put her arms around Isobel and pressed her mouth into Isobel's hair, inhaling the peppery scent that was almost her first childhood memory, inextricably woven into her heart's fibres. 'It's been so hard for you.'

'It's been ten years of catastrophes. Mummy dying, then Daddy. Then Roberto. And Paul. And now you, wanting to go into a nunnery. I can't stand any more.'

'Oh Isobel,' Felicity said in alarm, 'don't cry!' Nothing disconcerted her like Isobel's tears, rare as they were. Unlike Felicity herself, Isobel found tears difficult to shed, and did so with great reluctance, her shoulders heaving, her eyes squeezing tightly shut. They clung to each other in silence for a while. Isobel was first to break the embrace, pushing Felicity away and getting to her feet. She wiped her face.

'God, my cheeks are so chapped. I don't even have any cold cream.'

'We could ask Lieutenant Willoughby to bring us some from the house.'

'You heard him. They're looting the place. Clearing it out. There'll be nothing left. They're like disgusting locusts.'

'Don't think about it, darling.' She was relieved to see that Isobel had got herself under control and had shed no more than two tears, one on each smooth cheek.

Isobel smiled sadly. 'Do you remember when Mummy and Daddy went to America on the *Mauretania*, and we used to run down to read the newspaper every morning, hoping it had hit an iceberg? We so wanted to be orphans, like in *What Katy Did*. Now we really are orphans, and I miss them so much!'

'So do I,' Felicity said. 'I hate being an orphan. It's not nearly as much fun as I expected.'

Manuela called them to the table to eat.

◦◦◦

Willoughby did not return the next day, though Felicity remained on the alert from daybreak, listening for the sound of his motorcycle. The fog lifted somewhat and Manuela made a successful journey to the farmhouse, returning with a basket of onions and the news that, according to the gamekeeper's radio set, the Nationalists and the Republicans were locked in a fierce struggle, with no end in sight. The cottage was essentially surrounded, Franco's forces on one side and the Republicans on the other. Both sides were accusing the other of atrocities against civilians, which made them even more afraid of what might happen.

They also heard aircraft in the sky during the afternoon, though whether from the Nationalist or the Republican side they could not tell. A heavy explosion told them that a bomb had been dropped, and had them all running indoors for shelter, but there were no more alarms until nightfall.

In the evening, sitting close to the dying fire for warmth, they resumed their wrangling over Felicity's future, though more gently now.

'It's not just the waste of your youth that kills me,' Isobel said. 'You're going to give them all your money, too. You can't get that back until and unless you're released from your vows. And that can take years, under canon law.'

'Well, yes. But—'

'In the meantime, you'll be almost completely in their power. They can lock you in your cell and prevent anyone from seeing you for years at a time.'

'You make them sound like monsters,' Felicity said with a smile.

'We all went to a convent school,' Isobel replied tartly. 'We both know what nuns are capable of. The difference is that you loved it and I hated it. You never grew out of religion.'

'Religion isn't something one *grows out of.*'

'To me, being bullied by nuns for the rest of my life would be a vision of hell. When I was your age, I made a dreadful mistake with Roberto. I don't want you to do the same thing.'

'But Roberto is only a man, fallible and flawed. He wasn't worthy of you. The Church is not a single individual. It's the work of God.'

'I've never seen a happy nun.'

'How can you say that!'

'I never have seen a nun glow like a mother, any mother one can find with her children in the park on any morning. I've never seen that joy in the face of a nun. All I see is them creeping along with folded hands and costive faces, looking as though they were sucking a lemon.'

'That's because you can't see inside them. If you could, you would see a complete and unstained joy.'

'Fiddlesticks.' Isobel got to her feet wearily. 'I'm off to bed. Are you coming?'

'In a moment.'

'Don't be too long. I hate it when I've just got warmed up and you wrap your icy legs around mine.'

When Isobel had left, Felicity sat staring into the embers for a while. Then she went to the kitchen and unwound her bandages.

She bathed her fingers in salt water, as Willoughby had commanded her, then bound them up again. She glanced at the range, in her mind seeing him leaning there with that half-smile, amused but not mocking. He had occupied her thoughts a great deal lately. They were two of a kind, she thought, people with ideals and faith.

She retired to the darkened bedroom, where Manuela and Isobel were already competing with one other in ladylike snores. Gratefully, she got in with them, soaking up their warmth.

❧

They were awakened before dawn the next morning by the hideous music of a battle. The cannonades shook the ground beneath their feet for two hours, giving way, as the sun rose, to the long rattles of machine-gun fire. The fighting had never seemed so close before. As the sky lightened, they could see pillars of oily black smoke rising from beyond the hills. A few short miles away, men were killing one another and dying, mangling each other's minds and bodies, bringing God's great work to ruin.

At mid-morning they heard the roar of an engine, but it was not Willoughby's motorcycle. A military truck had stopped in the lane. Felicity felt terror seize her heart as she saw the soldiers walking up to the cottage, rifles at the ready.

There were five of them, and they were not friendly. Their leader demanded to see the women's papers. Isobel and Felicity produced their British passports, which caused immediate suspicion, and were not given back. They were not interested in Manuela. She tried to intercede, but, threatening her with rifle butts, they drove her away. After a curt interrogation, the two Englishwomen were ordered into the back of the truck.

They clung to the struts for support as the truck jolted off. The soldiers who rode with them watched them, unwinking, rifles on their knees. Felicity kept hoping this was a nightmare from which she would awaken, but the reality was all too present. The faces of the soldiers were hard-bitten, weary. Their hands were rough. On the sleeves of all of them was the hammer and sickle badge. The possibilities of being beaten or raped were suddenly not abstract, but horribly real. Felicity stared down at her sensible English brogues, her slender ankles in their woollen stockings. She and Isobel said nothing to one another. Isobel's normally ferocious tongue was silenced for once.

Had Willoughby denounced them? It seemed unlikely. He had been so kind and helpful. But perhaps that had been merely a front; or perhaps Isobel's harsh words had annoyed him sufficiently to make him give them up. There was no way of telling. Anything was possible.

A short while later, the truck lurched to a halt. The canvas was thrown aside, revealing that they had arrived at the castle. Behind the bleak stone walls, the sky was darkened with smoke, though there appeared to be a lull in the firing. The soldiers thrust them out of the truck and marched them through the front door.

The huge hall was bare but for a few soldiers carrying boxes of files. Felicity looked around, stunned. The great chamber with its vaulted, painted ceiling had once been a masterpiece of the Spanish High Baroque. It now was a ruin. The chandeliers and candelabra were gone. So were most of the paintings, many of them priceless masterpieces. The only one that had remained, a large, dark family portrait, was riddled with bullet holes.

Of the huge Sèvres vases which had stood on pedestals flanking each window, all had been removed, except three which had been smashed, their delicate fragments scattered on the floor, where they had not even been swept up. The carpets were gone, as were the heavy antique drapes. Even the gilded plasterwork had been chiselled off in long strips, perhaps in the mistaken belief that it was solid gold.

A marble statue of Diana which had stood in the centre of the hall was also missing. Deep grooves in the parquet floor showed where it had been lugged away. None of the furniture remained, except for a desk at one of the windows, where an officer now sat, assembling a pistol. The place had been ransacked with deliberate savagery.

Felicity shot a glance at Isobel's face and saw it was white and stiff. She took her sister's hand, but Isobel seemed not to notice, and her fingers remained limp and cold in Felicity's. She looked around anxiously for Willoughby, but he was nowhere to be seen.

Their captors marched them to the desk. The officer who sat there looked up at them coldly. He listened to the report, which was a rattle of Spanish too quick for Felicity to follow, then snapped his fingers for their passports. On each of the red shoulder boards was a row of gold stars. He had a thin, scholarly face and wore steel-rimmed spectacles perched on a bony nose. 'You are sisters?' he asked in English. They both nodded. He tapped the passports on his desk, pale eyes considering them each in turn. 'What are you doing in Córdoba?'

'We were on a motoring holiday when war broke out,' Felicity said, not trusting Isobel to tell the story. 'Our car was stolen by soldiers and we were marooned in that cottage. We've sent a message to the British Ambassador in Valencia, but there has been no reply so far.'

'Soldiers? From which unit? From which army?'

'To tell you the truth, I don't know which side they were from,' Felicity said. 'Does it matter?'

'If you have supplied a vehicle to the enemy,' the officer said coolly, 'you will be court-martialled for rebellion.'

Felicity let out a cracked laugh of pure nerves. 'But that's absurd. We didn't *supply* anything. Soldiers stole our car from us at gunpoint. They could have been from either side. We were powerless to do anything to resist them.'

The man's round glasses flashed at them. 'The punishment for rebellion is death,' he said.

'*What?*' Despite his ascetic appearance, Felicity realized, this was a very dangerous man. She felt breathless. 'We are British civilians! We are playing no part in your war. Our government is neutral!'

'What if the car was taken by your own men?' Isobel asked, speaking for the first time, her voice dry and bitter. 'Would we get medals instead of bullets?'

He turned his cold gaze to Isobel. 'You have already declared that you do not know to whom you gave your vehicle.' His English was good, if pedantic. He leaned back in the chair, the leather creaking. 'It is too late to change your story now.'

Their appearance in the hall had now begun to draw attention. Soldiers were crowding around them. All wore the same neat uniform, very different from Willoughby's rough battledress. Felicity looked around in panic at the hard faces. 'Please! This is a silly mistake. We're tourists, British tourists.'

'Perhaps you are not tourists at all,' the officer said. 'Perhaps you are spies.'

'That's ridiculous! Do we look like spies?'

'You call me ridiculous?' the man said thinly.

'I call the charge ridiculous,' Felicity said. 'We don't even have a radio. There's no telephone at our cottage, and even if there were, all the lines are down. Please, you must contact the British Embassy—'

'*Capitán*, look.' A soldier had approached the desk and now laid a silver-framed photograph in front of the officer. Felicity stared at it in horror. It showed Isobel standing next to a man in a dark suit. Both were beaming. The man was Adolf Hitler. As if to make the photograph more damning, the silver frame had been surmounted with a crest bearing a swastika. 'We found this in one of the bedrooms. There are others.'

The captain picked up the photograph and looked from it to Isobel. 'What is this?' he asked her.

'What does it look like?' Isobel replied shortly.

'The photograph is signed by Hitler himself.'

'I have met him. As you see.'

The captain took off his spectacles and polished them carefully. He put them back on his face and looked up at Isobel with an expression of cold triumph. 'You are Isobel Albarán, are you not?'

Isobel shrugged. There was no point in denying it. 'Yes.'

'A propagandist for the Fascists. The wife of their banker. This is your house?'

'Yes.'

'What were you doing in the cottage?'

'It's my property. You and your gang have taken my home. I have nowhere else to go. No car to go anywhere, all the trains and buses requisitioned.'

'Where's your husband?'

'I have no idea.'

'You're lying.'

'If I knew where he was, I would be with him.'

'He abandoned her,' Felicity said. There was little mercy to be expected from these hard-line Communists, especially now that they knew who Isobel was. The photograph alone was dreadfully compromising. But she had to try. 'He treated her shamefully. Everybody knows that. He's run off to the south of France, leaving her defenceless—'

'Your sordid private lives are of no interest,' the captain cut in. 'The facts are that you have written malicious lies about the Soviet Union and are an enemy of the people. You will be shot.'

'No!'

'Take them into the courtyard.' The captain began reassembling his pistol with no trace of emotion as the soldiers closed in on the two women. As the men took hold of Isobel, who seemed paralysed, Felicity felt something erupt in her, a volcano of anger and grief. She flew at the soldiers, trying to push them away from her sister.

A rifle butt slammed into her stomach, knocking the wind out of her lungs. Unable to breathe, she sank agonized to the floor. A boot thudded into her side. She curled up around the pain. Blackness roared in her head. Dimly, she heard angry shouting, felt hands grasping her. It was a terrifying age before she could draw breath. She felt she was going to die. At last she managed to take a few sobbing breaths. She could hear a familiar voice.

'What's happening here?'

'Willoughby!' she whispered.

'We captured them in the old cottage, hiding there like rats,' the captain said.

'*Captured?*' Willoughby replied. He hauled Felicity to her feet. 'While we were fighting the Condor Legion, you were "capturing" women?'

'She's Isobel Albarán.' The captain handed Willoughby the Hitler photograph. Lifting her head, Felicity saw that Willoughby was smoke-grimed and bleak, his face still tight with the stress of the battlefield. He looked at the photograph briefly.

'I see.'

'She will be shot.'

'No. We don't make war on women, Captain Reverte.'

'They make war on our women,' the captain said. 'And on our children.'

'They are beasts. We are not.'

The captain had assembled his pistol. He rose to his feet, holding the weapon at his side, his immaculate uniform contrasting with Willoughby's blackened battledress. 'This is not your affair, Willoughby. This is a decision of the Political Department.'

'Another order from Moscow?' Willoughby said contemptuously. 'Why don't you tell Stalin to send us something to eat? And some guns and planes. That would be more use than murdering a couple of innocent women.' There was a growl of assent from

Willoughby's men, who were gathered around him, all of them in the same smoky, battle-weary state. But as her senses cleared, Felicity saw that there were at least as many of the captain's political detail as there were of Willoughby's fighting men.

'Comrade Stalin knows what he is doing.'

'So does Franco. He's knocking the shit out of us. You should be on the front line with us, not sitting here using paintings for target practice. Unlike real Fascists, painted ones don't shoot back.'

The captain's pale face coloured. 'You do your part,' he snapped, 'and let me do mine.'

'What's your part? Shooting us in the back?'

'I advise you to be silent.'

'Do you think I haven't noticed my men disappearing? What do you do with them? Send them off to Moscow for political correction? Or do you just take them into the woods and shoot them?' There was another growl from Willoughby's men. The two groups were confronting each other with open hostility.

'You should have stayed in your comfortable bourgeois home.'

'And you should have stayed in Moscow.'

'Get out of my way.'

'I won't let you touch these women. They're under my protection.'

Reverte sneered. 'And what do you plan to do with them?'

Willoughby glanced at Felicity and Isobel. 'Maybe I'll give them a bath.'

An explosion of laughter broke the tension. There were cries of 'Yes, yes, the dirty Fascists!'

A man stuck his head forward, grinning. 'I'll get the men to fill your bath, Señora. It'll be cold, I'm afraid.' Felicity recognized him as the impudent fellow who had stolen their vegetables with Willoughby. She put her arms protectively around Isobel. 'Don't you dare touch her!'

'I'll wash the blonde one myself,' someone called. 'She's skinny. But I like 'em feisty!' There was more laughter.

Reverte raised his pistol, but Willoughby interceded, thrusting the other man's arm down. 'Don't even think about it, Reverte. Nobody touches them from now on.' The two men stared into each other's face. Willoughby was bigger and stronger, dominating the thin, clerkish Reverte. He had far more natural authority – and furthermore, the laughter had released the tension in a way that had robbed Reverte of his momentum. Felicity felt someone smack her backside, and kicked out furiously. 'You couldn't handle them, anyway,' Willoughby said pointedly. 'They kick and bite. Leave them to me.' There were mocking catcalls against Reverte.

'I'll have you shot for this,' Reverte said, so quietly that, in the general merriment, his words were unheard by most of those present.

'You'll have to get some ammunition first,' Willoughby replied, 'because we just used the last of it against the enemy. Ask Comrade Stalin to mail us some.'

There was death in Reverte's eyes. 'You refused to obey an order in the face of the enemy.'

Willoughby laughed wearily. 'You call these two women the enemy?'

'They are the worst kind of enemies. They are class enemies. This woman is a personal friend of Hitler. Her husband is the chief banker of the Falangists.'

'Go and tell Comrade Stalin all about it. I came here to fight Fascists, not women.' He grasped Isobel and Felicity by the arms and hustled them away from the desk.

There were more whoops and laughter as they left, the men jostling them and making coarse remarks. Felicity shot a glance over her shoulder and saw the political officer still standing behind his desk, watching them with a stony face.

Escorted by Willoughby's men, they were led into an adjoining chamber, which had once been a day room. It was, if anything, in even worse condition than the hall, everything of value having been stripped and removed. Isobel glanced around with a bitter expression, but Felicity threw her arms around Willoughby. 'Oh William, thank you! Thank you!' She would have kissed him, but he pushed her away roughly.

'You pair of idiots,' he said. 'Why didn't you tell me who you were?'

'We didn't know if we could trust you,' Felicity said apologetically.

'You're going to have to trust me now. Don't you think I would have helped you if I'd understood? Now that Reverte knows you're here, everything's changed. You can't stay. You're just lucky that my men are decent boys.'

'He's right,' one of the men said in unmistakably Cockney accents. 'Reverte's a nasty piece of work. He'll be on the blower to the commissars about you right now.'

'We've got to get you away from Córdoba,' Willoughby said. 'There's no time to lose. They'll shoot you out of hand. Pack up your belongings, but only the essentials. Just a bag each. Then wait for me. But not in the house. Go down the lane a little way and hide behind the big rocks. You know the ones I mean?' They nodded. 'Don't come out unless you hear me calling you. If anybody else comes, stay hidden.' His eyes were hard. 'You understand?'

'Yes, William,' Felicity said meekly. Isobel merely glowered.

∼

They crouched behind the boulders, shivering with cold and nerves. Manuela had made for her cousin the gamekeeper's place, where she would be able to blend in with the scenery. They had said tearful farewells, but as Manuela said, they were sure to meet again, in this world or the next.

The wind was blustering across the hills, blowing the sounds of further fighting to them, and now and then a choking reek of high-explosive fumes. Felicity had never felt so exposed or unprotected in all her days; her ribs were aching cruelly from the kicking she'd received. But at the same time, her blood was singing and she was keenly aware of her own existence, of every fleeting sensation that touched her nerves. Was this what Willoughby had meant by feeling alive? Was this vivid terror what had drawn him to Spain and a war so far from his home? Truly, men were strange creatures.

'He saved our lives,' she said to Isobel.

'Damn that bloody photograph. I'd forgotten about it.'

'He was so brave. The way he stood up to that political officer! He could have been shot.'

Isobel huddled into her coat. 'He's a complete fool.'

'How can you say that?' Felicity exclaimed.

'Well, he is. He just can't wait to die for some useless cause — democracy or Cervantes or us, it doesn't matter to him.'

'He's the noblest person I've ever met.'

'Mooncalf,' Isobel growled into her fur stole.

'Who's a mooncalf? Me or William?'

'Both of you.'

'I call that the height of ingratitude!' Isobel said indignantly. 'We would have been in front of a firing squad but for him!'

'Well, where the hell is our noble saviour?' Isobel demanded. 'What's the point of saving us from the bloody Reds if he leaves us to freeze to death like Captain bloody Oates?'

As if on cue, they heard the noise of an engine approaching down the lane. Obedient to Willoughby's command, they waited until they heard his voice calling them. They emerged from hiding, lugging their suitcases.

Willoughby had obtained a small and battered delivery van. He climbed out of the cab to meet them. He appeared tense and tired. He was no longer wearing battledress, but the faded dungarees and checked shirt of a labourer. He looked Isobel up and down, taking in the smart clothes, the bulging suitcases. 'Going on a cruise?'

'I'm not leaving my clothes behind.'

Willoughby turned his attention to Felicity, who was marginally less patrician-looking in her fawn coat and sensible walking shoes. 'Got any money?'

'Not very much,' Felicity said.

'Hand it over.' Without argument, she gave him her little sheaf of money. He counted it briefly. 'Is that all?'

'That's all I've got. I'm sorry.'

He turned to Isobel. 'How about you, Frau Hitler?'

'I'm not giving you a penny,' Isobel said grimly.

'Then you can walk to Valencia,' he retorted, turning to get back into the van. 'If you run across Reverte and his death squads, give them my love.'

'Wait, damn you,' Isobel snapped. 'What do you need money for?'

'For the card tables at Biarritz,' he threw over his shoulder.

'Don't be facetious.'

He faced her with cold grey eyes. 'I need to buy gas, food and at least one night's lodging for the three of us. I don't have a dime. Everything I had is at the castle, and if I go back there now, Reverte will put a bullet through my head.'

'Shit,' Isobel muttered. She turned her back on him and dug under her clothes to get the money out of her drawers. 'Here,' she said, handing it over.

'Trust you to have your underpants full of money,' he commented.

'I do not have my underpants full of money. That's everything. So be careful with it. I can't exactly walk into a bank to get more.'

Willoughby loaded their bags into the back of the van and helped them get up into the cab, where they sat three abreast on the hard bench seat. He slammed the van into gear and they lurched off down the road. 'So that old dump belongs to you?' he said.

'Yes, that old dump belongs to me,' Isobel replied.

'And I very hospitably brought you some bottles of your own wine?'

'You weren't to know,' Felicity said, trying to be kind.

'I was probably sleeping in your bedroom,' Willoughby said. 'Ceiling all painted with frolicking nudes?'

'Courtesy of Giovanni Battista Tiepolo,' Isobel said dryly.

'I tried to soak up the culture. Along with twenty others. I was lucky. I'm a lieutenant, I got the feather bed. The rest slept on the floor. We ripped down the gold curtains to make bedding.'

Isobel flared up. 'You're just savages!'

Willoughby slowed the van to a halt and peered up at the sky through the windscreen. Three planes were banking over the hills ahead. 'Stukas,' he commented briefly. 'Let's hope they don't decide to waste a bomb on us.' They waited without speaking as the crooked-winged planes completed their turn and flew straight towards the van. Felicity's heart lurched. She took hold of Willoughby's arm, her mouth dry, wondering if these were the last moments of her life. The Stukas thundered overhead, so low that Felicity saw the white-and-black crosses on their fuselages. Willoughby started the van into motion again. 'Emissaries of Aryan culture,' he commented. 'I've been bombed by them. It's not an experience you easily forget.'

Even Isobel seemed somewhat shaken. She sat in silence, staring at the bleak winter landscape through her dark glasses. The vastness of Spain was apparent here, barely a house to be seen for miles, only bare hills dotted with the monotonous rows of olive trees. The van was ancient and slow. Willoughby had to nurse it carefully up the hills, stopping now and then to let the engine cool down.

'What will happen to your men?' Felicity asked him.

'I've sent them in a convoy to Montoro to join the other International Brigades there,' he replied. 'I don't trust Reverte after this. I'll get back to them once I've delivered you to your embassy in Valencia.'

'I see that this soldiering business is something one can just pick up and drop again, like knitting,' Isobel said ironically.

'Not *exactly*,' he replied, caricaturing her upper-class English drawl. 'One stands *quaite* a good chance of a *rawther* inconvenient firing squad. That's one of the differences between soldiering and knitting.'

'We've really messed things up for you,' Felicity said.

'I couldn't leave you there.' The radiator was rumbling ominously, so he stopped at the brow of the next hill and got out to prop up the engine cover. The sisters also got out to stretch their legs.

'Couldn't you have found something better than this old crate?' Isobel demanded petulantly, lighting a cigarette in her black ebony holder.

'The Rolls-Royces were all in for a service,' he replied, using a rag to unscrew the radiator cap. A cold wind whipped steam into the pale blue sky.

Making a face at him, Isobel walked purposefully up the road, puffing industriously (he would not let her smoke in the cab, another source of contention between them).

'I really am sorry we've made you run such a risk,' Felicity said. 'I hope everything's all right when you get back.'

Willoughby grunted, getting out the tool kit. 'How, exactly, did she get so intimate with the Führer?'

'She's not, really. She went to Bayreuth three years ago with Diana Guinness and Unity Mitford. They're both besotted with Hitler, and well connected with all the other top Nazis. Diana got her an introduction to Hitler at the opera. Hitler collects beautiful women, especially beautiful Englishwomen. Not in that way,' she added, seeing his expression. 'He's apparently celibate. And a vegetarian. Rather a harmless sort of person, really.'

'You think Hitler is harmless?' Willoughby asked, sliding under the engine.

'To tell you the truth, I think it's more Wagner than Hitler, with Isobel. She's always been very sensitive to music.'

'She's the biggest bitch I've ever come across.'

Shocked, Felicity sprang to her sister's defence. 'You have no right to judge her! She seems hard, but you don't know what she's been through! Roberto was an absolute monster. He broke her heart. He was carrying on with other women even while she was pregnant. And her beautiful little boy died at only a year old. Are you even listening?'

His voice came from underneath the van, together with the sound of hammering. 'Yes. Keep talking.'

'I suppose it's hard for you to understand. But she takes herself very seriously.'

Willoughby slid out from under the van to get a spanner. There was a streak of oil on one cheek. He gave her a very old-fashioned look before disappearing again. 'I had noticed that.' The hammering resumed.

'Our parents died while we were still young, and Isobel more or less brought us up, me and Chiara, I mean. Chiara's the middle sister. She's the nicest of all three of us.' She laughed nervously. It was not easy talking to a man's dungarees while the rest of him was banging pipes under a van on a Spanish mountainside. 'I mean, Isobel's very fierce, and they say I'm a religious maniac.' She paused, but he did not contradict her. 'Chiara's the balanced one. The one everybody loves. Anyway, Isobel dragged the two of us up after our parents died. Then along came Roberto Albarán. He's terribly charming, of course, and very rich, or at least he led us to think he was. But the main attraction was political. He's a Blackshirt. Actually, they call them Blue Shirts here in Spain—'

'I know what they call them,' he growled.

'Of course you do, sorry. He took her off to that castle, like something in a fairy tale. Everybody was green with envy. But as it turned out, he wasn't a fairy tale prince after all. More like Bluebeard. Their little boy was called Paul.' Felicity looked at Isobel's distant figure, wandering down the austere roadway. All sounds of hammering from beneath the engine had ceased. 'I was with her when he died. It was the most pitiful thing. She was prostrate with grief. I didn't know if she would ever recover. And Roberto was even worse after that. I think he used to – well, used to hurt her. He left her in the end. He's living the high life with his fancy women. Isobel's been stuck all alone in that castle, like a hermit, with no money, no husband, no child.'

Willoughby emerged from under the van and began to pack his tools. 'I've tightened all the radiator hoses, but they're in bad condition. We've got a couple of hundred miles to go. I'll have to get some spares if I can.'

'I think she sees Fascism as something that gives order to her life. Can you understand that?' She looked at him anxiously. She was grateful for every scrap of his attention that she could win away from Isobel, yet, with a younger sister's loyalty, she wanted to defend and explain. 'Please don't hate her.'

Willoughby gazed at the distant figure, his hard expression softening. 'It's not easy to hate anybody that beautiful,' he said ruefully.

Felicity made no reply. She was thinking that she would give a lot to have him look at her with that expression of longing.

Willoughby refilled the radiator, which had now cooled. They got back in the van and set off, stopping to let Isobel get aboard when they overtook her. Willoughby leaned on the steering wheel, watching Isobel as she got into the cab. 'The cat that walked alone,' he commented.

'At this rate, it'd be quicker if I did walk all the way to Valencia,' she said, tossing her cigarette butt away after a last hungry drag.

'But then we'd be deprived of your charming company – and political wisdom. And what a loss that would be.' He was poker-faced.

They jolted off into the afternoon. For someone who'd had a sheltered upbringing, and who was shortly about to enter a convent, Felicity thought, she was seeing rather a lot of Life.

❧

This was a remote landscape where villages looked like tumbled heaps of rock, and tumbled heaps of rock looked like villages. Willoughby skirted any larger towns, minutely consulting his battered map each time they reached a crossroads. They were by now in territory nominally held by, and loyal to, the Republic. But as Willoughby said, local conditions were variable and anything could be expected. One municipality might be for Franco, the neighbouring one for the Republic; it was a war of brother against brother. Since he was a Republican soldier and Isobel a prominent Fascist, they could not count on a welcome anywhere.

'This is Spain, after all,' he said laconically, 'the land of Cervantes, paradox and absurdity.'

Things being what they were, people tended not to ask too many questions either way. Petrol – which he called gasoline – was in short supply, but they managed to get enough to keep going, and an extra can, along the way. The van, which Willoughby christened Rocinante, in honour of Don Quixote's horse, performed valiantly, though with frequent stops to let off steam. In the evening they reached a small hamlet called Santiago de los Vuitres, perched on the edge of a cliff. It was getting dark and cold.

'We'll spend the night here,' Willoughby decided. They found a fortress-like *fonda* or inn just outside the village, which appeared to have changed little since the seventeenth century. The innkeepers, an elderly couple, peered round the studded oak door at them, seeming at first frightened by their arrival; but once money was shown, they grudgingly offered a meal and a room for the night, and avoided asking what three foreigners were doing, driving around Andalucía in the middle of a war. There was only one room with a proper bed, a huge old four-poster that smelled of cats. The other rooms offered straw mattresses on the floor, which Willoughby declined. 'I'm not going to dislocate my spine to save your reputations. There's room for us all in the bed.'

'A delightful prospect,' Isobel said, lifting the valance to inspect the chamber pot under the bed. 'I'll guard your virtue, Fee.'

'How do you know,' Felicity replied archly, surprising herself, 'that I haven't lost it already?' Isobel rolled her eyes.

The meal consisted of pork and white beans, a hearty peasant dish washed down with large tumblers of rough red wine, drawn from a formidable oak barrel that stood on trestles, conveniently close to the single refectory table. For company they had a few ancient and silent villagers at the other end of the table, whose mottled red noses proclaimed the virtues of the cask. Warmed, filled and slightly drunk, they filed up the narrow stone stairs to their communal bed.

It was cold now and their bedroom was lit only by an oil lamp – there was no electricity upstairs and precious little down-stairs. They undressed as far as each thought decency permitted, Willoughby to his shorts and vest, Felicity only removing her shoes. Isobel stripped to her slip, which happened to be a rather pretty woollen one with embroidered rosebuds. Was it really neces-sary for Isobel to parade herself in this condition quite so blatantly, stooping to arrange this and stretching to reach that, like a nymph in some Bouguereau oil painting? Felicity saw Willoughby's eyes drawn to the outline of Isobel's bosom, which had always been more bountiful than her own. She felt a flash of irritation. If they weren't fighting, they were ogling each other, like a pair of panthers trapped in the same cage.

They clambered under the heavy eiderdown. The feral smell of cat piss enveloped them. Isobel put herself between Felicity and Willoughby. Willoughby blew out the lamp and they lay on the lumpy mattress, waiting to warm up.

'What were you two talking about when I left you this morning?' Isobel's voice came from the darkness. 'I presume Felicity regaled you with my tragic history.'

'What makes you say that?' Willoughby asked from the other side.

'She can't keep her mouth shut.'

There was a silence. 'Why don't you divorce him?' came Willoughby's voice.

'Divorce is for Americans,' retorted Isobel.

'Is that some European thing? Adultery is fine but divorce is not? And everyone lives in misery? I like the American way better.'

'American ways are wonderful. For Americans.'

'Would you mind not arguing all night?' Felicity said. 'I want to sleep.'

There was a silence. Then Willoughby said, 'One of my friends was killed the morning you were arrested by Reverte's men. He was hit in the thigh. We thought he was going to be okay at first. He was laughing about how he was going home, poor devil. Then something ruptured inside him. The blood pumped out. We couldn't stop it. He died surprised. We buried him on the battlefield. He was a New York boy named Rosenberg. He came over on the boat with me. A nice kid. Played the guitar. I have to write to his mother.'

'What did he expect?' Isobel said in a voice without emotion.

'What do any of you expect?' Felicity demanded, in tears. 'Fascists, Communists, you're all the same, telling yourselves you're doing God's work.'

'It is God's work,' Willoughby said. 'God wants blood. He needs an ocean of it. And by God, he's going to get it.'

43

They settled into silence. Felicity was exhausted. She felt as though her inner landscape had been rearranged by some careless hand, and nothing was where it was supposed to be any more. Sleep came, mercifully blotting out the images in her mind.

She slept solidly for hours and awoke as the room was growing lighter. Her aches of loss and grief had gone, to be replaced by a feeling of deep contentment. She realized that she was lying with her head pillowed on Willoughby's chest. Her sister had got up to go to the lavatory in the night, and somehow she had nestled up to Willoughby in her absence. His arms were around her, cradling her. She didn't know how she had come there. She dared not move. She had never been in such an intimate embrace with any man.

She didn't know whether Willoughby was awake or asleep. She was aware of his chest rising and falling, of the quiet thud of his heart against her cheek. Isobel was nestled into her back, like a child seeking refuge, still dreaming with little twitches of her hands and feet. Felicity floated on the surface of this happiness, knowing it was not hers to enjoy, snuggled up against a young male body. Her breasts were pressed against his side, the warmth of the contact uncurling in her like a bowl of honey being tipped over, sliding down her belly to her loins, warming and melting as it spread.

A phrase from her childhood came into her mind. *The sacred pleasures of my soul.* It was from a silk sampler that had hung in their playroom, embroidered by her mother's nurse. She couldn't quite remember how the words of the hymn had run, but that had been the last line. This was a sacred pleasure, she knew that. She had renounced this part of life. She had resolved that she was going to spend all the nights of her life in the small white bed of a nun, alone, never to lie in the arms of a man.

Having resolved to make that vow, was she not already bound by it? There could be no last flings, a voice inside her proclaimed, no last handful of sweets before renunciation. She should live now as she intended to live, renounce now what she intended to renounce. She was either strong enough for the life she had accepted – or she was play-acting.

And yet she found her mind forming the arguments that Isobel and others had thrown at her, arguments she'd laughed to scorn. *I'm committing myself to something that can't easily be undone,* she thought. *I'm so young. My life hasn't even begun. I know nothing about myself.*

It was so sweet to feel aroused. If it was so sweet to merely lie with one's head on a man's chest, how much sweeter must it be to marry, make love, have children, fulfil the destiny that Nature, and not God, had designed for her? That was a wrenching thought.

The golden cloud of her bliss began to dissipate, revealing visions of herself that were very different from the images she had cherished: not Felicity the angelic Carmelite sister, radiantly shining from beneath her snowy wimple – but Felicity the hypocrite and fool, Felicity the libertine, lusting after the body of a strange man.

She drew away from Willoughby. He released her instantly. It added greatly to her mortification to know that he had been awake all this time, aware of their entwined limbs and her soft breasts. She sat up. Isobel stirred into wakefulness with a groan, digging her fingers into her hair.

'God, my head. That wine, last night!'

Dishevelled and in various states of irritability, they climbed out of the bed. Downstairs, their hosts offered stale bread, hard cheese and mugs of the same red wine by way of a breakfast. There was no coffee to be had. Willoughby did not seem surprised by this, and calmly drained the wine. 'If there's anything about Spain I'll remember,' he said, 'it's red wine for breakfast. No wonder there's a civil war.'

A somewhat unwelcome presence materialized, as they breakfasted, in the form of the parish priest, a sour-looking, suspicious-eyed man who muttered privately with the landlord while watching them over his shoulder.

In his dungarees and checked shirt, Willoughby was a rangy figure, broad-shouldered and powerful-looking, with the level stare of a man who had been toughened. It did not take a feat of the imagination to see him in a soldier's uniform. And as a foreigner, the immediate suspicion was that he was a Republican volunteer. These were evidently the thoughts going through the priest's mind. To Felicity, his dark presence was like an accusation against her, a reminder that she had strayed from the Church's path.

'I think we'll be on our merry way,' Willoughby said, rising from the table. He settled up the bill, observed narrowly by the priest, who followed them at a distance and watched them boarding the van. 'I hope he's not arranging a warm welcome for us at the next village,' Willoughby commented as they set off into the cold, bright morning.

❧

Rocinante – whom Isobel rechristened Ruminant, due to her penchant for standing still and chewing the cud – covered the miles at a slow pace but without major problems. Felicity sat in silence, her unhappy thoughts churning round and round while Isobel and Willoughby wrangled or made desultory conversation.

An opportunity to speak came during one of Isobel's smoke breaks. They had stopped at the brow of yet another hill to allow the van's radiator to bubble. Isobel got out and perched on the running-board, puffing valiantly in the wind while Felicity and Willoughby remained in the shelter of the cab.

'About last night,' she began in a strained voice.

Willoughby was staring abstractedly across the rocky valley below them. 'What about last night?'

'I realize that we're forced into an intimacy that we might not otherwise have chosen. And I'm grateful to you, more grateful than

I can say, for what you're doing for us. But I don't think it was fair, or honourable, to take advantage of me.'

Willoughby's eyes focused slowly. 'What?'

'I said that it wasn't fair or honourable of you to take advantage of me.'

'What did I do?' he asked, genuinely baffled.

'Perhaps that's the way you would behave with a chance acquaintance,' she went on, her face pale and her mouth dry, 'but I'm not a chance acquaintance. You know what I have decided to do with my life. You should respect that principle, even if you have little respect for me as a person.'

'Felicity, what the hell are you talking about?' His voice was clipped.

She flinched a little in the face of his stare, which was now the colour and coldness of granite. 'Oh William, did it mean so little to you that you've forgotten? There was a contact between us that there should not have been – a contact which implied something that isn't there and can never be there.'

He glanced at Isobel through the windshield as though for guidance. 'You're madder than she is.'

'I am not mad! I woke up in your arms this morning. You were holding me in a way that you should not have done.'

He looked astonished. 'My God. Is *that* what you're talking about?'

'Yes. That's what I'm talking about. You were wrong to touch me in that way. Nothing of that sort must ever happen again.'

'You think I was *taking advantage* of you? Getting a kick out of it?' She watched as the expressions chased themselves across his handsome face. At first there was anger, which made her quail. It was succeeded by amusement. She cringed. To be laughed at now would be more than she could bear. But he did not laugh. His expression settled into a cool composure. 'It was you who crawled into my arms and put your head on my chest. You didn't need any encouragement from me. You slept like that for about two hours. However, you can be sure that nothing like it will ever happen again.' He turned away. 'You have my guarantee.'

'Thank you.' Her voice was thick, her face flaming.

The door opened and Isobel clambered in. 'I'm giving up smoking,' she announced. 'It's too bloody cold for vices.' She glanced from Willoughby to Felicity. 'What have you two been up to? Has he been singing smutty songs? You've got a face like a prune.' Shivering, she wriggled into the seat. 'Let's get going, I'm sick of this place.'

Whistling idly under his breath, Willoughby set Rocinante in motion again. They trundled down the hairpins into the valley, swaying together. Felicity sat hunched in misery, staring blindly at the road ahead. The memory of his astonishment, and then contempt, stung her worse than the salt water had stung her raw blisters. Couldn't she have been more diplomatic? She could have expressed it in a thousand different ways without offending him and making herself look like a fool or a prig. Why did what she said always sound so pompous? She was incapable of talking like other nineteen-year-old women. She sounded, even to herself, like a Victorian grandmother.

Now she remembered the words of the hymn that had been haunting her:

I shall be near and like my God!
And flesh and sin no more control
The sacred pleasures of my soul.

Flesh and sin. She'd had a taste of what sinners valued. But it hadn't been William who'd stolen from her; she had stolen those sacred, sinful pleasures from him. Trying to put the blame on him had been cowardly.

The mistress of novices had given her a bag of reading material to help her prepare for her Initiation. There was a book of the lives of Carmelite saints like St Teresa of Avila and St John of the Cross (Felicity had adored St John but felt repugnance for St Teresa). There was Thomas à Kempis' *Imitation of Christ*, two books of prayer and several pamphlets. Felicity realized with a sharp pang that she hadn't opened the bag for days. She hadn't even prayed for the past twenty-four hours.

She recalled something else, something the mistress of novices had said to her when they'd last parted: 'Each Carmelite sister carries the needs and hopes of all humanity to God, opening her heart to be a channel for his divine love. If a single sister wearies or weakens, the whole Mystical Body of the Church will automatically weary and weaken.'

She'd felt those words to be wonderfully exciting and inspiring at the time. Now she felt them as a crushing burden. She had failed, before she had even started. She had betrayed not only herself, but the whole Mystical Body of the Church. Her flame had blown out and she had become a spent candle, a place of darkness where there should have been light.

She closed her eyes and tried to pray now, but it was not easy in this jolting van, with Willoughby on one side and Isobel on the other. She prayed for forgiveness, for strength, for guidance. How far she had strayed!

'Shit.' Willoughby's profanity broke into her efforts at approaching God. Felicity opened her eyes. They had rounded a corner and found themselves at the entrance to a stony little village named Torrent. There was a striped pole barrier across the road and a knot of around two dozen men, headed by some dozen Guardia Civil in their olive green uniforms and ugly tricorn hats, carrying rifles.

Willoughby brought Rocinante to a halt. His eyes were watchful. 'That priest must have made a phone call,' he said tersely.

Isobel said, 'Let me do the talking. Neither of you speak Spanish, understood?' She got out of the cab. Willoughby and Felicity followed her, Felicity feeling her heart beating painfully hard.

The gang of villagers crowded round, the paramilitaries training their weapons on Willoughby. There was a babble of shouting voices. Slowly, Willoughby raised his arms, his face grim.

'Put your hands down, you fool.' Isobel snapped at him. He obeyed. She turned to the crowd. 'Who is in charge here?' she demanded, hands on hips.

A man strode forward officiously. 'I am the *alcalde* of Torrent. Who are you?'

'I am Isobel Albarán, the wife of Roberto Albarán.' She spoke with such serene confidence, and in such flawless Spanish, that the man doffed his cap, even if he had no idea who Roberto Albarán was. 'What is all this commotion?' she went on, looking around. 'Why are your men pointing their guns at us?'

The corporal of the Guardia Civil saluted. 'We had a report of a Republican soldier travelling with two foreign women on this road.'

Isobel laughed gaily. 'This is my sister, who is visiting me from England, and this gentleman is her fiancé. They speak no Spanish. We had the misfortune to encounter the Republican savages. They have stolen my house and my car. We're making our way to Valencia.' Casually, she produced her identity card. 'You know, of course, who my husband is?'

The men studied the card, frowning. 'Albarán,' one of them said. 'I've heard of him. He's a big shot with the Falangists.'

The rifles wavered, but remained pointed in their direction. Isobel showed no anxiety. 'A foolish misunderstanding. The priest at Santiago de los Vuitres telephoned you, I imagine? He's a suspicious fellow. We saw him looking at us. Of course, our appearance is wretched, but you must forgive us – the Reds stole everything we had. We were lucky not to be left stark naked.' She laughed her ringing laugh again, and was rewarded by sniggers from the villagers.

'Tell him to take off his shirt,' the unsmiling corporal ordered, indicating Willoughby.

'Certainly not,' Isobel said haughtily.

The corporal stepped forward and grasped Willoughby's collar. He ripped the check shirt down to Willoughby's navel, scattering buttons. Willoughby stood motionless. The soldiers bent forward to examine Willoughby's chest minutely, pointing to his muscular shoulders and talking among themselves.

'What nonsense is this?' Isobel demanded, glaring at them. 'What in hell do you think you're doing?'

'When a man has fired a rifle, the stock leaves bruises on the shoulders.' The corporal indicated the dark marks all over Willoughby's body. 'This one has been fighting. And look at his hands.' He lifted Willoughby's broad hand to show the roughened skin. 'He has the hands of a soldier.'

'Now look here,' Isobel snapped, 'my sister's fiancé is a very rich man, with a great deal of land. He hunts and fishes and shoots and rides his horses. Of course his hands are rough. He doesn't sit behind a desk all day. He has a pair of balls.'

The crude comment caused more laughter. The Guardia Civil corporal nodded, though he did not say that he accepted her explanation. He gave Willoughby a hard stare. 'I must make a telephone call to headquarters.' He marched off, taking Isobel's identity card with him. Isobel, unfazed, shook her head wearily. 'Damn this war. It's spoiling things for everybody.' There was general agreement from the crowd, and when she produced a cigarette, several hands thrust forward to offer her a light. She chose the silver lighter held by the mayor. 'But we'll soon have these damned Reds whipped back to their kennels,' she said. She put on her sunglasses, which caused a sensation, sunglasses evidently being a mark of great distinction in these parts. She smoked insouciantly, tossing her rich chestnut hair. Hungry male eyes devoured the curves of her body

Felicity was in awe. Isobel had the heart of a lioness. She was afraid of nothing, neither of Reverte's sinister thugs nor of these roughnecks. Felicity caught the way Willoughby was looking at Isobel and saw that he, too, was fascinated. As well he might be; his life hung on the casual way she waved her ebony cigarette holder and swung her hips, looking as though she were adorning the first salon of Spain, rather than some tumbledown village of Andalucía.

The wind flapped Willoughby's ruined shirt around his lean waist and lifted Felicity's golden mane of hair from her slender neck. Crows were calling ominously from the rooftops. Each of the three of them was compromising the other, Felicity thought. And yet clinging together was their only hope of safety.

After what seemed an eternity, the corporal returned. He snapped Isobel a salute as he returned her identity document. 'We have instructions to assist you in any way we can, Señora Albarán. We'll escort you to Badajoz. You can take the train from there to Bilbao – the line is protected by our forces all the way.'

'We are not going to Bilbao. We're going to Valencia.'

'Valencia is in the hands of the enemy,' he said sharply.

'But our embassy is there. We'll be put on a plane to London.'

The corporal was an ugly little man with a hard-bitten face. 'If you travel to Valencia, you will be going through territory mainly controlled by the enemy. I will have to send at least a platoon to guard you.'

'That won't be necessary,' Isobel said calmly. 'There is a war on. We want you to be free to give the Reds the thrashing they deserve. You have your hands full as it is, and we have no desire to take up your resources.'

'The countryside is unsecured, Señora. You will have to cross the front lines. I cannot permit you to continue.'

'You have been ordered to assist us in any way you can, is that not correct?'

'Yes, but—'

'I require you to assist us with food and petrol. That is all.'

She was so imposing that the man stepped back a pace or two. 'You may not be so lucky next time,' he said thinly.

'I am always lucky,' she replied. 'We're enjoying the drive greatly, I can assure you. And now, with your assistance, we'd like to continue.'

'I can spare you a can of fuel, no more,' the corporal said. 'We've been warned to stockpile as much gas as we can.'

'That will be better than nothing,' Isobel said loftily.

He gave the order. As his men scurried to obey, he surveyed the three of them with a small, cold smile. He clearly suspected he was being made a fool of. 'You're right, Señora Albarán. The Reds deserve a thrashing. Spain needs to be cleansed. We've started right here in our town. Putting things in order. Getting things straight. You understand what I mean?'

'Yes,' said Isobel, 'I believe I do.'

'Good,' he said briskly. 'I hope you will inform your esteemed husband that we are doing our part here in Torrent.'

'Of course.' The extra petrol can had now been loaded into the back of the van, together with a basket of provisions.

'Give my regards to your husband. And be careful with your sister's fiancé. Whatever you say, he has the eyes of a soldier. Take the road through the village square, if you please.'

Felicity could hardly believe that they were getting back into Rocinante and setting off. The striped pole was lifted and they jolted into motion. As the corporal had commanded, they took the street through the earthen village square. It was deserted except for five men, who sagged forward, dead, from posts in front of the church. The hands of each had been tied behind his back around the pole, and each had a placard around his neck.

Felicity stifled a cry of horror. This was what the corporal had meant by putting things in order and getting things straight. It was a grisly warning. Isobel turned her head away. Felicity clasped her hands and prayed. It was the first time she had prayed for the souls of men who had recently died by violence.

They drove through the narrow streets and out into the countryside. It was coming up for midday and the winter sun was at its brightest, turning the rocky landscape into chiaroscuro.

'I've just saved your life, William,' Isobel said.

'Am I supposed to kiss your feet?' He hauled off his ruined shirt and tossed it behind his seat. In his vest, his physique was shown to advantage.

'They would have shot you like those men in the square.' Isobel was cock-a-hoop. 'Did you see how I blew smoke in their faces? I had them eating out of my hand!'

Willoughby gave her a rare grin. 'Yeah, you did, as a matter of fact. I don't know how you got away with it.'

'Generations of breeding, darling. One has to know how to handle the peasants.'

'You were colossal.' This time it was Isobel who sat in the middle. Willoughby put his arm around her neck and gave her a smacking kiss on the cheek. Isobel laughed joyfully, pulling her hair back and pushing out her breasts. Felicity, who was still praying for the souls of the executed men, felt a sharp pang of annoyance. She preferred it when they were at each other's throats. If they were to start a mutual admiration society, it would be unbearable. She was almost pleased when they started wrangling again, Willoughby demanding to know whether Isobel was going to mention that execution in her next article and Isobel haughtily replying that any society needed to purge its rotten elements one way or another.

❧

Despite the war, the roads along which they travelled were largely deserted. They saw dark pillars of smoke on the horizon from time to time, signs of the fighting that was going on beyond the endless groves of silvery green olives and almonds whose bare branches were still stark.

They reached a small river and stopped to let Rocinante cool off. It was around four in the afternoon and they were all hungry. They decided to sit on the riverbank and investigate the basket which they'd been given. It proved to contain nothing more than bread, ham and wine, but that was enough to make a meal.

Willoughby and Isobel, to Felicity's dismay, were getting on better than they'd ever done. They were still wrangling, but now it was with laughter.

'Admit it,' Willoughby said, 'the only reason you got past those Fascists was because you're wearing a tight sweater.'

'*Filling* a tight sweater is a talent.'

'Nonsense! It's just an accident of birth.'

'*Your* birth may have been an accident, William Willoughby, but *mine* certainly wasn't.'

He smiled. 'You've got some nerve!'

As Felicity watched them spreading a blanket on the coarse grass, it was hard not to feel excluded. They were older than she was, of an age with one another. They knew what to say, what to do. She was outside their world in so many ways.

Isobel, still elated after her success in Torrent, carved ham and made sandwiches. She was charming and gay in a way that Felicity had not seen her since her marriage to Roberto. Willoughby opened the wine with his penknife, evidently entertained by her banter. He seldom took his eyes off her. When he laughed, there was a warmth in his laughter that would have given Felicity infinite pleasure if it had been she, and not her sister, who had provoked it. She felt wretched. Had they not seen poor murdered corpses today – and narrowly escaped with their own lives? There was something pagan in this gaiety, this swift forgetfulness of death.

They sprawled on the blanket, eating the rough sandwiches and passing the wine bottle around. Isobel, Felicity noted, did not even wipe the top of the bottle before passing it to Willoughby or taking it from him. She was normally so fastidious about such things; this was an intimacy that was very unlike her. How well they went together, she thought – Willoughby tall and athletic, Isobel womanly and graceful. They were each so handsome. Their bodies, side by side on the rug, seemed made for each other. They were all flowers and fruit, while she, the virgin, the apprentice nun, felt no more attractive than a bare stick. She half-expected to see Willoughby reach for Isobel and press his lips to hers. The image was agonising. She was in the throes of a pain more intense than anything she'd known before, an anguish she was completely unequipped to deal with. It crushed her lungs and made her unable to breathe.

'What's wrong, darling?' Isobel asked, suddenly noticing Felicity's face. 'Poor thing, you've gone quite white!'

'It's nothing, really.' But she couldn't bear to be with them any longer. It was too painful. She rose to her feet. 'If you don't mind, I think I'll take a little walk.'

As she walked away from them, she heard Isobel stage-whisper to Willoughby, 'Constipation.' She felt like screaming.

Felicity roamed along the bank of the river, which was narrow but swift, thrusting its way between boulders and exploding down little cataracts, making its impetuous way to the main artery. She had congratulated herself only days earlier on seeing rather a lot of life. She now felt she was seeing far too much.

She thought of St Teresa of Avila, whose life she had read with such squeamish fascination, and who had felt an angel thrust 'a long golden lance' again and again into her body, making her moan with 'the sweetness of this excessive pain'. Could anyone, in the age of Freud, see this in non-sexual terms? The path she had chosen was going to be a difficult one. The mistress of novices had interrogated her gently but insistently on her carnal needs; and on Felicity's mortified admission that she did, indeed, suffer from such hungers, had seemed pleased rather than otherwise.

'A difficult horse to master,' she had remarked obliquely, 'often proves the best steed once broken.'

She felt the cold wind flatten her clothes against her body, rubbing the fabric insistently against her breasts and thighs. *A difficult horse to master.* Yes, it was that, all right. And that cold word, *broken*. She didn't want to be broken.

She had tried, all her life, not to compete with Isobel. There was not just Isobel's greater strength and authority; there was also her own loyalty to Isobel and deep love for her, which had made her welcome the role of slave, into which Isobel had so often cast her.

When she looked back at her childhood, it was like seeing a play written and produced by Isobel, with herself and Chiara in the supporting parts, and Isobel unvaryingly centre stage. Games directed by Isobel, punishments ordained and executed by Isobel, rewards and treats dispensed by Isobel. A parade, led by Isobel, with herself and Chiara trotting adoringly behind.

In fact, in the age of Freud, it was probably no surprise that she had chosen a life of obedience – she had been groomed for it for nineteen years. She knew no other way to be.

But now, for the first time, she wanted to fight Isobel. She wanted Willoughby's eyes on her, not on Isobel. She wanted his smiles, the delicious warmth that he was able to bestow with a laugh. She wanted to take his hand and apologize for the idiotic way she had spoken to him. She wanted to tell him that she saw his nobility, his idealism, his courage, his gallantry.

She wanted to tell him that to lie with her cheek against his heart had been heaven itself.

Her dreams did not go further than that. Indeed, she had no experience of anything beyond that to draw on. Her imagination was chaste. She simply wanted it to be her, and not Isobel, who was first with Willoughby.

'Felicity!'

Her heart leaped into her throat at the sound of his voice. She whirled around to see that he was following her along the riverbank. She felt like weeping for joy. She stood with her hands clasped, waiting for him, the wind sweeping her hair away from her face.

'William!'

'Are you okay? Did something upset you?'

He was looking at her in concern. She took a step towards him and almost overbalanced. His hands closed around her arms, steadying her. She looked up into his face, rapt. He was so beautiful. She felt like St Teresa, pierced by a golden spear through her heart. 'I'm – I'm fine,' she stammered.

'Why did you rush off like that? Are you sick?'

'Oh, no! Nothing like that! I think – I think perhaps seeing those dead men in the square this morning—'

'Damn, I'm so dumb. I should have realized. Forgive me.'

'There's nothing to forgive! I'm the stupid one!'

'Listen, kid, we've packed the van. We better get going. It's going to be dark soon, and we need to find somewhere to spend the night.'

'Of course.'

As they walked back along the river, he put his arm around her and drew her close against his side. 'I've got used to horrible sights. I don't think twice about them any more. I suppose I should. You're right to be upset. You're sensitive. That's a great gift.'

Her heart was beating so fast that she could hardly speak. 'I don't know if it's such a great thing. Sometimes my feelings—'

'I understand. But it's better to have feelings, even painful ones, than to be indifferent. That's what I used to tell my students. You must be able to react. But don't let things prey on your mind.'

His body was lithe against hers, hip to hip and thigh to thigh, almost like dancing. He held her so perfectly, supporting her yet not crushing her, moving easily along with her. Felicity felt that warm flood of honey pouring into her loins again, making her aware of places she had sworn to be oblivious to. The sacred pleasures of her soul had been awakened again.

'Do you understand what I'm saying?' he asked, looking into her face.

'Yes,' she murmured, drinking in his concern like a sunflower turned to the sun.

'If you dwell on horrible things, they have a way of sickening you. But I believe that everything is sent to us – good and bad – for a purpose. So that we can learn.'

'You're a mystic.'

'Far from it,' he smiled. 'You just reminded me that I have an obligation to see things, and I am thanking you for that. But I shouldn't be touching you like this, I'm sorry.' He released her. She felt so bereft that she could hardly suppress a little cry of grief. She wanted his arm around her again, but they were already approaching the van.

Isobel was waiting for them. She, too, seemed to be concerned, and made a fuss of Felicity. 'Are you feeling better, dearest? You looked so wretched.'

'It was just one of my funny turns. I'm fine, darling, I promise.' And indeed, her heart was soaring. In her deepest misery, he had embraced her, comforted her, shared with her his inner thoughts. There was no greater joy.

It was almost dark before they reached the next village. In the twilight, they saw that the war had been here. They drove slowly past the burned-out shells of the church and the town hall, a street of houses that was pock-marked with machine-gun fire, the windows all shot out. None of the streetlights were working, but an icy moon was rising, shedding a lonely glow over the desolation.

They found a small, dingy bar in a back street with a light on. They went in. A solitary old woman was serving a handful of old men who were playing cards over wine and listening to a radio. Conversation stopped as they entered the bar. Someone switched off the radio, as though the very act of listening to the news was dangerous. In the silence, all eyes were fixed on them.

'We have nothing,' the old woman said brusquely in answer to Willoughby's greeting. Her face was white, her expression dazed. 'Please go.'

Willoughby looked around the shabby little place with pity in his eyes. 'I'm sorry for what happened here,' he said. He turned to the old woman. 'Is there somewhere for us to stay, mother?' he asked gently. 'We're on our way to Valencia but we won't get there tonight. It's cold to be sleeping out.'

'We have nothing,' the old woman repeated in a dry voice. She pushed them away with withered hands. 'There's nowhere to stay here. Go. Go.'

'Wait.' An old man in the corner leaned forward on a stick. 'On which side do you fight, young man?'

'On the Republic's side,' Willoughby replied without hesitation, 'I came from America to fight for Spain. These women were trapped by the fighting in Córdoba. I'm escorting them to Valencia. Then I'll go back to my brigade.'

The old man nodded. 'Give him the room, Maria.'

'I don't want more fighting,' the old woman said, a desperate note in her voice.

'There won't be any fighting,' Willoughby said. 'I promise. We just need a bed for the night.'

'Give him the room,' the old man said. 'He's our guest. And he's a good boy.'

The old woman seemed to crumple. 'There's a room upstairs.' She looked doubtfully at Isobel and Felicity. 'But these ladies are Señoras. The room is very simple.'

'We'll be glad of anything, believe me,' Willoughby said.

'I'll show you.'

She led them up the stairs to a small, very plain room which contained little more than a double bed and a crucifix on the wall. 'There's a bathroom next door,' she told them. 'I warned you, it's very simple.'

When they came down, the radio had been switched on again, and the news was bleak. Hitler had sent more tanks, warplanes and fresh troops to Franco. Mussolini had sent bombers, which were to be stationed on Mallorca, and could easily reach Barcelona and Madrid. Though the Russians had promised to supply equivalent weapons, they had not come. Appeals for help to the democratic nations, Britain and France, had been met with silence. The war was claiming thousands of lives. Spain was slowly succumbing to the Fascists, but fighting bravely as she went down.

The old woman brought them an omelette and a few slices of bread, and sat with them while they ate.

'It happened last month,' she told them. 'The Guardia Civil tried to arrest the young men of the town. They said they were traitors. There was fighting, and one of the boys was shot. The whole town rose up. They took spades and billhooks against the Guardia's rifles.' She drew wine for them mechanically as she told the story, speaking in a flat voice. 'They burned the *cuartel* and the police station and the church and the *alcaldía*. My son killed my brother.' Her haunted eyes searched their faces, one by one. 'He cut his throat with a scythe. How can such a thing be? That the nephew kills his uncle?'

'I don't know,' Willoughby said.

'Now all the young men have gone off to fight in the south. Only the women and the children and these old men are left.'

They ate without speaking after that. One by one, the old men melted away into the night. The radio was switched off. In the silence, ownerless dogs could be heard howling. The old woman shut the bar and did the dishes. They went upstairs and took turns to wash in the primitive little bathroom. Isobel went first. Felicity found herself crying. Isobel, too, was grim-faced as she emerged from the bathroom with her hair tied back.

'I hope you're pleased with yourself,' she said bitterly to Willoughby. 'This is the new Spain you wanted.'

'No, I liked the old Spain just fine,' he replied evenly. 'At least it was a democracy.'

'Ignorant people picking up billhooks and cutting each other's throats? Is that your democracy? That's just a disgusting shambles!'

Willoughby lost his temper with Isobel at last. He turned on her with hot eyes. 'Okay, let's try it your way, Isobel. First, we'll round up all the Jews and shoot them. Then we'll round up all the Socialists and shoot *them*. Then we'll take anyone who's still talking about elections and shoot them, too. Then we'll stick a big fucking picture of Adolf Hitler in every house and stick a big fucking swastika on every forehead, because that's really all anybody needs to know, isn't it? And we don't need any fucking arguments, do we?' His voice had risen almost to a shout. Isobel shrank away from him but he grasped her wrist and jerked her to face him. She gave a cry of pain.

'Stop it!' Felicity flew to him and seized his arm. 'You're hurting her! Look at her!'

Willoughby seemed to come out of his fury. Isobel's face was white and blank. She was trembling in every limb, hunched over as though protecting her womb. He released her and Felicity took her sister in her arms. 'Have you forgotten what I told you?' she threw at him over her shoulder. 'About what Roberto did to her?'

He turned away. 'I'm sorry,' he said thickly.

'Please stop fighting,' Felicity begged desperately, 'for God's sake. I can't stand it any more.'

'I'm sorry,' he said again. 'I'll go check on Rocinante.' He went out.

'Don't fuss, I'm all right,' Isobel said. But her voice was unsteady and her skin was like ice. She closed her eyes. 'I hate him sometimes.'

Although it gave Felicity some gloomy satisfaction to hear that, the hostility didn't last. As soon as Willoughby returned, he came to Isobel and apologized, gently and with dignity, for manhandling her. Isobel had stopped shaking by then and produced a few of her choking tears. Though Felicity suspected that she was laying it on just a little thick, Willoughby seemed convinced, and was stricken with remorse. It wasn't long before he was stroking Isobel's hair and murmuring in her ear, and Felicity was shut out completely.

'You don't realize how frightening you can be,' Isobel said in a pitiful little voice, looking up at Willoughby with a martyred face. Felicity rolled her eyes in disgust. Isobel, frightened? 'And I didn't know,' Isobel went on, 'how eloquent you can be, William. You're usually so quiet.'

Felicity hurried into the bathroom so as not to hear more. It was too nauseating.

The bathroom was tiny, and if there had been any warm water, Isobel had used it all. Felicity was grinding her teeth. The sink was littered with Isobel's chestnut hair and the sliver of soap was sticky with foam. Isobel's washed stockings and underwear were hanging shamelessly on the rail, where Willoughby would see them. Had she no modesty? She found herself longing for the little, neat, spotless cell which awaited her, where nobody fought or flirted, where all was holy and serene. She soaped herself as best she could and washed her underthings, balling them up in her shirt so as not to leave them on public display. She would rather wear them damp tomorrow than dangle them for Willoughby to see. She left the bathroom in spotless condition.

When she came back into the room, Willoughby and Isobel were sitting on the bed. Isobel had her back to Willoughby, who was massaging Isobel's shoulders tenderly.

'Am I interrupting?' Felicity said acidly.

'So sorry, darling,' Isobel said wearily. 'I think one of my migraines is coming on.'

Though Felicity was inclined to be sceptical, Isobel was very pale, and her eyes had become puffy, signs of the severe headaches from which she had suffered since Paul's death.

'It's my fault,' Willoughby said contritely, kneading her neck with gentle, strong fingers. 'I behaved like a savage.'

'You just spoke your mind,' Felicity said, feeling that, rough as Willoughby might have been, things were now going too far the other way for her liking. 'I've got some aspirins, if that will help.'

'That would be lovely,' Isobel said wanly. 'Oh, dear!' Clutching her mouth, she rushed to the bathroom and was noisily sick in the basin. 'Oh, so sorry! Always happens like this!'

The upshot was that Isobel became the centre of attention, lying on the bed with a damp cloth over her eyes, Willoughby fussing over her in a state of abject repentance, while Felicity cleaned up the vomit in the bathroom.

The aspirins had some effect after a while and Isobel grew sleepy. But the only way Isobel could get comfortable was with her head on Willoughby's shoulder and his arms around her. Nothing else would do. Felicity wanted to be sick herself. She was sure she could outdo Isobel in that department, at least. She was brimful with bile. But there was nothing for it but to lie beside them as Willoughby cradled Isobel – who soon began to snore, making sleep impossible for Felicity, even if she hadn't been on a bed of red-hot coals.

❦

They reached the sea the next morning and were approaching the outskirts of Valencia by midday. The air had become mild and warm after the dry cold of the interior. Rocinante was on her last legs, making pathetic noises whenever Willoughby changed gear. They were all subdued. They had slept badly. Isobel was heavy-eyed and silent.

Like the tolling a dull iron bell, Felicity was aware that their time together was coming to an end. She would have to say goodbye to Willoughby soon, and perhaps never see him again. The prospect was unbearable.

After the ferocious Nationalist assault on Madrid and the bombing of the city by Mussolini's and Hitler's planes, the Republican government had been moved to Valencia. The major embassies and diplomatic stations had followed suit. From here they would be able to get a plane to Paris or London, or a boat to Marseilles.

'We made it,' Willoughby said, as they passed a sign reading BIENVENIDOS A VALENCIA. He noticed the women staring through the window at the sea. 'What say we take a swim before we go any further?'

'We don't have any bathing costumes,' Felicity said.

'Oh, Felicity, for heaven's sake,' Isobel sighed. 'Yes, William, let's swim.'

They drove through orange groves down to the sea and found a beach deserted but for a handful of fishing boats, painted in a variety of faded colours. The sand was warm underfoot. They stripped to their underwear and Felicity found herself running hand in hand with Willoughby and Isobel into the sea, laughing hysterically.

The water was cold, but not unbearably so. As she threw herself into the waves, Felicity felt something wash away from her, the tension and misery of the past weeks. She splashed Isobel joyfully and was splashed in return. Willoughby struck out for the horizon with powerful strokes, as though determined to swim to Mallorca, until they grew alarmed and yelled for him to come back.

Afterwards, they sat on the beach to soak up the sun and dry off.

'I can't believe we're here at last,' Isobel said. 'God, this is heaven. Poor William, you have to go back to the fighting soon.' She put on her dark glasses and sprawled on her back, her splendid arms and legs outspread. The water had made her underwear more or less transparent, but then, of course, she enjoyed showing herself off to him, the more the merrier. 'How can you bear to go back to all that?'

'It's what I came here for,' he said sleepily. He, too, was sprawled on his back, eyes squeezed shut. Felicity longed to lay her palm on his muscled stomach. 'One day I'll come back here, when the war is won, and lie on this same beach and remember you two.'

'Oh, William,' Felicity cried, 'don't say that! We'll never lose touch!'

He smiled at her, squinting against the bright sunlight. 'You'll be in your convent, with the pink marble altar. You'll have forgotten all this.'

'I will never forget you,' she said passionately.

Something in her voice made Isobel sit up. 'What's wrong, poppet? Are you having one of your funny turns again?'

'No,' Felicity said miserably. 'I just don't want to think of us all saying goodbye.'

'Nor do I,' Willoughby said.

'You must be sick of us both, William,' Isobel said, laughing. 'You'll be dancing with joy once you get shot of us.'

'Matter of fact,' Willoughby said quietly, 'you two are the most interesting, beautiful, stimulating women I've ever known.'

There was a silence. Felicity felt her eyes fill with tears. Even though she'd been lumped in with Isobel, she would treasure his words forever. She was too choked to speak.

'Thank you,' Isobel said quietly. 'You're our hero, you know that.' There was a lump in Felicity's throat that prevented her from agreeing. A white seagull soared over the waves, mateless, lonely and pure. She fought back the tears. Isobel plucked at the whorls of hair at the tops of her thighs, along the elastic of her pants. 'God, I look like a gorilla. I've really been neglecting myself.' She raised her arms and inspected the stubble in her armpits. 'I need to find a razor.'

Felicity sighed. Trust Isobel to ruin every tender moment. Knowing that he was so smitten by her, why did she behave so vulgarly in front of him?

There were several roadblocks to be passed through on their way into Valencia, each one controlled by a different set of personnel, including two that were manned by ordinary men and women in civilian clothes, carrying rifles, who had taken responsibility for protecting their own districts. Nobody showed any interest in Felicity or Isobel, and Willoughby was able to talk his way through each one.

In this city of sunshine, palm trees and oranges, well within the Republican zone, there was an atmosphere of peace, even of holiday. The presence of the sea, dark blue and calm, added to the tranquillity.

The town was built on a large bay, basking in Mediterranean sunshine. Bougainvillea and geraniums bloomed against honey-coloured stone. Palm trees rustled around churches and hotels. Stalls were piled with oranges and lemons. There was little sign of the war here.

They found the temporary British Embassy on the seafront, facing the harbour. Willoughby parked Rocinante on the street outside. 'I'll wait for you here,' he said. He leaned on the wheel and stared at the sea.

Felicity and Isobel went in, carrying their precious British passports. The embassy had been set up in an apartment on the second floor that was far too small, and was crowded and noisy, but a courteous young attaché saw them quickly.

'We got your message, and we sent a reply, but of course you never received it. You'll be repatriated as soon as possible,' he told them across his desk, which was piled with forms and navy-and-gold passports. 'A matter of a day or two while we find you seats on a plane. We're trying to get all British nationals out of the country. The situation's getting considerably worse.' He looked at Isobel, obviously curious. 'If I may ask, Mrs Albarán, when did you last see your husband?'

'Several months ago.'

'Are you estranged?'

'Something of that sort.'

'Any idea how he sees the outcome of the war? Forgive me, but the situation is very confused and we welcome any information we can get from persons with – ah – their heads above the fray, so to speak.'

'Oh, Roberto is certain of a Nationalist victory,' she replied. 'And trust me, his head is well above the fray. I'm certain of it, too. Spain will very soon join Germany and Italy in the sisterhood of Fascist nations.'

'Ah. Thank you.' The attaché steepled his fingers, regarding Isobel with a somewhat quizzical air. 'That is, indeed, our own impression.'

'It's the only impression anyone can have.'

'Quite so. Well, I recommend that you find a hotel room – there are still rooms to be had along the *paseo marítimo*, if one is British – and stand by to be contacted. With luck, you'll be flying tomorrow.'

'Tomorrow!' Felicity echoed.

'Don't worry about money,' the diplomat said soothingly. 'Our priority is getting everyone out. Valencia hasn't been attacked so far, but it can't last for ever. You won't be asked for any expenses until you get back to Britain. Do you have enough for a hotel room?'

'I think so.'

'If you have any problems, refer them to us. We'll settle your bill, within reason. As soon as you have a room, call me and give me your address. We'll be in touch.' He rose. 'Let me know if there's any way I can help.'

Halfway down the marble staircase, Felicity stopped, unable to breathe. Her chest seemed to have closed up.

'Darling!' Isobel supported her. 'Don't take on so. What on earth is the matter?'

'I can't bear to leave him,' Felicity gasped.

'Who?' Isobel demanded, mystified.

'William, of course!'

'William?'

Felicity turned a white face to her sister. 'Oh, Isobel, this is frightful!' her heart felt as though it would break. She couldn't get her breath properly. She felt frightened and miserable.

'Come on, you're exhausted,' Isobel said, guiding the half-blind Felicity down the stairs, 'we've got to get you to a hotel.'

They found Willoughby sitting on the low wall overlooking the beach, licking an ice cream cone. 'Haven't had one of these since I was a kid,' he said. 'How did it go?'

'We've been told to get the best room in Valencia, courtesy of the British Embassy.' She appropriated Willoughby's ice cream and dug into it with a pink tongue. 'I don't see why they shouldn't pay for you, too. You're our knight in shining armour.'

'Okay,' he said, throwing the door of the van open. 'Let's go find the best hotel in Valencia.'

They were made welcome at the *Las Arenas*, a very grand spa hotel that seemed to be half-empty but for foreigners like themselves, waiting for a flight out of Spain. The *Las Arenas* was a dream in cream-coloured marble, flanked by tall colonnades like a Roman temple. Families dressed in white strolled under parasols along the vast expanse of beach in front of the hotel. A pier reminiscent of Brighton jutted out into the blue water. Pleasure boats bobbed on the water. The war could not have been further away. Wearing their ill-assorted clothes, still sticky with sea salt, and with beach sand in their shoes, Felicity felt distinctly conspicuous in the marble foyer. Nobody seemed to notice or care.

Willoughby had returned the remainder of their money to them but refused their offer of a room. 'Come on, William,' Isobel urged. 'Enjoy a little luxury. We'll pay for your room here. It's the least we can do.'

He shook his head, smiling slightly. 'I need to report to the local IB. They'll find me somewhere to stay.'

'A hard floor and a bowl of lentils!'

'If I'm lucky,' he agreed.

'We have lobster, oysters and fresh sea bass in the restaurant,' the receptionist fluted over the marble counter. 'And French champagne. Would the ladies like to book a table for tonight?'

'We damn' well would,' Isobel said. 'Hear that, William? Lobster and champagne for dinner. You'll join us, of course. Let us at least say thank you properly.'

He shrugged. 'Sure, why not?'

'A table for three,' Isobel told the receptionist. 'At seven.'

Felicity felt a horrible pang as Willoughby turned to leave. She hated to let him out of her sight, despite their rendezvous tonight. What if there was an air raid? What if – ? 'William!' she called.

He turned. 'Yes?'

Felicity threw her arms around him and kissed him clumsily on the mouth. 'Thank you for everything.'

'No problem.' He smiled slightly vaguely, as though his mind were already elsewhere. She watched him walk to the door, a tall figure against the dazzling sunlight. He turned and waved. Then he was gone.

∽

Their room was airy, with a big veranda and views of the Mediterranean. Felicity's chest still felt tight. She had to concentrate on each breath. The first thing she did was to book a call to Chiara, who let out a squeal of joy upon hearing Felicity's voice on the telephone.

'I've been so worried about you two! There hasn't been a word from you. I haven't slept for days. The war's all over the newspapers. I thought you'd both been captured by the Reds. And with Isobel's politics, they'd have put you up against a wall too.'

'We *were* captured,' Felicity said. '*And* almost put up against a wall! And as a matter of fact, it was a Red who got us out.'

'What!'

'Well, he's not really a Red,' Felicity went on. 'In fact, he's rather wonderful. Isobel says he's our knight in shining armour.'

'Who is this paragon?'

'He's called William Willoughby and he's an American volunteer. They've commandeered Isobel's house. You can't imagine the state it's in. He was billeted there and he came to our rescue. He saved us from a mad Bolshevik who wanted to shoot us, and drove us all the way from Córdoba to Valencia.'

'My God, he deserves a medal.'

'I'm going to see that he gets one,' Felicity vowed. 'He ought to be knighted. We've had such adventures. I can't wait to tell you all about it, but we've only got two minutes now, so it'll have to wait.'

'Willoughby, you say?'

'Yes. He risked his life for us. He's tall and handsome and brave, and – and—'

'Felicity! You're in love!'

Felicity flushed. 'Nonsense.'

'You are!' Chiara's bright laughter pealed down the line. 'Oh, goodness! That's dried my tears!'

'Don't be silly.'

'Does this mean the convent is off? Oh please say you've come to your senses, Fee!'

'It's not a question of coming to my senses.'

'Yes, it is. You've always lived in a dream, darling. That's why you get so many hopeless ideas in your head. Now you've had a dose of real life, and I hope it's blown the cobwebs away. Bring this Sir Galahad home, and let's take a look at him.'

'We're going to try,' Felicity promised. 'He's done his bit for the Spanish.'

'He certainly has. And for you. Oh Fee, what a wonderful phone call. To hear that you're safe – *and* that the nunnery is off!'

'It's not off at all,' Felicity said agitatedly. 'There's no question of that. And even if there was – which there isn't – it isn't me he wants.' She glanced at Isobel as she said the words, but Isobel was too busy investigating their room to pay any attention to what she was saying. 'He's only got eyes for you-know-who.'

'Has she been setting her cap at him, then?'

'She doesn't have to. You know what men are like around her.'

'Yes, I do. Pass me the sick bowl.' Chiara made an uncivilized noise. 'But you can't spend your life in Isobel's shadow. If you're in love with this Willoughby, then let him know. It's a fairy tale – the maiden fair, the shining knight and the dragon. And the knight's not supposed to go off with the dragon, you know. Give the adventure a happy ending. You'll be able to tell your grandchildren about it. Don't be so timid, Fee!'

Felicity couldn't help laughing. 'Oh, Chiara. You always cheer me up!'

'What colour are his eyes?'

'Cloudy.'

'Hair?'

'Black.'

'That settles it. I'll put up the banns!'

'Don't sit there gassing to Chiara all day,' Isobel interrupted. 'I want a spa treatment. We deserve it, after what we've been through. And Stanley Baldwin's paying.'

The peeps sounded to indicate their two minutes were up. 'I have to go, darling,' Felicity said to Chiara. 'Lots of love! Don't worry any more! We'll be home in a few days!'

They went down to the spa, where they were welcomed into a world of white-suited attendants, saunas, thermal baths, steam rooms, massage rooms, hydrotherapy and ice treatments.

'Mud, I think, to start with,' Isobel decided. 'And then steam.'

They lay back on marble slabs while the girls plastered their bodies with warm mud. Isobel sighed blissfully and drifted into a doze. After a while, the heat and the heaviness of the mud overcame Felicity and she too sank into a dreamless sleep. When she awoke, her breathing seemed easier.

In the steam room, they sat, naked but for towels, side by side on the bench.

'Heavens, it's good to sweat out all that grime,' Isobel said with satisfaction, as the drops rolled down her nose. 'Now, what's all this about William?' she asked, looking at Felicity closely. 'Have you got a little bee in your bonnet about him?'

'It's much worse than that,' Felicity said in a low voice.

'Oh Felicity!' Realization dawned on Isobel. 'Oh, darling. Really?'

'Yes.'

Isobel wiped sweat off her shiny face. 'Impossible, sweetheart,' she said decisively. 'Nobody can fall in love in a week, least of all a tough little nut like you. It's just indigestion. It'll pass off in a day or two.'

'I don't know how it happened,' Felicity replied miserably. 'I can't stop thinking about him. I can't bear the thought of losing him. I don't know how I'll get through the next two hours without him, let alone the rest of my life!' The last words came out somewhere between a wail and a laugh. Felicity took hold of herself and strove for dignity. 'But it's no bloody use. I'm going to be a nun. And even if I weren't, he's yours.'

'He's not mine at all,' Isobel retorted. 'What on earth makes you say that?'

Felicity shook her head. Could Isobel really be so dense? 'You can't take your eyes off each other,' she said.

'I think you've got this all topsy-turvy,' Isobel said, frowning. 'There's absolutely nothing between me and William.'

'When you're in the room, I don't exist for him. He thinks you're utterly wonderful. And you're so in tune with him. You know just what to say to make him laugh. I'm always excluded, the odd one out. Even when you fight each other, you're perfect together. And I have nothing, absolutely nothing, to contribute.'

Isobel took her hands. 'Listen to me darling. William and I are the same age, and you're younger. Of course we've got a lot in common, even though he's a complete fathead, politically speaking. That doesn't mean we're in love.'

'How can anyone *not* be in love with him?'

Isobel smiled. 'I grant you, if I were single, it might be a different story. He would be very interesting. He's the kind of man a woman could really make something of. But I'm not single. I'm a married woman. Whatever you may think of me, darling, I'm faithful to my vows. I would never betray Roberto. I may be a stinker in other regards, but not in that regard.'

Felicity felt as though a great, heavy stone was rolling away from her heart. Daylight was pouring in, piercing her. 'Oh, Isobel. I was so convinced – forgive me, I really thought—'

'That's all right.' She kissed Felicity's damp cheek tenderly. 'If he were mine to give, I would give him to you so happily. You deserve him. But I would never have guessed how you felt. You talk to him like a Mother Superior all the time. I'm sure the poor man has absolutely no idea at all. Are you sure about this?'

Felicity sat with her head in her hands. Her heart was beating heavily, a fist pounding on a locked door that was too frail to withstand much longer. 'I'm so confused,' she said wearily. 'I don't know what to do or think.'

'But that's wonderful. Confused is the way one *should* be at nineteen! Oh, darling, thank God for William. If he makes you reconsider your priory, I will be the best and most loving sister to him that any man could desire. *Does* he make you reconsider your priory?'

'Yes,' Felicity whispered. She could hardly believe that she had said the word. But she had. The stone was rolling away, gathering speed as it tumbled down, leaving her unbearably light, floating into the air.

'Hallelujah.' Isobel jumped up and did a little dance of joy, until her towel slipped scandalously. 'What wonderful news!'

'Don't be such a lunatic,' Felicity said, smiling despite herself. 'It's not as simple as that.'

'Of course it is! You've chosen Life, after all! Oh, darling, you've made me so happy! He's wrested you away from those festering nuns, after all!' She embraced Felicity, their damp skin clinging together in the sauna.

'I haven't got any clear ideas of any kind,' Felicity replied. 'And there's the small question of William's feelings. I've treated him so stupidly. He thinks I'm a complete fool.' Shuddering, she thought of the way she had lectured him about holding her in his arms. God, what an idiot she had been! If only she could take that back!

'No, he doesn't. He admires you enormously.'

'How can he admire me, after the way I've behaved!'

'He does. He told me so. He thinks you have a brilliant mind and wonderful principles.'

Even if, as she suspected, Isobel was making this up, Felicity felt a surge of joy. 'Truly?'

'Cross my heart.'

'When did he say all this?'

'At the river, when you went wandering off, white as a sheet. He gave me quite a wigging about how I don't appreciate you. He scolded me for mistreating you. I tried to persuade him that you're only an impudent insect, who needed to be stamped on regularly, but he wouldn't have it. He claimed you were a great soul and that he'd never met anyone quite like you.'

'You're making this up.'

'I am not, I assure you. And as for him only having eyes for me, haven't you seen the way he looks at *you*? Felicity, you're so beautiful! So much more beautiful than me!'

'Of course I'm not more beautiful than you!'

'But you are. I'm all worn out and used up. I don't have a heart any more to bestow on anyone. You're fresh and lovely and clean and young. Compared to me, you're a rose. I'm an old thistle, all spikes and thorns.'

Felicity laughed unsteadily. 'Some thistle.'

'Listen to me. If you want William, you can make him yours. He's the most romantic man. I mean, romantic in the real sense. He's just waiting to fall in love with you. You just need to show him that you see him in that way. He thinks you've set your heart on being a nun, so he treads on eggshells around you.'

'You always make me feel wonderful,' Felicity said. 'But before anything else, I have to make up my mind about the priory.'

'You already have.'

'No, I haven't.'

'Yes, you have. I'm not going to let you pretend otherwise any more. Falling in love with William has proved that you're not the plaster saint you so want to be. You've got red blood in your veins.'

'Red blood is not the point.'

'If you go into that convent,' Isobel said emphatically, 'you'll go stark, staring mad. You weren't made for that life. You'll end up like old Saint Teresa, sticking a golden pole up your whatsit and claiming it's God.'

'Isobel! You're disgusting!'

'I know I am. But the truth is usually rather different from our dreams, dear. Even if things with William don't work out – and I know that they will – the very fact of loving him means that you're not suited to being a nun. If it's not William, then it will be somebody else.'

'No. You don't understand.' Felicity smiled sadly at Isobel. 'If it's not William, then it will be nobody.'

Isobel studied Felicity's face as though deciphering some strange runes written here. 'Well,' she said at last, 'let's see about William, then.'

❧

They spent the afternoon in self-beautification and narcissistic pursuits. Felicity had her hair washed and combed out, so that it shone golden. Isobel bought them both new frocks with the last of their money, claiming Stanley Baldwin would pay for the rest, and that it was all he deserved for bullying that angel, Hitler.

'We've got to get William to see sense,' she said. 'This war is lost. You heard what that poncey little attaché said. No hope for the Reds. We'll get William on our flight back to London.'

'It won't be so easy,' Felicity said sadly. 'He's terribly committed.'

'He's done his bit. He fought for the Republic and he lost friends. They can't ask for any more than that.'

'It's not what they ask. It's what he's prepared to give.'

'The first thing is to open his eyes to you.' Isobel said practically. 'All else follows from that. This is how we'll play it. I'll stay for the lobster – damned if I'm going to miss that – and then I'll say I've got the megrims coming on. I'll retire to my room, leaving you unchaperoned. There'll be a band, and dancing. Wait until a slow number comes along, then tell him it's your favourite tune. He'll ask you to dance. Once you've got him on the dance floor, he'll be easy prey.'

'What a way to talk!'

'Just press up close against him, and look into his eyes. He'll get the message. If necessary, try and rub your tummy up against him in the strategic areas.'

'Isobel!' Felicity covered her ears and shut her eyes.

'Just, whatever you do, don't mention the convent. Or, if you do, say you've had second thoughts. Yes, that's it. Say you're not sure any more. Say something's happened that's making you change your mind. He'll ask you what. You just murmur his name and say you hoped he would understand.'

Felicity couldn't help laughing. 'Isobel, this is too corny for words.'

'Love is corny. Trust me.'

'I certainly do not trust you.'

'All right, then, write your own script. Just make sure he gets the message. Don't be subtle, that's all. Subtlety doesn't work with men.' She adjusted the fit of the flowered frock around Felicity's slight bosom. 'You look so lovely, darling. My golden angel! William Willoughby is the luckiest man in the world! And if you want to bring him up to the room, just call me from Reception. I'll melt away into the night. I won't even mess up the bed, don't worry. It'll be pristine. I might scatter a few rose petals on the pillow.'

Felicity couldn't help laughing. 'You're absurd. I can promise you that nothing like that is going to happen. And I promise I won't be subtle with William. I'm certainly not going to dance with him, either. I'm just going to tell him that I love him.'

Isobel met her sister's brilliant, wide grey-blue eyes and swallowed, as though she had suddenly lost her breath. 'Yes. That ought to do it.'

They waited at their table in their new frocks, drinking sherry and listening to the orchestra playing sweet old tunes. Oddly, it was Isobel who was jittery with nerves, smoking incessantly and fiddling with her freshly painted nails. Felicity felt as though she were floating, serene, high above the hubbub. She was very tired.

The restaurant was crowded. Whatever was happening in the rest of Spain, Valencia still conserved glamour. The women wore mantillas and combs in their hair, the men were sleek and brilliantined; waiters carried trays loaded with food and wine between the tables.

They amused themselves by criticizing the outfits of the women around them, until they ran out of victims. Felicity looked at the lipstick mark her own mouth had left on the rim of her sherry glass. 'I'm not used to make-up,' she said. 'I wish I could wipe it off.'

'Damn him, he's late,' Isobel fretted. 'What's he playing at?'

'He'll be here soon,' Felicity said tranquilly.

The band began playing the Bolero from *Carmen*. Several couples got up to show off their dancing skills. A waiter materialized at their table, offering a silver salver, on which was a note. Isobel snatched it up and unfolded it. She read it swiftly.

'Has he been delayed?' Felicity asked.

Silently, Isobel handed it over to Felicity. It was written with pencil on a sheet of lined exercise paper:

> *Sorry to let you down, but I hate goodbyes.*
>
> *By the time you get this, I'll be on the train back to Córdoba. There's heavy fighting down there and they need every man they can get. I couldn't stay here any longer. I donated Rocinante to the local militia. They'll fix her up and put her in service as a field ambulance.*

I'm glad you're getting out. It was a privilege to know you both. I won't forget you.

Enjoy the lobster!

Death to Fascism!

William.

Felicity looked up at Isobel, who was pale. 'I'm sorry,' Isobel said helplessly.

'It's all right.' Mechanically, Felicity folded the note and put it in her pocket. 'It's a lucky escape, really.'

'Oh, darling, don't say that!'

'But it is. I was on the brink of making a terrible mistake.'

'No!'

'I've been so terribly stupid. How embarrassing. It was just an infatuation, after all. But I've been saved. I'll always be grateful for that.'

'Felicity, please! We'll find him, get him back—'

'I'm constitutionally incapable of any sort of normal relationship. I can't share myself with anyone. I can't make anyone love me. I can only dream stupid dreams. I'm only fit to moulder away among others like me.' Felicity rose to her feet. There was a roaring in her ears. 'I know my path, now. This was a test, and thank God, I passed it.'

'Fee!'

She turned to walk out of the restaurant but somehow the floor wasn't there any more. She fell, as though from a great height, with a sound like the crashing shut of iron gates.

2.
ISOBEL

Holland, Autumn, 1938

It had been a long drive. The autumn scenery was lovely but sad, expanses of water reflecting a cold blue sky, leaves floating off the trees and making deep drifts along the sides of the roads. The Mercedes-Benz limousine swept them up into the air as it bowled along. Now and then, Isobel turned and looked through the rear window to see them swirling and settling in their wake. But, for the most part, she sat wrapped up in her sables, staring straight ahead. It was cold in the car. Max detested the heating, which he said was un-German.

'Besides,' he added, uncapping the silver flask, 'it gives us a reason for this little sin.' He swigged generously and held the flask out to her. Isobel barely tasted the fiery schnapps before passing the flask back to him. He grinned at her, showing large, white, tombstone teeth beneath his immaculately groomed black moustache. 'Too strong for you, *nicht wahr?*'

'I prefer champagne.'

'*Also gut.* We will endeavour to obtain a regular supply of that beverage for you, direct from the source.' He chuckled at his own joke, swigged again, and slipped the flask back into the inner pocket of his mantle. Max, who was a high functionary in Dr Goebbels's Ministry of Propaganda, had all the Nazi love of costumes. Today he was swathed in a travelling cape against the gales he wouldn't feel, and knee-length boots against the mud he wouldn't encounter. He stretched his long legs out now, admiring the gleaming leather with his head on one side. 'You are about to meet a piece of living history. How does it feel?'

'To tell you the truth, the whole thing gives me the creeps.'

'You are afraid?'

'Yes, of course.'

'Why?'

'Why?' she echoed. 'Max, this man was under my bed every night for years.'

His bright blue eyes widened in surprise. 'Under your bed? My dear Isobel!' Understanding dawned. He let out his rich guffaw. 'Ah! You mean he was the *Butzemann!* How do you say *Butzemann* in English?'

'The bogeyman.'

'The bogeyman!' He slapped his thigh with his gloves. 'The one who carries naughty children away in a sack.'

'Yes, exactly.'

'Do you think he will put you in a sack now?'

'He may. I haven't been a very good girl.'

'I have a special dislike for very good girls,' he replied. 'After all, I am a *Butzemann* myself, am I not?'

'Sometimes I think you are,' she replied. She looked out of the window at the melancholy, flat Dutch countryside, with its patchwork of well-kept fields and well-kept villages. It was, she thought, like driving through a painting by Jacob van Ruisdael, complete with cows and windmills.

He followed her gaze. 'What do you see out there?'

'Fields and cows.'

'I see a very nasty countryside for tanks. Wet and easily flooded, if the inhabitants should choose to open their dykes.'

They had reached the outskirts of a small village. Like all the villages they had passed through, it was picture-perfect, neat streets looking as though they were scrubbed daily by apple-cheeked women in pigtails. The chauffeur turned the car down a lane which brought them to an imposing gatehouse. The gates themselves were studded with iron, presenting a formidable appearance. An elderly Dutchman emerged from the gatehouse, and after a word with the chauffeur, swung the gates open for them. The task seemed almost beyond his strength. Max muttered impatiently.

'Why do they have such a decrepit old fellow in charge of the gate, God damn him? It's absurd.'

At last the gates were open and the Mercedes-Benz slid between them into the estate. They found themselves driving through a kind of forest. Half-buried in the greenery, they passed a chapel, like something from a fairy tale. The woodland was thick and dark around them, but soon opened out and gave way to a long avenue, lined with ancient elms. Here the leaves had been raked into piles. The tang of smoke in the air indicated that the gardeners were already starting to burn them.

At the end of the avenue, a rather severe chateau, built of red brick and stone, came into view. Flanked by two imposing wings, it was set in a rose garden where the last blooms of the year were still awaiting the pruning shears. An orangery lay to one side of the house. The golden glow of oranges hanging on the boughs could be seen through the glass.

'*This* is where he lives?' Isobel demanded.

'This is Huis Doorn. What did you expect?'

'I don't know. Something more like a prison, I suppose.'

'But it is a prison, my dear Isobel.'

'This is a mansion,' Isobel said, eyeing the liveried footmen who emerged from the front door to greet them.

'Nevertheless, any place which one cannot leave is a prison. Believe me. I am an expert.'

The doors of the Mercedes-Benz were opened for them by the footmen. They got out. Isobel surveyed the façade of the chateau with a feeling of apprehension. Max, however, was in high good spirits. 'I haven't been here in some years. They look after the place, one can see that.' A major-domo in a white jacket and white gloves led them inside. The entrance hall was dominated by a bronze equestrian statue and a number of busts and oil paintings. Max took Isobel's arm. 'Don't look so nervous. He can't eat you.'

'That's not what my parents told me,' she hissed back.

They were conducted silently to a reception room, wallpapered in yellow silk damask, crowded with furniture in Biedermeier style. There was no offer to take their coats, which would have been superfluous in any case, since the house was icy. There was a handsome tiled stove in one corner, but it was not lit. This was not a chamber where guests were made to feel welcome or would wish to linger. Family portraits frowned down at them from the walls, desks and tables bristled with ugly, costly ornaments.

'May I smoke?' Isobel asked. She was dying for a cigarette.

The major-domo shook his head slowly, managing to convey shocked disapproval without saying a word. The servants left them alone, but for the loud tick of an antique clock. Max surveyed her appreciatively.

'You look very beautiful. Stunning.'

Isobel nodded her acknowledgment of the compliment. Max had been trying to seduce her for months, using a combination of flattery, personal charm, lavish gifts and invitations to unique occasions (such as this one) designed to make her feel privileged.

She was now almost twenty-seven years old, and it was true that she had never looked more beautiful. During the time she had spent in Berlin, she had looked after herself. Her hair, skin and nails received regular attentions from the beauticians of the Kurfürstendamm. Her articles had been snapped up by the British and American newspapers, which were hungry for news of Germany, Hitler and Nazism. Her voice had become familiar on the BBC and CBS, earning her a decent income. In addition, Roberto had finally agreed to give her an allowance (out of her own money) so that she was relatively flush. She had been able to replenish her wardrobe. Certain extra-luxury items, such as the sable hat and coat she now wore, had come courtesy of Max. There were other admirers in the Nazi hierarchy who had laid tributes at her feet, including the striking (and reportedly lesbian) wife of a high Party functionary, though none with the assiduity of Max.

As a result, she was now better dressed and better groomed than she had ever been. Her legs were celebrated, her bust was described as divine by the elderly gentleman in the Friedrichstraße who made her brassieres. Her face was said to be rivalled only by that of Marlene Dietrich. Her photograph invariably accompanied the articles which she wrote. With her dark colouring, elegant clothes and free use of lipstick, Isobel did not conform to the female type held up by the Nazis, which was of blonde, unadorned domesticity. She did not even attempt to approximate it, as women like Magda Goebbels did, with their peroxided tresses and couture dirndls. Nevertheless, the attention she received indicated that, although unadorned domesticity might be all very well for the lower orders, what the Party insiders really desired was something more cosmopolitan. She had received compliments from Hitler and Goebbels themselves, the ultimate seal of approval.

But something Max had said earlier was haunting her. *Any place which one cannot leave is a prison.* If she was having a love affair, it was not with any individual, but with Fascism itself, with the style, logic, and power of a political philosophy which seemed to restore order to a chaotic world. However, she was aware that, as Germany's path diverged steadily from that of her own country, which she still loved deeply, she was in danger of being left with nowhere to call her own.

The fear of war was growing daily. Whether this was because Hitler was being driven to it by British and French aggression, or whether it was true that Hitler intended to conquer half of Europe, was a bitterly contested argument. Either way, if Britain and Germany went to war, her position would become impossible. If it came to that, what would she do? Remain in a country that was at war with her own? Or return to Britain to confront the failure of her dreams and the disapproval of her entire generation?

Spain was impossible; the Civil War was still raging. She recalled the drive from Córdoba to Valencia with Felicity and William Willoughby in the same way she thought of childhood holidays. Since that Quixotic jaunt, the Spanish war – and the world – had become much darker and more dangerous.

Poor Felicity! That awful evening in Valencia! What rotten luck that Willoughby had decided to go straight back to the front. Felicity's love for Willoughby had been the silly infatuation of an inexperienced girl, the sort of crush she might have formed for a matinée idol; but that was what girls were supposed to feel at nineteen. Otherwise half of them would enter convents. And Willoughby hadn't been a matinée idol. He'd been there in the flesh, high, wide and handsome. If he had only stayed one night, the course of Felicity's life might have changed. But he hadn't; and as so often, a woman's fate had depended on the whim of a man.

They were now aware of voices, the first they had heard in this silent house. Isobel heard the voice of an elderly man say imperiously in German, 'No, no, it makes no difference. I will see them.' The tapping of a cane approached their salon.

Max raised his silver flask to her, winked, and took a final swig, pocketing the flask deftly as the door opened. They both rose to their feet.

The old man who shuffled into the room was impeccably dressed in a pinstriped suit, with a white waistcoat and fawn spats.

His black silk tie was fastened with a diamond clasp. An enamelled cross was pinned to his lapel. In one hand he held an ebony cane. The other was tucked into the pocket of his jacket. Ignoring Max, he glared at Isobel like an elderly incarnation of the imperial German eagle.

Her heart was racing, but she had the presence of mind to curtsey deeply. He gave her no more than a nod in return. In addition to the legendary moustache, with its upswept, spear-like spikes, he now had a pointed beard. Both were white. The prominent beak of a nose jutted like the surviving buttress of a ruined cathedral, making him instantly recognizable as the bogeyman of her childhood, the slaughterer of infants and devourer of nations, Kaiser Wilhelm II.

'Your Majesty,' Max said, bowing stiffly and clicking his boot heels, 'thank you for this audience.'

The crêpe-hooded eyes finally left Isobel and gave Max a cursory glance. 'Well,' he said in a grating voice, 'you are thriving, I see.' He lowered himself slowly onto the edge of a chair, never removing his left hand from his pocket. Isobel knew that it had been withered since birth, and was always disguised in public. 'Who is this young woman?'

'Majesty, allow me to present Isobel Albarán, the wife of a valued Spanish colleague, Roberto Albarán—'

'You are still gallivanting around with other men's wives, I see.'

Max chuckled. 'With the full permission of their husbands, of course.'

'Why don't you get one of your own?'

'One day, perhaps, in time.'

'There is no time.' Wilhelm's voice had the hollow tone of a manhole cover being dragged open. The fingers which held the ivory top of his cane were in incessant, trembling motion. 'Death is at your shoulder. War is coming.'

'There is no necessity for another war,' Max replied smoothly. 'With reason and diplomacy, it can be avoided.'

'Is that the line that Berlin is taking these days?'

'Naturally, there are interests who want nothing more than another war.'

'Which interests are these?'

'The Jews, of course.'

'Ah, yes. The Jews.' These days, Isobel thought, no German conversation could continue more than a few minutes before it turned to the Jews. 'As individuals, they may be decent men.'

'As a people, they are pernicious. There has to be a solution.'

The Kaiser seemed more interested in Isobel than in Max. His lined eyes travelled slowly across her face and body. 'A solution?'

'Like any poison, they must be expelled from the body which they are destroying.'

'You mean, with violence.'

'I mean that we have been politely inviting the Jews to leave for many years, now. They have ignored us. They do not know the meaning of gentleness themselves, and therefore a firm policy is required. You are no lover of the Jews, surely.'

'I am opposed to the rough treatment of civilians.'

'Uncle, the only way—'

'Do not call me that,' Wilhelm said frostily, turning a cold blue eye on Max. 'How dare you?'

Max was unfazed by the snub. 'Your Imperial Majesty,' he began again, with the faintest of mocking smiles, 'the only way to dislodge the stranglehold of the Jews is to physically pry their fingers, one by one, from the throat of Germany. That is what the Führer has said, and Dr Goebbels—'

'I can just about stomach Hitler,' Wilhelm growled. 'Goebbels is pure poison to me.'

'As you wish. But I hope you understand that we have gone beyond pleading with the Jews and trying to reason with them. Things are changing.'

'Is that what you have come here to tell me?'

'We in the Party know that Your Majesty delights in seeing Germany great again. We value your encouragement.'

'Nonsense. You don't care what I think. Goebbels himself as good as told me that I am irrelevant to the glorious Third Reich.'

'I hope that was merely a misunderstanding.' Max was as slick as butter. 'However, to return to the point at hand, we intend to act, and we should be glad of your public support.'

'My support, eh?' Wilhelm showed yellowed teeth like an old dog confronting an annoying puppy. Turning back to Isobel, he examined her from head to toe. 'I know your face,' he said. His tone did not suggest any great pleasure. The trembling fingers worked incessantly at the ivory knob of the cane. 'You are British.'

'Yes, Your Majesty.'

He grunted. 'You have come to Huis Doorn to gape at your old enemy.'

'I have come to see a king,' she said tactfully.

The words, which had risen to her lips without thought, seemed to irritate him. 'I never wanted that war. Others wanted it. But not I. They blamed me. It was convenient to do so.' He dismissed the First World War with a weary shrug. 'You are one of these turncoat Englishwomen who are besotted with Adolf Hitler.'

'I admire him greatly.'

'Really! Then can you explain to me how the man can rant and rave for a whole hour and say absolutely nothing?'

'I find that Hitler is a deeply inspiring speaker.'

'Do you call yourself a Nazi?'

'I am a Fascist,' she replied.

'You don't know what Fascism is,' he said contemptuously.

'I have marched in the streets of London with Oswald Mosley and the Blackshirts,' she retorted angrily.

'Mosley! That popinjay! Is he another of your lovers?'

'I'm capable of joining a political party without becoming the mistress of the party leader,' she said. 'My beliefs are intellectual, not emotional.'

The Kaiser considered her, his wrinkled lids shrouding his rheumy eyes. 'In my experience, intellectualism does not go with that particular shade of lipstick.'

'Perhaps your experience with modern women is limited,' she snapped.

Max, who had been enjoying this exchange greatly, turned his snort of laughter into a discreet cough. 'Majesty, may we count on your support in the steps we need to take?'

Wilhelm did not look at him. 'You will get nowhere with this one,' he said. 'She won't open her legs for you no matter how many pearl necklaces you buy her.'

Isobel rose instantly. 'I will wait in the car,' she said icily to Max. She walked out of the room without looking back. A startled footman, lounging in the hallway, hurried after her.

'Fräulein?'

She ignored him. She was angry at the insults she had received, yet also relieved at a chance to escape that awful interview. She would always be able to say that she had walked out on the Kaiser himself, and settled a childhood bogey.

The Mercedes was not outside Huis Doorn. It had no doubt been moved somewhere so as not to defile the landscape. Fastening her sable coat against the cold wind, Isobel lit a cigarette and set off in an undignified hunt for the car.

'Madame!' Isobel turned. A dumpy little housekeeper had hurried out after her with an umbrella. She caught up with Isobel, puffing. 'It's starting to rain,' she said. 'You'll need this.'

Isobel looked up at the sky. The day had been bright so far, but now dark clouds had gathered. She accepted the umbrella. 'Thank you.' The courtesy was just in time. Heavy drops began to fall. She opened the umbrella hastily. She and the dumpy woman huddled under it as the rain plopped onto the silk. 'I was looking for my car.'

'It's been driven round the side of the house to be washed. Come back inside, and I'll ask them to tell your chauffeur to bring it to the front door.'

'Thank you, that's very kind.'

They went back into the house. 'Would you like a cup of tea while you wait?' the little woman asked.

'That sounds like a good idea.'

'This way, please.'

Isobel allowed herself to be led to a sitting room which was in marked contrast to the chilly chamber where Wilhelm had received them. A fire was burning brightly in a glass-fronted stove. A half-finished tapestry and a book in front of a cosy armchair spoke of a woman's leisure occupations. 'What a lovely room. Is it the Queen's?'

'The Empress's,' the little woman corrected her. 'Yes, it is.' She pulled a silk bell pull and a distant tinkle sounded somewhere in the house. 'Won't you sit down?'

Isobel perched on the arm of the Empress's armchair and picked up the book inquisitively to see what she was reading. It was a history of the royal house of Hohenzollern. She grimaced and put it down again.

The little woman was looking in a mirror and patting her damp, frizzy hair ruefully. 'I was going to wash it today, anyway. I hope my husband said nothing to offend you? He is very bad-tempered these days.'

'Your husband?' Isobel echoed. She met the other woman's bright, brown eyes in the mirror and jumped to her feet as though the chair were suddenly red-hot. 'Oh! Your Majesty! I do apologize!'

'What for?'

'I took you for—'

'For a housemaid?' She turned, straightening her black satin dress, which Isobel now saw, to her mortification, was not the uniform of a domestic servant at all, but old-fashioned mourning.

Isobel was about to exclaim that she had taken the Empress for a housekeeper, at least, but reflected in time that this was hardly better. A young girl in a starched white apron appeared in the doorway, curtseying. The Empress ordered tea and gave instructions for Max's car to be brought to the front of the house.

'You're so young, Your Majesty,' Isobel said hurriedly, when the girl had left. 'That's why it didn't occur to me. Please forgive my inattention.'

The Empress held out a plump hand. 'I am Hermine, Princess of Schönaich-Carolath.'

'Isobel Albarán.' Isobel touched the tips of the other woman's fingers. The Empress, Wilhelm's second wife, did not have the carriage of a great lady, though she had been born a princess. She was a small person of about fifty with intelligent, dark eyes and a mop of somewhat unruly hair. The hair was going grey, and had not been dyed. Nor had the Empress bothered to pluck her eyebrows, which were bushier than current fashions dictated. But she had authority and a decisive manner. She was now nodding at Isobel reflectively.

'I have a daughter of about your age. I have also lost a son.' She indicated the black fabric of her dress with a slight movement of her hands.

'I'm very sorry.'

'I saw you rush out into the rain and I felt sure that he had offended you. Please sit.'

'Your husband just spoke his mind,' Isobel said, choosing a comfortable stool by the side of the stove. 'I'm afraid I was very rude.'

'Speaking his mind is both his greatest virtue and his greatest fault.' She was studying Isobel. 'You are married, I think – but not to Max von Grimmel.'

'He's a friend.' Isobel hesitated. 'I shouldn't have come here with Max today. I think your husband took me for – well, for what I may appear to be.'

'But you are not what you may appear to be,' the Empress said. 'As I am not what I may appear to be. I was glad when I saw you walk out of the house. I ran after you because I wanted to talk to you. I never heard of a woman journalist until now.'

'I make my living from writing,' Isobel said with a smile. 'Many women have done that, surely.'

'But journalism – that is different.' The Empress's expression showed her disdain. 'The life is quite different from that of a lady writer. It is exposed to all kinds of insults and unpleasantness. And you live separated from your husband.'

Isobel realized that the Empress must know quite a lot of her background. 'I don't feel I need protection.'

'Not even from other women's tongues?'

'As long as I don't make a fool of myself, I'm not ashamed of anything. And, in fact, separation from my husband has given me back my freedom.'

'Hasn't it just made you lean on men other than your husband?'

'I've come to regard men and women as different species, who prey on each other in different ways. Each sex gets what it can from the other. Ideally, this can be done without shedding blood.' She had spoken lightly, but she saw an expression of distaste cross the

Empress's face. 'My husband lets me have a little of my own money. I earn what I can through writing and broadcasting. Whatever else falls into my lap, I accept with gratitude.'

'I can't say I understand your attitudes. But then, you're a New Woman and I am an old one.'

'I do what I must to survive.'

'You don't believe in divorce?'

'I believe in it, as I believe in murder. I don't condone it.'

'Ah, a fanatical Catholic.'

'Hardly fanatical. I made vows, and I will keep them.'

Hermine brushed crumbs off her ample bosom. 'They say your husband has ill-treated you.'

'I haven't complained of him to anyone.'

'Are you still in love with him?'

'I don't know.'

The Empress accepted this answer with a nod. 'I have been lucky. Both my marriages have been very happy. I married for love, both times.' She paused. 'I opposed my daughter's first choice of husband.'

'Did you disapprove of the match?'

'He was my own private secretary. A clever young man. Well-connected, but a commoner.'

'Does that still matter any more?' Isobel asked.

'If that doesn't matter, then what does?' the other woman replied with a touch of haughtiness. 'However, my daughter adored the man. She had given him her heart. I bestowed my blessing, at first. Despite the man's status. I thought that marriage to a commoner might smooth my daughter's path through life. With the Nazis, you understand. We old families live in difficult times. Hitler has declared that there shall be no more ranks and castes in Germany.' She produced a parody of Hitler's rasp. '*Ein Volk, ein Reich, ein Führer.*'

Isobel smiled, despite herself. 'Yes.'

'I think they would like to do to us what the Bolsheviks did to the Tsar and his family.'

'Surely not!'

'At best, they dislike and distrust us. So I thought that Caroline would be better off with a commoner. I soon realized that there was another, and insurmountable, obstacle to the match. The young man was a Jew.'

'I see.'

'I received a message from Dr Goebbels himself on the subject. Of course, I prevented the marriage. It would have been very difficult for Caroline. And I soon found a more suitable husband for her. They have been married for two years now. All is calm. But I wonder whether Caroline will ever forgive me. Or whether I will ever forgive myself.' The maid entered with the tray. The service was rose-patterned old Dresden, evidently in daily use. Hermine poured the tea and offered shortbread biscuits. 'I have them sent from Scotland. Do try them. And so young Max has come to talk to Wilhelm about the Jews. They appear to be the only topic of conversation these days. Are you yourself an anti-Semite?'

'I believe that the Jews pose a grave danger to Europe.'

'Graver than the Nazis?' Hermine asked, with that same, dark flash of irony. 'That is hard to believe. My husband has many Jewish friends, men he admires and respects. The Jews have made themselves rich by their own efforts, and Wilhelm approves of that. And yet, and yet.' She poured more tea. 'You mingle with people in power, people who make decisions in Berlin.'

'Only at a social level.'

'Can you tell me anything?'

'Anything? About what?'

'About what they plan.' Hermine touched her lips with her fingertips. Her dark eyes were no longer ironic, but contained something like pleading. 'For us. For my husband and my family.'

Isobel realized with a pang of pity that the Empress – empress in name alone – was begging her for some kind of reassurance. Exiled here at Doorn for years, she and Wilhelm were still waiting to hear the fate the Nazis had planned for them. She was not above begging a foreigner, a maverick like Isobel herself, for any scrap of information. 'I'm far less well connected than you imagine. But if I can find anything out, I'll tell you.'

The Empress poured tea, nodding her thanks. 'You are evidently intelligent. What do you see in Hitler? A handful of primitive ideas, a few catchphrases – what more is there to Nazism?'

'Those few ideas have transformed Germany. Perhaps their very simplicity is where their power lies. Hitler is a man who is able to grasp the fundamental elements of human nature and put them to work.'

'That is exactly what terrifies me about him,' Hermine said dryly. 'I think you may find that the fundamental elements of human nature work in a very ugly way.'

The men had finished their interview. A butler came to summon Isobel. She shook hands with Hermine and left her there in her warm room, next to the ornate, enamelled stove. The Kaiser was standing in the hallway with Max. He was not very tall, she was surprised to see; on first meeting, the man's presence produced such a dominant impression that one didn't notice his lack of height. Now, the impeccable, old-fashioned clothes gave him the air of a fastidious goblin from the Brothers Grimm. He looked exhausted. Whatever Max had told him seemed to have drained all the venom from his expression. Max performed his heel-clicking salute.

'Goodbye, Your Imperial Majesty.'

Wilhelm gestured at Isobel vaguely with his cane. 'They will make you learn to pull your skirts up, after all,' he said by way of a valediction.

She made no reply, taking this as a further insult, but once in the car, she turned to Max. 'What did he mean by that?'

'Who knows?' Max said. He was in a bad temper. 'The man is half-senile. Far from a *Butzemann*, he is a doddering, tedious old fool. He seems to understand nothing one tells him. You see the way he lives?'

'They seem to be very comfortable.'

Max snorted. 'You know that he was allowed to leave Germany with a trainload of treasures? Sixty railway carriages full of priceless objects! Including a yacht! He is treated very well. How dare he criticize the Führer ! What did the old bitch say to you?'

'Just that she is anxious about their future. She wanted to know whether their position would change in any way.'

'You can tell her that they can both rest easy if they have the sense to keep their mouths shut from now on.' He would add nothing to this, but sulked all the way to Osnabrück, where they were to spend the night.

Max had been born in Osnabrück, and was determined to show off the city, which Isobel found to be a somewhat dull place. Max, however, dragged her to all the sights, lecturing her on the galvanizing effect that National Socialism had had on its economy. Shattered by the Great War, it had sunk into Communism and unemployment during the 1920s. The Jews, Max said, had got their claws into the place. Osnabrück had turned to Hitler for help. Both Hitler and Goebbels had made speeches there during the federal elections.

'The town was electrified,' Max said. 'I myself was in the audience that day. It was a revelation to me. I heard the Führer's voice for the first time, and I knew at once that this was the man to lead Germany forward.' They were standing at the top of the church tower, with wide views across the city and the countryside. German flags and swastikas were hanging ostentatiously from ancient façades across the old part of the town. A red sunset was glowering after a largely rainy and blustery day. He waved expansively at the city. 'Look at this place, Isobel. Under Nazism, it has gone from ten thousand unemployed to a labour shortage in five years. Workers are flooding in from all over Lower Saxony. What better proof does one need of Adolf Hitler's greatness? Or that National Socialism is the only policy for Europe?'

Isobel had been jotting statistics in her little black notebook all afternoon. She would use them in an article about the economic benefits of National Socialism which she was currently writing. Serious articles like this one had been much sought after, as the world demanded to know the secret of Germany's mighty rebirth. Lately, however, newspaper editors had begun to ask for articles of a different type, criticizing Hitler's harshness and speculating on the probability of war. She refused to write that sort of rubbish. To her, Fascism was a force for peace, and she would continue to point out in her writing the social, economic and political benefits of the system.

She closed the notebook and fastened it with the rubber band. 'It's very inspiring, Max, but I'm cold and hungry.'

'You're right, my dear.' They made their way down the long, steep stone staircase and crossed the square to their hotel. Although Max's family home was in the city, he had not invited her there, saying that his parents would not understand their relationship. 'Besides,' he had added, 'it's a freezing, draughty old castle which you would hate.'

The hotel, in any case, was old-fashioned and comfortable, with a good restaurant, where they ate venison with seakale and *Salzkartoffeln* beside a roaring fire. The local beer was offered in foaming mugs. Isobel tried it, to please Max, though she was not fond of beer, especially the strong, bitter Saxon variety. He drank a great deal of the stuff, and became sentimental as the evening wore on, praising her lavishly for her beauty and her intellectual brilliance. She was accustomed to being told she was beautiful, which she did not regard as much of an accomplishment; and she knew pretty well what her own level of intelligence was, so his flattery did not impress her greatly, except in that it was a prelude to yet another attempt on her virtue.

That came as soon as they got upstairs. They had taken separate rooms, of course, but on the same landing. He escorted her to her door then leaned on the jamb, smiling down at her. 'Can I come in?'

'I don't think so, Max.'

He produced the silver schnapps flask from his pocket. 'I got a refill.'

'You've already had too much, and I don't want any more.'

'Let me try to change your mind.'

'Goodnight, Max.' She made the mistake of unlocking her door. He at once pushed his way in. 'Max!'

'Now I've got you,' he chuckled. He embraced her, pressing his mouth to hers. His lips were hot and wet, the smell of beer overpowering on his breath. Isobel fought away from him, dismayed. She had found Max an interesting companion, and had accepted his lavish gifts because he had assured her that these came from the Ministry. However, to be pawed by him like this was hateful.

'Max, for God's sake,' she exclaimed, wiping her mouth in disgust. 'I've already told you that I'm not interested in this kind of thing.'

'But *I* am interested.' He closed in on her again, kicking the door of the room shut with his boot heel. He was alarmingly powerful. This time she couldn't get out of his embrace. His tongue, extraordinarily large and strong, was forcing its way between her clenched teeth while a hand closed on her breast, the fingers and thumb pinching cruelly as they searched for her nipple.

She tried to cry out, but his mouth was crushing hers in a grotesque parody of a kiss. He had forced her against a chest of drawers. The sharp edge cut into her hip. He bent her backwards until she thought her spine would give way. She couldn't breathe, and she was starting to panic .

At last his mouth slid off hers, allowing her to draw breath. He was grinning at her, his eyes bright, his face flushed. 'That is better than champagne, yes?' He pulled her skirt up, fingers groping to get between her thighs and into her pants.

Her right arm was now free. She slapped him as hard as she could across the face. Her palm was stinging as he stepped back, his mouth open in astonishment.

'What the devil – ?'

'How *dare* you?' she demanded, shaking with rage and shock.

'Isobel!'

She thrust out her hand to keep him back as he tried to come back to her. 'Stay away from me, Max. You're insane. What in God's name made you assume you could behave in this way with me?'

Her palm print was now livid on his cheek. 'What made me assume this?' His big, white teeth were bared in a snarl. 'Did you think it was all take and no give?'

'I've told you before. I am not available.'

'But Max is available.' His smile was an ugly sneer. 'Max is available for trips to Bayreuth, introductions to the Führer, fur coats and fine restaurants. How many men, do you think, could have presented you to the Kaiser? You will dine out on that story for the rest of your life. But Max gets a kiss on the cheek and bye, bye, Max, good night and go fuck yourself.'

He was angry, and she was afraid he would attack her again. She tried to speak steadily. 'I would never have accepted any of that if I had thought you expected me to sleep with you in return.'

'And what did you expect?'

She laid a hand on her pounding heart. Her face felt as though it was on fire, and she was still dizzy. 'It has not been "all take", Max. I have always praised Germany and National Socialism in my writing. What I write is respected. I have access to newspapers and magazines which help to form the opinions of the world. You've given me a privileged insight and I've used that to promote a better understanding abroad.' She tried to pull her woefully tangled dress straight. 'It hasn't been easy. You know that there's hostility to Hitler and Nazism, especially in Britain and the States. A lot of hostility. Germany is not an easy country to promote right now. Especially since the takeover of Austria.'

His sneer had faded away. His expression was now calmer. 'I am not Germany. I am just Max. But, very well, I will not speak of give and take. I will say only that I want you. I want you very much indeed. I am at this moment blazing with desire for you. Is there nothing in your heart for poor Max?'

'Not in that way,' she replied. 'I'm sorry.'

'You don't know what I could do for you. I am a very expert lover.'

'I'm sure you are. But I am a married woman.'

A strange expression crossed his face. 'Are you serious when you say this? You know that, even now, your so-called husband is probably in bed with one of his five or six mistresses?'

'Yes, I know that,' she said quietly.

'You cannot keep parroting that you are a married woman. It is ridiculous. This is an attitude which is repugnant to National Socialism. It shows enslavement to an outdated superstition. And the Führer himself has decreed that useless marriages which are worthless to the Volk must be ended.'

Isobel was silent. She struggled to get her breathing under control.

'You must divorce him,' he went on. 'It can be done in a few weeks under the new laws.'

'And then?' she asked. 'You want to end my marriage just so you can get me into bed. That is not a very National Socialist attitude.'

'If you divorce him, I will marry you.'

She felt instantly that he was lying, but he had surprised her. 'I don't know what to say, Max. Even if I were to divorce Roberto, I would not rush into a second marriage. I would need time – a couple of years at least – before I could start thinking about that.'

'A couple of years?' He laughed. 'A couple of years to a woman of twenty-seven is like a couple of weeks to a cabbage in the market. You are getting past your prime, Isobel. Soon you will start to wither and stink.'

'I'm sure you're right,' she replied quietly. She just wanted him to get out and leave her alone.

'You need to understand who your friends are.' He looked her up and down with an expression of patronizing contempt. 'You are alone in the world. You need friends, my dear. Otherwise, you are alone. Utterly alone.'

At last he turned and left her, slamming the door behind him. She quickly locked it, and then, for good measure, propped a chair under the handle.

She went to the basin to rinse her face. Looking at her dripping self in the mirror, she first laughed, then cried. She didn't find crying easy, and forced herself to stop after the first few, jerking sobs. Her temples were throbbing. She could feel her migraine coming on, with nausea and a bad headache.

She went through her bedtime routine in a kind of daze, applying cleansing cream and then a face mask. She had assured Hermine that morning that she didn't need protection, but she had lied. Busy as her life was, it was tragically solitary. Max was right. The best years of her life were passing away and she had no lover, no friend, no companion, not a soul she could trust. Living on one's wits was a hard, lonely life.

She felt so in need of comfort that she picked up the telephone at her bedside and put a call through to her sister Chiara in London. The line was unusually good (another Nazi technological improvement) and Chiara's voice came through bright and clear.

'Darling!' she squealed, 'how perfectly wonderful to hear from you!'

'Hope it's not a bad moment?'

'*Actually* I was just going out with Charlie Grosvenor, but the brute can wait. You know how dull he is!'

'Which one is he?' asked Isobel, unable to pick the name out from the drove of Charlies, Jimmies, Reggies and Georgies who were her constant retinue.

'He's the big one with all the hair.'

'Don't remember him. Is he in the First Fifteen?'

'Just squeezed in,' Chiara said with a giggle, 'since his uncle died and left him a hundred thousand.'

'Very nice, too. Where's he taking you?'

'The Savoy Grill and then a couple of Mayfair nightclubs.'

'You poor thing.'

'*Actually*, I really am a poor thing – you've no idea what a bore he is!'

'Grin and bear it.'

'Yes, I'll drown my sorrows in pink champagne.'

Isobel imagined her sister in her Mayfair flat, her cropped hair gleaming rich as butter, the telephone cord wound around her finger, her elfin face glowing with life and happiness. 'What are you wearing?'

'Gold lamé. The Grecian goddess look.'

'You'll knock him out.'

'He's already knocked out. I can see him asleep in the taxi from my window. And you, darling? Where are you?'

'Osnabrück.'

'That sounds pretty dire. What have you been doing there, wherever it is?'

'Oh, I've been insulted by Kaiser Bill and half-raped by a Nazi.'

Chiara let out a merry peal of laughter. 'I never know when you're being serious or not. *Are* you being serious?'

'No, not really.'

'I bet you are! Which was worse?'

'The Nazi, I think. He told me I was a stinking cabbage on a market stall.'

'Golly, what a silver-tongued devil.'

'Yes, he has a delicate turn of phrase.'

'Why do you always attract such awful men? It's like iron filings to a magnet.'

'He has his moments. He's taken me to some interesting places.'

'I do envy you,' Chiara said. 'You lead such a glamorous life.'

'Don't be silly,' Isobel retorted. 'You're the only one of us who has any money left. Or any freedom. I could weep when I think of poor Felicity, buried in that convent, with all her money in the coffers of the church. And I've messed up my life good and proper. I just rattle around Europe, getting older and more disreputable.' She was suddenly close to tears again, real tears. 'I'm so lonely, Chiara.'

'Come home!' She could hear Chiara herself sniffing. 'Come back, darling. I miss you so much!'

'Do you hear anything from Felicity?' Isobel asked, swallowing the salty taste.

'Nothing. Except tracts. I write her screeds, and all she sends by way of an answer are little grubby leaflets with prayers or pictures of saints.'

'I don't even get that. She sees me as the enemy, because I tried to talk her out of becoming a nun in Spain.'

'You're very forceful. And she's always been terrified of you. You're a bit of a bully, you know.'

'What's happened to us? We used to all be such good friends. Now we never see each other. Felicity and I have made such a fiasco of our lives. Don't you do the same thing, Chiara. You have to make up for our disasters. Be happy.'

'Have you seen Roberto?'

'Not for six months.'

'Oh, Isobel. If only—'

'Please don't say, "if only Paul hadn't died". Roberto is what he is. Nothing will ever change him.'

'I'm worried about you.'

'I'm fine. And you're keeping poor Charlie waiting. Have fun, sweetheart. Keep your hand on your ha'penny.'

'Wait, Isobel!'

But Isobel was already replacing the receiver. Chiara was so bright and happy. She didn't have the right to unburden her own sorrows onto a younger sister. All she could do was pray that Chiara would avoid the tragic mistakes that she and Felicity had made, and have a happy life.

She could hardly think straight, now. Her migraine was raging, a dragon over her right temple that was devouring her brain in great bites. She took a handful of pills, knowing they would do nothing, and went to lie on her bed.

&

Isobel had expected Max to be shamefaced and apologetic the next morning, but he was his usual brash self, and made no reference at all to what had happened last night. They breakfasted on eggs and fat Saxon sausages and set off for Berlin in a fine drizzle. During the drive, he talked expansively about his chief, Goebbels, extolling him as a genius second only to Hitler himself.

'Ah, the brilliance of that man's mind,' Max sighed. 'He is like a god. More than a god.'

Isobel agreed politely with these extravagant sentiments, though Goebbels, with his skull-like face, snake eyes and hobbling gait, was one of the Nazis she liked least. On the occasions she had met him, he had made her skin crawl, most especially because he had turned on the charm for her benefit, his eyes caressing her in unmistakeable invitation. Like Max himself, Goebbels was notorious as a seducer of women, despite his marriage to Magda, who was one of Hitler's favourites, and their six children.

She had taken a decision overnight, and she told Max of it when they arrived in Berlin in the early afternoon and stopped in front of her apartment block in the Kurfürstendamm.

'I'm giving these back to you,' she said. She had laid the sable coat and hat on the seat of the Mercedes-Benz. 'I can't keep them.'

Max was astonished. 'What's this? You don't like them?'

'I love them,' she said regretfully, stroking the gleaming black fur for the last time. 'But they put me under an obligation which I can't fulfil.'

He frowned. 'Why can you not fulfil your obligations?'

'I tried to explain, last night.' She glanced at the close-cropped head of Fritz, the Motor Pool driver, who sat stolidly at the wheel in his khaki uniform. 'We can't discuss it now. But thank you for everything.'

'These belong to you. You cannot return them.' She got out of the car without another word. He followed her, and grasped her arm in the street. 'You cannot return them, Isobel!'

'You told me these were gifts from the Propaganda Ministry.'

'Exactly. Reichsminister Goebbels would be extremely offended.'

'I'm sure they can be given to some more worthy individual,' she said dryly. 'They won't go to waste. I've hardly worn them.'

'You're being very stupid. I don't understand you at all.'

'Max, surely you understand that your behaviour last night makes it impossible for me to keep these things. I don't even want to look at them any more.'

'My behaviour?' he said sharply. '*My* behaviour? It was you who struck me in the face!'

'You were behaving like a beast,' she retorted.

'My God! Is it bestial to offer a woman the greatest compliment that a man can give?'

'It's not a compliment to be mauled and pushed around.'

His eyes flashed. 'I offered to marry you!'

She didn't want to anger him further by telling him she didn't take that offer seriously. 'In any case, I don't want the things. I'm giving them back.'

'There is no "giving back", my dear.' His fingers tightened on her arm. 'It is too late to give back anything you have received. You have taken, and yes, you are under an obligation. Obligations are taken seriously in Nazi Germany. They are not thrown back in the giver's face. You understand me?'

She jerked her arm free, at the cost of some pain, for his fingers were very strong. Fritz the chauffeur had taken her suitcase out of the trunk, and was standing waiting impassively for her. He also had the sable coat over his arm. 'Sometimes you take a very ugly tone, Max,' she said. 'I don't like to be threatened.'

He was grinning again. 'Who is threatening you? Keep the furs safe. You'll be needing them again soon.'

'For the last time – I don't want them! Tell him to put them back in the car. Goodbye, Max.' She turned on her heel and walked towards the door of her apartment. That, at least, was paid for out of her own earnings. She was shocked to feel her head jerked back. Max had grasped her hair and was dragging her round to face him. She gasped in pain. 'Max!'

'You forgot something.' He kissed her mouth hard, his teeth crushing her lips. She struggled furiously, but he had a fistful of her hair, and the pain was excruciating. Her eyes were burning with tears of humiliation when he finally released her. 'That is better,' he purred, his blue eyes bright with amusement. The chauffeur was watching without expression. Max nodded his head at the man, who carried Isobel's suitcase – and the furs – into her apartment. 'We have many more entertainments planned,' he called after her. 'Soon!'

The driver insisted on taking her suitcase up with her in the lift. He set it down in her little sitting room, laid her furs on a sofa and snapped her a Nazi salute. 'Heil Hitler.' She stared at the sable coat as he left. It lay on the chaise longue like a crouching panther.

She went to her window and watched the big black car drive away. She had a breathless, panicky feeling that things were slipping out of her control.

∽

She sent a note to Empress Hermine at Huis Doorn, thanking her for her hospitality and relaying the rather sinister message that Max had given her:

'Max has assured me that your position is in no danger of changing, but has urged discretion on the part of His Imperial Majesty, especially in any public statements he may make about the Führer or the Reich Ministries.'

Within two days she had received a reply from the Empress, thanking her for her message. Isobel filed the letter away which, with its wax seal and heavy, crested notepaper, was an interesting souvenir of a strange encounter.

It was good to be back in her apartment. She had made it as pretty as she could, with pink silk shades on the lamps, chintz-covered furniture, old Turkey rugs and flower paintings picked up in antique shops. In London, she would probably have decried this style as over-feminine, even twee. Here in Berlin, however, it provided her with a refuge from the growing harshness of the National Socialist style. Its hard edges were everywhere, aggressive, strident, declamatory. There was hardly a building which had not sprouted swastika flags or other Nazi regalia. At first it had exhilarated Isobel, given her the feeling of living in a bright new world. Now it wearied her eyes and she had started to find it oppressive.

Fascism had been a philosophy which had always given Isobel comfort, the feeling that life was orderly and full of hope, despite her own tragedies. Now she had the feeling that blinkers were slipping from her eyes and that she was seeing how little she had really understood.

Was it hypocrisy to extol Nazism while she herself was free and able to do what she wanted with her life? She was starting to think that perhaps it was. She consoled herself by putting Wagner on her gramophone and floating on the music for hours.

The newspapers the next day were full of the vom Rath shooting in France. A seventeen-year-old Jew named Grynszpan had shot a German diplomat named vom Rath in the Paris embassy. The diplomat was in a serious condition. The Jew had been arrested and had confessed to the crime, making anti-Nazi statements which his French captors made sure got the maximum publicity. There was a roar of fury from the German press, denouncing the crime in jagged, black, Gothic headlines as an attack by international Jewry on the German people.

She returned from a shopping expedition to find the door of her apartment standing ajar. Her heart clenched in fear. Her first thought was not of a burglar. It was of the Gestapo, or worse, the SS. The vom Rath shooting had produced a wave of arrests and a heightened hostility towards foreigners which she had felt in the shops today. Yet she – she had nothing to fear. She was a friend of Germany, a proponent of National Socialism, wasn't she? Nevertheless, the instinct to flee was strong, and her knees had turned to water. With an effort, she forced herself to enter her own apartment and face what was within.

There were no black or brown uniforms. But, sitting in her favourite armchair in front of the gas fire, with his legs crossed, was Roberto.

She put her shopping bags down with a gasp. 'My God. What are you doing here?'

'Visiting my wife,' he said calmly. She had not seen him for months, and at first glance, he hadn't changed. He was smoking, holding the cigarette in his own peculiar way, between the second and third fingers. 'You look as though you've seen a ghost.'

'I thought you were the Gestapo!'

He seemed amused. 'What do you have to fear from the Gestapo, *querida*?'

'This business in Paris has made everyone nervous. They're picketing all the Jewish shops.' She struggled out of her coat and collapsed into the armchair opposite him. 'Anyway, you're worse than the Gestapo.'

'Much worse,' he agreed. He smiled. He was still the handsomest man she had ever known, dark-complexioned, with black wavy hair combed back from his temples, extremely dark eyes with thick black lashes, and features that were fine enough to have captivated his generation in Spain. He had been pursued by painters and sculptors, as well as by women of all ages, and had inspired a whole ideal of male beauty in his youth. People in Spain still spoke of Roberto Albarán as an Adonis. The only weakness she had ever been able to find in his face was his teeth; they were very slightly too sharp. He claimed this was because he had been born under the sign of Leo, and that this was the mark of the lion in him.

'How did you get in, by the way?' she demanded, her heart-beat settling a little, but not much. The shock of seeing Roberto was always great, for various reasons.

'I have a key.'

'How did you get the key?'

'You gave it to me.'

'I don't remember that,' she said suspiciously.

He looked around. 'You've made it very nice. What do the Germans say? *Gemütlich*. Very bourgeois.'

'It's not your style, of course. But it suits me. What has happened to your house in Córdoba?'

'Our house,' he corrected her. 'The whole of the South is in Franco's hands now, you know that. The house is being restored. Some things cannot easily be replaced, of course. The paintings, the sculptures. But I have access to similar items at very special prices.'

'You mean the spoils of war?'

'*Vae victis*,' he replied. He took a last drag and stubbed out the cigarette, narrowing his eyes against the smoke. 'They stole from us, now we steal from them. One should choose one's side carefully. As you and I have done.'

'These expressions of solidarity are alarming,' she said. Her knees felt as though they might support her now. She rose. 'I should offer you something, I suppose. Coffee?'

He glanced at the slim gold watch that adorned his slim brown wrist. He was wearing a superbly-cut charcoal grey pinstriped suit. She knew that he had cupboards full of them, as he had cupboards full of silk shirts and drawers full of gold watches and cufflinks. 'I think a whisky would be better.' He watched her as she went to the cabinet. 'You grow more beautiful each time I see you.'

'That isn't very often.'

'It was our eighth wedding anniversary last month.'

She was surprised that he had remembered. She had not marked the day in any way, except in feeling sad and angry. 'I heard nothing from you.'

'I celebrated. In my own way.'

'With some trollop, I presume.'

'Alone, with your photograph and my memories,' he replied.

She wanted to throw the whisky in his face, but refrained, and instead passed it to him with a flat smile. 'What a sentimental man you are, to be sure.'

'It's a weakness of mine,' he replied in the same deadpan tone. They toasted one another in silence and drank. 'You're well?'

'As you see. And you?'

'Getting older.'

'It doesn't show.'

He acknowledged the compliment with a nod. 'You enjoy life among the Germans?'

'It has its moments.'

'You're seeing a lot of this fellow, Max von Grimmel.'

'I don't think I'm "seeing a lot of him". He's in the Propaganda Ministry. My work dovetails with his.'

'*Dovetails*,' he repeated. 'What a soft sound that has.'

'Please don't pretend to be jealous, Roberto. That would really be rather rich.' She drained the whisky. 'It's an expression from carpentry. It has nothing to do with doves.'

'Nevertheless, you're a great deal in his company. And he's very attached to you, he says.'

'Who has he said this to?' she demanded, growing more irritated by the minute.

'To anyone who will listen to him. He claims to be your *preux chevalier*.'

'It's nonsense. He would like to get me into bed with him, but there's no romance involved, I assure you.'

'Nevertheless, you're a very beautiful woman.' His dark eyes travelled over her. She was wearing a plain blue dress with woollen stockings, and she did not look or feel very elegant. His eyes finally rested on her mouth. 'I miss you.'

She made no comment on that, but reached for the whisky bottle and poured herself a stiff one to steady her nerves. She found his presence very disturbing. 'And your work? Going well, I hear?'

'I've been moving into private investments. For a select group of very special clients. I've done it in Spain and now I'm doing it in Germany.'

'That sounds profitable,' she said dryly.

He shrugged. 'There's a lot of free money around.'

'Free? Can I get some?'

'I mean money that has been freed from its former owners. It all has to go somewhere. It percolates upwards. I assist those who are the final recipients.'

Her generous lips curled in distaste. 'Dirty work. The sort of thing you do best.'

'*Querida*, which class do you want to belong to, the *nouveaux riches* or the *nouveaux pauvres*? Don't take fur coats from the Nazis and then lecture me about dirty work.'

'I'm not lecturing you.' It had been a clear, cold day. The sunset was dying now and the light in the apartment was fading. She saw that he had brought a small pigskin bag with him. She could hear the strain in her own voice as she asked, 'How long are you staying?'

'In Berlin? Or with you, now?'

'Both.'

'I have a meeting with Hermann Goering tomorrow.'

'You can't spend the night here.'

He laughed softly. 'We are married.'

'You destroyed that marriage years ago.' She got to her feet. 'Excuse me. I must unpack my shopping. It was nice to see you, but now I think you should go.'

Isobel went into her tiny kitchen and started putting the groceries away. She heard Roberto come up behind her. He put his arms around her waist, drawing her against him. A familiar feeling swelled in her, of mingled fear, nausea and desire. She felt unable to move or react. His breath was warm in her ear. 'Don't be angry with me. Life treated us badly.'

'You treated me badly. I did nothing to you.'

'You turned against me. After the child died, nothing was the same.'

It was one of his peculiarities that he never referred to Paul by name. He was always, 'the child', as though Roberto were somehow distancing himself from the raw grief of his son's death. There was nothing raw about Roberto's emotions. Everything was calculated, everything controlled. She reminded herself of that now, as her heart started to beat faster again. 'Please let me go.'

'You became so cold,' he murmured. 'You blamed me. You still blame me.'

She stared without seeing at the packet of coffee she was holding. 'We blamed each other,' she said.

His hands moved, one drifting down her belly to cup her pubic mound, the other rising to caress her breasts. She wanted to tell him to stop, that he had no right. But the thought of the loneliness closing in on her once he had shut the door was crushing. She had missed him terribly. She could hate him as much as she would; she would also always love him. She put the coffee down and turned to face him. His face wore that look of refined desire which always made her heart turn over. She put her arms around his neck and kissed his mouth, at first tentatively, then with growing passion. She had been alone for so long. The

114

last time she had made love had been a year or more ago, and that had been with Roberto. She knew that he knew that. She didn't have the strength of will to turn him away and wait months more, perhaps, before she saw him again. 'You bastard,' she whispered. She was trembling. She touched his lips, his cheek, with unsteady fingers. 'Why do you do this to me? Are all your tarts busy tonight?'

She led him to her bedroom. They sat on her bed, which was covered with silk cushions, the mute companions of her loneliness. He kissed her for a long time, his mouth expert and meticulous. Familiar feelings of hot desire, mingled with regret and revulsion, flooded through her. Before Roberto, there had been no more than the bungled kisses of adolescence His was the only lovemaking she'd ever known. His lovemaking was calm and thorough – as though he were following some plan in his mind, she often thought, step by step, omitting nothing, waiting until each stage was complete before moving on to the next. She was ashamed of the fact that she so seldom achieved an orgasm with him. She could only do that alone. He certainly knew how to give her pleasure, so the fault, she understood, lay with her, and not with him. She passed through successive stages of delectation and arousal with Roberto, reaching a certain point, past which she so seldom passed that it was better to accept that state of affairs, and enjoy the journey, even though it led nowhere.

He helped her take off her stockings, and examined her feet with interest.

'You have started to paint your toenails. You never did that before.'

'I wore sandals this summer. All the Berlin women paint their toenails. I'll stop now that winter's here.'

'Don't. I like it.'

'You like it in me, or you like it in all women?'

'It suits you, in particular.' He rose and undressed, folding his clothes fastidiously and laying them on the chair. She leaned back on her elbows and watched him. It was like watching the actions of some lithe cat, a leopard perhaps, whose movements were precise, determined, not one hair of the lustrous coat out of place. As always, she found watching him undress highly erotic. She was very aroused. She crossed her ankles and squeezed the muscles of her thighs together, feeling the pleasurable pressure on her sex.

'No English gentleman ever takes such care of his clothes,' she said. 'One can see you're not one.'

'What does an English gentleman do with his clothes?'

'He drops them on the floor for his servants to deal with.'

'I have too much regard for my clothes to do that. Besides, you have no servants. So who would pick them up?'

'It's the principle of the thing.'

'I have no understanding of principles.'

'But why should you care about a shirt? You have so many.'

He examined the muscular definition of his own tanned stomach, a complacent Adonis. 'Just because one has many of a thing does not mean that one should neglect any of them.'

The answer displeased her. 'Are you referring to your harem?'

'There is no harem, *querida*.'

But just as he kept tabs on her, she kept tabs on him, and she knew it wasn't true. Though she remained faithful – absurdly but constantly – to the ruined moral structure of their marriage, he shared no such principles. She had no doubt that Roberto was fond of her, perhaps even loved her, in his own way. But it occurred to her now, as if for the first time, that they shared no beliefs. They had shared so little in the eight years of their marriage, which had begun when she was nineteen years old: a mutual excitement in one another's bodies; a home in Spain, which had been first abandoned by him, and then destroyed by the Reds, and which was now being refurnished with the stolen fragments of other people's lives. They had shared little else. Certainly not the grief of Paul's death. They had grieved separately over that. Or perhaps she had grieved and he had simply shut it off in his mind, refusing to participate in any emotions she might feel. He hadn't pitied her or tried to console her. In his calm, inexpressive reaction there had been nothing for her to pity or console.

He took her in his arms, looking down at her appreciatively. Even this lovemaking, which was performed so punctiliously, was not a shared thing. There was no communion. He was interested in her, but only in her body, and that as an object – or rather, a collection of porcelain objects, to be examined and admired, hands, feet, breasts, buttocks, each part of her intriguing him, but not filling him with any tenderness. He might as well be putting a jigsaw puzzle together.

She was not vain enough to enjoy being admired in this cold way, for her physical beauty alone, which she had always regarded as an accident. The touch of his lips on her nipples, the pressure of his fingers between her legs, were exciting but without emotion.

In fact, she felt now, there was a kind of contempt in him, well-disguised and almost imperceptible, but evident to her because she knew him so well. It was a distaste for the workings of her body, together with a condescension that came of his being able to manage her in bed, to control her reactions.

Was he like this with his other women? Was this what he was always like? Or did some of the others excite him more, provoke him to lose his self-control or lose his patience?

She remembered the occasions when he had lost his patience with her, when violence had erupted from his smooth façade like a monster bursting from the surface of a lake. It had happened twice, terrifying episodes that had lasted no more than a few seconds, but which had left an indelible mark on her mind. Both times he had struck her only once, a blow to the womb that had sent her sprawling and unable to breathe for the pain.

That memory made her whole body clench defensively. She felt she suddenly couldn't continue. She pushed Roberto away from her, rolled over, and sat on the edge of the bed, gasping for air.

'Did I hurt you?' he asked, propping himself up on one elbow.

Isobel didn't answer. She got up and pulled on her robe. She lit a cigarette and went to the window, looking out at the evening traffic on the Ku'damm. She was thinking of Felicity, of her silly infatuation with William, of the way she had cried when he'd gone back to the front. Those bitter, bitter tears, the first tears of love! One never forgot them. And then one cried so many tears in the years after that that eventually one couldn't cry any more, no matter what happened. One just lit a cigarette and waited for the pain to go away.

Perhaps it was better for Felicity to have retired into her convent, retired from life. One probably didn't have much occasion to cry in a convent.

She heard Roberto also light a cigarette. After a while, he dressed. He didn't ask her why she'd so abruptly withdrawn from their lovemaking. He was far too collected a man for that sort of question. He opened the pigskin bag he'd brought with him.

'There are some papers I need you to sign.'

'What papers?'

'I'm selling the house and land in Gloucestershire.'

'Why?' she asked.

'The price is very good right now. And with war coming, it's better to have gold in Switzerland than earth in Britain. It can't change hands so easily.'

'Is this why you came?' She turned to face him, not so much angry as despairing. 'Is this the reason for the visit? And the sex? Was that to make sure I did as you asked? Or just an incidental amusement?'

He held out the documents and the pen. 'Please sign.'

She didn't move. 'That land is the last thing I can call my own. You've got your hands on everything else.'

'You put things in an ugly light, Isobel.'

She stared at him, this handsome, cold man who was her husband, this stranger. 'My father never sold an acre in his life. Nor did his father.'

'And so?'

'I shouldn't accept something he would have despised.'

He uncapped his pen, a gold Mont Blanc that she had bought him. 'I'm doing this for you, *querida*. Don't be difficult.'

'No. I won't sign.'

'Do you need me to explain the logic of this transaction?'

'No. There won't be any transaction. I'm going to hold on to my British earth.'

There was a flicker of annoyance in his brown eyes. 'You talk as though I'm your enemy.'

'I don't know what you are, Roberto. You're not a husband, or a friend, or even an enemy.'

'I've offered you a divorce,' She made no reply. She turned away, just wanting him to go. 'If you choose to remain my wife, then please behave like one. I'll leave the papers here. Sign them by lunchtime tomorrow. I'll pick them up when I've seen Goering. I'm flying back to Zurich in the evening.'

Isobel stood at the window, finishing her cigarette, refusing to cry. She heard the door close and saw her husband emerge from the apartment block onto the street below her. He didn't look up. Within moments, he had hailed a taxi. Its red tail lights merged with the traffic, then were gone.

❧

The next day, the reaction against the vom Rath shooting intensified. Jewish children were turned away from schools, Jewish clubs and societies were banned, and every Jewish newspaper was shut down. There were anti-Semitic demonstrations in the streets.

Roberto returned at midday to collect the papers.

'You haven't signed them,' he said, frowning as he leafed through them.

'No. And I'm not going to.'

He glanced at her briefly. She knew that he was angry and she quailed inwardly. But she was determined to resist him. 'This is a bad decision, *querida*,' he said coldly.

'It's my decision. You have everything that was mine, Roberto. You don't need this, too.'

'I am trying to protect you.' But he didn't argue. He shrugged and put the papers back in his briefcase. 'What will you do if war breaks out?'

'I don't know.'

'The Germans will win.'

'Are you so sure?'

His black eyes met hers. 'I have incontrovertible proof of it. I have seen the preparations they are making. They cannot be defeated. By comparison, the British and the French are babes in the wood.'

'Hitler can't fight France and Britain at the same time.'

'Hitler will overrun France in six months.'

'Impossible.'

'And he will invade Britain as soon as that is accomplished. Mussolini will join him.' He snapped the briefcase shut. 'I repeat my question – are you the lover of this man, von Grimmel?'

'No.'

'Then why did you refuse me yesterday?'

'I just couldn't go through with it.'

He smiled slightly, whether in derision or amusement she could not tell. 'Choose your side well.' She said nothing as he pulled on his overcoat and hat. 'Goodbye, Isobel.'

'Goodbye, Roberto.'

She was left with an ominous feeling in the pit of her stomach. Was it possible that England, her England, would soon be no more?

The day after that came the news that vom Rath had died of his wounds in Paris. The newspaper headlines were even taller and more jagged. A furious tirade from Goebbels followed on the radio, spitting venom, promising vengeance. Then Berlin settled down to an ominous peace.

Isobel had just got into bed at midnight, with the draft of her latest article to correct, when she heard the pounding at her door and Max's voice calling her name.

'Isobel. Isobel!'

She got up angrily and went to the door, fastening her robe. 'What do you want?'

'Open the door!'

He sounded drunk again, and her heart sank. She could see his dark silhouette looming through the pretty stained-glass panel in the door. 'Max, it's late. Let's talk about this tomorrow.'

'Open! Or I smash it down!'

Unwillingly, she unlocked the door. Max thrust his way in. He was in high good spirits, grinning like a coal scuttle. He was wearing his official uniform of black jodhpurs and boots and a brown jacket with a swastika armband. He had a pistol on his hip. Her *preux chevalier*. 'Tonight you're going to see something. Get dressed.'

She was still holding her typescript. She waved it at him. 'I have work to do.'

'You will have better things to write by tomorrow.' He pulled the pages out of her hand and scattered them. 'Get dressed! And put on the sable coat, it's cold!'

In this mood, he was impossible to argue with. With a sinking feeling in her heart, she pulled on clothes. Max was holding her fur coat out for her. A hot reek of alcohol came from him. 'Where are we going?' she demanded as he hurried her down the stairs.

'You'll see. You'll thank me.'

'I've seen enough torchlight rallies and light cathedrals and Nordic bonfires to last me a lifetime.'

'This is better. This is the real thing!'

She fastened the sable coat. Fritz, Max's chauffeur, was holding the door of Max's Mercedes-Benz open.

The Ku'damm was unusually busy. By midnight it was generally getting quiet, but tonight trucks were roaring busily up and down the grand, wide street. The giant crimson banners glared in the sweep of headlights. She could hear shouting, and thought she heard the crash of a window breaking.

'What's going on?' she demanded in alarm.

Max hustled her into the staff car and climbed in after her. 'You know where to go,' he told the driver. 'Go.' The limousine set off with a roar, the acceleration pressing them back in their seats. Weaving between the trucks, which Isobel now saw were filled with men, the driver took them towards the Kaiser Wilhelm Memorial Church. Max wound down the window. 'Listen to that.'

The sound of smashing glass was everywhere, rising above shouts and screams. Isobel tried to focus on what was happening. Along the broad pavements, between the stately trees, men were running with spades, crowbars and pickaxes. Some were in the brown uniform of the SA, the Nazi storm troopers who had shattered the Communist front during Hitler's rise to power; most were in civilian clothes. In disbelief, she saw the plate glass window of a famous store shiver into fragments and cascade into glittering ruins.

'My God,' she said to Max. 'What are they doing?'

He lay back in his seat. He had his little silver flask, and between swigs, he roared with laughter. 'Wait, wait, wait.'

Fritz was driving fast, and the scenes flashed past her as they were repeated: trucks pulling up, men spilling out, running; the spades swinging, the glass crazing, hanging in the air for an impossible moment before spilling into the street. Some of the shop windows had been broken already and men were scrambling into the shops themselves. She saw a woman walking quickly with an armful of fur coats, a man stuffing necklaces into his pockets in the ruins of a well-known jewellery store window.

It was the Jewish shops that were being attacked. She understood that now. The smart, expensive Jewish-owned stores of the Ku'damm, symbols of the city's elegance and wealth, were being violently smashed open, their contents looted.

In the last few months she'd seen picketing of Jewish shops, with a handful of SA men standing outside each one, shouting slogans and urging Germans not to shop there. Woolworth's, in particular, always had a line of booted storm troopers in front of its window, since the SA had declared that the founder of the Woolworth empire was a Jew. But this was something else altogether.

They passed a graceful old hotel, which was receiving special attention from the rioters. Several trucks were parked outside. The doors had been broken down, the smashed windows disgorging furniture, sheets, carpets as the men inside hurled them out into the street. A bureau tumbled four stories down and exploded like a bomb on the pavement, scattering the residents who had been driven out of their rooms and into the road.

'Please,' she said, aware that she was trembling violently, 'I want to go home.'

'You are home, my dear,' he said, still chuckling, 'and we are doing a little spring cleaning. Oh la-la, what a night!'

Fritz set off again, honking imperiously at anyone who got in their way. Recognizing the car as a Party vehicle, the other traffic gave way. Several men gave the Heil Hitler salute as they passed. Faces were intent. Movements were brisk. This was serious work. Everywhere there was the glitter of broken glass. This was it, Isobel realized. This was what the Nazis had been promising. There was no going back, now. Nothing could ever be the same again. Not the Ku'damm, not Berlin, not Germany, not the world. Everything had changed.

At this end of the Ku'damm, crowds of spectators had gathered, cheering and clapping as the glass smashed. Max burst out laughing again. 'Hold on a moment, Fritz. Heavens, I wish I had a camera. What a circus!'

Fritz stopped the car. Isobel stared, her sense of unreality deepening. There was a Jewish old age home here, a refined Art Deco block located conveniently close to the parks and the shops. It had been broken into, every window gaping, the sidewalk a twinkling sea of splinters. Dazed scarecrows wandered along the road in their pyjamas and nightgowns, white hair fluttering, mouths open in bewilderment. Some were barefoot in the broken glass. A policemen stood, thumbs in his belt, watching impassively. Despite the plain clothes worn by the gangs, Isobel knew they were SA storm troopers by their discipline and deter-mination; they were instantly recognizable. The Brownshirts had a style that was all their own. They moved like one man, the product of years of training, years of concerted aggression. It was stunning and terrifying. She could see men being herded into a truck.

'Where are they taking them?' Isobel demanded.

'To the camps.'

The word struck her with dread. At first merely a shadowy rumour, regarded with scepticism as anti-Nazi propaganda, the camps had come to be spoken of more openly lately. Out in the German countryside, people said, concentration camps had been built to imprison all those whom the state deemed as undesirable – Gypsies, Communists, the disabled, Jews. 'Will they be killed?' she asked in horror.

'They'll be given a little health cure,' Max chuckled. 'You know Jews. They hate fresh air and exercise. By the time we've finished with them, they'll be almost human.' His nostrils flared, drinking in the smoky air. 'You smell that? Let's take a look, Fritz.'

They turned down into Fasanenstraße. Here, in a distinguished square, stood a large synagogue, one of the grandest in Germany, with a neoclassical basilica façade and an imposing dome. It was now about one o'clock in the morning. The square was crowded with people and trucks, including three fire engines. The doors and windows of the synagogue had been battered in, and were glimmering with the fire that had been started within. There were cheers as the flames began to appear at the upper storey windows. The firemen stood by, watching but doing nothing to stop the blaze. The SA storm troopers who had done the work were jovial, leaning on their sledgehammers and swigging from bottles.

'This was long, long overdue,' Max said in satisfaction. 'Imagine – a monstrosity like this, thrust in the face of decent Germans all those years. You know that old fool Wilhelm presented them with a marriage hall when he was Kaiser? How disgusting! Now they will pay.'

He got out of the car, holding his flask. Isobel got out, too, feeling that she was in some dreadful nightmare that would not end and that she couldn't escape from. The heat from the burning synagogue rushed into her face, together with the reek of the gasoline that had started it. The great stone face of the building seemed blank, like the faces of the old people she had seen being beaten on the street, but the windows flared red and orange.

She looked at the firemen, the pride of Berlin. Their faces, too, were blank. They stood with folded arms, wearing their greatcoats and helmets, immobile. Even if they'd wanted to help, the milling mass of Brownshirts between them and the burning building was forbidding.

A bonfire had been started on the sidewalk, pouring flame and smoke up into the night sky. Brownshirts were hurrying backwards and forwards with armfuls of paper, the sacred scrolls and books of the synagogue. Everything that could burn was dumped on the bonfire. As the ancient tomes flared, the faces of the men were illuminated. At last, a fire engine roared into life. The firemen were in action, unrolling a hose. A long arc of water rose into the air. But it was not to put out the fire in the synagogue; the firemen played the water on the roof of an adjacent building, to prevent it from being damaged. The fire truck's ladder rose into the air, the firemen diligently directing the jet anywhere except on the synagogue.

A roar of approval rose up from the crowd. A group of people were being thrust forward to the bonfire, men, women and children. They were in their night clothes, or random garments they had hastily dragged on. At the centre, an SA man grasping each arm, was a rabbi, a man in his seventies, his long earlocks and grey beard spreading down his chest.

'Look at that old brute,' Max said. 'My God, what a monster. Did you ever see anything so horrible?'

The Brownshirts pushed the man almost into the bonfire, so that he could see his sacred texts burning. His family, a wife of about his own age and several children of various ages, clustered around him, trying to protect him. The rabbi's face was impassive, like so many of the faces she had seen tonight, both victims and aggressors. There was a kind of resignation, of acceptance almost, in his eyes as they rested on the burning scrolls, as though this was something he had foreseen and foreknown. The younger children were crying helplessly in terror.

An SA storm trooper drew his dagger and seized a fistful of the old man's beard. He began hacking off the rabbi's beard with crude strokes, throwing the curls into the flames. Even this the rabbi endured in silence, but his older sons broke free and launched themselves at their father's tormentors.

The reaction was savage. Brownshirts waded into the young men with fists and clubs. Within seconds, all three of the rabbi's sons were beaten to the ground and boots were thudding into their faces and bodies.

'Stop them!' Isobel screamed, running forward to intervene. She was already clutching at the SA men when Max grabbed her and pulled her back.

'Are you mad?' he demanded.

'They're killing those boys,' she sobbed.

'So what? You want to be killed, too? For a bunch of Yids?'

The beating was remorseless. In the glare of the bonfire, Isobel saw the heavy boots swinging into lolling heads. Her screams did nothing to stop them. They did not even glance at her as she raged at them. Max held her tight, watching the beating with that detached expression. She saw a storm trooper drag the nightgown from a little girl. The child fled naked into the darkness. The other girls and women were being stripped, too. The rabbi was sagging under the hammering of the clubs. When they released his arms, he slid to the ground beside his sons.

Her ankle was wet. She raised the hem of her coat to see the dark stains on her stockings. She was so close to the beating that the blood of the rabbi and his sons had spattered her. She remembered the Kaiser's prophesy.

They will make you learn to pull up your skirts, after all.

Isobel stumbled away from Max to be sick. It poured up from the pit of her stomach and spewed into the gutter, all the dreams she had cherished, all the lies she had swallowed.

3.
CHIARA

I t's going to be a white Christmas,' Chiara said joyfully, getting out of the taxi at the rank on Brompton Road and looking up at the sky. Above the exuberantly palatial façade of Harrods, a grey sky was discharging constellations of large white flakes. Snow was already piled thick on the cornices over the windows and doorways of the great store. She closed her eyes happily as the flakes settled on her upturned face, melting in an instant on her warm cheeks and lips.

Charlie Grosvenor bumped her forward so he could get out of the taxi behind her. He was very drunk. 'Well,' he said, slithering on the sidewalk, 'which door shall we go in?' adding in a sepulchral tone, 'For Harrods, like Death, hath many doors.'

'This way,' she said, steering him through the throngs of shoppers jostling to get in and out of the store. There had never been a busier or a merrier Christmas, people said, despite the imminent threat of another world war. It was the jolliest on record.

A green-liveried doorman tipped his top hat as he let them in. 'Afternoon, Miss Redcliffe. Into the fray.'

Harrods was hot. A dizzying smell, as of the ten most popular perfumes of the season all mixed haphazardly together, blew into their faces. Charlie paused. 'I say. I feel rather sick.'

'I told you not to order that third bottle of champagne,' she said. Since the news of his inheritance, it had been his only drink – and plenty of it.

People were avoiding him. His mane of tawny hair, dishevelled by the wind and the champagne, gave him a wild appearance. He was a very big young man, but he was looking peaky. He mopped his brow with the end of his white silk scarf. 'No, I'm sure it was the oysters.'

'There's an R in the month,' she pointed out, trying to get him moving again.

'Doesn't matter, if you get a bad one. I need a brandy.'

'That's the *last* thing you need.'

'If I don't get a brandy, I shall be sick.' He made an ominous noise.

'Oh, Charlie!' she exclaimed impatiently. She couldn't tell if he was serious or not. They took the elevator up to the Georgian Restaurant, where the beaming head waiter, M. Alphonse, lately of Paris, greeted her.

'Afternoon tea, Miss Redcliffe? We're rather full, but I can squeeze you in.'

'It's only Charlie, Monsieur Alphonse. He says if he doesn't get a brandy, he's going to chuck.'

After a swift inspection of Charlie's face, M. Alphonse steered them to a quiet corner table. A brandy materialized in front of Charlie, who gulped it down, and then appeared to go to sleep, his chin on his chest. Chiara prodded him, but he did not stir. 'Oh, dear,' she said. 'And I did so want to get some Christmas shopping done. Do you think he's all right?'

'Sometimes it's just the thing to settle the stomach,' M. Alphonse said confidentially. He didn't bother putting on the French accent with Chiara. He sounded more like what he was, Mr Alfred, lately of Hackney. 'Though you'd hardly credit it. Hair of the dog, as they say. Lunched too well, has he?'

'I don't think he's been sober since he got the news,' Chiara said with a sigh.

'Well, good luck to him. Can I get you anything, Miss Redcliffe? Tea and something from the trolley?'

'Just a glass of water, thank you, Monsieur Alphonse.'

He hurried away. It was almost four o'clock, the high point of high tea, and the restaurant was buzzing with conversation and laughter. The tables bristled with silver cake stands. Waiters bustled with trolleys. The restaurant had been decorated for Christmas, with large wreaths hanging on the walls and fir trees festooned with silver baubles. The huge artificially-lit stained-glass skylight overhead made it seem like a sunny day, despite the snow outside. Chiara looked around, seeing a couple of faces she recognized. A few gloved hands waved to her gaily. She waved back self-consciously. There were also, she noted, several amused glances. She felt very conspicuous. She tried discreetly to nudge Charlie awake, but he made the cockling sound again, and she desisted hastily. His head was hanging forward now, his tangled brown hair half-covering his face. There could be no doubt to even the most inattentive observer that he was deeply asleep. M. Alphonse brought her a glass of water. 'Sleeping like a baby, is he?'

'Out for the count. How long do you think he'll sleep, Monsieur Alphonse?'

Alphonse inspected Charlie with an expert eye. 'In for the long haul, I should say.'

'And this is your busy time. So sorry. I'm afraid to wake him in case he – well, you know. Chucks.'

'Never you mind, Miss Redcliffe. Give him an hour to get over himself, then we'll try to mobilize him.'

An hour! Chiara pushed her white kid glove down and glanced at her watch. A Harrods full of temptations called her, with Christmas just a few days away, and here she was, stuck with Sleeping Beauty.

It would be so easy to slip away and get her shopping done, hoping for the best, but she dared not leave him unattended. He might disgrace himself publicly in any number of ways. And, being continuously plastered apart, he was a very nice young man. She felt responsible for him. Most of his friends were getting sick of his drinking – except the hangers-on who hoped to get something out of him – and had faded away.

Chiara sighed and rested her chin on her palm. She was generally considered the least pretty of the Redcliffe girls, but she didn't mind that in the slightest. She thought her sisters were the two most beautiful women in the world and she missed them terribly, Felicity veiled and wimpled in her priory in Westmorland, Isobel lost God knew where – Chiara had not heard from her in weeks – in the awfulness of Nazi Germany. She herself aspired to no extremes of religion or politics, neither of which she understood or cared about very much.

She had a snub nose and a mouth in the style which was politely called bee-stung, the upper lip slightly fuller than the lower. She was blonde, her golden hair cut short because its colour was so spectacular that when it grew longer, people stared at her in the street, and she hated to be thought a show-off. The wrong sort of girls had hair that colour, a male friend had once told her reprovingly, to which she'd exclaimed that the wrong sort of girls got theirs out of a bottle, while hers was natural. He'd said that didn't matter.

The Eton crop, unfashionable in an era which admired cascades of curls, gave her a puckish look. She was often described as *gamine*, an appellation she disliked, because it also suggested show-offishness; but it did express a certain elfin quality, a certain quaint aplomb, with which she struck others. Unusually for such a true blonde, Chiara had brown eyes which could appear mischievous, even when her thoughts were innocent. At twenty-three, she was growing rather long in the tooth to be rattling around London in a single state. Isobel had been married at nineteen and Felicity had plighted her troth with Jesus at the same age. Their mother had been married at seventeen. But here she was, a woman of means, attractive enough, well-dressed enough and amusing enough for most people's taste, yet still single, and sitting like Patience on a monument next to Charlie Grosvenor – who had now started to snore.

'What a charming picture. Una and the lion.'

Chiara looked up, startled, at the tall gentleman who had spoken to her. Lost in her thoughts, she hadn't realized that he had approached. 'I beg your pardon?'

'"Sad Una down her lays in weary plight,"' he quoted, "And at her feet the lion watch doth keep." Except that, in this case, the lion has laid him down in weary plight, and Una is keeping watch.'

'I don't know the poem,' she said with cool politeness. 'Is it Shakespeare?'

'Spenser. *The Faerie Queen.*'

'Lost me there, I'm afraid.' He was wearing a dove-grey suit with a pink hothouse carnation in his buttonhole and one might have thought him a dandy but for the maroon and navy striped tie he wore, which meant he'd been in the Brigade of Guards. She knew that because her father had worn one. She warmed enough to smile at him. 'I suppose Charlie is a bit of a lion to look at. But he's actually a poor lost lamb. He's inherited rather a lot of money and he's been celebrating.'

'So I've heard.' He wasn't looking at Charlie, but at her, with more interest than was appropriate, perhaps. But she was very glad he had appeared. The attendance of a distinguished gentleman at this juncture in her life was a salvation.

He was one of those impeccable men, whom you felt instinctively would always know the right thing to do and say. His hair was impeccably cut, to go with the impeccable suit and the impeccable accent. He was greying along the temples, a lean, tall man of around fifty. His eyes, she thought, were the grey-green of castle walls and the winter countryside, although he was more tanned than was usual for an Englishman at this time of year. 'Is Charlie your darling?' he asked.

'No, he's not my darling. I'm sort of his nanny, until he goes off his binge.'

'You've appointed yourself to this unenviable task, I take it?'

'Well – yes. Everyone else has fallen by the wayside.'

'And if Charlie is not your darling, then who is?'

'I don't have a darling.'

'Really. I understood that the younger generation was somewhat lacking in initiative, but I had no idea things had gone this far.'

He had a way of saying things that were teasing and yet flattering, with a sort of dry gallantry which amused her. M. Alphonse, spotting her companion, now came hurrying over to their table. 'Mr Courtfield! I thought you'd left.'

'I saw my mother to a taxi and came back to rescue this young lady, Alfred. A sad case.'

Alphonse/Alfred winked at Chiara. 'A sad case indeed, Mr Courtfield. May I get you something?'

'Well, now.' He turned courteously to Chiara. 'What shall we have? Perhaps a Campari?'

'I've no idea what that is,' Chiara replied.

'Then I think you must find out,' he replied. He pulled out a chair and sat down. 'Alfred, two Camparis. You know the way I like it.'

'Right away, sir.'

The head waiter bustled off again. 'Your mother?' Chiara asked.

'I'm sure it seems incredible that such an ancient creature as I should have a mother,' he said gravely, 'but there it is. She clings obstinately to life.'

'Is she so very old?' Chiara asked.

'A hundred and eleven.'

'A hundred and eleven!' Chiara said.

He had a very well-shaped mouth that seemed severe until he smiled. "She wouldn't thank me for giving away her age, but she's in her early sixties."

'Oh! I thought you were serious!'

He arched one eyebrow at her. 'I hope, now that I've taken the trouble to come to your rescue, that you're not going to turn out to be a dimwit.'

'You needn't stay if you're going to be disagreeable,' she said.

'I certainly won't stay if you are an example of the vacant, aimless young female who seems to infest London these days, usually in the company of vacant and aimless young males.' He glanced at her companion. 'What possessed you to bring young Charlie here in this state?'

'We had lunch at the Mayfair and then I wanted to do some Christmas shopping, like your venerable Mama. I didn't know he was going to pass out.'

'You're Chiara Redcliffe.'

'That's right. I'm sorry, I don't recognize you.'

'That's all right. We haven't met, but I've kept a sort of eye on you.'

'Oh? Really?'

'My name's Oliver Courtfield. I knew your father. We served together in the Machine Gun Regiment in the last lot.'

She was captivated. 'How thrilling that you were with Daddy!'

'I was very grieved when he died. He was one of the brightest and the best.'

The description of her father pleased her. 'Were you close friends?'

'He was my senior officer. We were companions of war, rather than friends.'

135

'Companions of war. That's a good phrase. When you say, "the last lot", you think there'll be a next lot?'

'There will be another war. It's just a question of time.' He was drumming on the tablecloth. She noticed that he had very strong-looking, refined hands. 'I don't say that to depress you, but because your sister is in Berlin.'

'Oh, do you know Isobel?'

'I know who she is. She's been supporting the Nazi cause, very misguidedly in my opinion, for a number of years now. This country will soon be at war with Germany. I think it's time she came home.'

'So do I! I'm terribly worried about her! I haven't heard from her since they smashed all the shop windows.'

'*Kristallnacht.*'

'Yes, that's what they call it.'

'They didn't just smash windows. They sent thirty thousand people to the concentration camps.' His eyes were no longer misty, but sharp and clear. His fingers had stopped drumming. 'You haven't heard from her since then?'

'She doesn't answer her phone. I've written and sent telegrams. I contacted the embassy, but the ambassador's been withdrawn and the staff there don't know anything about her. I spoke to one of her editors and he said he thought she was fine, but he didn't know any details.' Chiara took a deep breath. 'I expect she'll turn up. She'd hate me making a fuss, but I'm anxious.'

'I'll make some enquiries, if you like. I have a few contacts in the Foreign Office.'

'Oh, that would be wonderful!' she exclaimed.

He reached into his jacket and produced a little black leather note book and a pencil. Watching him write down the telephone numbers and addresses which she gave him was somehow very comforting. He was that sort of man. He had an aristocratic face, she thought, without quite knowing what she meant by that. He had a long, straight nose and firm cheekbones, a clean jaw. His gaze was intimidatingly direct when he looked you in the eye. He didn't look like a man one would want as an enemy.

Alphonse arrived with their Camparis. She was charmed by the colour of the drink, which she'd never heard of before, and taken aback by the taste. 'That's very sophisticated,' she said. 'Where did you discover this stuff?'

'On the Riviera.'

'Do you really like it? Or do you just drink it to draw attention to yourself?'

He threw back his head and laughed. She took a good deal of pleasure in having provoked that unaffected laugh, which showed his excellent white teeth. 'I'll have to be careful with you.'

'Yes, you will,' she agreed. She noticed that Courtfield's presence at her table had attracted attention. Several more gloved hands were waving. She also noticed that well-groomed heads were together and inquisitive glances were directed their way from women she didn't know. 'Did you have lots of adventures with Daddy in the Great War?'

'The usual thing,' he said vaguely. 'Stormed at with shot and shell. May I ask, do you have any Nazi sympathies of your own?'

'Good heavens, no. It doesn't run in the family, or anything like that.'

'You don't approve?'

'They're ghastly.'

'I think that's a good term for them.' He drained his glass and looked at his watch again. 'I must go.'

She was disappointed. 'Do you really have to?'

'Yes. But I'm going to dispose of Charlie for you.' He laid his hand on the sleeping Charlie's shoulder. 'Come on, old chap,' he said quietly. Though Charlie hadn't responded to her prodding, his eyes opened at once now, very red and bleary.

'All right,' he mumbled. 'Coming.' He rose unsteadily, supported by Courtfield. 'Sorry I was such a bore,' he said to Chiara.

'I'll be in touch,' Courtfield said.

'Thanks for everything!' she replied. Chiara watched the two men leave the restaurant, the older man supporting the younger with a hand under his elbow. Then she was alone, except for the crimson drink in front of her. She tasted it again, shuddering. She was not sure if she loved it or loathed it. She summoned Alphonse, but Courtfield had settled the bill. She was free to do her Christmas shopping.

❧

Of course, it was going to be a dismal Christmas without Isobel and Felicity. It would be the first they had all three spent apart. She was going to have Christmas dinner at the Savoy, with a whole crowd of other waifs and strays from her First Fifteen. The Orpheans would be playing and there would be dancing. The prospect was less gay than it seemed. Since their parents' deaths, the sisters had always tried to see each other for birthdays and Christmases. A Christmas that wasn't spent at one of their homes was a sad Christmas. The happiest Christmas she could remember was the year that little Paul had been alive. He had been an angelic baby and she'd adored him. She'd loved being an aunt. His death had been in some ways harder to accept than their parents' death. It was simply not fair. It had left a gaping hole. And since then it had become clear that Roberto was a stinker, and Isobel had become obsessed with Fascism, and Felicity – well, Felicity was lost to them forever now.

Chiara arrived home with her parcels to find that her French daily, Inès, had broken yet another vase, an antique Coalport one this time, which had belonged to Mummy. The pieces were piled on the telephone table, Inès's altar of shame, together with a tear-blotted note of apology. Sighing, Chiara threw the colourful fragments into the dustbin.

Her small Mayfair apartment was in Tisbury Mansions, a block close to the art gallery where she worked four days a week. It wasn't onerous work – the elderly owner, Mr Cavendish, doted on her – but it suited her. It was interesting, and it paid reasonably well, especially if she sold something important. She did some restoration in the studio at the back, cleaning and revarnishing old canvases, a delicate job at which she had become expert. She didn't really need anything more. As Isobel had pointed out recently, she was the only one of the three who'd held onto her inheritance. Their parents' estate had gone to them in three roughly equivalent sections. Felicity had inherited their mother's things, Isobel the house, and Chiara the financial investments. She'd used a lot of it to buy her flat in Tisbury Mansions, which was appreciating in value yearly, and there were a couple of thousand pounds in the bank.

She was also the only one of the three who hadn't 'done something' with her life so far. Isobel and Felicity had Ideas. She'd often wondered why she herself didn't seem to have any. She was very practical. She'd invested in paintings – a little Pissarro, a tiny Renoir. These speculations would appreciate, she knew. But she'd never been bowled off her feet by an Ism. She supposed she wasn't very emotional. Perhaps that was also why she couldn't fall in love, despite the throngs of eligible young men who surrounded her.

Because Christmas would be at the Savoy, she'd bought small-scale presents for her friends, pens and ties and bits of costume jewellery. She'd also bought wrapping paper and ribbon. She had settled down to wrap a few boxes when the phone rang. It was her Aunt Patsy, not a real aunt, but a cousin of her mother's, one of those who had 'stepped in' after their parents' deaths, and still regarded herself as *in loco parentis*.

'I hear you had tea with Oliver Courtfield in Harrods?'

'Goodness, the jungle drums are beating. I wasn't having tea. He rescued me from an embarrassing situation.'

'So he's back in England.'

'Unless it was his ghost. I thought he was very nice.'

'No doubt,' Patsy replied dryly. 'He's the most accomplished seducer of young females this side of Don Juan.'

'How exciting! Unfortunately, he didn't try to seduce me. He quoted poetry most of the time.'

'That's Step One, darling. You really are an innocent. He's not someone you should be seen with.'

She tried to finish tying her bow with the receiver tucked under her chin. 'Why not? I thought he was the perfect example of an English gentleman.'

'He's not even English,' Aunt Patsy snorted. 'His mother's French. Dreadful woman.'

'Oh. He said he was in the War with Daddy.'

'Which is the last time he behaved with any decency.'

'So that's true?'

'Oh yes, it's true, all right. Your father recommended him for the Military Cross.'

'He didn't mention that.' So much for *the usual thing*. 'He also said he was going to find Isobel.'

'He'll have his own axe to grind. He's some kind of spy with the Foreign Office.'

'Really?'

'Don't sound so enthusiastic. That lot don't have a moral scruple between them. They're notorious. Why, in my young day – what's all that rustling?'

'I'm doing my Christmas wrapping.'

'Well, look, all I want to say is that Oliver Courtfield is living proof of the adage that, the dishier the man, the less trustworthy he'll turn out to be.'

'I hadn't noticed that he was particularly dishy. He must be twice my age.'

There was a silence. 'Dear, sweet Chiara. You just keep out of his way. Pick up one of those nice young men and marry him quickly, that's my advice. There'll be conscription soon, you mark my words. Then they'll all be off. You're almost an old maid already.'

'Well, I don't mind being an old maid, Aunt Patsy, but I certainly don't want to be a war widow.' Chiara shook her head as she replaced the receiver. Aunt Patsy hadn't done a particularly good job of putting her off Oliver Courtfield. She was intrigued. She thought back to those few minutes in Harrods. Had he seemed especially seductive? He had been very courteous and helpful, nothing more. That he was a war hero and a secret agent made it even nicer that he had paused in his busy day to help a relative stranger. She was looking forward to meeting him again to see if she could gain some inkling as to why Aunt Patsy thought this kindly, middle-aged man was a ruthless seducer.

The next morning, at the gallery, she received another call. It was from Charlie, sounding very hung-over and contrite.

'Can't apologize enough. I'm a disgrace and I know it. You were a brick for sticking with me.'

'Did Mr Courtfield put you in a taxi yesterday?'

'Better than that, he drove me home in his Jaguar. Lectured me like a Dutch uncle, bless him. Put me straight. No more boozing for me, I swear it.'

'I hope that's true,' she said sternly.

'Cross my heart. Where did he spring from, by the way?'

'He was passing and saw my plight. He said we looked like Una and the lion.'

'Never heard of them.'

'Me neither. Charlie, do you know anything against Mr Courtfield's character?'

'Like what?'

'Well, that he's untrustworthy with young persons of virtuous morals.'

'He's a bit of a lady's man, so they say. His wife died years ago and he's never remarried. Why? Did he make a pass at you?'

'Nothing like that.'

'Then I shouldn't worry about it. He's highly unlikely to set his cap at you.'

'Oh?' she said haughtily. 'Am I so repellent?'

'You're half his age.'

She hung up on him and went to attend to a young couple who were studying a Degas pastel sketch of ballet dancers. She'd had her eye on the thing herself, a luminous study of flesh and acid-green gauze, but Mr Cavendish was determined to get five hundred for it, which was rather steep for her. She talked them into putting a deposit down on it. A sale would mean twenty-five guineas in her own pocket. She was pleased.

She'd been hoping that she would hear something from Courtfield about Isobel, but some days passed without a word from him, and she began to wonder whether it had been an empty promise.

Three days before Christmas, however, the man himself walked into her gallery, looking very debonair in a camel coat and swinging an umbrella (it was snowing hard).

'Good morning, Mr Courtfield,' she greeted him demurely. She brushed icy flakes of snow off the shoulders of his coat. 'Would you like to buy a painting?'

'What do you recommend?'

'We have some lovely French Impressionists. Mr Cavendish has an excellent eye.'

'I can see that.' He took in her shoes, dress and face. 'And the paintings are nice, too.'

'Are you toying with my affections, Mr Courtfield? I've been told to beware of you by my Aunt Patsy.'

'Very sound advice,' he said. He looked around the gallery. 'You're wasted here, you know.'

'Am I?'

'You should be doing something more useful with your life.'

'Isn't an art gallery useful? Anyway, I'm not fit for anything else. I was a dunce at school.'

He gave her an ironic glint. 'You mean you were lazy?'

Chiara frowned, offended. 'You're a very annoying man.'

'I find it hard to believe that you were a dunce. You have intelligence and character in abundance. That you wasted your schooldays is disgraceful, but you can still redeem yourself.'

'Oh good. I'll rush out and save the world, shall I?'

'I can certainly find work for you more worthy of your gifts.'

'I bet you can.'

'I have a bit of news about your sister. I believe it's your lunch break?'

'Until two.'

'Then allow me to offer you lunch at my club. It's just around the corner.'

'I'll get my coat and hat,' Chiara said with alacrity.

Snow whirled around them in the street. It was very cold. Courtfield took her arm and drew her close to his side under the umbrella.

'How is your mother?' she asked.

'She's stag hunting in Scotland.'

'Is that one of your jokes?'

'Not at all.'

Luckily, his club turned out to be Boodle's, which was indeed just around the corner in St James's Street. Chiara was intrigued.

She'd always wanted to see inside this bastion of male privacy, having passed its stately front so many times, and having peered up at the chandelier in its arched window.

She'd expected a fusty atmosphere of oak panelling and black leather, but the club was surprisingly beautiful inside, more like a country house than anything else, with Adam ceilings and fireplaces. After he'd given her a tour of the smoking room and the dining room, which were dominated by oil paintings of horses and hounds, he led her upstairs.

'Where are we going?'

'I certainly don't intend to share you with a lot of thundering old bores,' he said.

A table had been set in a small, private room with a fire burning brightly in the grate. The room was charming. Over the marble fireplace was a Stubbs of a mare and her foal. The centrepiece of the table was an arrangement of black hellebores. 'My favourite flowers,' Courtfield told her, pulling out a chair for her.

'Very masculine.'

A balding waiter with a row of medals on the lapel of his jacket attended them. Neither he nor Courtfield addressed a word to one another. The meal was simple but excellent, grilled lamb cutlets with sautéed potatoes and a good Beaujolais.

'Your sister appears to have had a change of heart about Fascism,' he told Chiara. 'She's been very pally with a nasty piece of work named Max von Grimmel, one of Goebbels's creatures. So long as she wrote approvingly of National Socialism, she was in the catbird seat. However, it seems she witnessed some of the atrocities of *Kristallnacht*, and wrote a furious article denouncing the Nazis. *Der liebe* Max intercepted the article and had her arrested.'

'Oh, my God.' Chiara put down her knife and fork, shocked.

He poured her another glass of wine. 'Drink up. You've gone quite white.'

'Is she all right?'

'Yes. She was thrown out of the country and arrived in Paris the next day. She appeared to be well. She gave a radio interview to CBS News.'

'The Nazis didn't hurt her?'

'Not physically, at any rate. But they've vilified her in their papers. Her article upset them. They regarded it as a stab in the back. She apparently contacted Kaiser Wilhelm in Doorn. He made a statement expressing his outrage at the treatment of the Jews. The Nazis are rather sensitive as regards Wilhelm. They don't like him criticizing them.'

'She said she'd met the Kaiser. I wasn't sure if she was joking or not.'

'She wasn't.'

'Where is she now?'

'I'm trying to find that out.' He paused and savoured a mouthful of Beaujolais, as though pondering his next words. 'I'm glad she's seen the truth. The Nazis have been successful in wooing a number of conspicuous Britons. It's part of Hitler's mythology that the Nazis and the British share a common philosophy. Like most of what comes out of his mouth, that's rubbish.'

Chiara toyed with her food. 'She must be broken-hearted. She set such store by Fascism.'

'Well, she's in an excellent position to persuade others that it's not the road to world peace. I'd like to talk to her.'

'Is that why you're giving me lunch? Because of my relationship to Isobel?'

He considered her with an assessing gaze. 'It's something to bear in mind.'

'I think I ought to be annoyed with you.'

'But it's not the only reason. I'm very interested in you for your own qualities – well hidden though they may be.'

'You really *are* offensive.'

'In the end, Isobel will have no choice but to come back to England. I'm trying to bring her home.'

'I hope you can.' Chiara studied Courtfield. She was beginning to understand why Aunt Patsy thought him 'dishy'. It wasn't that he had the dazzling good looks of a film star. His dishiness lay, rather, in other things; for example, in his absolute confidence of manner, the calm certainty that he was doing what was right, that he knew what he was talking about, that he was strong, inside and out. She hadn't met anyone with such a natural sense of authority. There was also the way he looked at her, so carefully and with such absorption, as though she were the only thing in the world that mattered to him.

'To many people,' he said, 'Hitler is just a fad. Uniforms, discipline, patriotism. It seems wholesome, until one realizes that it is all based on hatred.'

'Isobel often sees only the outside of things. She doesn't look deep enough. She acts without thinking. Felicity – she's my younger sister – is the other way around. She continually thinks without acting.'

'And that is the dichotomy of life. Or so I have come to think, after my forty-six years.' She made the mental calculation swiftly. He was twenty-three years older than she. Exactly twice her age. He smiled slightly, as though guessing her thoughts. 'It's also the main issue of *Hamlet*. And, as it happens, *Hamlet* is playing at the Old Vic. I've seen it once this season already. It's a superb performance, quite the best in history. I have tickets for tomorrow night. Will you join me?'

His eyes were holding hers. She found she couldn't look away, didn't want to. When he looked into her eyes like this, she felt a kind of prolonged thrill in her stomach, an excitement that came of suddenly seeing that something might happen, something that seemed impossible, unlikely, unwise, but which promised that the thrill could deepen and broaden and become overwhelming.

Chiara didn't answer. She felt that she was at a crossroads, that if she said no, her life would continue on its course unaltered, and if she said yes, it would take a completely different direction. She'd never had this feeling before. Courtfield's mouth still wore that faint smile, as though he'd made a bet with himself, and was waiting to see the outcome.

'All right,' she heard herself say.

'I'll pick you up at six,' he said.

'All right,' she said again. She was feeling dizzier than ever.

'And now for pudding. Bayliss tells me he recommends the Orange Fool. He has a point. It's rather good.'

The stolid waiter had in fact said nothing at all, but Chiara nodded. 'That sounds very nice.' And it was as easy as that, she thought, she had made her decision and her life was going to change. She leaned forward to whisper. 'I've never known such a silent waiter!'

'Who, Bayliss? The wretched man never stops talking. A perfect poll parrot. He was my batman in the War. I had to gag the fellow to stop him chattering.'

She scrutinized him, her chin in her hand. 'I'm starting to understand you.'

'Really?'

'You say outrageous things, but you're just teasing.'

'It depends upon the tease-worthiness of my interlocutor.'

'I'm very easy to tease, I'm afraid.'

'Then you're in for a hard time.'

'But how will I know when you're serious?'

Courtfield appeared to ponder. 'When I'm really serious, you will see a single tear steal down my cheek.'

'You're impossible.'

The Orange Fool was as good as he had promised, creamy and tangy and altogether luscious. They had coffee. And shortly after that, they were walking through the snow back to the gallery. He sheltered her with his umbrella while she unlocked the door. 'The bird goes back into the gilded cage,' he said.

'I like it in the gilded cage,' she replied.

'So you're not interested in my offer of work?'

'You haven't told me what you do.'

'Oh, I'm in metal exports.'

'Metal exporting sounds dreadfully dull.'

'It has its moments. The offer is open.'

'I'll let you know when I decide to spread my wings.'

'Good.' He left her with a smile and disappeared into the whirling white flakes. She felt absurdly happy.

❧

It had occurred to Chiara that she was out of her depth with a man who quoted poetry she'd never heard of, considered an evening of Shakespeare as a treat, and challenged her in so many ways; but it was part of the excitement. That such a sophisticated man should be interested in her was very flattering, even if the interest was fatherly. And she knew that his interest was very far from fatherly. He didn't flirt with her and he said nothing suggestive, but the way his eyes held hers made her heart race. It made her think of herself in a new light.

And though he teased her, he never made her feel a fool. Of the three sisters, only Felicity could be considered highbrow, and that was by choice, not education. Neither of their parents had approved of 'highbrow women'. It was bad enough that the family faith was Roman Catholicism, but that was inherited. The Redcliffes accepted that while certain men could be brainy, women should strive not to be, unless they wanted to become oddities like Cousin Fenella, who lived in Cambridge with a younger woman discreetly known as Fenny's Friend, or Felicity herself, whose ghastly fate was also now held up in the family as the consequence of over-braininess. Uncles and aunts who had stepped into the breach after their parents' death had perpetuated this philosophy. Isobel at least had been sent to a finishing school for a couple of months and was relatively accomplished. Chiara thought of herself as ignorant. But Oliver Courtfield seemed to think she was capable of great things – unless that was just part of what Aunt Patsy had called Step One.

She was exhilarated at the prospect of an evening with him. He was fun. He made her laugh. And being seen on his arm was one in the eye for everyone who thought they had her pigeonholed.

He picked her up at six the next evening, as promised, in a long, sleek Jaguar. Her attention was caught by the leaping silver beast on the nose. 'It's their new mascot,' he said. 'Not sure it'll take on. It looks like a scalded cat.' The car was new and smelled richly of leather. It felt very powerful. Crossing Waterloo Bridge, he said, 'There's something for you in the glove compartment.'

She opened it and found a little box of three chocolates inside. 'How thoughtful.'

'Eat them now. I can't bear people surreptitiously munching chocolates next to me at the theatre.'

'There's nothing surreptitious about the way I eat chocolate, Mr Courtfield,' she assured him. The chocolates were hand made, each one decorated with a C. 'They have your initial on them.'

'Actually, it's yours. And please call me Oliver.'

'I shall eat one now and take the others home to press in my album.'

'Are there many chocolates pressed in your album?'

'Not so far. Only a toffee presented to me by the King.'

The performance was in modern dress, with modern sets, which intrigued her. Sitting beside Oliver Courtfield in the dark of the theatre was a strangely intimate experience, for although she followed the play closely, she was intensely aware of his proximity; and she wanted to understand what it was he had praised so highly. Hamlet, a young actor named Alec Guinness, moped and brooded in a dishevelled suit and tie, delivering his lines in a measured, melancholy, weary tone. At the interval, they went down to the bar, where Oliver had ordered champagne. He asked her what she thought of the performance so far.

'He's very good. But he's ordinary. As though he were a junior bank clerk, rather than a prince.'

'Does that disappoint you?'

'I'm wondering why you think he's the best Hamlet in history.'

'Perhaps it's just the time and the place.' In the crush of people chattering, smoking and drinking, Oliver himself looked splendid in an evening jacket. She noticed that women always looked at him, but he never looked back. He was focused on her, studying her face constantly. She was wearing her little silver lamé dress, a choice she regretted, as the Old Vic was cold, though it did make her look very fairy-like. "Perhaps Hamlet's problems don't belong in medieval Denmark, but here, now, to all of us."

During the second half of the play, she thought about what Oliver had said. When Hamlet was finally provoked into action, killing the wicked king, it was too late, and he was already dying. Perhaps that was the warning Oliver had meant. She rose with the rest of the audience to give Guinness a standing ovation, tears in her eyes.

It had been a long performance and she was hungry. Oliver took her to Boulestin in Covent Garden. She hadn't been there before; her set tended to patronize the smart Mayfair hotels. This was very different, a Parisian restaurant filled with rich colours and scents, with modern murals of circus performers and low-hanging silk balloon lamps.

'How beautiful!' she exclaimed.

He seemed pleased. 'I think it's the prettiest restaurant in London.'

The place was crowded. Their table was in a corner, next to a mural of a vermillion clown and a bright blue horse in a yellow circus ring. Chiara felt elated. This was the perfect place to come to after the long, monochrome production of *Hamlet* they had seen. 'You really have the most exquisite taste, don't you?' she said to him.

'Your presence here confirms that,' he smiled.

'And that's another thing. You say the nicest things, but they never seem like compliments. I hate compliments.' She studied the menu, which was in French. 'You plan everything meticulously, don't you?'

He had put on glasses to read the menu, she noticed. 'I find that system yields the greatest chance of success.'

'And how would you measure the success of tonight?'

'By the brightness of your eyes.'

She looked up mischievously. 'Nothing beyond that?'

'What should lie beyond that, my dear Chiara?'

'For men, success with a woman usually means something more than bright eyes.' She turned back to the menu. 'I think I'll have the *sole meunière*. What are you having?'

'The *bouillabaisse*.'

'I'm terribly ignorant. I don't know what that is.'

'I recommend it. You can have *sole meunière* anywhere in London.'

'All right,' she said, closing the menu. 'What a pleasure it is to be guided by you.'

He folded his glasses away into his pocket. 'I'm not that sort of man, by the way. When I say that I measure success by making you happy, I mean it.'

'Good Lord,' she said, 'a single tear is stealing down your cheek.'

'Your eyesight must be defective.'

'At least I don't need glasses to read the menu.'

His eyes sparkled. 'Where are you spending Christmas, Hawkeye?'

'At the Savoy.'

'With Charlie?'

'And others of that ilk. Don't get me wrong, I hate spending Christmas in a hotel. But I don't seem to have any sisters left.'

Boulestin himself came to take their order, a jovial, beaky-nosed man who greeted 'Olivaire' with a great deal of chuckling and banter in French. He bowed gallantly over Chiara's hand and looked approvingly down her cleavage. When the order had been taken and Boulestin had left, Oliver said, 'You could always spend Christmas with me. I'm having a little family lunch at my place in Oxfordshire. You'll be able to meet my mother.'

'I thought she was stag hunting in Scotland?'

'She killed a thirteen-pointer yesterday at twilight. We're roasting it for lunch.'

'Whole, over the Yule log?'

'Exactly.'

'I can't,' she said regretfully. 'I've promised the others.'

'Then it will have to be another time,' he replied. He thought for a moment. 'I have to come up to London again on the 28th. Perhaps we could have dinner?'

'I think I'll be free,' she replied.

'Alone, except for the improving book which Aunt Patsy is sure to give you? What will it be this year? *A Girl's Guide to Church Architecture*?'

'You frighten me. You know everything.' She bantered with him but she felt rather as she'd felt in Oliver's Jaguar when he accelerated, that things were moving fast, and that although it was very exciting, it was also frightening.

By way of apéritifs they drank Negronis, a much more civilized way, in her opinion, of enjoying Campari. It was one of the happiest meals she could remember. They discussed the play, talked nonsense and teased one another. She made him laugh by recounting silly stories from her childhood, about Felicity and Isobel and their wonderful, eccentric parents, who would now never grow old.

'You can't possibly have been born in Adlestrop,' he said, laying down his knife and fork in surprise.

'Why not?'

'It's too perfect. That wonderful poem – "all the birds of Oxfordshire and Gloucestershire".'

'The poem is lovely, I agree, but Adlestrop is a tiny, very dull place. The house isn't even in the village. It's an old farmhouse about five miles away. It belongs to Isobel, now. I wouldn't have chosen to be born there. Even in the poem, it's just a one-minute stop at a railway station.'

'On the contrary. The gods chose wisely. There is nothing more beautiful than the English countryside. And your hair is just the colour of ripe summer wheat.' He smiled at her. 'Adlestrop is perfect.'

'Then Adlestrop it shall be.'

'And it's not too far from my own place. We're neighbours.'

He was very charming. The restaurant was delightful and the food was delectable. The *bouillabaisse* turned out to be a stew of fish, mussels and shrimps, redolent of garlic, a vegetable which had been forbidden at Adlestrop. Oliver told her that the British had the best fish in Europe, only they didn't know it and refused to eat it, except out of newspaper, with chips.

Several people came up to their table during the course of the evening. Oliver seemed to know half of London. There was only one moment when she felt uneasy, and that was when a couple named Langford paused to greet Oliver. The man was bluff and hearty, but the woman, a dark beauty in her thirties, was neither. She said little, but she gazed at Oliver with hungry eyes. Upon leaving, she shot Chiara a glance which seemed to be bitterly jealous.

'Who is she?' Chiara asked Oliver when they had gone out.

'Monica Langford? She has a stud farm in Devon. Racehorses, mainly.'

'I mean, who is she to *you*?'

'A friend. That's her second husband, Giles. He's a sort of colleague of mine.'

'She's stunning. I bet she's prepared to speak ill of you.'

'What makes you say that?'

'She looked at me in a very odd way.'

'Don't pay her too much attention,' he said dismissively. 'She's an odd sort of woman.'

She felt he was not telling her the truth, and that troubled her. However, it was his business; and besides, she was far more interested in the future than in the past.

It had stopped snowing for a while. He parked outside her flat in the early hours of the morning and they got out of the car into a silent, icy landscape, roofed with glittering stars. Chiara's breath clouded around her mouth as she looked up.

'This has been the most divine evening.'

'I'll remember it,' he said.

'So will I.' He walked her to the door. There, she turned and looked up at him. 'Thank you, Oliver.'

'We'll see each other in three days' time.' That suddenly seemed like an eternity to her, a vast gulf of time to get through somehow. She thought – hoped, with a squirming in her tummy – that he would kiss her on the lips, but he merely brushed her cheek with his mouth. 'Merry Christmas, Chiara.'

She skipped the lift and ran up two flights of stairs. She threw herself onto her bed and whispered, 'I'm so happy – happy – happy!'

❧

The gallery closed for Christmas the next day on a triumphant note: the young couple bought the Degas without quibbling over the price. Mr Cavendish gave Chiara her commission in crisp five-pound notes. She instantly gave them back to him and took home something she'd long had her eye on – a small, battered oil study of white clouds in a blue sky, which Mr Cavendish had optimis-tically attributed to Constable. It had not yet been cleaned. She went home and put her prize on the mantelpiece, delighting in its interesting composition and vigorous brushwork. When she had time, she would clean it and revarnish it. With a nice gilt frame, it would look lovely.

There was still no word from Isobel, but a Christmas card had arrived from Felicity, containing a rare treasure – a line or two in her own handwriting, saying that they would be celebrating nine Holy Masses over Christmas, and wishing her a happy 1939. The card went on the mantelpiece, next to the alleged Constable.

Whether Felicity so seldom wrote because the convent discour-aged her, or because she was unwilling to communicate, or even incapable of doing so, Chiara could not tell. She had visited Felicity only a handful of times since Felicity had taken the veil. None of the visits had been a success. On the two occasions when she'd made the mistake of arriving unannounced, she had waited in vain, only to be told after a couple of hours that Felicity could not see her. She hadn't repeated that mistake a third time. The other visits had been stiff and formal, almost unbearably so. Felicity, once so gay and open, had sat with folded hands and downcast eyes, answering

Chiara's questions with monosyllables, and quite clearly waiting only for her to leave. Chiara had understood that she was not a welcome visitor there. She could only hope that this was something which would change in the years to come.

Her letters to Felicity, full of news and gossip, seemed to cause annoyance, for Felicity responded only with little printed prayers or pictures of saints, which Chiara took to be admonitions for the frivolous life she was leading. So she seldom wrote now, either. She hoped these lines of handwriting were the first signs of a thaw.

⁓

It was a white Christmas after all, the whitest of the century, so the BBC said. Britain was blanketed in snow. Boys threw snowballs in Trafalgar Square, traffic slithered in Piccadilly Circus. The day was largely dry under the influence of a high-pressure ridge from Scandinavia, or some such thing. A few flurries of sleet scurried through London streets towards evening.

Christmas at the Savoy was very noisy and jolly. The huge dining room was filled to capacity and hung with extravagant decorations. Her usual crowd was there, dressed to the nines, occupying four large tables in a group. It was, everybody said, the best Christmas dinner ever. After the plum pudding, the Savoy's big band, the Orpheans, played Christmas carols very cleverly to a foxtrot beat in the glittering ballroom. Chiara was whirled around the floor by several members of what Isobel satirically called her First Fifteen. The Orpheans were hot, so hot indeed, that she found herself dancing a quickstep instead of a foxtrot.

Pausing for breath and a glass of cold champagne, Chiara found herself next to Moira Gilligan, an acquaintance. Pulling streamers out of her hair, Moira said to Chiara, 'You've put Charlie Grosvenor's nose properly out of joint.'

'Have I? How?'

'Charlie says he telephones you but you're never there. And you've been seen with Oliver Courtfield. Getting into his car, too.'

Chiara absorbed this. 'I don't know why Charlie should be upset. I don't belong to him.'

'Well, of course you don't *belong* to him. But everybody thought there was something between you. Including Charlie.'

'I only stuck around because all his friends abandoned him when he was drinking so much.'

'That's just it. You've proved yourself a true helpmeet. He thinks you're the cat's pyjamas.' Moira was rather a sly creature, with small eyes, freckles and a pointy nose that was always in other people's business. 'Why are you looking so po-faced? He's just inherited a hundred thousand pounds!'

She glanced across the ballroom to where Charlie was sitting with some of the other young men, looking mournful. 'I had no idea he felt that way.'

'He's been drinking soda water all night – at Christmas! And you haven't even noticed!'

'If he stops drinking, he should do that for himself, not for me.'

'And you've hardly spoken to him all night. Everybody's noticed.'

'Well, they shouldn't notice such things,' Chiara said irritably. 'I don't like being the subject of gossip.'

Moira put her curly head closer to Chiara's. 'Your Oliver Courtfield only wants one thing, you know. You watch out for him. Once he's had you, he'll drop you flat.'

'Have you met him?'

'Of course not. I don't move in those exalted circles.'

'Then you know nothing about him,' Chiara snapped, annoyed, 'and you shouldn't say such things.'

'Well, excuse me, I'm sure,' Moira said in mock-Cockney. 'I'm only saying what everybody says.'

'What does everybody say?' she demanded.

'That you're too inexperienced to be getting all starry-eyed around him. He's old enough to be your father.'

'Does that make any difference?'

'The difference is where he'll leave you, sweetie. You've got a spotless reputation. All the men know that. That's why they crowd round you like ants round a sugarlump. Charlie wants to marry you. They all do. But if you go with Oliver Courtfield, that will change. They'll want what he had. But not to marry you. You get the picture?'

'I don't want to marry Charlie. Or any of them.'

Moira looked at her quizzically. 'Would you marry Courtfield if he asked you?'

'He would never ask me.'

'Now you're getting the picture,' Moira said. Chiara didn't answer. 'It would be a couple of months of fun. Even I can see the attraction, sweetie. But use your head.'

The Orpheans struck up *The Lambeth Walk*, provoking a rush back to the dance floor

Charlie Grosvenor came hurrying over, looking like the melancholy lion in *The Wizard Of Oz*. She got up to dance with him, and they whirled away into the crush.

∽

The night had been fun except for two episodes, the wigging she'd received from Moira, and Charlie Grosvenor's impersonation of a whipped dog. Had everyone really assumed that she was going steady with Charlie? No good deed went unpunished, it seemed. She hadn't intended to give any such impression. But Charlie's reproachful demeanour last night had told her that this was the impression he'd received. She refused to feel guilty about it. She'd meant well. And with his hundred thousand in his pocket, Charlie would soon find a substitute.

She hated the idea that she was being talked about, that people were making her life a matter of public discussion. But that couldn't be avoided. Perhaps she was being irresponsible, after all. Maybe she wasn't the sensible sister, as she'd always thought she was. Whatever the rights or wrongs of it, she had found the love she'd been waiting for. Maybe she was just as queer, eccentric, misguided and unwise as Isobel and Felicity.

Three days later Oliver was back in London and took her to Quaglino's for dinner. She wore a new gown of pale blue silk which was daringly open all the way down her back, and a gold chain she'd inherited from her mother. He did not compliment her directly – he never did that – but the way his eyes rested on her was more than flattering. He made her feel desired, and that was something new, even though she'd always had men around her, like ants round a sugarlump, to use Moira's elegant phrase. No man had yet made her feel wanted in this way, wanted for herself, for what she was. Nor had any man yet made her feel that he would know what to do with her once he'd got her. And these impressions Oliver conveyed in force.

Quaglino's was crowded to capacity. Like Boulestin, it was the haunt of an older set than her own, wealthy and fashionable people who knew how to order a meal, dress and dance. The band was American, and very good. They played *Tea for Two, Christmas Swing, Honeysuckle Rose* and *Night and Day*. Once again, several people came to their table to greet Oliver and meet Chiara, though on this occasion she could not identify anyone who might be an old lover.

'I feel that all your friends are giving me the once-over,' she said. They had ordered a crab soufflé to start with, which had arrived in textbook condition, and was as light as sea foam. 'I'm surprised they don't ask to look at my teeth and hooves.'

'Your teeth and hooves don't need inspecting. They're obviously faultless.'

'It's true, though, isn't it? Everyone wants to know who you're with.'

'I think they want to know who *you're* with.'

'You're the focus of attention, Oliver.'

He shook his head. 'You really have no idea, do you?'

'About what?'

He smiled gently but didn't reply. That was one of his non-compliments, which made her feel warmer than any direct praise could do. 'I have a little news about your sister.'

'Tell me!'

'She's not in Paris any longer. She boarded a train at the Gare de Lyon a few days ago. She had two suitcases with her.'

'Where was she going?'

'She was probably going to Marseilles. But that's just a guess.'

'How do you find out these things?'

He shrugged. 'Just gossip.'

'I don't believe that. You *are* a spy, after all. Can't you have her followed?'

'There are no resources for that, my dear,' he said regretfully. 'As soon as I find out where she is, I'll contact her myself.'

'Do you know that she brought me and Felicity up? I was eight when Daddy died, twelve when Mummy followed him. That's a tricky age to lose your parents. We were superintended by uncles and aunts, but it was really Isobel who took over as clan leader.'

He was interested. 'What was she like as clan leader?'

'A darling. A tyrant. It's hard to believe now that she was only about fifteen then. Felicity and I were in such awe of her. To tell the truth, we still are, Or at least *I* am. Isobel shaped our lives. She made up the rules. She bullied and protected and consoled and moulded us. Where would we have been without her? She was magnificent. And yet she's as mad as a March hare. No wonder we all turned out so odd. Oh, Oliver, if you know how, please bring her home!'

'I will try,' he promised.

The meal and the service were not to be faulted. Quaglino prided himself on doing everything *comme il faut*. It was the one place in London, according to Oliver, where one could be attended as luxuriously as in one's own home. As proof of this, Chiara caught glimpses through the crowd of Prince George, the King's brother, and his wife, the Duchess of Kent, seated with friends near the bandstand. The royal party appeared very animated. 'He's quite handsome when he laughs,' Chiara observed.

'He's doing everything he can to persuade everyone that Hitler is harmless,' Oliver said. 'Like his brothers, he imagines that war with Germany can be averted.'

'Isn't that a noble idea?'

'Very noble,' he said dryly. 'A noble mouse assuring the common mice that the cat won't eat them. What can one expect? We've already been treated to the spectacle of the Duke of Windsor reviewing a battalion of SS troops.'

'Don't you think that we can avoid a war?'

'No,' he said flatly. 'That's a pipe dream. My idea is quite different – that war is inevitable and that we must prepare to win it at whatever cost.' Oliver looked around. 'I wonder how much of this will be left in a few years' time? The next war will be fought with heavy bombers. Fleets of them, in their hundreds. The destruction will be terrible.'

She was struck by the look on his face. She laid her hand on his arm. 'It may not come to that.'

'You're right.' The look faded and he smiled into her eyes. 'And we may still be here, enjoying this perfect happiness.'

'Are you really perfectly happy?' she asked.

'At this moment, yes.'

'So am I.'

They held one another's gaze for a moment. Chiara felt that heat in her belly again, that excitement of possibilities, of promises. Even if London lay in ruins, she thought, she wouldn't care, so long as she could be with Oliver.

A couple had arrived at their table. The man was elderly, with white hair and a ravaged face, the woman very handsome, dramatically-dressed in green. She was foreign looking and appeared to be of Oliver's own age. Oliver rose and kissed the woman's cheek. 'Hello, darling. I didn't know you were here tonight.'

'I saw you coming in, *chéri,*' she replied with a noticeable accent. She shot a sharp glance at Chiara. 'And of course, your beautiful companion.'

'Let me introduce you to her. This is Chiara Redcliffe. Chiara, this is my mother, Cécile de Robillard.'

Chiara took the white, red-nailed hand that was offered her. 'How do you do,' she said. So this was Oliver's mother, described by Aunt Patsy as 'a dreadful woman!' It was clear at once that this was not someone Patsy would admire. The low-cut green silk dress, the jet-black hair and the lipstick were all solecisms of the worst sort in a woman of sixty. Not that Cécile de Robillard appeared to be a day over forty. Chiara had seldom seen skin of such unlined whiteness. Nobody bothered to present her companion, who stood in the background talking to someone else, looking like Father Vice in evening dress.

'*Vous êtes si jolie, ma petite,*' Cécile said. '*Quel âge avez-vous?*'

'*J'ai vingt-trois ans, Madame.*'

She turned to her son with a raised eyebrow. '*Tu l'as arrachée à son berceau?*'

Oliver nodded his head lazily at his mother's companion. '*Tu l'as arraché à son cercueil?*'

This exchange shocked Chiara somewhat, but neither Oliver nor his mother appeared to be discomposed by it. 'We're going on to a nightclub, *chéri*,' she said. 'Angus says Quaglino's has become too middle class for words. Even the Royals have started coming here. It's the kiss of death. Will you join us?'

'I think not. We're not as fashionable as you. But thank you, darling.'

Cécile de Robillard patted Chiara's cheek. Her eyes, Chiara saw, were a lighter green than Oliver's, and far colder. 'Be twenty-three forever,' she said. 'That is my advice.'

They departed. Looking at Cécile's rear view, Chiara saw that she had an hourglass figure, accentuated by the bold tailoring of her dress. The curvaceous bottom and shapely white shoulders disappeared among the crowd. 'Fresh from the Scottish crags, I see,' she said.

'I didn't say she was on the crags. I said she was stag hunting. And as you see, she has killed a noble beast.'

'You didn't roast him at Christmas, then?'

'He's already roasted,' Oliver said equably, 'and I assure you, will soon be picked clean.'

'I don't like it when you talk so cynically,' Chiara said, feeling for some reason that a shadow had fallen over her perfect happiness.

'With a mother like mine, my dear, it's best to be clear-eyed. She makes her living from gentlemen of that sort. When the flavour of this one bores her, she'll digest for a while, and then find another.'

'You make her sound like a vampire.' He merely shrugged by way of an answer. Their next course arrived, *suprêmes de volailles à l'archiduc*, but the melting chicken breasts did not appeal to her. 'You must have enough money to look after her, Oliver.'

'Of course I have,' he said. 'I could keep her in comfort and dignity for the rest of her life.'

'Then why does she behave in that way?'

'Because she is Cécile. She's a solitary huntress. She prefers to get her own dinner with her own claws. Don't look so shocked.'

'That makes me sad.'

'It shouldn't. She has lived that way since she was a girl.' He indicated her plate. 'The chicken is excellent, try it.'

She tried a mouthful. 'You talk to her rather cruelly.'

'It's the way we've always talked to one another,' he said, showing the first touch of impatience she had yet seen in him. 'She had me when she was seventeen. Having done her duty by my father, as she saw it, she went on her merry way. Being a doting mother and wife were not for her. She was very beautiful, after all. She broke my father's heart and, insofar as a little boy can have a heart to break, she broke mine. I love her, but I am not sentimental about her.'

Chiara ate in silence for a while, her mind occupied with the images his words had evoked. She remembered the sharp glance of those green eyes, the flawless white skin that was somehow like marble. 'Are you like her?' she asked.

'I don't need anyone else's money, Chiara.'

'I don't mean that. I mean, are you cold?'

She didn't think he was going to answer. The handsome face was like a mask. 'In some ways,' he replied at last.

'And do you go from woman to woman, taking what you want and moving on when you are bored?'

Again, he thought about her question. 'I have been like that at some stages of my life.'

She met his eyes. 'Are you like that with me?'

He leaned back in his chair. 'Why do you bother your head about such things now? We haven't even begun.'

'I have begun, Oliver,' Chiara said quietly.

'I hope you don't intend to express the sentiments of a penny novelette,' he said, smiling.

'My sentiments are not those of a penny novelette,' she replied evenly. 'I simply want to know whether I would be a fool to continue seeing you.'

'Have people been suggesting that?'

'Yes. But I don't give much account to what people say. I'm asking you on my own account. If you've always treated women in that way, am I to expect anything different?'

He thought for a moment, as though this were something he hadn't considered up until now. 'I behave in a certain way because I don't find love.'

'You've never loved a woman?' she demanded, incredulous.

'I loved a woman very much once. But she has been dead for years.'

Chiara felt an agonizing pang of jealousy. She could hardly breathe. How could she hope to compete with a dead woman, embalmed in his memory, never growing old or fading in her loveliness? And yet she knew already that Oliver was the great love of her life, come what may. 'Don't you hope to find love again?'

He seemed indifferent to the question. 'I suppose I do.'

'And women are willing to have you experiment on their hearts?'

'Perhaps they enjoy the experiment. In the interests of science.'

'So the offer is a good time, with no strings attached, no regrets and no reproaches when it ends?'

'There are worse offers,' he smiled. But his eyes were cool, now.

'And my only chance of keeping you is to make you fall in love with me?'

'You put things too simply sometimes.'

'I can't help it. I'm simple.'

'Darling, how can we make promises to each other now?'

'But you talk as though our having an affair is inevitable.'

'That's another issue. And you're letting a very well-prepared dish go cold on your plate.'

Chiara sighed. 'I wish I knew what makes you tick.'

'Knowing that I'll be dead one day makes me tick.'

The shadow over her seemed to have deepened. 'Oliver!'

'It's no more complicated than that. Remembering it is what guides my decisions. All the small things – fear, vanity, shame – all those things become unimportant in the face of death, leaving only the things that matter.'

'I hate to think that I have to die.'

He nodded. 'Of course you do. You're young.'

'But you're not old. Why do you think of death?'

'I saw rather a lot of it from 1914 to 1918. It's hard to forget. Now let's stop this, my dear girl, and eat, drink and be merry.'

He refused to let her continue in any serious line of questioning after that. She drowned her sorrows in the nectar-like wine and tried to be content with what he had told her.

The Lambeth Walk was the signal for the dance floor to fill up. Watching the well-heeled patrons of Quaglino's strut and toss their heads and shout, 'Oi!', Chiara thought she would always associate this lilting tune with Oliver's arrival in her life, long after his departure from it.

They went onto the dance floor together to a slow version of *My Honeysuckle Rose*. He danced beautifully, holding her lightly but firmly in his arms. His body was strong and warm. It was so easy to fall into Oliver's rhythm. He could get anyone to do what he wanted. The syrupy melody enveloped her, lulling her into a moving trance of drowsy eroticism. They were not dancing, they were making love. Their bodies brushed together, their fingers twined. Their souls, she felt, were in union. This was not something that could be judged by the standards of Aunt Patsy or Moira Gilligan. They wouldn't understand any of it, the sorrows or the joys. All they could see was what Oliver called the small things, fear, vanity, shame. He was right. At the end of life, one surely didn't look back and congratulate oneself on having been governed by those emotions.

Oliver drove her home in the early hours of the morning. He parked outside her mansion block but they didn't get out. In the dim light, she looked at his silhouette and said, 'I don't want this evening to end.'

'Mine isn't ending. I must pack now,' he said. 'I'm leaving London in a few hours. I'll be away for a couple of weeks.'

Chiara's heart sank. Had her nagging over dinner put him off her? 'Where are you going?'

'Abroad.'

'Where, abroad?'

'Oh, various boring places,' he said vaguely.

'Metal exports?'

'Yes.'

'Will you be in any danger?'

'No.'

'Will you write to me?'

'No. I'll be home in the middle of January. I'll call you when I get back in town.'

'I'll miss you, Oliver.' She slipped her arms around his neck and lifted her mouth to his. He seemed to hesitate for a moment. And then he took her in his arms and kissed her. She felt that she was enveloped in heat, as she'd been on the dance floor, but this was more overwhelming. She kissed him back in a frantic way that owed nothing to art, her lips crushed painfully against his. It was a raw expression of her need, of not wanting to lose him. The kiss was almost clumsy in its passion, and over in seconds.

He drew back and gently unwound her arms from his neck. 'Don't think too much while I'm gone,' he said.

He walked her to the entrance but would not let her kiss him again. She thanked him in an odd, formal way for the evening and ran upstairs, hoping to see him drive away; but she was too late, and by the time she got to her window, his Jaguar was gone.

❧

Despite his injunction 'not to think too much', she did little else over the succeeding days, which were dreary and empty. She rehearsed their conversations again and again in her mind. She found Alec Guinness's Hamlet haunting her thoughts. Faced with evil, ordinary people had to act. But Oliver's description of vast fleets of bombers smashing London to rubble horrified her. Was it worth such a sacrifice? Wasn't it better to just give Hitler what he wanted and avert the war?

She forced herself to be gay. She went out and saw people. On New Year's Eve she went to the Chelsea Arts Ball with Charlie and a group of others. She went as an unlikely Cleopatra, Charlie as an even less convincing Anthony. It didn't matter. In a crowd of over five thousand, most of them students, filling the Albert Hall with noise and colour, nobody noticed their costumes. There was a frantic quality in the dancing and merrymaking, as there had been in her kiss with Oliver in the car, and for the same reason – a sense that this age was coming to an end, a sense that this might be the last happy moment for a long time. They had a table on the balcony, but went down into the mêlée to dance.

On the stroke of midnight, thousands of balloons were released from the dome above. They drifted down onto the revellers, fragile, rainbow bubbles that popped and bobbed and drifted and rose with the heat and the noise. The racket in the hall was deafening. Every fire station across London rang its fire bells. Tugs and barges blew their sirens on the Thames. Someone played *Auld Lang Syne* on the immense Grand Organ and they all sang to the booming notes. Among the hysteria Chiara saw some people crying and could not help crying, too. The year 1939 was under way.

They went out. The streets outside the Albert Hall were thronged with wild, cheering people. They threw snowballs, jumped onto passing taxis and climbed the lamp posts and scrambled over the railings into the Park, where they built a snowman. A group of skimpily dressed girls clambered up the Albert Memorial, waving champagne bottles and singing. Police arrived, blowing their whistles. The boyfriends of the girls did gallant battle with the officers.

She had no appetite for the all-night revelling of previous years. Reluctantly, Charlie was persuaded to get her home at 1 a.m. She extricated herself from his drunken attempts to talk to her, and when that failed, kiss her. She got rid of him and went up to her bed. In her mind she wished Oliver a happy New Year, wherever he was. She was missing him dreadfully. She wondered what Isobel and Felicity were doing, and how they had celebrated the New Year.

She had just fallen asleep when she was roused by an insistent ringing of the street doorbell. Thinking it was Charlie being importunate, she tried to ignore it, but it went on and on. She got up and lifted the intercom handset.

'Who is it?'

'It's Cécile de Robillard. Let me in.'

Greatly surprised, she pressed the button. A few moments later, Cécile arrived at her door. She was wearing a mink coat, her raven hair dishevelled. She spoke clearly and articulately, but somehow Chiara got the impression that she was very drunk. 'Will you pay the cabby? I have no money.'

Too taken aback to argue, Chiara went downstairs in her dressing gown and paid an impatient cabby an extortionate fare. He roared off to find more revellers. When she got back up to her flat, Cécile had tossed the mink onto a sofa and was trying to light the gas fire in a very tight white dress and high heels. '*Mon dieu, il fait froid ici*,' she muttered. 'You English have ice in your veins.'

Chiara lit the fire. It popped into life. Cécile stood in front of the glowing bars, rubbing her hands. 'What do you have to drink?'

'Only whisky.'

'That will do.'

Chiara poured her a stiff shot. 'Has something happened?'

'What? No, nothing. Angus was impossible. Vile. He locked me out.' She gulped the whisky without thanks and shuddered. 'He is a pig.'

'How did you find my address?'

'Oliver told me to keep an eye on you.' She drained the glass and held it out for a refill.

'That's very kind,' Chiara said dryly, 'but I'm quite all right.'

'I will spend the night here,' Cécile said. She made it sound like an unchallengeable decision, but she shot Chiara a frowning, questioning look from the corners of her green eyes.

'That's all right, if you want to,' Chiara said. But she corked the whisky bottle and put it away. 'I'll make up a bed on the sofa.'

'No bed. I'll sleep under the *vison*. It will be warmer than your spare blankets.' She kicked off her high heels and hoisted her dress to unclip her stockings, showing an expanse of pale thigh. She staggered a little.

'Be careful!'

'Then come. Help me.' Chiara helped Cécile take off her stockings. She smelled of whisky and *Après L'Ondée*. Chiara saw that there were bruises on one white arm where a man had dug in his fingers. She would undress no further, but curled up on the couch under her mink coat. She stared around her with those cold eyes. 'You have some taste in paintings, at least. Or did your lovers buy them for you?'

'I'll go back to bed now,' Chiara said, moving to the door.

'No, wait.' There was a pleading note in her voice. 'Stay with me a little while.'

'I think you should sleep.'

'Just a little while,' she said in a wheedling tone. Chiara sat wearily back down beside her. 'You like Oliver?' she asked Chiara.

'Yes.'

'I like him, too. But I made him what he is.' Cécile closed her eyes. 'I didn't treat him very nicely. I had my own life to lead. *Que voulez-vous?*'

Chiara sat, watching repose steal over Cécile's face. As she relaxed, she looked more innocent, the anger fading from her mouth. When she thought the older woman was asleep, she rose quietly.

'*Il a été trahi par les deux femmes plus importantes de sa vie,*' Cécile said dreamily. 'His mother left him and his wife died young. He will never trust another woman. Leave the fire on.'

Feeling very tired, Chiara went to bed.

She awoke early, thinking of the thousand and one questions she could ask Cécile – about Oliver's work, his women, his childhood, his wife, who Monica Langford was, whether he was really a spy. But when she went into her sitting room, Cécile and her mink coat were gone. The gas fire had been turned off, and all that remained was a trace of *Après L'Ondée*.

❧

On reflection, Chiara decided that it was far more likely that Oliver had given his mother her address in case Cécile needed a refuge – rather than, as Cécile had claimed, 'to keep an eye on' Chiara. That thought pleased her, because it implied that he thought she was dependable. She heard no more from Cécile. But Cecile's Delphic words, like the dreamy oracle of some prophetess, haunted her. Oliver had been betrayed by the two most important women in his life. He would not trust again. She would never be able to make him love her. In any case, he had vanished from her life.

The year 1939 began drearily, the snow alternating with rain and sleet until London's pavements became rivers of slush. The news was alarming. The newspapers were full of reports that the Germans were planning to invade Holland imminently and use the Dutch airfields to launch a bombing onslaught against Britain. In the blizzard of accusations and denials, tensions rose, and the prospect of war became even more real. People no longer talked about *if*, but *when*.

In Spain, Fascism was triumphing. The Nationalists, aided by Mussolini, were poised to take Barcelona, which would mark the end of the Spanish Civil War. Refugees were streaming from the city into France already. The newspapers said there would a terrible purge when Franco took Barcelona, that he had sworn to kill all those who had turned their hands against him. She thanked God that Isobel was no longer in Spain. But where *was* she?

In the meantime, numbers of Jews began to appear in London, pathetic and bewildered families who obviously had little more than the clothes they trudged the streets in.

She occupied herself by cleaning the little canvas of sky and clouds she had bought. The yellowed varnish came off, revealing that it was a very fine sketch. Perhaps Mr Cavendish was right, and it was a Constable after all. The old art dealer had an excellent eye, as Oliver had said.

She had thought of him a great deal. At first, the idea of a fortnight's separation at this crucial point had seemed unbearable. But it had given her time to catch up with her emotions, which had been racing ahead of her intellect. It had given her time to reflect, and to assess what her future with Oliver was going to be.

It was perhaps silly to talk of being in love when she'd known him a bare few weeks. But she knew that if she didn't love him now, she would do soon; and that her love would be real and lasting. Exactly how she knew this was a mystery, at least in part. He was authoritative, kind and sexually compelling. But that was not enough to explain her passion. That was something which came from deep inside her, as though it had lain dormant all her life, waiting for this moment and this man, and no other. It had lain the root's white core and had sprung out of her.

She knew so little about him. And yet she knew him intimately. How? Perhaps from a time when he had been a king in Babylon, and she a Christian slave, as in the old poem. She longed for his return now, yearning to be in his arms, to lie with him and tell him all that was in her heart.

Inès came back from her holidays and together they gave the flat a spring clean. The gallery reopened and Chiara went back to work. There were several customers and a sale on the first day. Perhaps, in the face of war, people were putting their money into tangible things. People said that gold jewellery was unobtainable. It was being bought up by the dealers to hedge against inflation.

On her second morning back at work, a refugee couple arrived at the gallery, a husband and wife in their thirties. Both wore clothes that had once been very good, but were now made shabby by constant wear. Their faces showed the bewildered exhaustion of people whose lives had been shattered. They spoke little English. They were carrying a brown-paper parcel, which they gave to Chiara to open. She was astounded to find that it contained a Rembrandt portrait of a young girl, possibly his daughter, Cornelia. They had somehow managed to smuggle it out of Germany, despite the vigilance of the Nazis.

'This painting is very valuable,' she told them.

The man nodded wearily. 'Of course, I know. How much you give?'

'You should take it to Sotheby's,' she said. 'It's close by. I can give you directions. It would make at the very least ten thousand pounds.'

'You pay this money?' the woman asked, looking at Chiara with haunted eyes, 'this ten thousand?'

Chiara looked at the painting, an undoubted masterpiece. 'My employer would give you half that, at most. Perhaps only two or three thousand. Take it to Sotheby's.'

'They pay us now?'

'I'm afraid not – it's an auction house. It would take a few months.'

'We need money now,' the man replied. 'We cannot wait for months. You understand?'

She telephoned Mr Cavendish, who arrived at the gallery half an hour later. His eyes gleamed on seeing the painting. He went off with the refugees, elegant in his pinstriped suit and bowler hat. She never found out how much he paid for the Rembrandt, or what he did with it. He didn't tell her. Perhaps it went into his bank vault.

In the second week of January, her spirits started to rise again. Oliver had said he would return around this time. She began to tremble with excitement. When a letter arrived, addressed to her in handwriting she did not recognize, her heart leaped. It was not from Oliver, however. It was typewritten on notepaper headed with the name of Felicity's convent in Westmorland. The contents were terse:

Dear Miss Redcliffe,

I write with regard to your sister.

I am sorry to tell you that she has been in ill health for some time, although the doctor assures us that there is no imminent danger.

However, the prioress feels that a visit from you might prove beneficial.

The weekends are not a suitable time for visitors. Any weekday is acceptable.

Kindly contact the priory by telephone should you wish to arrange this.

It was signed by Sister Teresa Margaret, Felicity's novice mistress. The letter put Chiara into a panic. 'Ill health for some time'? What sort of ill health? Why hadn't she heard anything about this? 'No imminent danger'? What did that mean? That there might be danger later? Was Felicity dying?

She immediately began planning her visit, which would mean taking a day off work (weekends not suitable? Did they think nobody had a job?) and finding somewhere to stay overnight in Appleby. Mr Cavendish agreed to give her Thursday off. Since she didn't work on Fridays, that would give her a day and half to see Felicity, if she returned on the Saturday. She telephoned the priory and confirmed the time of her visit. The nun she spoke to couldn't or wouldn't give her any details of Felicity's condition.

Getting to Appleby from London necessitated two train journeys, the Flying Scotsman to Carlisle and then the Carlisle-Settle Railway. The second part of the journey was popular in the summer, because it was among the most scenic routes in the North, crossing arched viaducts and running past fells and wild moorland. In this midwinter, however, the vistas were bleak. The hills were covered with snow; the valleys were brown and windswept. Pen-y-ghent was as white as death. How lonely it was! Chiara gazed out of the window of her carriage, reflecting on the strange fate of her younger sister. Why had she chosen such a path in life? She and Isobel had tried so hard to talk her out of it. Felicity had even been sent to Spain to get her away from England and the influences that were pushing her to the nunnery. That hadn't worked out, either. The civil war had necessitated a hasty retreat from Córdoba, and on her return from Spain, Felicity had immediately entered the priory. Chiara had never found out the details of that adventure. She suspected that Isobel, as so often, had been too heavy-handed, and instead of rescuing Felicity, had ended up pushing her the other way.

She had booked a room at the Merton Arms, a small hotel in Appleby, which was almost empty. The weather was too bad for walking, with constant flurries of snow and a cutting wind, so she arranged a taxi to take her to the priory, which was a mile or two out of the town.

The buildings of the convent always struck Chiara as fortress-like. Built from the local grey stone and roofed with slate, they presented a forbidding aspect to the eye, despite the touches of beauty in the oriel windows and the intricately carved mullions. She was admitted through the heavy iron gate and entered the silent world of the priory.

The courtyard was filled with mist, making the sisters, in their year-round habits of heavy brown stuff, their faces framed with white wimples, appear like disembodied spirits. They seldom raised their eyes from the ground and Chiara received no more than a murmur from the few who passed her. She was taken to a waiting room where she was told to sit. The rhythms of the convent were smooth and steady, marked by muffled bells and silent processions of veiled figures from one part of the buildings to another. Was this what had drawn Felicity, this orderly calm, so different from the chaos of their childhood?

Sister Teresa Margaret appeared at length, a middle-aged woman whose face might have been kindly if she'd allowed herself to smile. She greeted Chiara without warmth.

'Your sister is in the infirmary,' she said. 'I will take you there shortly. Before you see her, however, I should like to ask you to be very quiet in her presence, and not to agitate her in any way.'

'Yes, of course. Sister, please tell me – what is wrong with Felicity?'

'*Wrong* with her?'

'What is nature of her illness?'

'Oh, I see. She has had a persistent cough, which has not yielded to any treatment. She's been tested for tuberculosis and emphysema. Also for consumption. She has none of these.'

'Then what does she have?'

'For one thing, she is suffering from physical exhaustion. Her coughing tires her greatly. It is sometimes hard to tell whether it is the cause or the symptom of her malady.'

'How long has she been like this?'

'Some weeks.'

'With no improvement?'

Sister Teresa Margaret hesitated for a moment. She stood as all the sisters stood, with her hands clasped at her waist. The pose seemed at once self-contained and defensive. Her lean cheeks and long nose were reddened with the cold. 'The doctor thinks otherwise, but it is my belief that your sister's illness is largely imaginary.'

'I'm not sure I understand,' Chiara said. 'What do you mean, *imaginary*?'

A flicker of irritation crossed Sister Teresa Margaret's face, as though she thought Chiara were very stupid. 'Perhaps you should go to see her, now. Please come this way.'

Chiara followed the nun. Sister Teresa Margaret's steps were almost noiseless, even on the stone staircase which led down to the infirmary. There was only the faintest rustle from her clothes. What must it be like, Chiara wondered, to put on the same habit day after day, never varying in its drabness, swaddling one in its monotony?

The infirmary was small. Felicity was the only patient. The elderly sister in attendance, introduced as Sister John, took over from Sister Teresa Margaret and led Chiara in. Felicity lay on a narrow iron hospital bed beneath a window, set high in the wall, whose light fell on her in a wintry swathe. As Chiara approached her bed, Sister John sat herself on a chair not far away. It was evident that she intended to remain there for the duration of Chiara's visit.

Chiara looked down at her sister. She was barely recognizable as the Felicity she'd grown up with. She was bare-headed. Her hair, once bright and abundant, was now a close-cropped, colourless wool. Her face was thin, her cheeks and eyes sunken. She looked gaunt. She stared up at Chiara as though confused for a moment. Then she said, in a quiet voice, 'Chiara! You came!'

'Oh, Fee!' Chiara's eyes blurred with tears as she bent to kiss the once-plump cheek.

She felt Felicity's slender arms embrace her. For a while, they held each other. Then Felicity lay back. 'You look wonderful, darling.' Her eyes, at least, were still Felicity's, the bright grey of their father's, fringed with long, dark lashes. 'Have you heard anything from Isobel?'

Given Felicity's evident fragility, Chiara thought it best not to go too deeply into the reports of Isobel's turbulent existence which Oliver had gleaned. 'Just that she's in France now, and seems to be well.'

'I'm so glad. I think about her such a lot.'

'So do I.'

'Is she over her Nazi-mania?'

'Yes, I think so.'

'Thank heaven.'

'You're awfully thin, Fee.'

'I'm not so bad.' But Chiara could see that her arms were trembling with the effort as she lifted herself to sit up in bed. Chiara helped her, arranging her hard pillows to make her comfortable. 'I've only been in the infirmary for a week. I'm sure they'll let me out soon. It's cosy here, isn't it?'

Was there a glimmer of her old humour in Felicity's eyes? Chiara looked around at the bare walls. There was nothing but a plain wooden cross to relieve the monotony. The place did not even look very clean. It had certainly not been painted in years. 'It's lovely.' She stroked Felicity's cropped head. 'You feel like Ambrose.'

Felicity laughed quietly. Ambrose had been Chiara's teddy bear for years until he had fallen apart under the pressure of her love. 'I feel a bit like him in the last stages of his existence, all pulled to pieces,' she said.

'Why? What's happened to you?'

'Nobody knows. I'm a Medical Mystery. And a terrible nuisance to everybody.'

'You always were a terrible nuisance, so that's nothing new.'

'True. Did you have a lovely Christmas and New Year?'

'I missed you and Isobel. I miss the Christmases we used to have.' Chiara heard Sister John shift her weight in the chair behind her. She tried to ignore the silent wave of disapproval. She'd thought that Felicity's arms had trembled because of the effort of moving, but now she saw that Felicity was all atremble, her fingers unsteady, her hands shaking. Even her face was unsteady, one eyelid dropping now and then in the parody of a wink, her lips twitching. She tried to hide how dismayed she was to see this. 'I had Christmas at the Savoy and New Year at the Chelsea Arts.'

'Doesn't sound like you missed me at all.'

'Well, the Savoy was rather dull, but the Chelsea Arts was a riot. Almost literally. Some girls got thoroughly plastered, and climbed up the Albert Memorial, wearing practically nothing at all—'

Sister John rose to her feet. 'Please! I shall have to ask you to leave!'

'I'm so sorry,' Chiara said repentantly. Was there that ghost of a smile in Felicity's face again? Or was it simply a nervous tic? She couldn't tell. 'Anyway, I got your card, thank you very much.'

'Our Christmas was beautiful. We had Midnight Mass. Then we—' Felicity seemed to run out of words. She plucked at her lower lip. Her eyes drifted away from Chiara to the wooden cross on the wall. 'Don't you think that Christmas is very sad? That little baby, so innocent. And then what they did to him. Do you think about what they did to him? He was born for *that*. One can hardly bear to think of it.'

'Then don't think of it.'

'But I must!'

'Not now. While you're in here, you must rest.'

'Tell them to let me get up, darling. I must get back to work. I'm just wasting everyone's time in here!'

'Shhh. Just get better. Nothing else.'

Felicity was trembling more violently now. Chiara could hear her teeth rattling. Her eyes were very wide and staring, the whites visible right around the irises. 'I don't know why they keep me here. I'm perfectly strong. It's silly.'

'What does the doctor say?'

'He says – he says—' Chiara was silent, waiting for Felicity to continue. Felicity seemed to be staring at some invisible horror.

'Shouldn't you be in hospital?' Chiara looked around the primitive little infirmary and lowered her voice. 'I'm sure they love you here, but they don't have the resources they need to look after you properly.'

'I'll be all right.'

'Sister Teresa Margaret told me you've been sick for weeks.'

'Shhh,' Felicity said urgently.

'You've lost so much weight.'

'*I'll be all right.*' Felicity said this in an odd, breathless voice. She gave a wheeze and then began to cough. It was not the tubercular cough Chiara had anticipated. It was an odd, barking cough that shook Felicity's slender frame as though she were being struck.

Sister John got up with a sigh and began to stir some mixture in a glass.

'Sorry—' Felicity said. 'Didn't mean – to – do this.'

'Don't be sorry, darling.' Chiara held Felicity's shoulders. Sister John brought her the medicine, some kind of chalky suspension, which she managed to drink in little sips. But the coughing went on, percussive and relentless, each cough ending on a rasp.

'Shouldn't we call the doctor?' Chiara asked the nun. Sister John shook her head impatiently. She started to thump Felicity on the back, between her shoulder blades. Felicity didn't object, but that didn't seem to help either. The harsh coughing went on until Felicity's lips turned blue. Chiara was frightened. Her sister's body had become rigid. A string of saliva drooled from her lips. She seemed so frail, the coughing alone giving her a kind of ruthless energy, as though it possessed Felicity and wanted her to shake herself to pieces.

At last, Felicity was able to lie back on the pillows, shuddering. She was breathing again, but with difficulty, as though there were a heavy weight on her breast. Chiara saw that there were little pools of sweat in the hollows of her throat. She laid her hand on her sister's chest and felt Felicity's heart beating wildly. Felicity couldn't speak. The attack had exhausted her. 'Oh, Fee,' she said, 'you can't go on like this.'

Felicity smiled wanly. 'That – was – a mild one,' she gasped. 'Sorry to alarm you. But I'm just – just a bit tired now, darling. I think – I'd better – rest for a while.'

Chiara kissed her brow. 'I'm staying overnight at the Merton Arms. I'll come and see you tomorrow.'

Felicity nodded. Her eyes were already closing.

Chiara went to find Sister Teresa Margaret. As she ascended the stone stairs two at a time, she told herself to restrain her temper. But it wouldn't be easy.

Sister Teresa Margaret was waiting for her at the top of the stairs, standing in her usual pose.

'She can't be left like that,' Chiara greeted her sharply. 'She should be moved to a hospital immediately.'

Sister Teresa Margaret's face was stony. 'We will continue this conversation in my office, if you please.' She led the way in her silent, gliding walk. Her office was a tiny cell, mingling the bureaucratic, in the form of a filing cabinet and a desk, with the spiritual, in the form of several religious prints on the walls. She seated herself behind her desk, her hands clasped, and looked at Chiara through her rimless spectacles. 'Now. What is it you wish to discuss?'

'Felicity can't stay in that wretched little dungeon. She should go to a hospital straight away. She's very ill.'

'I disagree with you there,' Sister Teresa Margaret replied. 'I don't believe that she is very ill.'

'Have you heard her coughing?'

'Day and night,' Sister Teresa Margaret replied dryly.

'And you don't consider that being ill?'

'I consider it a very good way of attracting attention.'

Chiara was astounded. 'She isn't play-acting, if that's what you mean!'

'The doctor has found no organic cause for the coughing. In my experience, Miss Redcliffe, a thing either is or it isn't.'

'Then if the cause isn't organic, it's psychological!'

Sister Teresa Margaret produced a small, cold smile. 'Ah yes. *Psychological*. That word is much in vogue these days, isn't it? I'm afraid I don't believe in psychology, myself. I think there's far too much of it around. Psychology encourages weakness and excuses faults that should be addressed and rectified. I believe that things have much simpler causes and effects than psychologists would like us to imagine.'

Sister Teresa Margaret seemed to be taking a suppressed delight in saying this, her eyes gleaming. Chiara tried to stay calm. 'And you believe that Felicity is shamming.'

'You chose that word, not I.'

'What word would you choose, then?' she demanded.

'I would say that she is convincing herself of something which does not exist.'

'That's the definition of a psychological problem!'

'It is the definition of folly.'

Chiara wanted to scratch that smug face. 'I insist that my sister is taken out of the priory and sees proper medical staff in a proper clinic,' she said tautly.

'You may insist what you please. You have no authority within these walls.'

'You can't imprison her!'

'She is not being *imprisoned*,' Sister Teresa Margaret said in an icy voice. 'If she wishes to go to hospital, she will be taken at once. She has expressed no such wish. As for the infirmary being "a wretched little dungeon", as you call it, she has already taken up a great deal of our meagre resources, our limited time and our patience.'

Chiara's heart was pounding with anger. Her voice shook. 'Then she should leave.'

'She wishes to stay. I have no authority to expel her.' She raised a pale hand to forestall Chiara's retort. 'I think that you should take this up with Sister Helen, the prioress. I can pursue this subject no further with you.'

'Then I want to see Sister Helen.'

'I believe you are spending the night in Appleby. Sister Helen will see you tomorrow morning.' Sister Teresa Margaret rose to her feet and indicated the door without a further word.

Chiara trembled with rage all the way back to the village. Arrogant, cold, vicious woman! How could Felicity survive in such an atmosphere of repression? She must be got out of the priory as soon as possible, and now was an excellent opportunity. If she remained, she was doomed.

The weather closed in. By mid-afternoon, it was dark. The wind howled around the hotel. Depression settled over Chiara as her anger left her. She had an early supper in the dining room and went to bed early and lay listening to the wind and thinking about Felicity. That bright, angelic child, to have come to this!

Snow was still falling heavily the next morning, blanketing the world in even deeper white. She arrived at the priory at nine, and was told that the prioress would see her straight away. There was no sign of Sister Teresa Margaret. A young postulant led her to Sister Helen's office.

Sister Helen, the Mother Superior of the convent, appeared to be at least eighty. Her face, framed in its white wimple, was warm, with serene blue eyes set in a mesh of lines. She took Chiara's hands in both of her own. 'Thank you for coming all this way to see us,' she said, giving Chiara's fingers a light pressure. 'I'm sure you would like a cup of tea.'

Disarmed by this greeting, which was so different from Sister Teresa Margaret's, Chiara accepted the offer of tea and sat in the comfortable chair which Sister Helen indicated. All that hung on the bare walls was a photograph of the Pope and a crucifix. Through the leaded panes of the arched window, snow could be seen falling endlessly onto stones already burdened with white.

'When my mother gave someone a good scolding in Donegal,' Sister Helen began, 'she would say, "I've had words with so-and-so." I am told that you *had words* with Sister Teresa Margaret yesterday.'

'I'm sorry if I was rude, Reverend Mother. I'm very worried about Felicity.'

The prioress inclined her head. 'Of course you are.'

'Sister Teresa Margaret seems to think she's putting it on to get attention. I can't accept that. It's not in Felicity's nature.'

'I make it my policy not to interfere between novices and their supervisors. And whatever the impression you may have received, Sister Teresa Margaret is very far from a cold or unfeeling person. She's an excellent novice mistress. I trust her judgment absolutely.'

'So you also put the blame on Felicity.'

'There is no blame to be put anywhere. She is sick, and when we find the right treatment, she will get better again – if that is God's will.'

'I think Felicity should be in hospital. That coughing can't go on. It's wearing her out.' The tea arrived, accompanied in Chiara's case by a biscuit. Chiara ran on, telling the prioress of her concerns about Felicity, her indignation at Sister Teresa Margaret's coldness. Each time she paused, the prioress nodded and waited for her to marshal her thoughts and continue. Only when she'd run out of words did the older woman speak.

'You and your family were opposed to your sister's decision to become a nun.'

'It wasn't that Isobel and I don't respect the vocation of the Carmelites. We simply felt that it was the wrong decision for Felicity.'

Sister Helen nodded calmly. 'But it was your sister's calling, and her decision.'

'She was so young, Reverend Mother!'

'When your sister first came to us, I was not struck by her youth, but by her certainty. She is approaching the third year of her novitiate. She may soon profess her first vows. I believe that she has a special contribution to make to our sisterhood, our congregation. I believe that with God's grace, she will lead a long and blessed life among us. I see Christ working in her and that fills me with joy. However.' She folded her little hands under her habit and smiled at Chiara. 'The religious life is not the dull monotony which some lay people believe it is. I often compare it to this landscape around us. It has towering heights and it has dark valleys. One can remain trapped in a marsh, or one can run in the sunlight. One can fall and bruise oneself. One can find oneself crossing a moor which appears endless. One can take the wrong direction, be hopelessly lost. And one can come home again. It is a journey. Like all journeys, it has its moments of crisis. And there is no doubt that Felicity is in a crisis.'

'Then she needs help!'

'She is receiving it.'

'Not from Sister Teresa Margaret!'

'The help that I mean comes from God. God sends these crises to us to teach and strengthen us.'

'What if she's not strong enough?'

'Some things are achieved by will and some are achieved by grace alone.'

Chiara felt her hope ebb away. Serene as she was, the prioress had a steely core. 'Then what's to be done?'

'I promise you that your sister will receive the medical attention that she needs. The doctor will see her again next week and we will start investigations again. And I promise that you'll be kept informed of her progress. And she *is* progressing. She is making her own journey. And she is on the right path.' The prioress pushed herself to her feet with arthritic slowness. 'Go to her now and be with her. Try to understand what God is saying through her.' The interview, unsatisfactory as it had been from Chiara's point of view, was at an end. She thanked the prioress without much enthusiasm and they walked to the cloisters together, where a bitter wind was piling snow onto the grey flagstones. 'One last thing,' the prioress said.

'Your sister received her name in religion some time ago. She is not Felicity any longer. Her name is Sister Albert. We should learn to use it.' She made the sign of the cross, conferring a blessing on Chiara.

Felicity had changed since yesterday. She was sitting up in bed and seemed more alert. She was also colder and more contained.

'I'm sorry I made such a spectacle of myself yesterday,' she greeted Chiara. 'I know that I alarmed you.'

'I've just spoken to the prioress,' Chiara said, sitting beside Felicity's bed. 'She says I'm to call you Sister Albert from now on. It's a bit of a mouthful. Can I call you Bert?'

Felicity did not smile. 'I was named for St Albert of Jerusalem, who wrote the Carmelite Rule.'

'What did his friends call him?'

' "Your Excellency". He was a bishop.'

'How about "Bertie", then?'

'Just call me Felicity. It doesn't matter.'

'Sorry, I shouldn't tease you. What would you *like* me to call you?'

'Anything that doesn't express your contempt for me too openly.'

'Oh darling,' Chiara said, stricken, 'I don't feel contempt for you.'

'Yes, you do. You and Isobel both do. It doesn't help. Can't you see that? It doesn't help!'

'Please, darling.' She didn't want to precipitate another coughing fit. 'We don't feel contempt. We just worry about you, as you worry about us.'

'Then don't. I'm all right.'

'I know you are,' she soothed.

'They asked you to come and see me because I was *sick*.' Chiara saw that Felicity was trying to stop herself trembling by clenching her fists, her elbows pressed hard to her sides. 'Not so you could throw your weight around. Play the saviour. Insult everybody.'

'Felicity—'

'Not so you could start a campaign to get me out of the priory.' Her eyes were like pale fire. 'Not so you could make demands and assert yourself, as though you *own* me.'

Felicity had heard of her conversation with Sister Teresa Margaret. Chiara felt crushed. 'I'm sorry.'

'How *dare* you?' Felicity was quivering with outrage. 'How dare you come into this place and behave like that? This is my *home*!'

'I'm sorry,' she said again, 'but—'

'I don't want you to come back any more.'

Chiara's heart twisted. 'Oh darling, you can't ask that of me!'

'I can and I do. I have been here for three years, and you and Isobel still talk as though I'm a child who doesn't know her own mind. I've had enough. There's nothing more to say between us.'

'Felicity!'

'I'm sorry you were brought all the way up here. Now please go back to your wonderful life in London.'

Chiara reached out to Felicity. 'Don't do this to me.'

Felicity ignored her outstretched hand. 'Go.'

'Forgive me, darling. I was so afraid when I saw you so ill. I just wanted them to take you to a hospital.'

'Get out of here!' Felicity screamed. The sound echoed on the stone walls.

Chiara stood up. 'Can I write to you?'

Felicity's face was turned away now. 'It would be better to just forget me.'

'I can never do that.'

'Please go, Chiara.'

As she walked up the stone stairs, she heard Felicity begin to cough again, those harsh, animal barks. By the time she got to the cloisters, they had become shrieks, rising from under the ground, fading on the wind.

᠊ᢙᦉ᠊

When she got back to Tisbury Mansions, Alf the porter poked his bald head out of his cubbyhole. 'Your young gentleman called and left a note for you, Miss Chiara.'

'Thank you, Alf.' She thought it might be from Charlie, but to her delight, it was from Oliver. To Alf, a veteran of Omdurman, Oliver was no doubt a 'young gentleman'. The note was written on a page torn from his little black notebook, and read simply, 'Can you come to a concert & dinner tomorrow night at 6.30?' A Whitehall telephone number was written beneath the message. Her delight dimmed somewhat at this less-than-sentimental greeting after two weeks of separation. It was the first time he had given her a telephone number on which to contact him

She called the number and was answered by a clipped woman's voice which agreed to relay her acceptance to Mr Courtfield and then rang off immediately. Chiara didn't even know which concert she was going to. However, he was back in London at last, thrillingly, tantalizingly close!

Over the day, her feelings about Felicity had hardened. The long trip to the priory had been a fiasco, but that wasn't her fault. If Felicity was determined to stay in her nunnery, then so be it. Let her stew there. Even her novice mistress was sick of her posturing; Sister Teresa Margaret had all but called Felicity a fraud. Neither Sister Teresa Margaret not the prioress had felt Felicity was in any danger. The best thing she could do was ignore Felicity until Felicity came to her senses of her own accord and saw the madness of what she was doing. Chiara had her own life to live – and Oliver was back. There was nothing more important.

Because the invitation had sounded very formal, she wore a black evening gown which left her shoulders and neck bare. An advantage of her Eton crop was that no great attentions were needed to her hair. Looking at herself in the mirror, it seemed to Chiara that she looked absurdly young and innocent. No wonder those old crows at the priory hadn't taken her seriously. Did Oliver, too, see her as an ingénue? How could she make herself appear more sophisticated? There didn't seem to be any way. Plastering herself with make-up would be silly. She had never used cosmetics much, a legacy from her mother, who'd discouraged 'warpaint' (though Isobel loved make-up, which she used liberally).

Oliver arrived promptly at 6.30. She asked him to come up to her flat – she didn't want to greet him in the street. Her heart was racing with excitement. She threw her arms around him when he appeared, feeling an explosion of joy.

'I've missed you!'

He looked down at her, smiling. 'I've missed you, too.' He was in evening dress, looking extremely dishy, but there were lines of strain in his face which hadn't been there two weeks earlier. She could see tension around his eyes and mouth. She showed him her flat. He walked around, looking at her paintings, taking books off the shelves and opening them. 'It's very charming,' he said.

'I've got a Christmas present for you.' She had decided to give him the little cloud study while he'd been away. She presented it to him, carefully wrapped in gold paper. She watched his face as he unwrapped his present, seeing his expression change.

'Chiara, this is beautiful. I'm deeply touched.'

'Mr Cavendish thinks it's a Constable. He may be optimistic, but I think he's right.'

'I'll take your word for it. It's a precious gift. Thank you.' He kissed her tenderly on the lips, leaving her trembling to her fingertips.

In the car, she asked him where he had been.

'I had business in Paris,' he said.

'Metal exports?'

'One day I fear we will be exporting a great deal of metal in that direction.'

'Was your business successful?'

He hesitated. 'You remember I told you that our duty is to prepare to win this war?'

'Of course.'

'Well, I believe that my business in Paris was very successful. Successful enough to give us a strong advantage.'

'That's wonderful!'

He glanced at her. 'But it's not to be spoken of, Chiara.'

'I will never breathe a word,' she promised. She told him about her trip to the north, about her battles with the prioress and Sister Teresa Margaret.

'Childe Roland to the dark tower came,' he said.

'That's what it felt like.' She told him how she had found Felicity. He listened, seeming intent.

'She's having a nervous breakdown,' he said briefly when she'd finished.

'What does that mean?' Chiara asked, looking at him anxiously.

'There's a strain on her emotions which she can't cope with. We saw soldiers like that in the War. They called it shell shock. The coughing fits are probably attacks of asthma. She feels she's being suffocated, that she can't breathe.'

'What would do that to her?'

'A life which she's forcing herself into, despite her distaste for it.'

'But she's so hostile, Oliver. She won't hear of leaving the priory, even to go into hospital. She insists that she knows what she's doing. I can't go back there if she doesn't want me.'

'She'll either learn to cope with it, or leave of her own accord.'

'Was that what soldiers did in the War?'

He gave her a grim smile. 'The ones who left of their own accord were shot at dawn, if they weren't lucky enough to have sympathetic officers, and most officers weren't very sympathetic. Rather like your Sister Teresa Margaret. They called it cowardice. Sometimes I think we all had shell shock. We lived with it.'

'And if you couldn't?'

'We lived with it whether we could or we couldn't.'

'Did people get over it?'

'Most of us did. I hope Felicity will get over it. I imagine that all those who attempt to follow that path suffer some kind of crisis. Of course, you must stay in contact with her, even if she forbids it. You mustn't abandon her.' He paused. 'I could visit her myself and give you an opinion, for what it's worth.'

'It would be worth a great deal! Why are you so kind?'

'I feel I owe it to your father. And to you.'

'Thank you, Oliver.' She hesitated. 'Aunt Patsy said Daddy recommended you for the MC.'

He didn't seem pleased by the reference. 'Your father recommended me for various things. I didn't object at the time but later I wished I had refused.'

'Why?'

'They seemed so futile.'

'But they were given to you because you were brave. And I'm so proud that it was Daddy who saw your bravery.'

'My dear Chiara,' he said wryly, 'I did as many cowardly things as brave things. They're words that don't mean very much. I've seen men throw their medals into the river.'

'Will you tell me about it one day?'

'One day,' he agreed.

They arrived at the Royal Albert Hall. This was a very different occasion from the New Year's Eve carnival Chiara had attended a fortnight earlier. A cultured London audience was assembling to hear the great Spanish cellist, Pablo Casals, perform three cello concertos, including Elgar's, which had almost never been played in public since its disastrous first performance just after the war. It was a poignant occasion, since Casals's native Catalonia was at that moment being overrun by Franco, aided by Mussolini.

'It's a bloody mess,' Oliver told her as they settled into their seats in the stalls. 'Barcelona raided by heavy bombers, thousands of refugees pouring into France every day. The French are keeping the border open for the time being, but they simply can't cope with the numbers. They herd the Spanish into camps where they have barely enough to eat, no medical attention, and only tents to sleep in. It's cold and rainy. Ankle-deep in mud. Children are dying. And more coming every day.'

'You talk as though you've seen it with your own eyes,' Chiara said, looking at him. 'Is that where you've been?'

'It's what one hears.'

She laid her hand on his arm. 'Oliver, I beg you not to lie to me. I care about you enough to always want the truth.'

He watched the orchestra assembling on the stage and did not reply for a while. Then he said, 'I have to tell you something, Chiara. Your sister is in Barcelona.'

Chiara almost shot off her seat. '*Isobel?*'

'I couldn't find her. I'm so sorry. I searched high and low, but the city is in complete chaos. It's hard to travel around. The streets are blocked with rubble from the bombing, the trains aren't running. Electricity and water supplies are cut off for days at a time. There's no fuel and no food. I'm sorry to have to tell you this. I'd hoped to bring you better news.'

Chiara was appalled. 'But what is she *doing* there?'

'She told someone that after Berlin, she wanted to show Fascism for what it really is. She apparently decided to cover the civil war from the Republican side. She took a train to Marseilles and somehow got to Barcelona from there.'

'Oh, my God. Did anybody ever have madder sisters than I do? They both belong in lunatic asylums. Why didn't she *tell* me what she was doing?'

'I don't know. She's written an article, but the British papers won't touch it because of her previous association with the Nazis. The American press has published parts of it. And she's done another radio broadcast for CBS. I'm sorry, Chiara. I had an address for her, but she's not there any more.'

'How much longer will Barcelona last?'

'It's a matter of weeks.'

'Will she have the sense to leave before the end comes?'

'Let's hope so. I've asked people to listen out for her. If they find her, I promise you I'll go back and get her myself.'

'I don't know whether to cheer her or burst into tears. Isobel is the only woman I know capable of doing such mad things. You went all the way from Paris to Barcelona to look for her!'

He smiled. 'I wish I'd found her.'

She searched his eyes. 'It's the most wonderful thing anybody's ever done for me.' She laid her head on his shoulder. 'You're a very perfect, gentle knight. Thank you, Oliver.'

He kissed her hair. The conductor arrived to loud applause, but the arrival of Casals himself was greeted with a deafening roar and a standing ovation. Now approaching sixty, the unassuming, balding Catalan was regarded as the greatest cellist in history. The fate of his country added to the drama of his appearance here tonight. It was almost as though this crowd of music lovers was shouting their defiance of Franco, Hitler, Mussolini and the other Fascist dictators of the age, who between them had already destroyed so much of the world's artistic heritage.

Casals played magnificently. The highlight of the long performance was the Elgar, which brought Chiara to tears. It seemed to alternate between hope and despair, throbbing with pathos and passion. Chiara sat clasping Oliver's hand and thinking of her sisters. As an encore, Casals played a solo piece, a Catalan folk song which had become a symbol of resistance against Fascism. It brought the house down.

After the concert, Oliver took her to Maison Prunier, a few streets from her flat, reputed to be the best fish restaurant outside of Paris. The restaurant was crowded with theatregoers in evening dress. They opted to sit at the bar and dine on the delicious snacks which Madame Prunier was famous for, starting with oyster brochettes and a bottle of Meursault.

'I've been thinking about Isobel all evening,' Chiara said. 'She must be in as much anguish, in her way, as Felicity is in hers. She's ashamed of having believed in Fascism. But she's bitterly disillusioned, too. It's taken away something that she needed. Poor Isobel! Life has taken everything away from her.'

'There's work for her to do here, when she gets back,' Oliver said.

'You mean with you?'

'With people I know.'

'I can just see Isobel as a Mata Hari,' Chiara said, 'seducing foreign diplomats in her boudoir.'

'Well, the work I had in mind was less romantic, but much more useful,' Oliver replied with a smile. The light at the bar illuminated his face. 'This coming war is going to shake things up. It's going to change Britain. Women are going to work in places they've been kept out of until now.'

'That sounds rather exciting.'

'Oh, it is. For years we've neglected half of our workforce, half of our genius, half of our strength. We can't afford to do that any more. We have to use every ounce of manpower and womanpower that we've got. This war won't be like the last one, fought by young men far away, with life at home going on pretty much as usual. This will be total war, fought by every man and woman, and if necessary, every child.'

'You think about the war all the time, don't you?'

'My job is to prepare for it, my darling girl.'

'You give me butterflies in my stomach when you call me your darling girl.' She leaned on the bar and gazed at him. 'And just what *is* your job, my darling boy?'

'I told you,' he said, amused, 'I'm a humble businessman.'

'And I'm the Dowager Empress of Cochin-China. You're a spy. Admit it.'

'If I was, I certainly wouldn't talk about it in a smart restaurant,' he replied. 'I'm sure the lady in the mink wrap behind you is an enemy agent.'

Chiara glanced over her shoulder. 'She's the Duchess of Halifax, and you know it. Anyway, nobody's listening to us. I like it when you look stern and talk about our national duty. I'm sure you think I'm a frivolous butterfly.'

'Not at all.' They were eating dainty salmon sandwiches. He poured more wine into her glass. 'But I do feel that, with a brain like yours, you're utterly wasted in old Cavendish's gallery.'

'Oh, it's my brain you're after, is it? How disappointing. I thought it was my little retroussé nose.'

'I'm after all of you.'

'Then Aunt Patsy was right.'

'I'm afraid so.'

She sighed in mock despair. 'I shall have to resign myself to being devoured, like this poor little sandwich.'

His eyes were laughing at her, now. 'You could save yourself.'

'How?'

'You could flee.'

'What if I would rather be eaten?'

'Then you could cry, "Eat me, eat me", like the pigs in the land of Cockayne.'

'Don't you want to eat me?' she asked.

'I prefer you here in front of me,' he said softly.

She put her mouth close to his ear. 'But I want to be eaten by you, more than anything in the world,' she whispered. She saw his expression change. 'Am I too bold?'

He studied her face. 'No. You're perfect.'

'Of course,' she said, raising the wine to her lips, 'you will be the first.'

He raised his eyebrows. 'The first?'

'You look surprised. What did you imagine?'

'When you said that – I suppose I assumed—'

'That I'm what they call a woman of the world? No, Oliver. I'm not. I said that because I've never been more sure of anything in my life. And I told you that I'm a virgin because you are a very sophisticated man, and I'm afraid that you will find me very naïve.'

He seemed confounded by her. 'Oh, Chiara. I don't know what to say.'

'I'm rather offended,' she said, picking up another sandwich, 'that you thought I was that sort of girl. I thought my innocence radiated out of me.'

'It does.'

'Then why did you imagine otherwise?'

'Well, times have changed. Young women don't bother with all that sort of thing nowadays. Keeping themselves pure – and all that. Do they?'

'This one does,' she said simply. 'You look disconcerted. Does it really present such a challenge?'

'Not in the practical sense,' he said solemnly. 'You're right. I am ashamed of having thought anything else.'

'You should be. I don't know what sort of "young women" you've been associating with, Mr Courtfield. Or am I as mad as my sisters? Would you rather I had "been around", as they say?'

'No. You are different from all others.'

'Then I hope you're conscious of the great honour which I'm offering to bestow on you,' she said mischievously.

'I am.'

She clinked his glass with her own. 'But – ?'

'But I'm also conscious of the difference in our ages.'

'Oh, nonsense,' she retorted. 'What does that have to do with anything?'

'People may say I'm taking an unfair advantage of you.'

'I didn't think you were the sort of man who cared what people say, Oliver.'

'I'm not – except insofar as what they may say about *you*. People are vicious.'

Two little pots of lobster salad had arrived. Chiara toyed moodily with hers, picking out the leaves of tarragon. 'I don't like tarragon. Why do they put it in? It tastes peculiar. And anyway, people are already saying things about us.'

'What do they say?' he asked gently.

'That I'm too young for you. That you'll destroy my reputation.'

'I see.'

'That you would never consider marrying me.' She raised her eyes to his. 'That all you want is a conquest, after which you will leave. Are those things true?'

'I don't want a conquest. You're not Mount Everest. As for marriage, wouldn't that be even worse than a conquest?'

'I don't see how.'

'I am exactly twice your age.'

'Thank you, I've worked that out.'

'If we were to marry, I would be fifty-three when you were thirty. When you were forty—'

'I've done all those sums, Oliver,' she said impatiently.

'Then you know that as time passes, you would be a young woman married to an old man.'

'An *older* man,' she corrected him briskly. 'It's not the same thing at all. And you hardly give the impression of decrepitude, my dear. Quite the reverse. You're an oak tree, and they last forever.'

'You're very kind. But nothing lasts forever. In the end, even oak trees fall. At which point you would be left a widow.'

'You don't know that. I could be run over by a bus tomorrow.'

'So could I, for that matter. Barring homicidal bus drivers, however, the first condition is the more likely outcome.'

'Then it is far better that we embark upon our life together sooner, rather than later,' she replied calmly. 'Why wait?'

'You're being a bully.'

'And you're being excessively vexing. Would we be having this conversation at all if I hadn't told you I was a virgin?'

He thought for a moment. 'Perhaps not.'

'So would you rather I went to bed with a few young men of my acquaintance and then came back to you, well run in?'

Oliver's eyes glittered. 'No. I would be obliged to kill them all.'

'Ah! At last a sign of passion! Your coolness is infuriating.'

'I am trying to be sensible.'

'Aunt Patsy would be very impressed. But I am not Aunt Patsy.'

He smiled at her. 'Aunt Patsy wouldn't play with her food.'

'Aunt Patsy can have my bits of tarragon. I'll post them to her. She can stick them up her jumper. I refuse to have my life ruled by what Aunt Patsy thinks, or anyone else, come to that. Stop laughing at me!'

'I'm not laughing at all,' he replied.

'Your eyes are laughing. Your mother told me you would never trust another woman, you know.'

He raised one eyebrow. 'And when did she tell you that?'

'On the crags, in the Highlands.'

'What else did she say?'

'She asked me if I liked you. I said yes. She said she liked you, too. But she said that she had left you as a little boy, and your wife had died young, and so you were incapable of trusting any woman.'

'Cécile habitually talks like a character from a nineteenth-century melodrama. It would be extremely unwise to take her seriously. So you like me?'

'I'm mad about you,' she said, looking into his eyes. 'I don't enjoy the spectacle of you "being sensible". If you don't plan to either seduce me or marry me, then you're going to have to stop seeing me.'

He seemed to be hiding a smile. 'Is that an ultimatum?'

'It soon will be. You have to make a decision, Oliver. I will not be treated the way you've treated other women in your life.'

'And how is that?'

'As a pastime.'

He looked away from her. The bar at Maison Prunier was lavishly decorated with golden fish, crabs and seaweed motifs. He studied these reflectively. 'I don't consider you a pastime,' he said. 'I've never considered any woman a pastime. But the circumstances of my life are not conducive to cosy domesticity. I don't spend much of my time in England. I am called abroad at short notice and I can never be sure when I'll return.' He met her eyes with his calm, cool gaze. 'Or if I'll return.'

'Oliver!'

'I don't say that to be melodramatic, but to explain the facts to you clearly. I'm in an odd line of work. I associate with an odd line of people. There are no set hours, no nine to five and weekends off. Even when I'm in England, my time is not my own. I can't talk about what I do to anybody, not even you. I tend to pop out of sight like the white rabbit in *Alice In Wonderland*, but one day I will fail to pop up again, and that will be that.' He traced circles on the bar with the foot of his wine glass. 'I'm a very devious man, but not in the sense you fear. If the world were different, I would tell them all to go to hell, and live the life of a country squire with the darling of my heart – as it might be you. But Adolf Hitler has made sure that none of us are going to retire any time soon. This has nothing to do with my mother or the death of my wife. It's simply the way things are.'

'So I have to accept you as you are – on your terms – or not at all?'

'Is that impossible?'

'No,' she replied slowly. 'It's not impossible. I understand your terms. I don't want to do without you. If you want me as your lover, then that is what I'll be. But you must be *my* lover, Oliver. For the time that we are together, until the day I free you – and that may be never – you will belong only to me. There will be no others. Only England and me. Those are *my* terms. Do you accept them?'

He looked very serious for a moment and then smiled into her eyes. 'Yes. I accept.'

'Then take me home.'

4.
ISOBEL

Spain, Winter, 1939

The ward sister's office presented, as did the whole hospital, an air of having been overwhelmed by events. It was lined with battered filing cabinets, their doors open and their contents half pulled out. Stethoscopes, blood pressure cuffs and other pieces of equipment were piled on the desk, together with huge rolls of gauze, bottles of iodine and a towering stack of files. The noise of the hospital was unceasing and tumultuous, like a railway station. Isobel sat in the little room, listening to it. This was not a quiet refuge of healing; it sounded like what it was, an extension of the war that was raging outside the city. *Sagrado Corazon* was filled with thousands of injured men – and now, with the increasingly heavy air raids, women and children, too. The sick and the wounded were spilling from the wards out into the corridors and even (despite the cold and the rain) into whatever shelter they could find in the hospital grounds.

She was severely dressed in one of her dark Berlin suits, wearing a hat with a little lace veil that hung in front of her eyes. The veil helped. Her face was well known, and even now people sometimes recognized her in the street, with unpleasant results. Even if she was not recognized (and her photograph had been everywhere) people stared at her clothes. Barcelona was a dying city and its people were shabby. She continued, however, to wear the clothes she had brought from Berlin. She had no others.

She looked at her watch. She had been waiting for an hour already, although she had arrived at the exact time she had been told to arrive. Punctuality was no small feat in Barcelona nowadays, and she was irritated. Her typewriter was waiting for her in her apartment, with a fresh sheet of paper in it. It was late afternoon, and raining hard. The cloud cover might keep the bombers away tonight. But then again, it might not. In any case, even without an air raid, the barricades that were erected every evening throughout the city would make getting back home a nightmare.

At last the ward sister arrived. She marched briskly into the office, a wiry Scotswoman in early middle age, with hard red cheeks and hard blue eyes. She wore a starched white cap with a red cross on it. Her apron, Isobel saw with a shock, was spattered with gouts of blood. She gave Isobel a curt nod, and began at once to take off the apron. She made no apology for this, or for having kept Isobel waiting. 'I'm Sister Harris. You'll be Mrs Albarán.'

'Yes, I am.'

'You can see him shortly,' she said. 'No more than ten minutes, please.'

'Ten minutes! I've been kept waiting an hour already.'

'I can't help that. Don't make him speak unnecessarily. And no theatricals, please. He's suffered enough already.'

Isobel controlled her annoyance. 'I'll avoid theatricals,' she said quietly.

'And he doesn't like to be touched.'

'I'll avoid that, too.'

The sister folded the blood-spattered apron and dumped it into a bin. She began tying on a new apron. She was looking at Isobel's clothes. 'If you don't mind my saying so, shouldn't you be doing some sort of war work?'

'I'm a journalist. My work is reporting the war. They don't make us wear a uniform,' she added.

'How nice for you,' the sister replied, straightening her fresh apron.

'Not really. Can you tell me about his injuries?'

'Apart from the exhaustion and the fractures, loss of vision.'

'Loss of vision? What does that mean?'

'What do you think it means?' Sister Harris said sharply, compressing her thin lips. 'He's blind.'

It was an effort for Isobel to ask, 'Is he going to be blind for the rest of his life?'

'I really couldn't say,' the sister said, picking up a folder. 'You'd best hurry if you want to catch him awake. Ward Thirteen. Up the corridor, second left.'

'Thank you.' Isobel rose. As she left the office, the sister called after her.

'Would you be so good as to come and see me again before you leave?'

Isobel made her way through the crowded corridor. As she reached the ward, a young nurse was backing out, pulling a trolley. On it was the body of man, partially covered with a bloodstained sheet. Isobel was growing accustomed to the sight of death. She stood aside to let the nurse pass, catching a glimpse of one glazed, staring eye from the face on the trolley.

She entered the ward. It was crowded with people. There were sixteen beds, all of them full except the one which had just been vacated. An orderly was stripping off the red-blotched bedclothes. Willoughby was at the far end, by the window, which was crisscrossed with brown paper tape, like every window in Barcelona. His eyes were bandaged but she knew his face at once.

She sat quietly on the chair next to him. He was propped up in the bed, his hands resting palm upward on the blanket. Isobel checked her watch. She had ten minutes. Willoughby slowly turned his head to face her.

'Hello, William,' she said. 'It's Isobel.' There was no reaction. 'I didn't expect ever to see you again. They said I mustn't upset you or touch you. And you're not to say anything to me. And they've only given me ten minutes.'

He was silent for a long while and she thought he hadn't heard her. At last he asked, 'How's Felicity?'

'She went into her convent, after all. Shortly after we parted company in Valencia. She's safe in the north of England.'

He nodded slightly. His face – what she could see of it – was drawn and pale. She remembered the handsome nose and mouth well. 'I'm sorry they called you,' he said.

'I'm not sorry they called me. It's good to see you.' She meant the words. She had come across town wearily, full of resentment; but seeing Willoughby in this condition, she was glad she had come now, and somewhat ashamed of her earlier reluctance. 'I want to get something out of the way, William. I changed my mind. About Fascism, I mean. I was in Berlin. I saw what they're doing to the Jews there, and—' She stopped. 'I'm ashamed of the way I was,' she went on, after a pause. 'I came back to Spain to write about the war. To tell people what's happening. And to admit that I was wrong. That's why I'm here. It isn't easy. But I'm learning.'

'They wanted a name.' He spoke with no emotion. 'Yours was the only one I could think of. I don't have anyone else.' He gestured in the direction of the empty bed. 'He was the last man from my old company.'

'I'm sorry.'

'You met Sister Harris.'

'Yes. She doesn't like me very much. The feeling's mutual.'

'She's all right. She tried to save him.' His face was still turned in the direction of the empty bed, as though he could see it somehow. 'We got our wounds together. Me and him.'

Isobel looked at her watch. He hadn't reacted to her declaration of faith. She tried again. 'I was wrong, William. Terribly wrong and terribly stupid. I don't want you to think I'm the same person I was two years ago.'

'None of us are the same people we were.' He touched some letters on the locker beside him. 'Do you want me to read these to you?' she asked. He nodded. They were already open. She picked them up and unfolded the first one. It was written on pink-tinged paper in violet ink. A little dried flower had been pasted on it. Isobel began to read. '"Dearest William, I hope . . ."' She paused, her eyes scanning the lines, seeing the clichés, the commonplace phrases that had been trotted out one after another. 'Ah. She married the haberdasher, after all.'

William nodded. 'You were right,' he said.

'Of course I was. At least you can't see the colour of the ink,' she added dryly. 'That's a blessing in disguise. Let me read the other. It's from your mother. "My darling boy, we all miss you so much. We are so proud of you – but we long for you to come home to us. You have done more than your share. We are so afraid for you. We want your bright, smiling face back amongst us. To lose you would be more than I could bear, and your sisters – "' She stopped reading. He had lifted his hand.

'It's okay,' he said. 'You don't need to read any more.'

'None of it's very jolly, is it?' She folded the letters and put them back. 'Where did you get your wound?'

'At Toledo. On my birthday.'

'How old are you now?'

'Twenty-seven.'

'So am I. I always thought you were younger. Funny. What happened at Toledo?'

He seemed to be thinking. 'I can't really remember,' he said at last. 'They told me it was a shell . . . but . . . I don't remember. I was very tired.'

'It doesn't matter. Do you ever think about that trip to Valencia? I often think about it. Wasn't it fun? You were our knight errant. On a very rusty old Rocinante.'

'Yes,' he said quietly.

She took off her little hat and arranged the veil. 'God, it seems a lifetime ago. We were so young. It was all such a lark. We had no idea what was in store for us. I never really believed that Felicity would go into that convent. I thought I would be able to change her mind.' She studied Willoughby's mouth. 'She fancied herself in love with you, you know.'

Willoughby turned his bandaged face to her. 'Felicity?'

'Yes, poor little thing. I don't suppose you even noticed. It was just an infatuation, of course. But when you didn't show up for dinner, she was broken-hearted. If you had come, everything might have been different.'

He was silent for a long while. 'I didn't know.'

'Of course you didn't. I shouldn't have told you anything. Forget it.' A bell had started to sound. The visitors began packing up to leave. She put her hat back on her head and arranged the veil over her eyes. 'I'd better go.' She was, she was ashamed to admit, somewhat relieved to be going. 'I'll try to come again,' she said, without much conviction. 'Is there anything you need? Anything I can bring you?'

Willoughby shook his head slowly. 'There's nothing. You needn't come again. I'm all right.'

'Well . . .' She hesitated. 'Goodbye, William.'

He nodded, turning his face away from her. Isobel thought about kissing him, then changed her mind. She left the ward. She'd been hoping to avoid another meeting with Sister Harris, but the nurse emerged from the doorway of her office and called out to her.

'Mrs Albarán! In here, please.'

Reluctantly, Isobel obeyed the peremptory command. 'I really don't have a lot of time,' she said, seating herself.

'I won't keep you long.' Sister Harris sat behind her desk and opened a file. 'May I ask what your relationship is to Captain Willoughby?'

'I'm a friend. More of an acquaintance, really. Why?'

'Naming you next of kin suggests something more,' the sister said in her terse way.

'I assure you that there's nothing more than that, Sister Harris. His family are in the United States and from what he told me, his companions are all gone.'

'Yes. The last one died of a haemorrhage an hour ago. That's why you were obliged to wait.' She raised her cold blue eyes to Isobel's. 'There's not much more we can do for him.'

Isobel frowned. 'That sounds very ominous.'

'I mean that he'll be out of here soon. His bed is needed by more urgent cases.'

'More urgent? What could be more urgent than William's case? He's been blinded!'

'Quite. He sustained his injuries while trying to rescue some members of his platoon who were wounded and pinned down by heavy fire. He showed extraordinary bravery in getting to them. The shell which injured him killed most of the men he was trying to rescue. He himself suffered a number of burns and fractures, which are healing well. The loss of vision was attributed to flash burns on the corneas. However, these are also healing well. The doctors now say that there must be irreparable damage to the optic nerves. But I suspect that the loss of vision may be caused by another factor.'

'What factor?'

'Blindness is a documented feature of shell shock.'

'You mean some damage to the brain?'

'No,' Sister Harris replied impatiently, 'I do not mean damage to the brain. Shell shock is a psychiatric condition.'

'Then he should be on a psychiatric ward.'

'We don't have a psychiatric ward, Mrs Albarán. We have enough to do attempting to repair their bodies. We can't repair their souls as well. There are simply too many of them. And in my experience, they're all psychiatric cases. What is needed is a period of convalescence.'

'What does that have to do with me?'

'I'm going to discharge Captain Willoughby into your care.'

Isobel was too shocked to reply for a moment. 'That is absolutely impossible, I'm afraid.'

'Why is it impossible?'

'I simply don't have the emotional resources to cope with it. I'm something of a psychiatric case myself.'

'I don't follow.'

Isobel was growing tired of Sister Harris's coldness. 'Don't you? Perhaps that's because you're devoid of any human emotion.'

'I don't cultivate my emotions,' the sister said flatly. 'I simply do my duty. Most of his company are dead. He doesn't have a relation within five thousand miles. And he may never see the sunlight again. You don't need to expend any of your precious emotions. Just look after him as he deserves. Don't you feel you owe him something?'

'Is that what he's said?'

'He's said nothing.'

'Then you can't hold me to—'

'His condition is not going to improve in here,' the nurse interrupted. 'He doesn't need much care. You'll be able to do your writing all day while he rests. It's very little to ask.'

'He got himself into this,' Isobel said resentfully. She was being pushed into a corner by this tough, insistent little Scot.

'That is true. Then, if you feel no ethical obligation to him, isn't there a personal obligation?'

'I don't know what you're getting at.'

'He would not have given us your name if he didn't feel that you owed him something.' Sister Harris's eyes were very cold, as though she already knew the answer to the question she had asked. She closed the file. 'It's up to you to decide whether you can pay him back.'

❧

Isobel had found an apartment close to the Park Güell in Gràcia, overlooking Barcelona. The block was built against a hill, reached up a steep, winding road, and commanded sweeping views. The area had so far escaped the bombing, which had been concentrated on the port and the downtown areas. But from her balcony, Isobel had a panorama of the city and the destruction which the bombers had brought. Each day brought new columns of smoke, rising up to form a pall which lay over Barcelona and did not seem to dissipate.

She had two bedrooms, one of which she had set up as her study, with her portable typewriter perched on a rickety little table. Beside it was a stack of pages – the novel which she had begun writing. She had started it soon after her arrival in Barcelona. She had a commission from *LIFE* magazine for a 5,000-word article on the last days of the city. She also had an informal commission from *Time* for a shorter piece. But she had felt that journalism was not going to be enough for her to describe what she saw and felt. She could not express, in articles alone, the scale of a war whose beginning she had seen, almost four years earlier, and whose end she was witnessing now. Like Ernest Hemingway, whose novel about the Spanish Civil War was eagerly anticipated, she had turned from reporting to a freer form of writing, a form of writing which she believed would allow her to tell a deeper truth than simply recording the facts. Because this war was not a triumph. It was a tragedy.

She had found fiction a great release after journalism. It had opened a part of her which had always remained closed, the ability to dream. So it was with considerable irritation that she now moved her old Remington and her rough drafts to her bedroom. Having Willoughby in her apartment was going to be a considerable burden. Feeding herself was difficult enough; Barcelona was under siege and the daily search for fresh produce meant long queues in the shops to obtain scraps here and there. Electricity, water and gas supplies were intermittent at best. Getting a cup of coffee required ingenuity. Cooking a meal was often beyond her. Had Willoughby been able-bodied, he could at least have been some help. As it was, he would simply be an extra mouth to feed.

But the most serious challenge was going to be the loss of privacy. She had lived alone for so long. To have a man about the house might be intolerable. She burned with resentment as she prepared Willoughby's bed, cursing Sister Harris and cursing herself for allowing herself to be pushed into this. He had helped them in 1936, that was true, but she should not be blackmailed because of it. That was not just or fair.

Nevertheless, she made his room as comfortable as she could, and it was ready for him when they brought him from *Sagrado Corazon* at mid-afternoon. She went to meet the ambulance. The orderly who had driven Willoughby had brought her a small package of supplies, all that Sister Harris could spare – some gauze bandage, a bottle of drops which she was supposed to put in his eyes four times a day, and a bottle of aspirin. Willoughby himself was now back in uniform, with a sheepskin jacket against the cold. All he had with him was a duffel bag.

She took his arm to guide him to her apartment, but he shook her hand off impatiently.

'I'm not a cripple. Just tell me where I'm going.'

She controlled her irritation as he stumbled up the stairs and groped down the corridor. He seemed stronger today, and was in no better mood than she was.

'I didn't ask to come here,' he said, almost as soon as they reached her apartment.

'And I didn't invite you,' she replied shortly. 'However, here you are.'

'If I had anywhere else to go, I would go there.'

'It doesn't matter. I owe you something, anyway.'

'Is that what Sister Harris told you? You owe me nothing, Isobel. As soon as I can get away, I'll go.' He reached for his duffel bag and opened it. 'I've got some money. It's not much, but it will help.' He held the sheaf of notes out to her. 'Take it.'

Isobel hesitated for a moment, then took the money. 'Are you hungry?'

'No.'

'I have instructions from Sister Harris to make sure you eat. You're as thin as a stray dog.'

'That's what I feel like.'

'I warned you to choose your side wisely.'

'So what are you doing here?'

'What I do best – making unwise choices.'

Willoughby grunted. 'That makes two of us.' He felt his way around her little apartment, guided by her spoken directions. Sister

Harris had warned her that he disliked being touched. He preferred to bang his head and bark his shins. By the time he had navigated the place, he seemed tired. He lay on his bed, a tall figure with bandaged eyes. His body looked far from relaxed. He was tense and angry, but she could not help that. It wasn't her fault.

'I'm going to write,' she said. 'Let me know if my typing disturbs you.'

'After that hospital,' he replied, 'nothing disturbs me.'

She left him there and worked for a couple of hours. Although she was aware of his presence, it was not as intrusive as she'd feared. She had been so desperately lonely for so long that it was a kind of pleasure to know that there was someone else in the apartment. When evening came, she made a bowl of soup and they ate their first meal together. It was a largely silent meal, but at least they didn't fight.

'I'm supposed to put drops in your eyes now,' she said when they'd finished.

'They don't do any damn good,' Willoughby growled. But he submitted to her. The operation, Sister Harris had told her, must be done by candlelight. No stronger light must ever be allowed to touch his eyes, or any chance of recovery might be destroyed. Sister Harris had also warned her that the drops were agonizingly painful and that Willoughby would resist. However he didn't argue with her, and stripped off his shirt. He sat patiently as she unwound the gauze from his eyes. When she laid the bandage aside, he opened his eyes slowly.

'Can you see anything?' she asked.

He shook his head almost imperceptibly. 'No.'

She passed the candle flame three or four times in front of his eyes, as Sister Harris had told her to do. She saw the flame reflected in them but there was no reaction from his pupils, which remained dilated and immovable. If this was the result of shell-shock, then it was a very powerful effect. Her instinct was that this was permanent. She found that thought very depressing.

'I'm going to put the drops in now.' He sat on the bed and raised his face to her. His eyes stared at her and yet not at her, seeming to see her and yet seeing nothing. She put two drops in each eye. His body stiffened and he clenched his fists as the tears ran down his cheeks.

'Sorry,' she said, wincing in sympathy. 'I know it hurts.'

He was leaner than she remembered, his stomach hard as a washboard. He couldn't speak for a while. 'Do you remember,' he said at last, 'when you gave me a bath?'

Isobel smiled. 'I remember.' She dried the tears from his face and tied the bandage around his eyes again. 'Do you need something for the pain? All I have is some aspirin Sister Harris gave me.'

'I think I'll just go to sleep.'

She found his pyjamas in his duffel bag – he seemed to have almost no kit – and helped him put them on. She saw a long, jagged scar on his side. 'You've been wounded before.'

'Shrapnel,' he said laconically, 'on the Segre. It looks worse than it was.'

'You should have gone home after that.'

'I didn't see any point in starting a job and not seeing it through.'

'Still the white knight,' she said wryly.

'No. I've given up the white knight business. It doesn't pay.'

'Who's going to save the world, then?'

'Nothing can save the world,' he said tiredly. 'It doesn't deserve to be saved.'

'What are you going to do now?'

'I don't know.' There was an edge of desperation in his voice. 'I'm not much use to anyone like this,' he added bitterly.

'You could go back to teaching,' she said.

'Yeah.' He lifted his arms and crossed them over his face. 'I'll go back and teach people not to be so Goddamned stupid.'

She lay awake for a long while after she left him, thinking about the last time they had met. He had been so full of life, so spirited. It was sad to see what had become of that idealistic, beautiful young man – this embittered, blinded cynic who was probably lying awake, just as she was, thinking about living the rest of his life in darkness.

❧

The next days were relatively quiet. Bad weather continued and the Italian bombers, sent by Mussolini to aid his fellow dictator Franco, stayed away. The battle for Catalonia was being lost, however, and the enemy would soon be at the gates of the city. The exodus into France was building up, despite the terrible conditions that refugees met there. Many would rather face starvation in the French mud than the retributions that Franco had promised.

She was already growing accustomed to having Willoughby there. In an odd way, she was reminded of how it had felt to have a child, someone who depended on her care, who would be bereft without her. Not that he was demanding. He accepted much less care from her than she was prepared to give him. It seemed to her that he was locked in a Chinese puzzle of boxes, the blindness locked inside the psychological damage he had already suffered, that damage locked inside the box of his political disillusionment. To reach him seemed almost impossible. But they were able to talk, in the manner of people who had shared an experience, about the last time they had met.

After he'd left them in Valencia, Willoughby had gone straight back to the front line. He'd spent most of the past three years fighting along the River Segre, a series of savage skirmishes in a losing war against the increasingly powerful Nationalist army, bolstered by Hitler and Mussolini, as well as by Moroccan mercenaries paid for by Franco. He had been wounded several times, and in a bag, jumbled together, she'd found a handful of military decorations that the Spanish government had given him. She was interested to hear that he had met Ernest Hemingway, a journalist whom she admired greatly.

'We spent two days discussing Jean-Paul Sartre, John Steinbeck and Ayn Rand while the Nationalists shelled our position,' he told her. 'It was one of the strangest experiences of my life. He's a clever man but not a happy one. He drinks very heavily.'

Diffidently, she told him about the novel she had started. 'I don't see myself as a great writer, or anything like that. There are just some things that are easier to say in fiction.'

'I can understand that. Would you read me some of it?'

'I think you've suffered enough already,' she said ironically.

'Please,' he said.

For a number of reasons, Isobel was uncomfortable with the idea of using Willoughby as a captive audience. But he seemed genuinely interested. That evening, after they'd eaten, she read him the first three chapters of her book. He listened carefully. Somehow, the bandage over his eyes made it easier for her to read her work to him; there was less shyness. He sat motionless, listening intently. When she'd finished, he nodded.

'It's what I expected.'

'Ah. Superficial, juvenile rubbish?'

'No. It's brilliant.'

She laughed out of sheer surprise. 'Oh, William! You don't need to flatter me.'

'I'm not a flatterer,' he replied quietly.

'You can't tell me you expected brilliance from me. You told me I was in the wrong often enough.'

'We were on opposite sides,' he said. 'But that doesn't mean I didn't see – and respect – your brilliance. You are brilliant. And your novel is brilliant. If you want me to tell you why I think that, I will. But I think you know your own qualities. And you know that it's going to be a fine book.'

Unexpectedly, she felt a lump in her throat. 'Thank you. It means a lot to me. I've lost a lot of my self-confidence. I've been—' She paused. 'I've been very alone.'

'So have I.' They were both silent for a while. 'I'm sorry about Felicity,' he said at last. 'But I don't agree with you that it was a silly infatuation. You can have very strong feelings in a short space of time, feelings that don't go away or diminish. I've never stopped thinking about you these past three years. I knew that we would meet again. Maybe only one last time. But I knew it wasn't over.'

Isobel shied away from that subject. 'I saw my husband just before *Kristallnacht*,' she said. 'He just turned up in Berlin out of the blue. He's been living in Rome for a while, seeing a lot of different women. He wanted me to go to bed with him. I was so lonely that I agreed. We took our clothes off and got into bed.' She didn't know why she was telling Willoughby this. Perhaps, with his blindfolded eyes, it was like being in a confessional with a priest who could not see her. 'But I couldn't go through with it. And then, afterwards, he wanted me to sign over some property to him. I think that's the only reason he wanted to make love to me – to make sure I would sign.'

'I'm sorry, Isobel. I know that you love him.'

'I love him and hate him.'

'I read your articles. All those pieces you wrote about Franco and Mussolini and Hitler. I collected them all.'

'I'm very ashamed of them now.'

'You're eloquent. You write and reason superbly. You just hadn't seen the true face of Fascism yet. Hitler is so successful because he

217

insists he wants peace while waging war. Most people are fooled. They look at what he says, not at what he does. It's not until you see what he does that you understand what a good liar he is.'

She put the drops in his eyes, an operation she was starting to dread because she knew how much it hurt him. Afterwards, he asked her to leave the bandages off for a while. They sat in the dark and listened to the radio. *La Pasionaria*, the militant revolutionary who had been such an inspiration to the Left in the early years of the war, made a speech. Her rolling oratory was as fiery as ever but Willoughby was bitter.

'She's run to Moscow, where she belongs. You know what sickened me most about this war? Not the Fascists and their bombers. The way the Communists stabbed us in the back. We asked them for help. They sent torture squads, apparatchiks and assassins. You're ashamed of once supporting Hitler. Well, I'm ashamed of wearing a hammer and sickle on my shoulder. Both of us were fools, Isobel. There's nothing to choose between us.'

La Pasionaria's speech was followed by a programme of classical Spanish guitar music. The gentle sounds drifted through the night, dreamily evoking a time of peace, before war and betrayal. It had been a day of rapprochement. She had enjoyed his company and the warmth of his good opinion. The next day, however, Willoughby seemed colder and more withdrawn than ever. He hardly said a word to her all day. He sat in an armchair with his eyes blindfolded and his head bowed. What he was thinking of, or remembering, she couldn't begin to imagine. When their hands touched accidentally, Willoughby flinched at the contact, as though her skin had burned his.

That evening, as she put the drops in his eyes, he said, 'I don't think I can take much more of this. It's not doing any good.'

'Sister Harris said we shouldn't give up,' she said.

'It feels like fire eating into my brain.'

'Let's give it another few days,' she pleaded. 'It's all we have.'

'Okay.' He braced himself and she dropped the liquid into his unseeing eyes. He dropped his head and shuddered with the pain.

'I hate doing this to you,' she said.

'It's the quack eye doctor's theory,' Willoughby said. 'He thinks there's scar tissue covering my pupils and this stuff is going to burn it away. I think it's just making me worse.'

'You see nothing at all?'

'Nothing,' he said in despair. He wiped away the tears. The candle flame flickered in his wide, staring eyes, but the pupils did not respond.

'Don't give up,' she said.

'I'm sorry I'm such a coward,' he said.

'You're not a coward, William. Sister Harris told me that you were trying to rescue some of your men when it happened.'

'I do most of what I do because I can't bear seeing anyone suffer. I couldn't bear seeing those men killed. I couldn't stand it. So I went to get them, even though I knew none of us stood a chance. It was stupidity and cowardice.'

'I have the same kind of cowardice.'

He raised his face. 'I'm afraid of the dark.'

'I'm afraid of it, too.' She touched his hand. 'You're not alone. I'm here.'

'You must be exhausted. You should sleep.'

'And you?'

'I'm okay. I just think about things.'

'Maybe you shouldn't think so much.'

'What else is there for a blind man to do?' he asked ironically.

'Talk,' she said. 'Is that too hard?'

He was silent for a while. 'Your voice changes at night.'

'In what way?'

'It becomes less assured. More open.'

'How does my voice sound in the daytime?'

'Like a closed door.'

'Perhaps the room is empty.'

'I think you're just sad and lonely.'

Isobel sat beside Willoughby on the bed. 'I'm sorry about your girl in the States. She wrote a very stupid letter.'

'She thought I was a fool for coming to Spain.'

'Has there been anyone else? Since you came to Spain, I mean?'

'Nothing serious.'

She felt an unaccountable pang of possessiveness. 'What do you mean, "Nothing serious"?'

'It was the sister of a friend, Vasquez. I went to Madrid with him for a weekend. We wrote to each other for a while after that.'

Jealousy made her voice cruel. 'Is she beautiful?'

'She was.' His voice was flat. 'She was killed in an air raid.'

'Oh, William, I'm sorry.'

'Vasquez was captured on the Segre. The Fascists shot him, even though he was wounded.' He shrugged. 'The end of a short story.'

She could find nothing to say. Repeating that she was sorry seemed futile. She said good night to him and went to her own room. As always, sleep came reluctantly to her.

❧

The next day, the rain had gone. A hard, empty sky arched over the city, promising air raids that evening. Willoughby was silent and tense, answering her questions with monosyllables. Pity him as she did, she seemed unable to reach him in his locked world. He groped around the apartment, trying clumsily to do everyday things like make his bed and wash his clothes. When she told him she would do those things for him, he reacted with a growl; and when she pressed, the growl became a snarl.

She went out to meet the photojournalist *LIFE* magazine had sent, a young Hungarian named Robert Capa, who already had a formidable reputation as a war photographer. They had a drink in a small bar not far from her apartment. Capa, a Jew, made no secret of his distrust of Isobel.

'Yesterday you were a Nazi. Today you're all for democracy. What you gonna be tomorrow, huh?' He was a strongly Eastern European-looking man with a strong accent, who fiddled constantly with the cameras around his neck. His black eyes were suspicious. 'I don't trust people who change their mind halfway through. You know what I mean?'

'If people don't change their minds, there's no hope for the human race.'

Capa grunted, winding on the film in his camera. 'Yeah. You just better not be back in Hitler's lap by the time this story gets printed.'

'I won't be. And if I wanted to be on the winning side, I wouldn't have changed, would I?'

He shrugged. 'The Fascists are gonna lose the war. Nobody can fight the United States. Spain is one to them. The next one, the big one, goes to us.' Grudgingly, he passed her a sheet of contact prints. Small as they were, Isobel could see the drama of the shots: people hurrying to air-raid shelters, looking up in dread; shattered buildings; desperate-eyed Republican soldiers and haunted-looking civilians. She agreed to tailor her story around the shots so the article would follow a coherent thread. By chance she mentioned Willoughby. Capa looked up, interested.

'Willoughby? Yeah, I came across him a couple times. Big guy, intellectual. Totally blind forever?'

'I think so.'

'This sounds like a great shot. You take me to him, okay?'

'Let me speak to him first. He's in a bad way. He might not agree to be photographed.'

Capa tapped the contact sheet. 'I didn't get these shots by speaking to the people first, okay? You know what I mean? I shoot first, ask permission later. This is war.' He grinned, showing stained teeth. 'What kind of a journalist are you, anways? You don't see the human interest in this story? You not gonna write about him in this article?'

'He is not a story. He's a friend.'

'Yeah, sure. He's my friend, too. A blinded American? What better propaganda you want! Let me speak to him, okay?'

'All right,' she said, with misgivings.

They emerged from the smoky bar into a cutting *tramontana*, the wind that blew down from the Pyrenees. Capa hunched into his coat and cocked a wary eye at the sky. 'Clear. Bombers gonna come tonight.'

They climbed up the hill to her apartment. She was not sure how Willoughby was going to react to Capa. The Hungarian was already checking his cameras. They went up the stairs. Isobel unlocked the door of the apartment and opened it. The apartment was small, and from the front door there was a clear view to the balcony. Willoughby was standing on the balcony, silhouetted against the cold sky, holding a revolver to his temple. It took a second for her to absorb the significance. She screamed his name.

'*William!*' Capa was already snapping photographs as she ran out onto the balcony, desperate to stop him before he pulled the trigger. She grasped Willoughby's gun hand in both her own and dragged it down. He seemed dazed, and allowed her to tear the pistol from his fingers. She hurled it off the balcony into the bushes below and turned to him furiously. 'What are you *doing*? Are you mad?'

'I wouldn't have done it,' he mumbled. 'I was just . . . thinking . . .'

But she didn't believe him. 'You fool! How could you be so *stupid*.' She was crying, hitting him in the face and chest with her fists. 'How could you do this to me?'

'Isobel—'

'You coward! Coward! I would have found you dead. What do you think that would have done to me?'

'I'm sorry.' He grabbed her arms clumsily to stop her hitting him. Her knees were turning to jelly and she sagged against him. He held her in a rough embrace while she cried against his throat. 'I'm sorry, Isobel. I didn't mean to scare you.'

They stood in silence for a while, pressed close together. She was dimly aware of Capa's camera clicking, but when at last she pulled away from Willoughby, the Hungarian had gone, leaving the front door open. She was shivering with the cold and the after-effect of shock. They went inside and she poured them the last of her precious cognac, the neck of the bottle rattling against the rim of the glass.

'You bastard,' she said shakily. 'I'll never forgive you for this.'

He was silent. He found his way to the sofa and sat down. There was no expression on his face.

'What the hell is in your mind, William?' she demanded. 'I never thought you were a quitter.'

'I'm not a quitter,' he said in a low voice. 'But I can't go on being a burden to you.'

'You are not a burden, damn you!'

'What else can I be? I can't do a single thing to help you. Every moment I'm here is an imposition on you.'

She was stricken by the thought that she had given him that impression. Her anger began to fade. 'If I ever made you feel like that, please understand, it wasn't intentional.' She studied his face, which seemed to her like a closed door. 'I was a selfish bitch at first. I didn't want to get involved. I admit it. I'm ashamed of the way I felt then. I don't feel that way any longer. If you were to—' She hesitated, then said, more gently, 'I'm glad you're here, William.'

He gave one of his rare, bitter smiles. 'It's ironic. All these years, I dreamed of being with you again. I never imagined it would be this way. I can't even see your face. And now I'm no use to you. Just a liability A weight you have to carry.'

She was silenced. She gulped down her cognac, feeling it burn into her stomach. 'I had no idea you felt like that,' she said at last. 'I always thought you and Felicity—'

'Felicity?' he retorted. 'Felicity's a child. I felt sorry for her. But that was all. There was never anybody but you.' He put his head in his hands wearily. 'Did you really have no idea?'

She was thinking back. 'Once or twice Felicity said things . . . but I told her she was wrong. I suppose I wanted you to care for her. God knows, she cared for you, right up until you disappeared. I hoped it would stop her mad ideas about becoming a nun. I hoped you would be the end of all that.'

'That's all you thought?'

'I wasn't in a very good state of mind, William. I certainly didn't have any romantic inclinations.'

'I disappeared because I had lost you. You were flying home the next day. And I knew you would get on that plane without looking back. I didn't want to say goodbye. Perhaps that was cowardly, yes. But you haven't been out of my thoughts a single day since then.'

'I didn't see the way you felt. But if I had, William, I would have told you that it was out of the question. I wasn't in any state to be wooed.'

'I had no intention of wooing you. I just wanted to get you safe. Along the way . . . my feelings changed.'

'It was an infatuation, William. Just like Felicity's for you.'

'It was more than that.' Lifted his head from his hands. 'Or I would have gotten over it.'

Isobel laughed shortly. 'Have you forgotten how we fought?'

'No, I haven't forgotten.'

'We were like cat and dog. You called me every name under the sun. Remember how you shook me that night at the inn? I was terrified of you! You loathed me from the moment you set eyes on me.'

'You weren't very nice to me.'

'You had to be punished.'

'I didn't want to fall in love with you,' he said. She winced. 'It just happened, fast. Even when we fought, I kept thinking, how spirited this woman is, how beautiful. That's why I got so angry with you. I couldn't bring myself to hate you as I should.'

'You certainly didn't spare me your sarcasm.'

'It was my only weapon.'

'A sharp one.'

'You're strong, Isobel. It's hard to get through your defences.'

She shook her head. 'Unfortunately, that's not true. I'm very easily wounded. I've just learned to hide it.'

'Well, you made me feel like a jerk. You were so superior, looking down your nose at me, talking to me like I was a fourth-grader.'

'Funny. I thought that's how you talked to me.' She drained her glass, her nerves starting to settle. 'As a matter of fact, you got through to me, though I didn't want to admit it. It was you who first showed me what a fool I was being. You started me thinking, at any rate. The end of the process was *Kristallnacht*. That was when the penny finally dropped.'

He grunted. 'You and everybody else. The world sees Hitler for what he is, now. When I first came to Spain, nobody understood. They called us Commies. Now it's too late for us to be rehabilitated. Half of us are dead, anyway. We're a lost generation.'

He spoke so bitterly that she was beginning to understand why he had held a pistol to his head. 'At least you have the satisfaction of being right. And you did a noble and brave thing. That's all we can hope for in life.'

Willoughby sighed. 'You shouldn't even be here in Barcelona. You should get out, now, while you can.'

'I'm seeing it through,' she said brusquely. 'To the bitter end.'

Now it was his turn to be angry. 'Don't be a fool, Isobel. The bitter end will be a firing squad. If the Fascists capture you, they'll put you up against a wall as a traitor. They will never forgive you. Franco doesn't know the meaning of mercy.' He had turned his face to her. The blindfold somehow made his words even grimmer.

'It hasn't come to that, yet.'

'Don't leave it too late to get out. Promise me.'

'I'll promise you that if you promise me never to think about killing yourself again.'

He frowned. 'I can't promise not to have thoughts. But I promise I won't do it. Least of all in your house. I wouldn't have done it today.'

'Then what were you playing at out there?' Isobel demanded. 'You can't preach at me about getting out while you hold a gun to your own head.'

'I was just wondering how it would be. What happens next. Whether we're free. Or whether there's nothing.'

'We've both seen a lot of death,' she said wearily. 'It rather looks like there's nothing.'

'I thought you were a staunch Catholic?'

'That went by a long time ago.' They fell into a silence. After a while she went down into the garden and hunted for his revolver in the oleanders. She found it at last and took it back to Willoughby. 'You gave me your word.'

With deft fingers, he took the bullets out of the chambers and handed them to her. 'Happy?'

Their fingers brushed. She took the heavy, cold things and held them in her palm for a moment. She suddenly felt that she had no option but to trust him. She gave them back to him. 'Keep them. I'm not your jailer.'

They spoke little for the rest of the day. She was digesting what he'd told her. Strangely, Isobel felt no awkwardness since he'd told her he loved her. Instead, she was moved. She'd always thought of him as Felicity's property. Now Felicity was in a nunnery and he'd never had any interest in her anyway. Poor Felicity. But he was here, and he was hers, and his presence gave her warmth and, oddly, a sense of being safe. Blind as he was, Willoughby had a reassuring strength. And she knew that he, in turn, relied on her strength. They were a pair. She was seeing him in new ways.

~

In the evening, she bathed his eyes again. She was starting to feel that this was an unnecessary torment for him. She hated to see him shudder in pain. It cut her to the quick.

'I think this is doing more harm than good,' she said, bandaging his eyes again. 'I don't want to do it any more.'

'Thank God,' he muttered. 'Pour the damned stuff down the sink.'

She did exactly that. Willoughby lay back on the bed, covering his eyes with his arm, breathing deeply. Isobel stood looking at his lean, muscled body, at the scars and the bruises that still hadn't faded. She recalled watching him step naked out of his uniform on the first day they had met, so youthful and innocent. He'd always been good to look at. She remembered the joy that he'd had in life, the flashing smiles that had now disappeared. She felt like crying for the destruction of youth and happiness.

Later in the night, she awoke from a bad dream, the details of which started fading the moment she opened her eyes. Felicity had been in it, and William, too. It had left her with a feeling of acute loneliness. She had come to a decision.

She got up and went to Willoughby's room. He was lying on his back, the bandage over his eyes, but she could tell that he was not sleeping either.

'Did I wake you?' she asked in a low voice.

'I heard you cry out.'

'I was dreaming.' Her hair was tied up, as she always wore it in bed. She unfastened the ribbon and let her hair fall. She sat beside him, leaned forward, and kissed his naked shoulder.

He tensed. 'What are you doing?'

She kissed him again on the other shoulder.

'Isobel—'

'Shhh. Don't speak.' She kept kissing him, lightly and gently, on his chest and nipples. She was in no hurry. She was determined to make this beautiful for them both.

At last she touched his lips with hers. He took her face in his hands and kissed her hungrily. He tried to take off his blindfold, but she stopped him. 'Leave it on.'

They began to kiss, with growing urgency. She was the more experienced, more deliberate, but Willoughby was the more passionate. She saw tears slide down his face from under his blindfold.

Her marriage vows had kept her faithful to an unfaithful husband for years. Now those vows – and that husband – had stopped meaning anything. She felt free, and in control of her own sexuality, for the first time since she'd met Roberto.

But she didn't want to think of Roberto. She did not question the impulse that had brought her to Willoughby's bed. She knew that she was not in love with him, and knew that she might never be. But she was a lonely woman and he a lonely man; and for the moment, that was all that mattered. She had come to seek comfort for them both. Compassion for Willoughby made her gentle at first, but her desire was surging . It had been so long since she had felt skin on skin.

Willoughby didn't speak again. Though he could not see her, he was intensely focused on Isobel. He explored her skin with his lips and fingertips, inhaling her scent, drinking her in. He kissed her belly, moving down between her parted thighs. She wrapped her legs around him as he learned about her body, exploring her with his mouth. Her fingers knotted through his.

Now it was her turn to explore him. It was clear that Willoughby had never experienced anything like the pleasure she could give him. He reacted to her every touch as though it were a revelation. He was in a world, with no light, but with all the other senses heightened and aflame.

Finally, he entered her, and then nothing else mattered. The pent-up hunger of years was pouring out. With Roberto, sex had been methodical, carefully planned and executed. Willoughby was not like that. He was overwhelmingly powerful, thrusting into her deeply and passionately, covering her face and throat with kisses. His body touched all the right places in hers. She couldn't form a single coherent thought. It was like riding a galloping stallion who took her surely and powerfully to her destination. She heard him gasping her name again and again.

Afterwards they lay together, drained, embraced. They didn't speak.

At length she felt him slip into a deep sleep, but she was awake for a long time, holding him in her arms, not wanting to lose this feeling.

෴

The next day, she took him to Santa Eulalia, the great Gothic cathedral of Barcelona.

'Are you trying to convert me?' he asked as she led him into the vast, dark, echoing space.

'No. I like you the way you are.'

'Then what are we doing here?'

'Hush. Keep your voice down.'

'There's nobody here,' he replied. 'Even I can tell that.' He was right. The huge cathedral was deserted. Official disapproval of religion and the disappearance of priests had emptied the churches. Mass was celebrated seldom and furtively, if ever. Even the bells were no longer rung. 'I thought you didn't believe any more?'

'God is here.'

She covered her hair with a mantilla and lit candles. He waited patiently while she prayed, her eyes fixed on the altar. As if her presence was a seed, life crept into the deserted cathedral. After a series of thumps and scrapes, the organ began to play softly, the fingers of the player seeming to grope after half-forgotten notes and chords. An old woman appeared and began to sweep away the litter that had blown in the door. At length, an unshaven priest arrived, yawning, and entered the confessional. He shot Willoughby a grim, suspicious look as he drew the curtain. Men in uniform were not a welcome sight when so many churches had been desecrated and vandalized. Isobel knelt beside the grille and made her first confession in many years.

She held tightly onto Willoughby's arm as they left the cathedral and wandered through the narrow streets of the Gothic Quarter. People stared at them. Willoughby was a striking figure, tall and vigorous, walking without hesitation despite the bandage over his eyes.

'What did you confess to the priest?' he asked her.

'About you. What we're doing.'

'Is it such a sin?'

'It's adultery. It's a mortal sin.'

Willoughby seemed amused. 'What did he say?'

'He asked if I intended to repeat the sin. I said yes. He said my confession was not valid. But he was very nice.'

'That very nice priest would put me in front of a firing squad if he could.'

'And you would burn down his church.'

Willoughby laughed. 'You know I'm not an Anarchist.'

'You're not a believer, either.'

'I might still be a believer, too – if the priests weren't with the Fascists.'

'Not all of them.'

'In Spain,' Willoughby said dryly, 'Mother Church has a revolver on her hip. Jesus wears jackboots, Mary drives a tank. Did you light candles, too?'

'You are impossible. I won't talk to you.'

'You did light candles. Can you really believe in all that mumbo jumbo?'

'Yes,' she said shortly.

'Okay. I'm just wondering what that was all about.'

Isobel looked at his face. 'I wanted to introduce you.'

'To God? He's not interested in me.'

'Well, I reminded him of your existence.'

In the middle of the square they stood in, oblivious of the people around, he took her in his arms and kissed her. 'Let's go home and repeat the sin. You promised the priest you would. I would hate you to break your word.'

❧

The sin was repeated, again and then again. The sin was so sweet that they could not live without it. It possessed them, as they possessed each other.

She lay face down on the bed, naked. Willoughby rubbed her back. He, too, was naked. His hands were sensual, strong. He couldn't see her but he was intensely aware of every grain of her skin, focused on her to the exclusion of everything else.

'What do you see in your mind?' she asked him.

'I see you. Like a painting by Goya.'

'I'm not young any more. I'm sure your imagination is much better than the reality.'

'I know every line of you. That's my reality. There is nothing better.'

'You're learning to be a lover and to say the right things.'

'You must have had many.'

'Thousands.'

His voice changed. 'Really?'

She smiled. 'In my imagination. I was a virgin on my wedding day.'

'So . . .' He paused. 'I am only your second?'

'If you want to think of it that way.'

He resumed the massage. His hands were sure, kneading her muscles into serenity. 'Did you think this day would come?'

'When Manuela brought you into the cottage that day, I was so angry with you, I could have shot you there and then.'

'All because I was taking your cabbages?'

'Because you were stealing the last thing I had to steal. I wanted to strip off your ugly uniform, humiliate you, the way I had been stripped and humiliated.' She rolled over lazily. Willoughby kissed her breasts, then poured a little oil on her skin and began to smooth it across her curves. She watched his face. 'I am supposed to be the one caring for you.'

'We're caring for each other.'

They made love slowly but with mounting passion. They knew one another's bodies well and everything happened with grace and ease. In the last moments, Willoughby pulled the bandage from his eyes and appeared to be looking into her eyes. When they had finished, she touched his face.

'I almost feel you can see me.'

'I almost can.'

'In your mind? Or with your eyes?'

'I can't tell the difference.'

'You are a very strange man.'

'We're two very strange people.'

Her novel was forgotten, her typewriter lay idle in its carrying case. They lived only for each other, and everything else – the war, the fate of Europe – lost its meaning. She hardly knew that she had a husband, sisters. William was her life.

The winter deepened. The war had ground to a stalemate and there was relative peace. The bombers had stopped coming. To the south of the city, both sides rested and licked their wounds. A kind of emptiness descended, which they filled with their passion.

Days became weeks. They hardly noticed. They made love twice each day, sometimes three times. It was necessary to their existence, more necessary than food. Their bodies, lean and hollow from hunger, cared only to be fitted together, like pieces of a puzzle that only made sense when assembled and was incomprehensible when apart.

❧

They put some of their precious firewood into the ancient boiler to make hot water for a bath, a great luxury, and got in it together. The atmosphere was dreamy, steam rising around the dim glow of the bulb. She lay in his arms, her head on his shoulder.

'Why are you crying?' he asked.

She hadn't realized she was; she wiped her eyes. 'I don't know.'

But she did know. Her period had not come for the second month in a row. She'd been pregnant before. She knew the feeling. She was almost certainly expecting her second child. It could hardly be a surprise. They took no precautions, as though all she wanted was his child. The unspoken, unthought wish had come true.

Her diffused attention was caught by a deep concussion that squeezed her chest. She felt the bath water slide up her chest. Dust drifted down from the ceiling onto them. She tensed. Another explosion rocked the bathroom. Then another. They were coming closer, and now through the window they could hear the drone of bombers and the wail of air-raid sirens. The pale fingers of searchlights probed the night sky.

'It's an air raid! We have to get to the basement!'

They scrambled out of the bath and groped for clothing as another bomb rocked their building. Isobel screamed and covered her head as chunks of wood and plaster rained from the ceiling. The dim light went out, leaving them in blackness. She and Willoughby grabbed each other's hands and ran through the apartment.

The stairwell was in chaos. There had not been raids for a fortnight, and people had stopped preparing for them in the hope that they had somehow, miraculously, stopped. They joined the mob of tenants running down the stairs to the basement, parents clutching half-awake children. An old woman lugged a parrot in a cage. The only light was the glare from the anti-aircraft battery near the block. Another bomb exploded in a nearby street, blowing in the windows. Broken glass showered in, slashing faces.

Knees and elbows thudded into Isobel. Willoughby did his best to shelter her from the frantic clawing of the others, using his strength to forge a way down. They were among the last to reach the basement.

The basement was crowded to capacity, the dusty air lit by a small oil lamp. Families cowered under the low brick arches. A few babies cried, but as always, the children were silent, huddled against their parents.

She and Willoughby squeezed into a space at the far end of the vault. The bombing was all around them. The floor shuddered beneath their feet with each impact. The mortar holding the bricks together seemed as frail as chalk. Isobel felt the bricks working loose, like rotten teeth. The thought of a direct hit was terrifying. The apartment block, already a hundred years old, would come down like so many other blocks in Barcelona, crushing them all under tons of rubble in the cellar. Or an incendiary would pour blazing phosphorous down here and they would die screaming in a man-made hell.

The raid was prolonged, as if to make up for the long period of peace they had enjoyed. Willoughby put his arm around Isobel and held her close, but she was unable to respond. A single thought was going round and round in her brain: she didn't need to be here. This was no longer her country, no longer her war. She belonged in her own place. She felt little empathy with the trembling people around her; this was their fight, and it was going to end badly. Though she'd lost all her infatuation with Fascism, she could not espouse any other cause. She'd tried, but she had been fooling herself. All she felt was a profound disillusionment.

The bombing faded away, returned, faded again. The hours passed. After a long silence, the All Clear sounded. They rose, stiff and aching, from their huddled positions and left their refuge, jostling to get out, as they had jostled to get in.

It was now dawn. They wandered outside, peering blearily through the grey smoke. A stick of bombs had fallen close by their block, uprooting trees in the park and buildings in the street with indifference. Everything was altered. Piles of rubble blocked the road, like guts that had spilled from opened bellies. Shop windows had been blown in, their glass glittering for yards around. Here and there lay the body of someone who hadn't been able to find shelter in time. Dazed and distraught civilians were trying to help a few parties of ambulance men load the dead and wounded onto stretchers. Still, people looked anxiously up at the skies. The bombers sometimes returned in daylight to continue the carnage.

A crying child stumbled past, calling for her mother. Isobel knelt and embraced her, trying to comfort her, or perhaps comfort herself. The child pulled loose and ran on up the street. She saw that Willoughby's blindfold was off and that his eyes were on her. 'You can see.'

He nodded wearily. 'Yes.'

'When did that happen?'

'Last night. On the stairs.'

She rose to her feet. 'Why did you suddenly start seeing then?'

'Because I had to.'

She regarded him steadily. 'Has this all been a game, William?'

'You know it hasn't been a game.'

'So this is a miracle cure? You couldn't see, and now you can?'

'I didn't want to see.'

'You've been pretending.'

'No.'

'What, then?'

'The last thing I saw was the bodies of my last remaining friends, torn to pieces by a shell. After that, I didn't want to see anything more.' He looked down the shattered street. 'Now I wish I was blind again.'

'Very convenient,' she said bitterly. 'Just answer my question: Have you been able to see clearly all this time?'

He shrugged. 'I have worn a bandage.'

'And when you took it off?'

'I saw nothing. Until now.'

'Okay.' Isobel turned away. She remembered Sister Harris saying that Willoughby's blindness had been a form of shell shock. But somehow, Willoughby's abrupt cure had deepened her disillusionment still further. She felt wearied, spent, used. She'd entered into a relationship with him which she probably wouldn't have contemplated without his blindness. This had been yet another of life's snares, another of the traps men had set for her, and which she'd trustingly walked into. She'd abandoned her work for him. And now she was probably carrying his child. Her life had been hijacked in mid-passage, and she had lost control of it.

Reading her thoughts, he said, 'I didn't try to deceive you, Isobel.'

'But you did deceive me.'

'It wasn't deliberate. I thought I would never see anything again.' He paused. 'You healed me, Isobel.'

'Oh, William,' she said tiredly, 'that's so banal.'

'Not to me.'

'I'm not a saint. I don't perform miracles.'

'Every minute with you has been a miracle,' he said gently. 'Darling, you can't be angry that I can see again.'

'You've been able to see all this time,' she retorted. 'You just blindfolded yourself to keep the world out.'

He took her arm. 'It wasn't like that. You're talking as though I deliberately faked the whole thing. I didn't. My eyes were burned and I believed I couldn't see. Aren't you happy for me?'

She looked up into his eyes, grey-blue and clear. She had lost herself in him for a while. But now she felt that she was emerging from the other side of a fog. As he had learned to see, so must she. 'I'm happy for you,' she said, and tried to smile. 'Of course I am.'

They went back into their building without talking.

❧

The bombing continued nightly after that. The weary armies resumed their fighting. A pall of black smoke gathered over Barcelona and hung there, impervious to the cutting *tramontana*, which did not blow high enough to move it.

Isobel got up early one morning, without waking Willoughby, and made the long journey back to *Sagrado Corazon*. The hospital was more crowded and chaotic than ever. The bombing had brought a flood of injured civilians, most of them women and children, who filled the corridors. She was lucky enough to catch Sister Harris in her office, and was granted a few minutes.

'He can see again,' she said tersely, without preamble. 'You were right. It was psychological.'

Sister Harris showed no reaction. 'Hysteria. Subjective paralysis and blindness are not uncommon. Any residual symptoms?'

'No. In fact, he's full of energy.'

The dryness of Isobel's response made Sister Harris raise her gingery eyebrows. 'Are you having an affair with him?' she asked bluntly.

'That's what you wanted.'

'It is not what I wanted,' Sister Harris retorted. 'I asked you to take care of him. Not to use him for your own ends.'

'It's the other way around, if you ask me.' Isobel was coldly angry. 'He has been using me for his ends. He pretended to be blind to get my sympathy. Now that he has me, he doesn't need to keep up the pretence, so his sight has conveniently returned.'

'The blindness vanished with sexual intercourse?'

'It wasn't as prosaic as that. He allowed me to lead him round like a tame bear for a few weeks, first. It was very touching. The miracle occurred during an air raid, but I think he had started to tire of the charade long before that.'

'Charade? Are you so sure it was a charade?'

'What else would you call it?'

'I would most certainly not call it a charade, if by that you mean a systematic, deliberate deception. Psychological injuries are complex. It's very difficult to impersonate them convincingly. When Captain Willoughby was in my care, he was totally blind. His pupils were fixed and unresponsive. A man can say he does not see, but he cannot control the opening and closing of his pupils.' Isobel shrugged wearily by way of an answer. 'I should like to see Captain Willoughby,' Sister Harris went on. 'I'm very glad to hear that his sight has been restored, but his psychological problems are unlikely to be over.'

'Oh, I'll tell him. You and he can congratulate one another. It all worked out very well. You wanted to get him off your hands. He wanted to get into my bed. I was the perfect stooge.'

Sister Harris shuffled a sheaf of files with her blunt, freckled fingers. 'Is that all?' she asked impatiently.

'No,' Isobel said. 'That's not all. I did you a favour. Now you're going to do one for me.'

༄

She came back to the apartment in the evening, carrying a loaf of stale bread which was all she'd been able to buy in this increasingly hungry city. Willoughby was sitting at her typewriter, pounding on the keys. The use of her machine – and her precious stock of paper – filled her with acrid resentment. She walked stiffly past him to the kitchen and began unpacking her bag.

She heard the sound of him pulling a sheet of paper out of the Remington. He came up behind her and put his arms around her waist.

'Are you okay?'

'I'm fine,' she said tightly. But she was as stiff as a poker.

Willoughby rested his chin on her shoulder and stared out of the window at the grim, glaring twilight, the heavy shadow of smoke. 'It looks like the end of the world. I was worried about you. You were gone so long.'

She felt like a cat, ready to hiss and slash with claws. 'Don't. You're too heavy.'

'Sorry.' He removed his weight, but tried to kiss her neck. 'Where have you been?'

'Leave me alone, just this once.' She pushed away from him and went to the bedroom. He followed her, puzzled.

'Did I do something wrong?'

'No.' she replied shortly. 'I'm going to wash.'

'I'll light the boiler.'

'No need. Cold water is fine.' She started taking off her clothes, her back to Willoughby. Willoughby watched her from the doorway, not seeming to understand that she wanted privacy.

'You're so beautiful.' Isobel didn't respond. 'What happened to you today?' he asked.

'Nothing.'

'Tell me the truth.' Again, he tried to take her in his arms and kiss her, but she fought away from him. She was unsteady on her feet.

'Don't!'

'What the hell is wrong with you?'

'Nothing! It's finished.'

'What's finished?' he demanded.

'Everything. Everything's finished.'

'Isobel!'

She broke free of him and went to the bathroom, shutting the door in his face. She sat on the edge of the bath and removed the bloodstained bandage from between her thighs. The flow seemed to have slowed down. She could no longer suppress her shuddering sobs.

Willoughby pushed the bathroom door open. 'Are you okay?'

'Get out of here,' she choked. 'I don't want you here!'

But he had seen the blood in the bath. His face was pale. 'What have you done?'

'What do you think?'

'Is this normal? I mean—'

'No, it's not normal,' she snapped. 'I had an abortion.' She leaned on the wall and closed her eyes. Willoughby was frozen.

'Why? Why did you do it?'

'Why do you think?'

'You should have told me.'

'Why should I?'

'I had a right to know.'

She heard herself laughing. 'A right to know! You are absurd.'

'Jesus, Isobel! Am I so far beneath you that you had to kill my baby?'

'I didn't want *your baby!* Isn't my life ruined enough?'

'You make it sound like *I* ruined your life!'

'You did your part, William.'

'What the hell did I do? You did it all! You pile ruin on ruin. And now you've killed our child!' He clenched his fists. 'Why?'

'Look out of the window, William! Look at the world! Look at yourself! Look at me! Is this how to have a child?'

'The war will end. Life will go on. Except for our child. What sense does this make?'

'It makes no sense to rant at me now. I couldn't have this child. It's finished.'

He covered his face with his hands. 'Where did you go? Some back street?'

'I went to Sister Harris. She gave me the name of a doctor.' She showed Willoughby her hand. The wedding ring she always wore was gone. 'It cost me my wedding ring.'

She rose from the bath and dressed. There was a deep, dark ache in her womb from the procedure. She wanted only to lie on the bed and seek oblivion, but Willoughby stood in her way. His face was tight and bitter. 'By your own insane standards, you've committed a mortal sin.'

'That's my business, not yours.'

'So much for your religion.'

'I am being punished. This is my hell.'

He exploded. 'Praying and killing is all you people know! Was this what you did with the last one? Is that why your husband left you?'

'What do you care? The war is lost. You'll be gone in a week, a month.'

'I'm not going anywhere.'

'Of course you'll go. I can't be tied to a bastard child that nobody wants. I did what I had to do. You didn't have to do anything, suffer anything. This is not for you to judge. What are you, William? A boy having a grand adventure. This isn't our country, this isn't our war. You've spent your life in books. Why did you come here? To fire your gun and lose your virginity with the first Spanish girl who would spread her legs for you. Do you think you would make any kind of father to my child?'

Willoughby slapped her across the face. There was a terrible silence. She didn't look at him any more. 'Go.'

'Isobel, I didn't mean to do that.'

'Get out. Pack your bag and go. You can see your way, now.'

'Please let me—'

She found she was screaming at him. 'Just go! Get out! Go!' She thrust him away from her, furious and implacable.

'All right,' he shouted, 'I'm going!' He strode to their bedroom and began throwing things into his duffel bag.

She was still not able to cry. She went to her typewriter and stared down at the keys. The day, which had passed in a blur, was suddenly becoming razor-sharp in her mind, a camera lens focusing: the journey to the hospital, the interview with Sister Harris, the noncommittal blue eyes of a useful woman staring at the strange phenomenon of a useless one. The gynaecologist's room, the impatient way he'd interrupted her stammered explanations.

'I'll do it now,' he'd said brusquely.

'*Now*? I thought perhaps tomorrow—'

'Tomorrow none of us may be here. I am ready.'

'I hadn't expected to do it now!'

'Then why did you come to me? You will be able to leave immediately afterwards. I have other patients waiting. Do you want the termination or not?'

She'd felt herself cornered, even though she'd already taken the decision – or thought she had. 'Yes, I – I want it,' she'd said.

'*Pues, no le damos mas vueltas a la cosa*. What have you brought?'

She'd fumbled in her purse for the money. 'Is this enough?'

'No money. I only take gold.' His eyes were fixed on her left hand.

She would never forget the feeling, after so many years, of drawing Roberto's ring from her finger, twisting it over the knuckle, slipping it from the last joint, her hand feeling suddenly weightless, the alarming sensation of being unanchored. And seeing the little gold band slide into the pocket of his white coat, a part of her amputated, alienated, sold and passing into the possession of others.

Lying on the couch with her thighs spread. Trying not to cry out at the sharp, cold pain of the instruments that pushed into her body, cranked open the red chamber of her womb, revealed the secret life, part hers, part Willoughby's, part someone else's, which clung there.

And then the scrape, scrape, scrape of the curette, no anaesthetic offered or asked for, the pain raw and unbearable. Her own weeping. The silence of the doctor and his nurse after the single comment, 'You are no longer pregnant.'

They'd allowed her to lie in the anteroom for fifteen minutes. Then she'd had to make way for a heavily pregnant woman. She and the other women hadn't looked at each other. It was a toss-up as to which was more wretched, the one about to deliver a child with the Fascists at the gate, or the other having destroyed a child by her own hand. She couldn't remember how she'd got home.

Suddenly, she wanted to write about it. To put it down in black letters on white paper. Record it for ever. She sat at the desk and wound a sheet into the machine. Her fingertips rested on the cool, concave keys. She was only half-aware of Willoughby standing in the doorway, watching her.

'Goodbye, Isobel.'

She didn't look up. 'Goodbye.'

Her fingers began to type, at first slowly, then faster and faster, the clatter drowning out the sound of retreating footsteps and the front door closing.

5.
FELICITY

London, Summer, 1942

The young man in the labour exchange had a squint, so Felicity was never quite sure whether he was looking at her, or at the wall behind her, upon which was spread a dingy map of the British Isles, covered in rusty thumb tacks, and a number of posters exhorting Britons to dig for victory and eat less bread. The expression on his face, however, was unequivocally one of scorn.

'No shorthand or typing?'

'No.'

'No bookkeeping experience?'

'None.'

'Can't cook?' he asked disbelievingly.

'Can't even boil an egg, I'm afraid.'

'Sewing?'

'Sorry.'

'Got no trade at all?'

'Sorry, no.'

'And you can't join the Land Army?'

Felicity glanced at the poster of the robust young woman wielding a pitchfork. 'I tried to explain. I've been ill. I get asthma with physical exertion.'

The young man picked a pimple on his chin. One of his eyes roved over her still-cropped head and pale face, the other following, as it were, two steps behind. It was obvious why he hadn't been called up. One wouldn't want to see him aiming a rifle, with that strabismus. Yet even in front of this boy, who was about the same age as she, Felicity was abashed. She felt a little like Rob Wilton in the radio sketch: *The day war broke out, my wife said to me, What good are you?* 'You never had a job of any kind? Never worked?'

'Well, yes, of course I've worked. I've been in a convent for five years.'

'Like a nun or something?'

'Yes, like a nun or something.'

'And what did you do in this convent of yours?'

'I was the librarian.'

'I got no openings for *librarians*,' he said. 'I got secretarial, agricultural, trades and manual.'

'I thought I might get a job in a munitions factory.'

He sucked his teeth disdainfully. '*Munitions factory*. Everybody wants a job in a *munitions factory*.'

Felicity, who had thought this would be a rather dangerous and unpopular line of work, was put out. 'Do they?'

'Good pay, good hours, canteen, secure position. They only take the cream.'

'Oh, I see.' She was very much conscious of not being the cream.

'Librarian in a convent,' he said incredulously, shaking his head. 'So why aren't you there any more?'

'That's none of your business,' Felicity retorted.

'Yes, it is,' he countered. 'It's your previous work experience, isn't it? I have to know about your previous work experience. So I know where to send you next.'

'My previous employer dispensed with my services,' she said stiffly, after a pause.

He picked up his pen. 'What's his name?'

'God.'

He frowned. 'Did the nuns throw you out?'

'I resigned. And here I am,' she said, heading off more questions. 'There's a war on. I want to do my bit. What about the NAAFI?'

'They wouldn't have you,' he said. He opened a ledger. 'You can serve dinner, then, can you?'

'Yes, I can do that.'

'I can get you in a British Restaurant. You would have to sign a form saying you don't object to working in a danger zone.'

She had been hoping for something more heroic, and she was put out. 'A restaurant?'

'A British Restaurant. Don't you know anything? They're public kitchens for people who can't feed themselves. Where the Germans like to bomb.'

She brightened. There was something noble about the sound of that. 'Oh, that sounds as though it would be all right.'

'Three pound six shillings a week.'

It didn't sound very much. 'Is that enough to live on?'

'You'll have to find out, won't you?'

'Yes, I suppose I will.'

He filled out several forms of different colours, blotting the ink carefully. 'Know what I reckon?' he said, as he handed her the relevant cards. 'I reckon you ought to have stayed in your convent. Next, please!'

She gathered her gas mask and her torch and made her way through the crowded waiting room and down the murky stairs.

As always, coming out onto the street was a shock. After the years protected behind convent walls, the streets of London were overwhelmingly hectic. Taxis hurtled ruthlessly, buses careered, crossing the road was a test of nerve which she often failed. She felt dazed and breathless much of the time, out in the street.

And London was transformed. Barrage balloons hung like sullen fleets of giant slugs in the sky. Shop windows were boarded up, except for little gaps for passers-by to peer into, the parks were criss-crossed with trenches, walls of sandbags had been erected around important buildings. Most shocking was the evidence, throughout London, of the German bombing, which had torn chunks out of the city, apparently indiscriminately, blindly flattening churches, the dwellings of the poor, factories, the mansions of Belgravia and the theatres of the West End alike. It was blind spite, she thought, Polyphemus hurling rocks at Odysseus without seeing or caring where they landed.

She went down into the Tube station, passing the crushed-looking, homeless people who had been bombed out and had nowhere else to stay, who huddled in any corner they could find. Her nerves felt raw. They had done so ever since she'd left the priory. Her unhappiness in the priory had at least been scabbed over. Now the scab had been picked off, leaving a raw wound, and everything hurt her, every impression made her wince. Seeing these wretched families living in the dirty passages of the Underground, reduced to little more than beggars, was unbearable. She scattered some small change, which she could ill afford, and hurried past.

Chiara, who worked at the Censor's Office until four, was in her kitchen, producing mouth-watering fragrances. The flat, with its rich colours, rich smells, glowing paintings and Tiffany lamps, was like the nest of some shimmering fairy. By contrast, it made Felicity herself feel like a moth, colourless and grey. Checking herself in the hall mirror as she came in, the image was confirmed. With her gaunt cheeks, she was a wraith of what she had been. Where her once-luxuriant tresses had grown, strange, colourless tendrils had sprouted in all directions. She was twenty-four, but she looked worn out.

Her clothes – a hodgepodge of Chiara's cast-offs and a few garments she'd bought in a second-hand shop – didn't help. Mostly, she wore a very baggy and faded pair of corduroy pants and a sweater. Chiara said she looked like a refugee from the Left Bank.

Chiara glanced out of the tiny kitchen. 'It's chicken *chasseur*. Won't be long, darling.'

'It smells wonderful.' Chiara's skill in producing gourmet meals out of a few scraps was astonishing. Felicity started to set the little dining table for two.

'How did it go?' Chiara asked, clanking pots.

'Very well,' she replied, trying to sound bright.

'Really?'

'I got a job.'

Chiara executed a jig, brandishing her ladle. 'Oh, well done!'

'Working in a canteen.'

'Is that what you wanted?'

Felicity was determined to sound cheerful. 'Well, as the clerk said, they're not looking for librarians with a special knowledge of sixteenth-century spiritual literature.' They sat down to eat. The chicken stew was wonderful, and Felicity said so.

'It's half a hare from under the butcher's counter,' Chiara said. 'But don't tell anyone. Where's this canteen of yours?'

'It's a British Restaurant in Canning Town.'

'When do you start?'

'Saturday.'

'Poor darling. You'll be up to your armpits in greasy dishwater all day,' Chiara said. 'You won't like it. I wish you'd have let me fix you up with something at the Ministry.'

It was something of a sore point. Oliver Courtfield, whom Felicity had never met, and who was on some mysterious service somewhere abroad – he was said to be in MI5 – had pulled strings to get Chiara a post in the Ministry of Information. Her job was to quell newspapers which were too pessimistic in their reporting, and force them to sound jolly. Chiara called her work, 'Yes, we have no bananas', after the popular song about the relentlessly optimistic grocer who refused to say 'No'. Felicity disapproved of string pulling, and had rejected Chiara's offer to find her a place. 'I don't mind hard work,' she said, rather stiffly. 'I'm not looking for a cushy billet.'

She regretted the words the moment they left her mouth. But it was too late. She could see that Chiara was offended. 'My job isn't a cushy billet,' she retorted. 'Trying to control what the newspapers say is like stopping a steamroller. You should try it sometime.'

'Well, I won't criticize your work if you don't criticize mine.'

Chiara pushed her plate away. 'I wish you hadn't given all your money to the Church. Isobel told you this would happen and she was right.'

'They'll give it back to me.'

'When?'

'I don't know. In God's good time. In the meantime, I have exactly forty-two pounds and six shillings, and I must work or beg.'

'You were better off in the priory.'

'That's what they told me at the employment exchange today.'

'There you are, then.' Chiara rose from the table, leaving her plate half eaten, and went to the window, where she stood with her arms folded, looking out. She and Felicity were still not on good terms. Whether they ever would be was an open question. That disastrous visit before the war hung between them like a spectre. Chiara's bright helmet of golden hair gleamed in the evening light. She had changed, Felicity reflected. She was no longer the vivacious, rather silly ingénue she had been. She was quieter, tougher. Perhaps that came from battling newspaper editors every day. In any case, war and love had wrought changes in Chiara, making her more womanly, less a girl. 'But of course, you never listen to anybody's advice.'

Felicity, too, had lost her appetite. She put her knife and fork down. 'I listen and I am baffled. You were angry with me for going into the priory and now, apparently, you're angry with me for coming out.'

'Perhaps that's because you never bothered to explain either your going in or your coming out to anybody,' Chiara said dryly.

'Why should I explain either?' Felicity replied. 'It's nobody's business but mine. And in any case, I doubt you would understand.'

'I understand that you've made a mess of your life,' Chiara said sharply. 'And it's absurd to think of hard manual labour in your condition. Look at you – you're as thin as a rake and as white as a ghost. You won't last a day in a busy kitchen.'

'Thank you for that vote of confidence. Does it ever occur to you that your so-called advice consists chiefly of telling me I'm no good for anything?'

'That's not true.'

'Ever since I can remember, you and Isobel have been browbeating me. Every little achievement was sneered at, every aspiration I had was mocked. Whatever I wanted to do, you told me I wasn't fit for it.'

'Darling, listen.' Chiara turned to her. 'I'll lend you money until the Church disgorges your dowry. Go and live in the country until you're stronger. Get some fresh air and healthy food.'

Felicity shook her head. 'Do you want me out of your way so badly?'

'Don't be horrid. I'm worried about you. I want you to get out of London, away from the bombing, to where it's safe and quiet.'

'Thanks, but no, thanks. I've had quite enough of safety and quiet to last a lifetime. And quite enough of doing nothing. I want to contribute. And as soon as I can find somewhere to stay, I'll go.'

'I don't want you to go,' Chiara said irritably. 'You're my sister. I've missed you awfully all these years. You can stay as long as you like, of course. Don't be so prickly.'

But Felicity *was* prickly. She couldn't help it. She felt like a hedgehog, prickles on one side and vulnerable on the other. Unless her prickles were facing the world, she was helpless.

They washed the dishes and tidied the kitchen. It was a pleasant evening and the flat was stifling, all the more so since the atmosphere between them was uneasy. 'I'm going to take a stroll in the Park,' Felicity said, and went out again.

It was a five-minute walk from Chiara's flat in Tisbury Mansions to Hyde Park, where Londoners were gathering after the day's work to seek whatever wartime recreation they could find. Motley squads of Home Guard soldiers were drilling with antiquated rifles, boys were playing cricket, families were bantering with the workmen filling in craters made by stray bombs. She wandered away from the crowds and into the trees, where there was more peace, apart from the couples who kissed in the long grass, oblivious of the sheep which had been put there to graze.

What gave Chiara the authority to talk to her as though she were a child? There was certainly no moral superiority on her part. Though she always spoke of the priory as something somehow obscene, the truth was that Chiara was the acknowledged mistress of an older man who came and went as he pleased. And despite her stout denial, Oliver Courtfield had made her life very comfortable – the high-ranking job at the Censor's office, the gifts of impossible-to-get silk, chocolate and perfume. Where was the morality in that?

Men and women did as they wanted nowadays – evidence the writhing couples in the grass around her, the hands groping up petticoats, the mouths locked like morays. War and death were great aphrodisiacs, it seemed. The world had changed dramatically in the five years that she'd been in the convent. Women swore and smoked, painted their faces, showed their legs, dyed their hair. Soldiers swaggered and whistled, thumbs in belts, blatantly on the make.

And Felicity knew she was wrong in everything she did. She didn't look like them, couldn't talk like them, didn't dress like them or swear like them or think like them. And it was even worse when she revealed that she had been in a convent for five years. People shrank away from her as though she had said 'a leper colony'.

It was a bare three weeks since the priory gates had opened to let her out. Looking back, only the last few days were in focus. The period between her decision to leave and the granting of her dispensation was similarly a blur. She had spent most of it alone in her cell. Nobody, not even Sister Teresa Margaret, had made any attempt to talk her out of leaving; in fact, she was conscious of a silent sense of relief from many of the sisters, or at least of their having known all along that this would happen.

She'd sat in her cell, suspended from her work in the library, immobile and yet battered by alternately searing and freezing tempests of the spirit. God no longer wanted her. That devastating conclusion had come to her like a thunderbolt, explaining why, for five years, she had endured the utmost wretchedness. He had summoned her – of that she had no doubt – and then had turned his back on her. Like the wedding guest in the parable, she had been thrown out of the feast.

Why? What had she done wrong? In what way had she offended? Was it because she had allowed herself to be swayed by William Willoughby's broad shoulders and blue eyes? Was God such a jealous God? There was no answer. But she knew that she was no longer a welcome guest.

She had emerged from the priory like a hedgehog, blinking and scuttling. She'd made no coherent plan for her life on the outside. And indeed, what was she equipped to do? All the things she had learned in the priory, all the progress she had made, all had vanished on passing out through the gates. Not a scrap of it had any meaning outside of the convent. She'd gone in at nineteen and had come out at twenty-four with nothing to show for it – nothing, at least, that the world could recognize as a talent or a skill. And she was still not a member of that distinguished group that one might call The Grown-Ups Club.

If she was to survive in this terrible year of our Lord 1942, she was going to have to start at the bottom and work her way up, learning through each hard knock, until she was indistinguishable from the 'normal' people around her, even these who copulated shamelessly at her feet under the trees of Hyde Park.

The bus that took her to work on Saturday drove the length of East India Dock Road. It was a journey into devastation. The East End had borne the brunt of the bombing. Craters yawned among piles of rubble. She could only guess at the misery and the loss of life that had been inflicted. Factories had been razed, gasworks had burned with devastating heat, leaving mangled skeletons of steel behind. Railway yards, workshops and warehouses had been torn apart.

Most pathetic of all were the ordinary homes whose sides or fronts had been ripped away, leaving their inner workings exposed like the rooms of doll's houses. Whole communities had been reduced to wasteland, since the crowded, narrow, terraced streets had made ripe targets for high explosive and incendiaries.

The people who wandered among the ruins looked dazed, standing in huddled groups or queuing for assistance, like sleepwalkers.

Heaps of rubble punctuated the landscape, which had never been anything but a grim vista of docks, railways and industry. She understood why she'd been made to sign a form agreeing to work in a danger zone.

In this part of London, the barrage balloons filled the sky, thousands upon thousands of them, receding to infinity. It was an eerie and imposing spectacle. Between the factories she saw the dull, grey river and caught glimpses of a ship which had been hit, and now lay half-submerged in the Thames, barges jostling around it trying to get up or down the stream.

The conductor tapped her on the shoulder. 'Your stop, love.'

Felicity got off the bus. The air had that stink of recent bombing, which she was already so familiar with, of fires recently put out, broken drains and leaking gas. She found the restaurant easily enough. The sign read, 'Trinidad Street British Restaurant', but there was little romance about the place. It was located in one of the arches under a Victorian railway bridge, a brick vault between a car repair workshop and an auction house which sold second-hand baths, toilets and furniture from bombed houses. The door was locked, so she knocked. She was two hours early, but she had resolved to make a good impression, and to start as she meant to go on.

'Can't you read? We're closed.' A sullen young woman holding a mop had opened the door an inch. Before she could shut it again, Felicity blurted out:

'I'm Felicity.'

'Who?'

'Felicity Redcliffe. I'm reporting for duty.'

'What you on about?'

'I'm supposed to start work today.' She held up her card.

'Well, why didn't you say so?' Grudgingly, the girl let her in.

The restaurant had the Spartan atmosphere of all wartime institutions. Chairs were stacked on the long, board tables while the sullen girl mopped the floor. The walls were stark, the ceiling a brick vault. At the far end was the serving counter.

'Who do I report to?' Felicity asked.

The young woman jerked her head towards the kitchen, which was partitioned off behind the counter. 'Manageress.'

Felicity entered the kitchen timidly. The first sight that greeted her was a vast pile of dirty dishes, pots and pans heaped on a sink. A very straight-backed woman was sitting at a table, filling in forms. She looked up briefly, showing a narrow, rather masculine face framed in horn-rimmed spectacles.

'Well?'

'I'm Felicity Redcliffe. I'm supposed to start work today.'

The woman pointed at the sink. 'You'd better get started then, hadn't you? Good job you're early. Your predecessor didn't turn up last night. We'll get on to introductions later.'

Felicity's heart quailed. It looked like Chiara's dire predictions were coming true. She found a pinafore hanging on a peg, put it on, and set to work. The remains of food on the dishes were crusted and hard by now. The water was cold enough to make her hands ache. She was too timid to ask about lighting the boiler. And the bar of green soap began to burn her fingertips at once. She persevered. The pots were the worst, baked and burned, the enamel refusing to give up ancient black layers even when she scrubbed with Vim. Her back began to seize up and her arms grew numb. She surely wasn't going to crumble in the face of mere washing-up?

'Do you know what you're doing?'

The sharp question pulled her out of a trance. The manageress was standing beside her. 'What?' she gasped, wondering what gross error she had committed.

'You're building the New Jerusalem.'

'Am I doing something wrong?' Felicity stammered.

'The New Jerusalem, in England's green and pleasant land. You may think this humble work.' Her eyes gleamed from behind the tortoiseshell spectacles. 'But it's glorious. Oh, yes. Even this. This is the future, Redcliffe. The New Britain. My name's Miss Allsop.'

'How d'you do?' Felicity said. Miss Allsop was a fortyish, spinsterish woman of a type which Felicity had already encountered in religious life, burning with holy zeal – in this case, apparently, for Socialism. 'I hope I'm not—'

'They told me about you. Don't stop working, you've a lot to get through. Privileged background, but that didn't satisfy you. Joined a nunnery, but that didn't do the trick either.' Felicity winced. The youth at the employment exchange had obviously Told All. She'd been hoping to avoid such disclosures. 'Well,' Miss Allsop went on, 'you've come to the right place, Redcliffe. This is the Melting Pot. You'll find the whole of society here. Upper-class ladies like yourself—'

'I'm hardly an upper-class lady,' Felicity put in hastily, but Miss Allsop ignored her.

' – shop girls, domestic servants, plenty of Cockneys of course. All united in the common cause: to aid the Proletariat in this great struggle against Fascism.' A bony hand clamped on her aching shoulder. 'And the New World Order will be built, Redcliffe. It will be built.' Miss Allsop inspected her face closely. 'You still have that convent pallor on your cheeks. Pretty girl, though.' Her breath smelled of XXX Mints.

Felicity was too overwhelmed by the task at hand to anticipate the New Jerusalem. In a few hours, there would be hundreds to feed. How on earth was it to be managed? The pile of washing-up had scarcely diminished. Her strength was running out and she had barely worked an hour. To collapse before she had even started in her new job was too humiliating to contemplate. But she could feel her chest closing. An asthma attack was not far away. She had been so ill for so long at the priory; her physical strength had gone long ago. She had survived the last months on spiritual energy alone. She tried to summon up the same fuel now.

After another hour, the kitchen filled with young women, all about her own age, but very different from her in every other way. With primped hair and bright lipstick, they chattered like so many brilliant parakeets as they bustled in. Felicity glanced over her shoulder with wide eyes at tight slacks stretched over broad bottoms, short skirts showing bare legs (some still bearing the smudged lines of last night's painted-on 'stocking seams') and blouses straining over ample bosoms.

'Who's this Gawd-elp-us?' said a loud Cockney voice behind her. Felicity shrank into herself like a threatened mollusc.

'Blimey, that's the nun,' someone else said.

There was a burst of laughter which made Felicity cringe even further. Her secret – if it had ever been a secret – was well and truly out. A large female body bumped up beside her, and a large face, topped with sculpted red hair, peered into hers. 'What *have* they done to you? Made you look like a proper pollywog, that's what. Did they use your hair to stuff Mother Superior's pillows?'

'It hasn't – hasn't grown yet,' Felicity replied, flushing scarlet.

'I can see that, darlin'. Here, you look peaky. You're not used to this, are you?' A sturdy hip bumped her aside. 'You dry and stack, I'll wash.'

'Did you hear about the two nuns in the bath?' Another large, and tightly clad body with a heavily made-up face had materialized on Felicity's other side.

'No,' Felicity said innocently.

'One said, "Where's the soap?" And the other one said, "Yeah, doesn't it!"'

Felicity understood neither the joke nor the hilarity which followed it. She concentrated on drying and stacking, wedged between the two hefty bottoms of her assistants, who, it turned out, were known as Ginger and Eileen. Their vivacity was comforting somehow; she no longer feared fainting on the floor.

Some of the girls had started cooking. An Irish stew was on the go, and what smelled like steak and kidney pudding. The conversations all around Felicity, half-heard and punctuated with kitchen noises, were eye-opening. All were unmarried. Shirley had 'got off with' not one but two American soldiers last night and was very pleased with herself, and hoping to meet up with them again tonight. Marlene had got a factory job at Scoreswick, far from the bombs. Lily had 'missed' for three months and was calculating whether Eddie would be home in time to make it a white wedding. Ivy had been so drunk last night that she'd had to be carried home by some men and nobody knew what had happened after that. Maudie's family had been bombed out and had gone up to Newcastle.

Most of their talk seemed to be about men and sex. The war appeared to be of little interest to them. In the priory, talking about one's feelings at all – let alone one's physical being – had been taboo. This brazen baring of the most intimate and anatomical detail was shocking to her. Though she belonged to the same generation as they did, Felicity felt like a different species. She knew nothing about sex or men. Their jokes (when she understood them) were scandalous, their language crude.

They knew, at least, what they were doing. Ovens and sinks and kitchens were as familiar to them as drawing rooms were to Felicity. Miss Allsop did not have to issue many commands, but sat contemplating the New Jerusalem through glinting spectacles. The food was cooked, the crockery set out and the canteen readied for service by noon. An impatient queue was already forming in the street outside the door, hollow-cheeked faces peering in through the glass. Londoners, Felicity had learned, were always hungry. In the priory, at least, hunger could be assuaged by bread and margarine and a cup of tea, and mealtimes were approached in a mood of calm contemplation. She was already regretting those days. Her own stomach was growling.

She and five other girls took up their stations behind the counter, armed with ladles to dish up with. There were three meat courses, one of macaroni cheese and one of scrambled egg. There was also a pudding (apple crumble) as well as bowls of watery mash and limp cabbage. Felicity was on the macaroni cheese, which was a pale, glutinous mass exhaling a miasma of long-imprisoned feet.

'Right, girls,' Miss Allsop called, 'smiles on faces, please!'

They all obediently bared their teeth. The door was opened and the public jostled in. Here Miss Allsop came into her own, raising her voice to a parade-ground level.

'No pushing! Keep in line, please! Only one meat dish per customer! Tickets at the till!'

The system was a simple one. For a set price of sixpence, customers could have a meal consisting of one meat, egg or cheese dish, a pudding and a cup of tea. The steak and kidney pie was ninepence. The macaroni cheese was popular, and Felicity was thrown at once into the fray, taking tickets and dolloping portions onto the plates that were held out to her.

The parade of faces in front of her was bewildering at first. There were mothers with smudged eyes and drawn-looking children, obviously recently bombed out of their homes; elderly bachelors or widowers in cloth caps; some prosperous-looking couples who'd run out of ration coupons and who inspected their plates dubiously, as though this fare were not what they were used to; young people who looked as though they were runaways sleeping rough; a few tramps and alcoholics, some soldiers and sailors on leave, some Poles and Czechs, a wide assortment of humanity with hunger in common. None were refused. Some smiled and thanked Felicity, some avoided her eye and scowled as though they hated to accept this charity. Some muttered pleas for a larger helping, which invariably drew a rebuke from the eagle-eyed Miss Allsop.

As they worked, the girls around Felicity continued their conversations in asides.

'So I said, I'll be buggered if I will. 'E says, you'll be buggered if you won't. Next, please!'

'No, I can't give you egg *and* cheese, lovey, sorry. I turned around and 'e's only lookin' up me skirt, ain't 'e? I gave 'im such a slap 'is silly glasses fell off. Next!'

By two o'clock the ladles were loudly scraping the bottoms of the warming trays. The last stragglers were ushered out and the task of clearing up began. Tired as she was, Felicity found herself back at the sink. But by now she had been caught up in the humming energy of the women around her, which buoyed her above her weariness. Besides, the great task of feeding the hungry had been accomplished; and lo, there was now hot water.

Apart from a few jokes, most of which had passed over her head, the other girls hadn't singled her out in any way. However, now that the meals had been served, a group formed inquisitively around her.

'What's it like, then, being a nun?' The questioner was a little, bird-like woman with curls and circular glasses, named Peggy.

Felicity was nonplussed for a moment, wondering how to explain something so remote. 'Well, for Carmelites it's a very quiet life,' she said. 'There's a lot of time to pray . . . and think . . .'

'Oh, that sounds lovely,' Peggy said with a sigh.

'Sounds dead boring,' someone else said.

'Can't be more boring than the bloody war. I'm sick of it. And you got to wear the same outfit, day after day?'

'Exactly the same outfit,' Felicity said gravely.

'They say you 'ave to bath in a shift 'cos otherwise God would see you naked?'

'God sees us naked anyway,' Felicity said aphoristically, wanting to stay off the subject of baths.

'Why'd you leave?' asked Ginger, the confident redhead who'd first come to Felicity's rescue at the sink. 'Did they throw you out?'

'I threw myself out,' Felicity said.

'You didn't get up to any hanky-panky or nothing?'

'Oh, no. I was just — I was very unhappy there for a long time.'

'Well, what did you expect when you signed up?' Ginger demanded in her forthright way.

'Actually, I expected great happiness.'

'What, with no men, no music, no booze, no dancing?' Ginger was a handsome, strapping young woman who would have plenty of success with the opposite sex, Felicity guessed, and seemed to have no interest in anything else. 'You might as well bury yourself alive.'

'I didn't see it that way.'

'How long was you there?'

'Almost five years.'

'Five years of your life gone.' This came from Gladys, a pretty Welsh girl with very pale skin and green eyes which searched Felicity's face. 'Don't you regret it?'

'I regret making the wrong decision,' Felicity replied. 'But I thought I was doing the right thing at the time.'

'I can't stand religion,' Gladys said. 'I had enough of it rammed down my throat when I was a kid. You'd have to drag me kicking and screaming into a chapel now. But I s'pose you came from a religious family.'

'As a matter of fact my family were horrified. They thought I was insane. Most of them still aren't talking to me.'

'And you still went in,' Ginger said.

'Yes.'

'And now you're 'ere.'

'Yes.'

'Well, you shouldn't be.'

'Why not?' Felicity asked.

'Yeah, why shouldn't she?' Gladys said protectively. 'Why d'you want to go and make her feel unwelcome?'

'She ain't unwelcome,' Ginger said, hefting several dozen plates in her arms, 'but she don't belong here.'

'Why ever not?'

'For one thing, she's a lady. She's never been in a kitchen in her life, except to order the dinner. She don't know the sink from her arse. For another – well, look at her.' Ginger set down the plates with a crash on the counter. 'She's a pollywog.'

There was a chorus of mingled laughter and protest. Ginger's Cockney voice cut through it easily. 'I'm not saying it's her fault, or nothing. But she ain't cut out for hard work. She can hardly pick up a bar of soap, she's that weak. She's half-fainting already and it's only her first day. She's going to go falling in fits by and by, and probably take two dozen of His Majesty's best china plates with her.'

They all stared at Felicity, who stood frozen, with her hands in the sink, wishing the earth would open and swallow her. Even Miss Allsop was looking at her speculatively. She felt a wave of dizziness, as though Ginger's prediction were about to come true and she were going to flop to the ground. She opened her mouth. ' "I know I have the body of a weak and feeble woman," ' she heard herself say, ' "but I have the heart and stomach of a king, and of a king of England." '

There was a silence. 'What's she on about?' Ginger asked, looking baffled.

Miss Allsop laughed quietly. 'Over your head, Ginger Perkins. She's quoting from History. Back to work, please, girls.'

The bustle resumed. Gladys nudged Felicity. 'Well done,' she murmured. 'Don't let her get you down. She's too full of herself by half.'

Felicity, however, felt battered by the encounter, a frail rowboat that had somehow avoided being sunk by a trawler. At least nobody bothered her again and she lapsed back into being invisible. She got through the next hour of work, by which time it was four, and they were ready to knock off.

As Felicity was putting on her coat, Ginger came over to her. Felicity's heart sank. Ginger put her fists on her hips, glowering. 'What was all that about the stomach of a king?'

'Queen Elizabeth said that in 1588 when the Spanish were about to invade.'

'Yeah?' Ginger still looked suspicious. 'You weren't being snarky about my size?'

'Oh no! You're a perfect size!'

Ginger sucked her full lower lip, surveying Felicity dispassionately. 'Well, I can't have you going around like that. Your hair's in a shocking state. You got eyebrows like George Robey. And a moustache like Lloyd George.'

'Am I really that bad?' Felicity said with a weak smile.

Ginger took her arm in red-nailed and proprietorial fingers. 'You're coming with me.'

The girls poured out of the restaurant in a noisy group, instantly attracting the attention of every man in the street. Their peals of laughter and squeals of mock dismay, Felicity realized, were mating calls, recognized as such by the opposite sex. Several of the girls had men waiting for them, and paired off. She allowed herself to be led unwillingly along the street by Ginger. 'Where are we going?'

Ginger ignored the question. 'You watch out for that Gladys Williams. The Welsh are all tea leaves.'

'Tea leaves?'

'Thieves. You can't trust 'em.'

'Any of them?' Felicity asked.

'Nor the Irish, nor the Jocks. Northerners are the same. The only people you can trust is Londoners. And only East Enders, out of them.'

They reached a door where Ginger rang the bell. The woman who opened was a surprisingly soignée apparition in that dingy street, wearing a long dress and pearls. Middle-aged, with heavy-lidded eyes and a cigarette in an amber holder, she surveyed Felicity slowly from head to toe. 'Now. What have we here?'

'This is Felicity, Mrs Hunt.' Ginger pushed Felicity forward with a firm hand. 'She's just escaped from a convent.'

'So I see,' Mrs Hunt drawled, drawing on her cigarette.

'Can you fix her up?'

'One can but try.'

'I'll leave you to it, then,' Ginger said, setting off down the street. 'Ta ta!'

Felicity was alarmed to see her go. 'Where are you going?'

'It's Saturday night,' Ginger threw over her shoulder. 'No time to waste!'

'Come into my parlour.' Mrs Hunt extended a languid hand and drew Felicity in.

❧

Mrs Hunt's parlour was set up as a beauty salon, with various little tables, on each of which was piled an assortment of greasy bottles and implements. The woman herself had the drowsy air of a sleepwalker, emphasized by her dark eye shadow and thickly made-up lashes.

'Did you climb over the wall, dear?'

'Something like that.'

'How long were you a nun?'

'Almost five years.'

'Half your life, then. Well, the girl is out of the convent. I wonder if we can get the convent out of the girl.' She led Felicity to the window and studied her, slowly champing the mouthpiece of her cigarette holder. 'At least you're skinny,' she said at last, 'that's a mercy. And the facial bones are good. Here's what I'll do for you. Eyebrows, one and fourpence. Upper lip, two shillings – I'll use the machine to do that, it won't grow back. Manicure, a shilling. Hair, half a crown, but I don't guarantee anything. And I'll throw in a facial for free. You'll come and see me next Saturday and we'll see what more needs to be done. How's that?'

It was almost seven shillings altogether. The cost of beauty was exorbitant. Felicity took out her purse and counted her change anxiously. 'Can I owe you the half-crown until next week?'

'You look trustworthy, dear,' Mrs Hunt drawled. 'Shall we get started?'

Felicity looked around at the shabby little room. It was the memory of being called a pollywog that decided her. She decided to embrace the future. 'Yes, please.'

Very little of what followed was comfortable. The electrolysis (which Mrs Hunt dispensed from a small suitcase, using a device like a stylus attached to a battery) was the worst, each hair on her upper lip giving up its ghost with a sharp pang. Her eyebrows, dealt with by means of tweezers, were scarcely less painful. Her nails were trimmed, filed, shaped, buffed and coated in pink varnish.

Mrs Hunt then set about her hair with a pair of very sharp scissors. While she was doing this, the front doorbell rang twice. Each time a man came in, who was ushered tactfully into the back parlour.

'Customers, dear,' Mrs Hunt informed Felicity in her drawling way. 'Don't worry, they'll wait.'

'Are they having beauty treatment too?' Felicity asked innocently.

'Not exactly, dear. But I'll make them feel beautiful, don't you worry about that. Hard to tell what your natural colour is. You're a blonde, I take it?'

'Well, I used to be.'

Mrs Hunt reached for the peroxide. 'And shall be again, dear.'

The result of the cut, bleach, wash and dry was surprising. Looking in the mirror, Felicity saw that Mrs Hunt had somehow turned her crazy tendrils of hair into a mop of curls that was almost flattering. Even the colour had changed, from a drab grey (which it had taken on in the priory) to something like its former gold. Her eyebrows had been thinned and shaped, giving her a more appealing expression. Her upper lip was less than beautiful, being swollen and reddened by the electrolysis, but Mrs Hunt assured her that would fade in a day or two.

'I'll do your facial now,' she said. 'And then a mask. You've got good skin, I must say. Another blessing.'

After the prodding, pinching and scrubbing, she plastered Felicity's face with some mud-like, marshy smelling substance. 'You'll have to lie still for twenty minutes, dear, which will just give me time to attend to one of my gentlemen. Think pure thoughts.'

Felicity tried to obey, and lay feeling the mud slowly dry and pull tight on her face. From upstairs (where Mrs Hunt had gone with one of her gentlemen) came a series of rhythmical, muffled thuds, as though someone were dancing the rhumba on a sofa. The pace increased steadily and ended *prestissimo*. A short while later, the gentleman came down the stairs and let himself discreetly out. Could it be that Mrs Hunt had . . . her mind sought a polite word . . . *entertained* him? And would shortly entertain the other gentleman? Today had been a day, Felicity thought, on which she had Seen Life.

Before Felicity left the house, Mrs Hunt had sold her (and shown her how to use) a stub of someone's red lipstick, a half-used eyeliner, a battered compact containing a trace of face powder and half a pot of Vaseline for her eyelashes.

'That's gold, dear,' Mrs Hunt said. 'Cosmetics are very hard to come by these days. Come back and see me next week. I'll continue your education.' One midnight-blue eyelid descended in the ghost of a wink.

On the bus home, Felicity studied her hands. Mrs Hunt's creams and treatments had made them young and pretty again. She hadn't realized how chapped and dry they had become. And the pink nail varnish had been an inspired choice. The problem now would be to defend them from the daily battering of her new job. She would have to ask Ginger Perkins how she kept her hands nice-looking.

Hearing murmurs, she looked up. Annoyingly, two soldiers were staring at her. Then she realized that it was not the sort of stare she had been accustomed to. It was a new sort of stare, of frank admiration. One of them winked and grinned. She kept a straight face and looked away. Was that all it took to turn from a freak into an object of desire?

She got back to Tisbury Mansions at nine in the evening. It had been a long day. She was exhausted but happy. She let herself in. Chiara, who had been listening to the radio, got up to look at her.

'I was so worried about you.' She stopped short. 'My God. What have you done to yourself? Are you wearing lipstick? And your eyebrows!'

'I went for a hairdo and a beauty treatment,' Felicity said airily. She held out her nails for admiration. 'And a manicure.'

Chiara inspected her in silence. 'Well, you've certainly joined Modern Womanhood. With a vengeance.'

Felicity touched her upper lip. 'The swelling will go down. I had electrolysis. I thought you'd be pleased! Don't I look nice?'

'You certainly look different, darling. Not exactly respectable. In fact, not to put too fine a point on it, you look a bit of a tart.'

'One of life's ironies.' Felicity retorted. 'I look like a tart but I'm perfectly respectable. Whereas you're the other way around.'

She'd spoken hastily – and bitterly – but she'd had enough insults for one day. She went to her room, leaving Chiara open-mouthed.

It was not a good start to their weekend, and they hardly addressed a word to each other after that. Chiara was missing her Oliver, who had been abroad since the spring, but Felicity resented the implication that Chiara had to be treated with the deference owing to a widow. Half the women in Britain had a loved one overseas. Chiara's notion that she was to be an object of pity annoyed Felicity. She herself had nobody to love – and nobody who loved her – and the desolation of that state of existence was something Chiara knew nothing about.

And then there was Isobel.

Isobel had burst back onto the world's stage with a vengeance. Last seen as a supporter of Hitler and Mussolini, reviled in the British press as a Fascist, she had somehow reinvented herself as a champion of the underdog. Her lurid novel – one couldn't really call it an autobiography, though it was clearly meant to be understood as such – had been a sensation when it had come out last year, complete with explicit sex scenes and a detailed account of the miscarriage which had ended the affair.

Then there had been the obviously staged photograph in *LIFE*, of Isobel averting Willoughby's suicide by dragging his gun away from his temple. Despair saved by Hope. It was all a rich and steamy concoction, and it had upset Felicity terribly. Truth be told, it was after reading *A Country of the Heart* (smuggled into the priory and read under the library counter in a brown paper cover) that Felicity had realized she could no longer remain in the priory.

William Willoughby had occupied a special place in her heart for years. Her love for him might have been a juvenile infatuation, but she had preserved it exactly as it was, enshrined it, locked it away in her soul as something sacred. Isobel's book had torn open the tabernacle and profaned the contents. By her own admission, Isobel had treated William brutally, squeezing the emotional juice out of the relationship and then discarding him. That filled Felicity with bitterness. William had been *hers*, and Isobel had sworn not to touch him. Now she had not only touched him, but desecrated him.

Finally divorced from Roberto and enjoying her notoriety, Isobel was currently in America, mobilizing support there for the British war effort – with all the zeal of a reformed alcoholic preaching against the demon drink.

'I have met Adolf Hitler and I have looked into his eyes,' her lectures began. They ended to rapturous applause and a rain of dollars.

Which left only herself, Felicity the Infelicitous, with nothing. No home, no friends, no money, no comfortable male protector, a pollywog at the mercy of every jeer and snide remark.

How had it happened? She had followed a course which she had believed with all her heart to be right and good and true. It had left her washed up in her sister's flat, unwanted, unlovely and unloved, wearing other women's clothes and other women's make-up. She had only herself to blame, but what had it all been about?

៚

She had learned one thing, at least, which was that working women in their twenties did not go to their jobs without make-up; so on

Monday morning, she used the lipstick and powder as Mrs Hunt had shown her, and set off for Trinidad Street.

'You look lovely,' Gladys Williams said approvingly. 'Nobody's going to call you names, now.'

'Who's called her names?' Ginger said aggressively. 'I'd like to see them try, Gladys Williams.' Later in the morning, Ginger passed by Felicity as she was peeling a mountain of potatoes and paused to examine Felicity's hair and nails. 'She fixed you up nicely.'

'Oh yes, thanks so much, Ginger. She was very nice.' Felicity hesitated. 'There were some men there . . .'

'So?'

'She went upstairs with them.'

'Yeah?'

'Well, I wanted to ask, is she . . .'

'Is she what? A prozzie?' Ginger looked scornful. 'What do *you* think?'

'Well, I don't know what to think. Only, if I'm to go back there—'

'Know what the men call her? Mrs Something-that-rhymes-with-Hunt, but ain't. Don't worry, you won't catch nothing off her. She's very select, even if she is on the game. And she knows her stuff. At least you look human, now. You stick with her and you could soon be in the same line of business.' Amused by her own humour, Ginger went her way.

The week that followed was hard. The physical labour of the kitchen – peeling vegetables, scouring pans, mopping floors – would have been well within the capabilities of any ordinary woman of her age. But Felicity had lost weight drastically in the convent, and the long bouts of asthma had weakened her system. She ended each day exhausted, and returned to face her sister's icy disapproval, which didn't help.

But she willed herself to keep going, whatever her feelings were. And each day at Trinidad Street was like going to a play, full of bawdy humour, social drama and rough kindness. There were occasional flare-ups. If they got too fierce, Miss Allsop would command the participants to 'take it outside', which meant into the malodorous back alley, where the dustbins stood. Contestants sometimes returned from these excursions with scratched faces, but generally the restaurant ran smoothly and the girls all got along – and Felicity found that she was Fitting In. It was not a feeling she'd experienced much in her life.

And her strength slowly returned. By the end of the week, Miss Allsop had an approving word for her.

'This has been good for you, Felicity. I knew it would be. I'm pleased with your work.'

It had been a long time since she'd had such warm praise from anybody. 'Thank you, Miss Allsop.'

'You're putting your back into it. I admire that. And your personal appearance has improved enormously. We may be Socialists here, but that does not mean we need frighten the horses!' Miss Allsop chuckled. 'You've been in the Melting Pot and you're turning to gold.' She touched Felicity's hair fondly. 'Literally.'

'I reckon she's a bit of a lezzie,' Ginger said as they walked out, 'but you're probably used to that.'

'Why should I be used to that?' Felicity snapped. 'Everybody thinks they know all about nuns! None of you know anything!'

'All right, keep your 'air on,' Ginger said, laughing. 'You going to see Mrs H?'

'I owe her half a crown.'

'I'll walk with you.' Eileen, Ginger's large friend, accompanied them along the road. 'Nice to see you getting a bit stroppy. I reckon you're going to be all right. You coming out tonight?'

'Where to?'

'The Paramount.'

'What's that?'

'Don't you know anything? Paramount Dance Hall, Tottenham Court Road.'

'I don't think so,' Felicity said quickly.

'Why not?'

'I'm not a very good dancer.'

'Who cares about that?' Eileen said, laughing. 'It's Saturday night! Everybody goes to have fun, not win prizes. Most of the girls from the canteen will be there. What you going to do instead? Sit by the radio and wish you were someone else?'

The thought of a Saturday evening doing exactly that – under Chiara's disapproving eye – was crushing. What could be worse? 'I might come,' she said reluctantly.

'You better,' Ginger threatened, 'or we'll come and get you.'

'But I don't have anything to wear.'

'Get yourself a frock from Mrs H. I'm sick of the sight of those corduroys, anyway. Give 'em back to the tramp you pinched 'em off.'

'We'll be waiting for you,' Eileen said. 'Eight-thirty. Don't stand us up!'

Mrs Hunt had a rail of pretty rayon frocks, all at seven and sixpence. Like much of what Mrs Hunt sold, including herself, most had been used by others. Felicity picked out one with a pattern of pink roses on green leaves. She had never in her life chosen anything so colourful or gay. But the porridge colours she'd been brought up with were now as ancient as the Ark. Some further attention to her hair was necessary, as was another mani-cure, and she left Mrs Hunt to her gentlemen, eleven shillings the poorer.

It was an unfortunate coincidence that Chiara should have cho-sen that day to offer an olive branch.

'I've been given two tickets to a piano recital,' she said when Felicity arrived home. 'Moura Lympany playing Brahms. Shall we go?'

'Oh, I wish you'd told me earlier,' Felicity said in dismay. 'I've promised the girls at work I'd go to a dance with them.'

'You? Going to dance?'

'The Paramount in the Tottenham Court Road,' Felicity said uncomfortably.

Chiara's face closed. 'Oh, well, I'm sure you can pick up a nice sailor there. Beats Brahms any day.'

'I'm sorry, Chiara,' Felicity said remorsefully, but Chiara was in a huff and remained aloof. There was nothing further to be said.

Wearing the frock Mrs Hunt had sold her was a new experience in itself. It was such a light, gauzy garment that she felt all but naked. After the years of wearing layer upon layer of clothing, winter and summer, this scrap of coloured rayon felt positively indecent, as though she were contemplating going out in her underwear. Luckily it was a warm evening.

And à propos of underwear, when she tried a few experimental pirouettes, the skirt billowed up airily almost to her hips. Could she wear such a thing to a dance? It was improper in the extreme. She wanted to ask Chiara, but there was no support to be expected from that quarter. She would simply have to restrict her movements to the most sedate steps – waltzes and foxtrot at the most. And embrace the future. Her heart was beating faster. The last time she'd been to a dance had been a lifetime ago, as a teenager. She was looking forward to the evening ahead with mingled dread, curiosity and excitement. Her stomach was in too much of a knot to feel hunger, so she had nothing to eat. She put on a coat and said goodbye to Chiara.

Felicity emerged from the Underground station to find the Paramount right across the road. It was hard to miss. Under a pulsing neon canopy, like the opening to an electric fairyland, a crowd of several hundred people was jostling noisily, with several sweating police officers trying to keep order. Wishing she had an escort – say one of the many large males in uniform who abounded – she entered the fray. Bumped and squeezed on all sides, she made her way to the entrance and finally entered the dance hall with her heart racing.

It was a gaudy, glittering, wonderful spectacle. The huge hall was crowded with dancers. At the far end, a big band was playing jazz. From the roof hung a mirrored ball which scattered shards of light in all directions as it turned. Spotlights played on the crowd, changing colour as they revolved, bathing the dancers in warm and dappled rainbows. She stood in a dream, her mouth open. She had not expected this magic. Under these soft, radiant lights, everybody was beautiful – the women with glowing cheeks and arms, faces tilted up to look at the men. At least half the men were in uniform, as were many of the women. The civilian men were in tuxedos or dark suits, the women in vivid prints that added to the spellbinding effect.

Somebody grabbed her arm, shaking her out of her trance. It was Eileen. 'You've just earned me five bob,' she shouted. 'They all bet you wouldn't come!' She dragged Felicity round the dance floor to the far side, where a row of plush velvet settees was arranged against the wall. The settees were crowded with girls, men standing over them attentively. She recognized the Trinidad Street girls all in a group, with Ginger in the midst, her flaming red hair blazing in the moonlight gleams of the mirror ball. But if she'd thought them heavily made-up at work, that was nothing to their appearance now. Now they were queens, all flaws of complexion or features erased by cosmetics, hair immaculate, movements graceful, surrounded by assiduous courtiers bringing them drinks and cigarettes.

Suddenly Felicity understood why they lived for Saturday night. In this kaleidoscopic nirvana, the war ended. Bomb craters, austerity, air raids, work, danger, tomorrow – none of that existed here. This was a dream world of swinging jazz, swirling dresses and flowing colour.

'I never thought you'd turn up,' Ginger greeted her, grinning. 'You just cost me a shilling, young Felicity. One of you lot – get her a drink!'

Introductions were made. Ginger was with her 'steady', Albert, a corporal built on the same scale as she was.

'Oh,' Felicity said brightly, 'Sister Albert was my name in the convent.' She regretted the words at once as a silence fell, and Ginger rolled her eyes. Albert came to her rescue with a funny story. He had an apparently endless supply of off-colour jokes, which made the girls writhe with laughter.

Most of the other men around the girls were American servicemen, their uniforms more elegant than their British counterparts (whose rough wool battledress never seemed to look anything but bulky). Several of them were black men, the first of their kind that Felicity had met. One of these, a softly spoken giant named Earl, whose voice she could hardly hear over the music, got her a drink, a bright pink confection that tasted innocuous but had her head spinning in no time.

Alas for her visions of stately waltzes and quicksteps! The dancing she remembered from her teens bore no resemblance to the joyous cavorting she saw here. Even the slow numbers were full of movement, and the fast numbers were frenetic. Every now and then the drummer – who was, even to Felicity's untrained ears, very good – would take a solo, whereupon the couples would separate and prance wildly to the pounding rhythms.

'Shall we dance?' Earl said, his lips close to her ear.

'I'm afraid I don't know any of these!' she replied in embarrassment.

'This is a nice slow one. You just hold on to me. You'll soon pick it up.'

He led her onto the floor and took her in his arms. The rhythm of the number was leisurely, but had a swing to it nevertheless. She saw at once that Earl was a very good dancer. All she had to do was keep her arms around him and follow his movements. She thought of William Willoughby and closed her eyes.

The floor was springy under her soles. In the press of the crowd, there was no need to be self-conscious. It was almost impossible to make small talk over the music, and Earl didn't try. However, when the band began to play a really fast number, she made a move to escape.

'It's the jitterbug,' he yelled, yanking her back. She had no idea what was required, but Earl didn't seem to mind that. He twirled her and twisted her with easy strength. All she had to do was maintain the stiff-legged posture that would keep her from collapsing. Like a rag doll, she spun. Her skirt swirled up around her waist, exactly as she had feared, revealing her bloomers. It didn't matter. Every other pair of bloomers on the dance floor was also seeing the light of day. More than that: some girls were being turned upside-down by their partners, their legs spread wide to give everyone an eyeful of their underwear. She giggled breathlessly. Earl swung her over his shoulder and the room whirled crazily.

Earl bought her another drink after that and then, to her disappointment, went off with another partner who was a far better dancer than she, marooning her on the purple velvet settee. She gulped at the fizzy concoction, feeling dizzy and drunk.

She was not alone for long. Ginger came off the floor with Albert, flushed pink, and grabbed her arm, hauling her to her feet. 'I need the ladies'. Come along.' The ladies' was a hubbub of jostling women, smelling of sweat and scent. Ginger fought her way to a sink and powdered her cheeks and nose, speaking to Felicity in the mirror. 'I'm glad you got rid of that Earl. The darkies are fun but the coppers don't like them, and there's always trouble outside. Listen. There's a Yank who wants to meet you. He's very interested in you.'

'Really?'

'He's an airman. A dreamboat, but quiet with it. Just your type.'

Felicity looked at her reflection in the mirror, a pale, insignificant-looking blonde with very short hair and big, frightened eyes. What dreamboat would be interested in her? 'I don't think I've got a type.'

Ginger glared at her. 'Don't be so bloody stupid. And don't mess this up. Okay?'

'Okay,' she saw Felicity-in-the-mirror say.

Ginger made her mouth into an O and applied crimson lipstick. A cubicle door swung open. She made a dash for it, pulling Felicity inside with her. There was scarcely room for the two of them. Ginger pulled down her knickers and sat on the loo, looking up at Felicity. 'Have you got a johnnie?'

A week at Trinidad Street had taught Felicity what a johnnie was. She was shocked at the question. 'Of course not!'

Ginger produced a little package from her purse. 'Make him put one on, even if he says he's got one of his own.'

'Oh, Ginger! I'm not going to—'

'Take it,' Ginger said impatiently. 'You never know your luck.'

Red with embarrassment, Felicity took the little packet from Ginger. 'I have no intention of sleeping with a complete stranger!'

'Well, of course not. But you'll be old pals before the night is out, darlin'. His name is Frank. And there are three in the packet.'

The orchestra was taking a break as they made their way back to their group, so animated conversation had broken out all over the dance hall. The bar was doing a roaring trade. The room lights had gone up and the coloured spots were off, but the mirror ball continued to revolve, sending glances of silver around the room. The boys had bought more drinks, and Felicity found herself clutching another brightly coloured, sweet-tasting potion. Why did they imagine that women only drank sickly things like this, she wondered.

'This is Frank,' she heard Ginger say. Felicity looked up from her drink. He was a tall, dark-haired man with velvety brown eyes and handsome, somewhat Latin features. His uniform was immaculate, the jacket tightly buttoned, and apparently tailored to his slim form. Silver wings gleamed over his breast pocket. He also had a campaign ribbon. He took her hand.

'I'm so happy to meet you,' he said. 'I've heard a lot about you.'

'Then I'm sure there's very little more to know,' she said with a nervous laugh.

He continued to hold her hand, looking into her eyes. 'I doubt that very much.' His voice was as velvety as his eyes, caressing her. They were about the same age, but he exuded the confidence of a much older man. He noticed her lime-green drink. 'That looks pretty nasty.'

'It is,' she assured him.

'What would you rather have?'

'My father always used to drink Scotch,' she said valiantly.

'He sounds like a man after my own heart.' He reached into his jacket and produced a silver flask. 'I guarantee this is better than the stuff at the bar.' He uncorked it and passed it to her. Having made a brave boast, she was compelled to take a swig. A rush of heat passed through her. She swayed against him.

'Oh, that's strong.'

'I have a buddy who's stationed up in Scotland. He gets it from the local distillery. Twelve years old.'

'It's wonderful,' she said hoarsely.

He had a lazy smile. The warm, hazel eyes never left her face. A lock of dark hair hung over his forehead. Ginger was right. He was a dreamboat.

The band struck up again. The lights dimmed to a misty haze and the swirling coloured spotlights began to spin. 'Shall we?' he asked, offering her his arm.

He was smooth in every way. He danced stylishly, holding her close to him with quiet confidence, putting his cheek against hers and talking in her ear so they could converse despite the music. The evening had suddenly become a lot more interesting.

He was very engaging. His name was Frank Carrillo and he was born in New York's South Side, the son of Italian immigrants. He had several brothers and sisters. He had been stationed in Norfolk for almost a year. When she asked him if he was a pilot, he laughed. 'I'm only a second lieutenant. I'm the bombardier in a Flying Fortress. But if I survive another couple of dozen missions, I'll apply for pilot school.'

His talk of surviving his next missions upset her. Frank was the first man on active duty she had met. He seemed to take the danger calmly. He had already flown twenty-two sorties over Germany. He rode in the nose of the plane, in a Plexiglas bubble, from where he controlled the dropping of the bombs.

'How did you get such a terribly dangerous job?' she asked him.

'I had much better depth perception than the other guys,' he replied. 'Which is why I'm so interested in you. I perceive that you have great depths.'

'And I perceive that you're on the make,' she replied tartly.

He smiled. 'Do you?'

'Yes. I have very good depth perception, too.'

'Then we have much in common.'

'You're very smooth.'

'I hope so.'

Felicity stroked his shoulder. 'Even your uniform is smooth. I'd be on the make, too, if I was risking my life every day, and was far from my home, and didn't know if I'd ever see my family again.'

'I like the direction this conversation is taking.'

She laughed. 'Unfortunately, I don't intend to be made. But there are plenty of much prettier girls who'll be happy to oblige.'

'I'm not interested in any other girls. Only you.'

She found him charming and exciting, even though she knew the alcohol had lowered her inhibitions. Everything in her life had always been so serious. A serious childhood, a serious adolescence; going into the convent with great seriousness, coming out with great seriousness. She had hardly known what fun was. But this was fun: dancing and flirting with a handsome young man in the combined haze of the music, the lights, the movement and the alcohol.

He wanted to know about the priory. 'There's nothing to tell,' she replied. 'A very boring story. I was called, but God changed his mind about me.'

'Maybe you were wrong about being called.'

'I don't think so. I think he just couldn't find a use for me once I'd got there.'

'So you haven't lost your religion?'

'No. Have you?'

Frank reached into his collar and pulled out a little St Christopher on a chain around his neck. He kissed it. 'This keeps me alive.'

'That's not religion, that's superstition.'

'You wouldn't say that if you saw what I see.' He dropped the medal back into his collar. 'Sometimes there's so much flak that it looks like midday at two in the morning. You can feel it ripping through the wings. Sometimes the fuselage is so full of holes, it looks like a cheese grater. After the bomb run, I have to check that everybody's okay. If they don't come back to me on the radio, I go down the plane to check on them. Sometimes I find my buddies dead or dying in their seats. Sometimes we have to land with an engine down, or two engines down. But me? Not a scratch. How do you explain that?'

'God is looking after you. But that's got nothing to do with that bit of tin round your neck.'

He smiled, showing teeth as white as cuttlebone. 'I can see why the Almighty fired you.'

'Ginger says I'm getting stroppy.'

'Is that another word for a smartass?'

'Probably.'

'Well, my Sicilian grandmother gave me this bit of tin round my neck, and I'm not letting it go.'

They watched the competition dances, which included some amazingly acrobatic jitterbugging, and then Frank suggested they go to a nightclub. They trooped out of the Paramount, in an excited group of nine or ten. On the pavement, Felicity caught sight of Earl, her first partner of the evening, in an altercation with some white soldiers, who were trying to pull his companion, a white girl, away from him. Fists started to fly. The police were already galloping over with truncheons drawn as they got into their taxis. She didn't want to look. Ginger had been right about that, too.

The nightclub was in a basement in Piccadilly. It was very crowded and the three-piece band was contending hotly with the laughter and conversation. However Frank, who seemed to have no shortage of money, passed the head waiter a ten-shilling note and some tables were pulled together in a corner for them. They had a view – through a dense haze of cigarette smoke – of the dance floor, which was so packed that the dancers could do little but struggle against each other. The place seemed to be a favourite haunt of American soldiers, each of whom had a girl hanging round his neck. Platinum blonde seemed the hair colour of preference. She was faintly disgusted until she recalled that she herself was yet another blonde with an American soldier.

Frank ordered food and drink. He had taken over leadership of their party without effort. The other Americans had opened their collars and loosened their ties, but Frank was still immaculate. Some bottles of Algerian wine materialized, together with a tray of *coquilles St Jacques* and half a dozen grilled partridges. They were all ravenous, and set to work eagerly.

'You're a miracle worker,' Felicity told Frank.

He shrugged easily. 'One does what one can.'

'You must be spending all your pay on us.'

'That's what it's for.'

That seemed to be the spirit of the age, Felicity reflected. Dance your heart out, spend your money, sleep with anyone, because tomorrow might not come. How different from the philosophy she'd lived by all her life, of denial, of storing up treasures in heaven. Here, the treasures were within reach, and heaven could wait. The scallops were served on real shells. She slipped one into her purse as a souvenir of the evening.

There was more dancing, more drinking, more shrieks of laughter. The evening turned into an Arabian Nights blur of colour and music. On the dance floor with Frank, she started to feel giddy and breathless. She was plastered, she realized. Another first.

When they got back to their table, some of the girls were falling asleep, heads lolling on their partners' shoulders. It was time to go home. Felicity's brain was throbbing as they made their way up the stairs and into the cool night air at three in the morning. Ginger was even drunker than she was, and went behind a telephone booth where she was copiously sick. Felicity went to help her, but Ginger seemed none the worse. 'Fucking wine,' she said, 'give me a

Guinness any day.' She accepted the hanky Felicity offered her, and wiped her mouth. 'I told you he was a dreamboat, didn't I?'

'Yes, you did.'

'He looks at you like you was the last slice of cake on the plate. My Albert used to look at me like that. You still got your johnnies? You ain't used them on some other bloke?'

'No,' Felicity laughed, 'I won't be using them on anybody.'

'More fool you, then. Don't lose him!'

Frank insisted on seeing Felicity home. They all said goodbye with much hugging and kissing. By luck, two taxis came along together. She and Frank got into one, the rest all piled into the other.

In the darkness of the taxi, she turned to Frank. 'I've had a lovely evening,' she said, her words a little slurred.

By way of an answer, Frank took her in his arms and kissed her on the mouth. She was so taken by surprise that she didn't react at first. It was literally the first time a man had kissed her. The sensation swiftly became electric. She squirmed, but she was not certain whether she was trying to get closer, or to get away. She had been admiring his mouth all evening. It was full and curved, and reminded her of certain film stars, like Cary Grant and Gregory Peck. And now it was pressed against hers.

She pushed him away, breathless. 'I'm not ready for that!'

'But I am,' he said, closing in on her again. 'I've been waiting all night. You're so goddamn sexy.'

She'd had no idea that kissing was so sweet, or so physical. When you saw it in the movies, it looked noble and usually quite dignified. Frank's mouth was alive, tender and strong. Moreover, he had cupped the back of her neck in one hand so she could not escape again, and the other – she was thrilled and appalled to feel that the other was unfastening the buttons of her dress and slipping inside to cup her breast.

'The cabbie!' she hissed.

'He's seen it all before,' Frank said, applying his mouth to hers again. And indeed, with one eye she saw that the cab driver was looking stolidly at the road ahead, munching on a sandwich. Frank's fingers were gentle but strong. They made short work of her brassiere, which was rather old and tired, and then explored her breasts. She'd spent so many years repressing the moods of her body that it was a shock to remember that her breasts were capable of erotic sensations; especially when he possessively squeezed her nipples. That sent the electric impulses shooting down into her loins. This was sin, or had been until a short while ago. Waves of conflicting discomfort, excitement and curiosity struggled in her. She dug her elbows into him.

'Frank! You're hurting me!'

'Sorry,' he said remorsefully. 'I've been aching to do that all evening.' They were driving through the streets of Mayfair now. He started to kiss her again, but this time more gently, and this time with his mouth open. The warm, wet touch of his tongue was yet another shock. It was a surprisingly strong organ. The sensation of it inserting itself between her teeth was at first intrusive, then pleasant. She had backed away from him as far as she could, but now she was wedged in the corner of the seat, with no further retreat possible. She gave herself up to the shared luscious caresses of their tongues. It was all part of the magic of the evening, another intoxication.

Frank's hand, having withdrawn from her breasts, now began to stroke her knees. 'You drive me crazy!' he whispered. 'You're such a little snow-white virgin, with those big eyes and that adorable pink mouth. I can just see you in a wimple.' His fingers roamed higher, delicately stroking the sensitive skin of her thighs. This produced a sensation of almost unbearable anticipation in that part of her body which she had relegated to the lowest rank of consequence during the priory years, but which was now growing very swiftly in importance.

However, when his fingers slipped into her bloomers and touched the melting flesh there, a dart of such intense pleasure leaped through her that she knew at once it was a mortal sin. She clamped her knees shut and pushed him away with a firm, 'No!'

Luckily, they were just arriving at Chiara's flat and further explorations into this uncharted territory were curtailed. 'Can I see you next weekend?' Frank asked.

'If you promise to behave.'

'I promise. Give me your number.' He wrote it down, then walked her to the entrance. 'I'll be dreaming about you all week, Felicity.'

'Will you be flying a mission?' she asked. Her legs were wobbly and her heart was still pounding.

'I'm not supposed to talk about that,' he replied.

'Oh, I'm so sorry! I forgot!'

He smiled. 'Don't worry about anything. St Christopher will protect me.'

'I'll pray for you.'

They embraced tightly on the doorstep. She let herself into the building and Frank drove away in the taxi. She found she was trembling, her underwear in disarray, her buttons still undone. It had been an unexpected evening. The most unexpected thing of all was that he wanted her, and wanted to see her again. She found herself laughing out of sheer happiness.

※

Chiara was cool the next morning, when Felicity finally dragged herself out of bed.

'I hope I didn't wake you up last night when I came in,' Felicity said apologetically.

'I was already awake. I don't sleep very well, as you know.' She examined Felicity's bleary eyes and pale face dispassionately. 'You look awful.'

'I don't feel too good. I think I had too much to drink.'

'You certainly smell like it.'

'Sorry. How was the concert?'

'Ravishing. How was the dance?'

Felicity poured herself a cup of tea from the pot Chiara had made. 'An education.'

'Did you pick up a sailor?'

'No. But I met a very nice American airman.'

Chiara sighed. 'Oh, God. Darling, please be sensible.'

'His name's Frank. You'd like him. He's charming and generous and so handsome. And he has a terribly dangerous job – he's the bombardier in a Flying Fortress.'

'Really.'

'Lots of his friends have been killed already. They're making such a great sacrifice.'

'You're such an innocent. He's probably a cook in the camp kitchen.'

Felicity put her cup down in shock. 'How can you be so cynical?'

'How can you be so naïve?' Chiara replied. 'Men like that will say anything to get a girl into bed. It's the oldest trick in the book to pretend to be a war hero. Sleep with me now, I might be dead next week.'

'He is not one of those!'

'How do you know? You meet a complete stranger at a dance and take him at face value. Well, good luck to you, but don't expect me to sing hallelujah.'

'I don't understand you,' Felicity said. 'You've become so bitter.'

'And you've never grown up.' Chiara retorted, folding her paper. 'Listen to yourself, Fee. A month ago you were in a convent, sworn to eternal chastity. Now you're in love with some cowboy you've just met in the Tottenham Court Road—'

'I am not in love with him,' Felicity interrupted.

'The last time you looked at a man, you were nineteen years old. You know absolutely nothing about the world. It's absurd to hurl your virginity at the first plausible male you encounter.'

'I haven't hurled my virginity at anyone!'

'Well, you're clearly planning to.' Chiara tossed something onto the table. It was the little package of condoms that Ginger had given her last night. 'All prepared, are we?'

Felicity felt her face flush hotly. 'One of the girls gave that to me. She wouldn't take no for an answer! And how dare you dig in my bag?'

'I didn't have to dig, darling,' Chiara said in her most maddening drawl, 'it fell out of your bag, along with a scallop shell.'

Upset, Felicity snatched up the package and threw it into the wastepaper basket. 'You're doing it again! Tearing down everything that's precious to me!'

'I just wonder,' Chiara said in the same cool way, 'how you can have the barefaced cheek to call me immoral when you behave in this way.'

'I never called you immoral.'

'You make it clear that you despise me. You called me a tart.'

'You called *me* a tart!'

'I said you *looked* like a tart. Which you do. And now your behaviour matches. You transform yourself with bewildering dexterity, Fee. I can hardly keep up.'

Felicity tried to control her dismay and anger. She didn't want any more fights with Chiara. 'Yes, I made a terrible mistake with my life. And yes, I'm trying to reinvent myself now. It's not easy. I know I have a lot to learn.' She gulped down the tears that suddenly came. 'In fact, I've realized that I know nothing at all. That's the hardest thing to accept. I'm halfway through my twenties and I have no wisdom, no experience, no background. Nothing. There's no dexterity about it. I'm floundering, Chiara.' She paused. 'I don't despise you. I envy you so much.'

Chiara's face changed. 'Why on earth do you envy me?'

'Can't you see? You have everything that I don't. A home, a life, someone who adores you and whom you adore. You've made a success of your life.'

'Not so much,' Chiara replied quietly. 'If the truth be told, I have also made my own path thorny. I was as free as a bird until Oliver. Now I'm bereft without him. I wait every day to hear that he's been killed. And even if he does come back to me, he'll never be truly mine. I can only ever have a part of him. I'll probably be hanging around on the outskirts of his life until I'm grey. I won't have his children, and when he's gone, I won't want anyone else's. You're the one who's free. And I'm the one who envies you. You can make your life any way you want to. I just hope you won't be a fool, and waste more years on a bad decision.'

'I don't want to do that, either.'

Chiara drummed her fingers on the table as though debating what to say next. 'Isobel and I were both dismayed when you wanted to become a nun. We thought it was a terrible waste of your life, and we were certain you'd be wretched. That's why we tried to talk you out of it, not because we wanted to stop you from fulfilling yourself. When I came to see you in the priory, I was terrified. I thought you were dying. That's why I made that fuss. I was convinced I would never see you again. I cried all the way back to London.'

Felicity was silenced. At last she said, 'I'm sorry I put you through that. I still thought I could make a go of it at that point. I didn't understand that God was telling me to get out. I shouldn't have screamed at you. Forgive me.'

'I forgive you,' Chiara said. 'But you're an insufferable little prig, and I feel like strangling you sometimes.'

Felicity smiled weakly. 'I'm not really going to jump into bed with Frank. I'm not such an imbecile.' She held out her hands to Chiara. Chiara took them in her own. 'Let's be friends again.'

'All right,' Chiara said with a sigh, 'let's be friends. But maybe we can only do that if we forget we're sisters.'

'I don't ever want to forget that. Can't we be both? And I'll try and join the Grown-Ups Club, I promise.'

They held each other tight.

At Trinidad Street on Monday morning she was greeted with much curiosity. Everyone, it seemed, had heard about Frank. Ginger led the questions.

'So what 'appened after?'

'He took me home in a taxi,' Felicity replied, embarrassed by the attention.

'Did he spend the night?'

'Of course not!'

'So what, then?'

'We said good night and he left.'

'You didn't get off with him on the back seat or nothing?' Eileen demanded.

'Absolutely not,' Felicity said stoutly, feeling her cheeks grow hot.

'He's a real dish,' Ginger announced, 'and he fancies her something rotten. Written all over his gorgeous mug.'

But later in the morning, Gladys Williams had something else to say. 'He's only interested in you because you've been a nun,' she told Felicity. 'You being a virgin, that's the attraction.' She smiled, showing the tips of pearly teeth. 'Mind you, you got to give it to someone, haven't you? May as well be him. 'Course, once he's had you, you can say ta-ta.'

This poisonous little comment festered in her mind all day. Some of the things Frank had said to her on Saturday night suggested it might be true. Men loved to boast of having taken a woman's virginity, she knew that. The Don Giovanni syndrome. She was certainly not planning anything carnal, but it clouded her happiness to think that Frank's attention might stem from an ulterior motive.

A week of hard work followed. A bombing raid set alight the docks not far from Trinidad Street, and for days they worked in a miasma of soot and ash, with the constant clangour of fire engines passing down the street. The raid brought extra customers to the restaurant, dazed-looking, dirty families who had lost their homes. Extra food had to be brought in and the ticket system was waived for the new arrivals. It also meant that everybody worked extra hours each day, so Felicity got home late and tired.

She thought about Frank from time to time during this week, but the warnings given by Chiara and Gladys Williams had cast a cloud over her happiness. Her virginity had not been an issue for many years. She had given herself entirely to God, as a Bride of Christ, and had never expected to think of it again.

Before that, it had hardly been relevant either. Her mother had died long before such issues could come up, although there had once been a brisk little talk from Aunt Patsy about 'keeping pure', which had not, in the event, been necessary. Pure she had been and pure she remained. But she was no longer either a nun or an adolescent. And in this summer of 1942, keeping pure was as irrelevant as the rituals in the 'Etiquette for Young Ladies' she had learned in the early 1930s.

On Saturday afternoon she went for what was becoming her regular weekly visit to Mrs Hunt.

'The girls tell me you've got a beau,' Mrs Hunt said, squinting through cigarette smoke as she did Felicity's nails.

'He's not my beau,' Felicity said.

'But he does exist?'

'He's just someone I've met.'

'Seeing him tonight?'

'I think so. At least, he said he would come down. He's stationed in Norfolk.'

Mrs Hunt sucked her teeth. 'An American fly boy? Plenty of them about. Just as well. A lot of them take off and don't come back again.'

Felicity snatched her hand away. 'Don't talk like that!' she said angrily.

The creases in Mrs Hunt's face were artfully lined with powder, and her eyelashes were clotted with mascara. In a dim glow, she looked thirty, but in the harsh light of her work lamp she looked closer to seventy. 'And you say he's not your beau,' she said dryly. 'I didn't mean anything by it. Keep your hair on.' She retrieved Felicity's hand and resumed filing. 'Plenty more fish in the sea, that's all I'm saying.'

'I hardly know him, Mrs Hunt.'

'You hardly know anything, dearie,' Mrs Hunt retorted in her deadpan way. 'You're not in the convent any more. Things are simpler on the inside, as my Alf used to say. On the outside, there are no rules to follow.'

It was, in its way, yet another warning. She wished, however, that somebody would tell her what to do, rather than what not to do. But on the tube train to Tottenham Court Road that evening, her heart was fluttering like a snared bird; and when she saw Frank, dazzlingly handsome in his uniform, his white teeth flashing in a grin, she could not help throwing her arms around him, just as the other girls did with their beaux. The outside world ceased to exist from that moment.

The evening was more frenetic than last time. The big band, glamorous against a backdrop of quilted purple satin, pounded out the hot tunes of that summer, and the dance floor was jammed all night. The music was too loud for conversation, but the way Frank smiled at her made Felicity's stomach quiver with butterflies.

Instead of going to a nightclub, they went to a large and very grand private house in Chelsea, which was thronged with people. The crowd was mixed, some of the men in dinner jackets and the women in long dresses, others in various uniforms. In the drawing room, a man was playing Cole Porter numbers on a grand piano. A woman in green sequins was singing. A few couples were dancing in the crush. There didn't seem to be a host or hostess, but from time to time a grave butler dispensed champagne on a huge silver tray, which he locked carefully into a cabinet after each round.

'Come on,' Frank said, 'You gotta see this.' Drinks in hands, they migrated down the stairs to the basement. A large room had been set up as a private cinema, and here at last they met the host, a very respectable-looking middle-aged man selling tickets at the door. Frank produced a sheaf of money and they were admitted to the darkness.

The film being projected was silent, but the action was self-explanatory. A naked man and woman were making love on a divan, watched by a French maid from behind a curtain. The camera investigated every angle to ensure that no detail of the coupling was missed.

'Hot stuff,' Frank whispered into her ear.

Felicity looked around. The projection room was crowded; there was hardly anywhere to sit. Some people were lying on the floor. The bluish light from the screen flickered across faces mostly blank, a few avid. Frank found them a perch on the arm of a sofa. He put his arm around her waist and pulled her close.

The film was graphic in the extreme, but oddly unshocking to Felicity. She had, instead, a desire to laugh during the close-ups of the male organ disappearing into the female one and popping back out again, like a squirrel storing nuts. Occasionally it missed its mark, whereupon hands hastily reached to reinsert it.

'He knows what he's doing,' Frank said approvingly.

The maid in the film now had her hand down her own knickers and was jiggling busily between her thighs. Some of the Americans made appreciative comments out loud, but the British sector of the audience maintained a dignified silence. The maid, apparently aroused at last to an unbearable degree, emerged from behind her curtain and – after tearing off her uniform – flung herself onto the amorous couple, wearing only stockings and suspenders. Far from being outraged at this intrusion from the domestic staff, the master and mistress welcomed her eagerly, and it was not long before they were fitting themselves together in a variety of mutually advantageous jigsaw puzzles.

Frank's arm tightened around her. 'What do you think?' he whispered.

Felicity was hot and prickly all over. 'I've never seen anything like it. But if you don't mind, I think I've had enough.'

'I couldn't agree more. Let's go.'

They found a way through the chairs to the lobby. Holding her hand, Frank led her round the house from door to door, trying the handles. 'What are you doing?' she asked.

'They're all locked,' he said. 'Busy night.'

'We can't just wander round in someone else's house,' she giggled. 'What are you looking for?'

'Here's one!' Frank opened a door and pulled her into the darkened bedroom.

'Put the light on!' she commanded, uncertain in the dark.

He found the bedside lamp and turned it on. It was rather dim, and revealed a four-poster bed with an ornate canopy. Frank grinned at it. 'Perfect!' He locked the door.

'Oh, Frank,' she said anxiously, 'we can't!'

'Oh, Felicity,' he mocked her, 'we can!'

He pulled her onto the bed with him. The drinks of the evening, with the champagne to finish off, were making her head spin. He started kissing her, in the same intimate way as in the taxi, his tongue probing her mouth, hands reaching under her skirt.

'Frank,' she whispered, feeling heat rush through her belly and thighs, 'darling Frank . . . I can't do this . . .'

But she was starting to kiss him back, her arms around his neck, her mouth open. His hand searched between her thighs. She struggled against him, feeling that everything was going too fast, that she did not have enough choice in the matter. His fingers were insistent and strong, and found their way to her. She writhed with mingled discomfort and pleasure as he groped at her privates, feeling herself rapidly approach the abandoned condition of the French maid in the blue film. His finger slid inside her, making her gasp. He, however, sat up, frowning.

'I thought you were a virgin.'

'What?' she said, her tongue feeling thick in her mouth.

'I stuck my finger right in you!' He examined his fingers by the light of the little lamp. 'You're not a virgin! You've been with somebody!'

'Of course I'm a virgin,' she retorted, rearranging her clothes hastily. 'And I certainly haven't "been with anybody", if that's how you want to put it.'

'I don't believe you.'

She felt as though she'd been doused with a bucket of cold water. 'My God! Is that all you care about?'

'Of course not,' he said, 'but how do you explain that I was able to—'

'I don't have to explain anything to you!' she said sharply.

'Who was it?'

The last of the intoxicating warmth was slipping away from her fast. 'It's none of your business who I've been with or haven't been with,' she said, pulling up her stockings. 'No gentleman would ask such things!'

'I never claimed I was a gentleman,' he said. 'Where are you going?'

'Home,' she said. She was already unbolting the bedroom door. She just wanted to get far away from him.

He jumped up. 'No! Don't go!'

'I'm not going to stay in a locked bedroom in a strange house with you, Frank. You've obviously got the wrong idea and the wrong girl.'

He put his shoulder against the door to keep her from opening it. 'You can't leave me like this.'

'Why not?'

'Look at me.'

Felicity looked down. To her dismay, he had opened his flies. An obviously engorged male member was protruding from his well-tailored fawn pants. She recoiled. 'Put that away!'

'I can't help it. It's what you do to me. I'm desperate for you!'

She heaved at the door. 'Let me out!'

'Please, honey. I want you so much.' He tried to embrace her. 'You drive me crazy!' She could feel his erection prodding her insistently at crotch level. Her feelings had been outraged, but he was so very handsome, with his melting, hazel eyes and his lock of dark hair all dishevelled on his brow. And there was something thrilling about being desired so urgently. Besides, he was now contrite. 'Forgive me, sweetheart. I was a beast. A brute. Of course I believe you're a virgin. Come back to bed and take your clothes off.'

'Absolutely not.'

'I'm begging you,' he said piteously. 'If you leave me in this state, I'll be sick for days.'

'Really?' she asked, starting to feel sorry for him.

'It's very bad for a man. You know that, don't you? My glands'll swell up. I'll be in agony.' He cupped her breast in his palm tenderly and started kissing her neck.

'I'm not getting back into bed with you,' she said decisively. She rattled the door handle. 'Not now, and not here. It's not how I want it.'

'Okay, okay,' he said pacifically, 'not here and now. I get it. But if you care about me, sweetheart, you have to do something for me. To stop me getting sick.'

'What?' Felicity asked suspiciously.

'Be nice to me.'

'I've already told you—'

'Not like that. I'll show you.'

'Oh, Frank!' Unwillingly, she allowed him to lead her back to the bed, where he removed his elegantly tailored taupe trousers and lay back down, apparently very proud of his tumescent manhood.

'Be nice to me.' He guided her reluctant hand onto him and showed her what to do. She sat awkwardly on the edge of the bed, trying not to look. But there was a certain interest in the proceedings. She found herself thinking of William Willoughby in Spain, her first lover, if he could be called that, and of the antique casts gallery in the British Museum, where she, Chiara and Isobel had giggled as they drew the naked male form with ink-stained fingers.

Having secured her cooperation, Frank stretched luxuriously on the bed, hands clasped behind his neck. 'You'll get the hang of it,' he said. 'You're a real sport, Felicity. I'm crazy for you. You know that, don't you? I can't take my eyes off you. You're like a lovely white candle in a church. You absolutely glow. One day you'll be mine. Promise me that.'

'I don't know,' she said, pumping away vigorously. Was this giving him pleasure? It seemed rather rough. But he appeared to be responding. He was starting to pant.

'You will.' He was growing more excited. His eyes glazed over. 'Oh Jesus, you drive me wild! My Felicity, my little virgin, you make me crazy! Oh, God!' He groped urgently in his pocket and thrust a handkerchief at her. She wasn't sure what it was for, but she soon found out, when Frank's animal spirits gushed out like a geyser. After the mopping-up operations were over, Frank was in high good spirits and extremely affectionate. 'You're a pearl, a peach,' he said, pulling on his pants. 'My God, I'm wild for you!' He hugged and kissed her. His eyes were shining. 'Wasn't that swell?'

Felicity was happy that she had pleased him, and glad that she hadn't 'gone all the way', as the Trinidad Street girls put it. It had been educational. However, she was feeling far from comfortable. 'Being nice' to Frank had hardly been a romantic experience, yet it had left her restless, also wanting to be satisfied. Frank, however, made no enquiries about her own state, being blissfully happy with his own.

They unlocked the door and went out. The others of their party were all either still in the projection room or had vanished to bedrooms of their own. In fact, the entire household seemed to be engaged in an orgy. Half-naked figures flitted in the corridors, and muffled shrieks came from behind locked doors.

'Have you been here before?' Felicity asked.

'Once or twice,' he admitted.

'With whom?' she asked, struck by a swift pang of jealousy.

'Oh, just some of the guys from the base,' he replied airily, but she was not sure that she believed him. 'Let's see if there's any more of that champagne.'

On the way home in the taxi, later, he didn't bother trying to neck with her or put his hand up her dress. In fact, between the sexual release and the champagne, he seemed to have lapsed into a state of self-satisfied torpor, with one proprietorial arm around her. Felicity, who was still unfulfilled, began to feel that she had been used and discarded in a heartless way. He was good-looking and generous, and could be fun, but he was no White Knight.

'It'll be better for you next time,' he said, as they arrived at Chiara's. 'I'll get us a little place. Somewhere we can go without a lot of people around. Maybe a little apartment somewhere.'

'That's not necessary,' Felicity said hastily.

'Don't worry about it. I'll work everything out.' He kissed her, smiling. 'You were wonderful tonight. I'm the luckiest guy in the world to have you.'

Somewhat mollified by this, Felicity went up to the flat. To her surprise, the lights were on and Chiara was still awake. The reason immediately became obvious. Oliver had returned.

∽

Felicity found Oliver Courtfield to be an extraordinarily charming personality. Never having met him, she had formed an image in her mind of a somewhat depraved and predatory old man who'd got his claws into her sister. Instead, he turned out to be vigorous, courtly and amusing, unmistakeably authoritative, but carrying his authority lightly. She liked him very much from the start.

And Chiara was transformed. Her shrewishness had vanished. She was once again the bright, happy person Felicity was used to. Even her expression had gentled, and her elfin face glowed with love. She was very much in love with him, and whatever the miseries of their long separations, it was clear to Felicity that Oliver was the love of Chiara's life. She felt ashamed of having cast them as a lecherous sugar daddy and his concubine.

They had obviously been in bed together before she arrived, and were in their dressing gowns when she came in, but there was no awkwardness as they shared a glass of champagne brought by Oliver (it had been a night for champagne). In fact, Felicity felt a new sense of solidarity with them, since she too now had what people called 'a sex life'. Her own sex life was somewhat embryonic at the moment, but it definitely existed. She could still smell it faintly on her hands. For the first time in her life, she felt she was a grown-up among grown-ups.

This happiness was tempered by the realization that if Oliver was staying in London, she would now have to move out of Chiara's flat.

They slept for a few hours and then Oliver took them to the Savoy for a Sunday morning breakfast. The great hotel had suffered some bomb damage. They had to negotiate piles of rubble and broken glass in the street. However, once inside, the smoothly oiled machinery of a luxury hotel surrounded them, and the temporary inconvenience of the Blitz ceased to be relevant. At the Savoy, at least, rationing seemed not to exist.

Oliver Courtfield was interested in Felicity. Over eggs Benedict and more champagne, he questioned her courteously about her job.

'It's not what I would have chosen,' Felicity concluded, after she had explained what she did in Trinidad Street, 'but they had nothing else. I'm not strong enough for the Land Army or a factory.'

'What did you do in the priory?' Oliver asked.

'I was the librarian.'

'Did you enjoy it?'

'To tell you the truth,' she confided, 'it was deathly dull. So I set myself tasks to stop myself from going mad with boredom. I catalogued the whole library. It hadn't been done since the nineteenth century – and there were thousands of books, some of them valuable old tomes. I devised an index, and re-shelved the books, so they could be found easily. I also invented a card system, just like in a regular library.' She smiled. 'Nuns don't steal, as a rule, but it's amazing how forgetful they can be. Anyway, after I'd done all that, it was much easier to track what we had and who had borrowed which volume.'

Oliver was watching her with shrewd grey eyes. 'Where did you learn to do all that?'

'Oh, I just made up my own system. Eccentric, I'll admit, but it worked. It'll do for another hundred years, I expect.'

'You're clearly wasting your gifts in the canteen,' Oliver said.

'They said my experience in the library isn't useful for anything.'

'That's a matter of opinion. Do you like crossword puzzles?'

'Yes, very much.'

'She got all the brains in the family.' Chiara patted his hand. 'Sorry, darling, you ended up with the dumb one.'

Oliver took out a little black leather note book and a pencil. He made a few notes. He was the sort of man who gave you the impression he could sort out any problem with no effort. 'I'll speak to some people,' he said, putting the notebook away again.

'Don't say that,' Chiara said. 'Felicity disapproves of string-pulling.'

'It's not a question of pulling strings,' Oliver replied calmly. 'It's a question of getting the right people into the right jobs, so we can win this war. It's Felicity's duty to serve her country in the best way she can. Isn't it, Felicity?'

After that, Felicity could only nod obediently. Chiara smiled at Felicity. The change in her was wonderful, Felicity thought. With

Oliver gone for so long, and in such danger, the strain on Chiara must have been immense. No wonder she had been overwrought. Chiara had warned her not to ask Oliver where he had been, or any questions about his work, but he seemed to know a lot about what was happening in Nazi-occupied France.

'There is a resistance movement, of course,' he told them, 'and it fights back where it can. But the government, the civil service and the police generally do whatever the Germans tell them to do. It makes one wonder what would happen in Britain if the worst came to the worst.'

'It won't come to that, will it?' Felicity asked anxiously.

'It may,' Oliver said calmly. 'And if it does, each of us will have to ask whether he or she will lie down before the invader – or, as the Prime Minister has said, fight in the fields and in the streets and the hills and never surrender.' He helped them to a little more champagne. 'The French police have just rounded up thirteen thousand Jews in Paris. They were herded into a vélodrome and handed over to the Nazis for disposal. All French citizens, mostly women and children.'

'What will happen to them?'

'They were shipped to a camp in Silesia called Auschwitz. They'll be exterminated there. The Resistance saved a handful, but the French authorities collaborated fully with the SS.'

'That is disgusting.'

'As I said, it makes one wonder what would happen here. The Nazis have built most of their death camps in Poland. If they were to invade this island, however, the inconvenience of shipping British subjects such a long distance would be too great. They would have to build camps here in Britain, probably in North Yorkshire, Northumberland or Scotland. The existing rail system would work very well in transporting candidates from London and the midland cities.'

The matter-of-fact way in which he talked was chilling. Felicity shuddered. 'I thought we were safe from invasion, now that the Americans have joined the war.'

He gave her one of his urbane smiles. 'No island can ever be said to be safe from invasion.'

Oliver, it appeared, might be home for the foreseeable future. Felicity was determined not to spoil her sister's joy in any way, and over the next days began looking for somewhere else to stay. However, Oliver's promise to 'speak to some people' bore fruit with unexpected swiftness. On Wednesday, returning home from the East End, she was met by an excited Chiara with instructions from Oliver.

'Oh, darling, don't take your coat off. You're to go straight to the War Office for an interview.'

'Now?'

'Yes, right now! Hurry!'

Chiara went with her for solidarity. The War Office was an ornate stone monstrosity with a tower at each corner, occupying an entire block in Whitehall, just opposite Downing Street. They walked into the immense entrance hall, which echoed with the boots of those passing through it, and presented themselves at the desk, where a pair of burly sergeant majors checked Felicity's papers and made guarded phone calls. Chiara was then told to wait in the lobby while Felicity was conducted up the sweeping staircase to the second floor.

She was shown into an office where a mild-looking man in an improbable colonel's uniform surveyed her over his pipe.

'They tell me you like puzzles.'

'Yes,' she replied.

'Well, you're in luck. I've got a few juicy ones for you here. Sit down, Miss Redcliffe.' The colonel, whose name was Parker, gave her some pencils and a sheaf of paper. Despite the summer sunshine, he had an electric fire burning. A malodorous spaniel dozed in front of it. He stood at the window and puffed at his pipe while she tackled the 'puzzles', which were of different types, some numerical, some linguistic, some involving shapes.

'It's come to something,' Colonel Parker mused, looking out over Whitehall, 'when we start pressing nuns into the defence of the realm.'

'I'm not a nun any more,' Felicity replied, poring over the conundrum she was working on. 'And looking back, I wasn't much of a nun to start with.'

He gave her no more than half an hour to complete the tests. She hadn't found any of them particularly difficult. He sat looking through them, tapping his teeth with the stem of his pipe, then tossed all the papers into the wastepaper basket. Her heart sank. 'You've got digs in London, I take it?'

'Yes, I'm staying with my sister in Mayfair.'

'Good. We don't have much barrack or billet accommodation in London. You'll be expected to get here at 9.00 every morning, seven days a week. You'll get Saturday afternoons off and one day a week off at the Ministry's discretion.'

She was astonished. 'Do you mean – I've got the job?'

He gave her a dry smile. 'Not a job, Miss Redcliffe, but you'll start training at once.'

'But – but what about my work at the canteen?'

'You'll have to give notice, won't you?' he said. He knocked the ash out of his pipe. 'You're in the army now. You start on Monday.'

∽

'Give notice indeed,' Miss Allsop retorted. She was seething. 'I never heard of such a thing! You can't give notice. You're here for the duration! It's out of the question, Redcliffe. Absolute nonsense.'

'I've signed up, Miss Allsop!'

'You can jolly well unsign.' She went off angrily to telephone Colonel Parker.

But the girls were all in favour – and impressed with Felicity's audacity.

'Cor, you're going to be a spy or something,' Eileen said.

'Hardly,' Felicity laughed.

'Better than being here, any rate,' Ginger declared. 'Good for you, kiddo. Never mind old Allsop. She can't do nothing to you. You don't need her permission – all that about your signing on for the duration is rubbish. She just wanted to get into your knickers.'

Shortly afterwards, Miss Allsop returned, looking even more annoyed. 'Well, Redcliffe, it seems you've been called to higher things. Nothing I can do. We'll have to dispense with your services. Don't just stand around gawking, get to work.'

The New Jerusalem, it seemed, would be built without Felicity. 'But you'll still be coming to the Paramount with our lot,' Ginger said decisively.

'No fear,' Gladys Williams said. 'Our Felicity's leaving all that behind her. Ballroom of the Ritz, more like.'

'Well, what about Frank, then?' Ginger challenged.

It was a good question. Last Saturday's experience with Frank – and his promise to 'get a little place' where their sexual activities could be expanded further – had been on her mind. A certain disillusionment had set in after what had happened between them. She didn't care for Frank that much any more. She had decided she didn't want any long-term relationship with him. She wasn't ready for anything like that just yet, in any case. She still felt what Miss Allsop called 'that convent pallor' on her. Nor did she want to be made to feel guilty because Frank's life was in jeopardy; that wasn't the basis for a relationship. So she skipped the Paramount that

Saturday. She felt a little guilty about not going. She was a coward but she didn't feel that she owed him a great deal.

She began her training at the War Office the next week. She'd hardly known what she was letting herself in for, but it soon emerged that she was to be instructed in the use of codes and ciphers. A vast amount of communications traffic poured in and out of the War Office each day, all of it encoded, and all of it needing to be processed as quickly and as accurately as possible. She was one of a group of twelve young trainee clerks who had been selected for what was described as 'accelerated instruction' in the use of the most secret codes.

They were made to sign the Official Secrets Act, and then assembled in a cramped, windowless room with four desks, on each of which was a bulky object covered with a cloth. Their instructor was a dry civilian Scot named McTaggart, who addressed them as 'young leddies'.

'You're in the presence of one of the biggest secrets of the war,' he told them. 'None of you are to speak one word to anyone about what you're going to see now. Understood?'

'Yes, sir,' they chorused.

He lifted the cloths carefully off the machines, one by one. Revealed were four alarming contraptions resembling typewriters, but with large and complicated systems of wheels and cogs attached on either side. 'Behold the Typex, young leddies. It will turn plain English into something the Almighty himself couldn't make head or tail of.'

They began to learn the workings of the Typex, three to a machine. The incessant rattling of the cogs and thumping of the keys was to be the tenor of their days from now on. The machines were adjusted to a different setting for each message. As McTaggart said, the Typex converted the text into columns of unintelligible letters, which could be transmitted without fear that the enemy could understand them. All that was required was that the operator at the other end knew the setting, which was put at the beginning of each transmission. She could then adjust her Typex accordingly. Keying in the apparently meaningless figures would turn the cypher back into readable English.

'The system is unbreakable,' McTaggart said. 'Isn't it, young leddies?'

'Yes sir,' the girls chorused dutifully. But Felicity shook her head.

'It's not unbreakable.'

'And why would that be?' McTaggart asked her, turning a gimlet eye on her.

'Because if just one of the machines fell into enemy hands, they would be able to read everything we sent.'

'Exactly so,' he said in his clipped way. 'And that means that your Typex must be guarded at all times – with your lives, if necessary.' He went on to list the security measures that were needed in dealing with the machines. They were to be kept in locked rooms at all times, never photographed, never spoken of to outsiders, completely destroyed if there was any possibility of their being captured. 'All the messages you will deal with are High Priority,' McTaggart warned them. 'They need to be encoded and decoded quickly and delivered to the right person – without mistakes or delays.'

It was a complex, laborious system, but required accuracy rather than brilliance, and Felicity knew she could be accurate. Most of them picked it up swiftly. In their way, they were not so different from the Trinidad Street girls, a mixed group from all walks of life, thrown together by the war. However, three of the class were soon dismissed by McTaggart for being too slow or making too many mistakes, and one dropped out for biological reasons, being obviously about to give birth, which left eight of them with the requisite skills. Felicity found herself at the top of the class.

She was the only one who never jammed her machine, or forgot to include the setting code in her messages, a ghastly error which would make the text impossible to decipher.

During the course of their training they were issued uniforms, were taught how to recognize the rank of officers (and to salute them) and were taken to a pistol range to have marksmanship training with a Webley pistol. Her life was changing fast. A few weeks ago she had been in the silent world of the priory, where time crept from bell to bell and life was prayer and contemplation. Now she was holding a heavy revolver in both hands and taking satisfaction in firing six .38 bullets into a target in the shape of a German infantryman.

'Head and chest, ladies, head and chest,' the instructor bellowed. 'We want to kill the bastard, not wing him. Otherwise he'll just keep coming. And we know what he'll do to you, don't we?'

Felicity noticed that the woman next to her was squeezing her eyes tightly shut as she fired, her bullets going wide of the target. She herself took careful aim, as the instructor had taught them, placing four shots neatly in the chest and two in the menacing, helmeted head. If it ever came to the real thing, she wanted to survive the encounter.

The uniform was a khaki skirt and blouse, worn with a tie and a jacket adorned with brass buttons which caught on everything. They were also issued with thick, black woollen underwear which caused Chiara much hilarity. 'Authentic passion-quellers,' she said, holding up the voluminous bloomers. 'These'll put a crimp in your love life.'

Her love life was in abeyance, anyway. Frank made several attempts to contact her, calling the flat (Felicity refused to take the phone from Chiara) as well as writing a rather piteous letter asking whether 'there was someone else.' She ignored this, too. Eventually, he arrived at their door one Saturday night, very drunk.

'I got us a room in Bayswater,' he said, holding up a key. 'Hot water and everything. You know how difficult it is to get a room with hot water these days?'

'You'll find somebody else to take there,' she replied.

'Don't want anybody but you. I'm in love with you.'

'I'm sure you're not, really.'

'You're so cold.' He swayed, and had to put a hand on the doorjamb to steady himself. His eyes were moist and swollen, like gooseberries. 'Icy cold.'

'There are lots of other girls, Frank. You'll find someone much nicer than me.'

'You broke my heart.'

'Go home. You're drunk.'

'Damn right I'm drunk. You should be drunk too! You should be drunk, and having fun with me! Life's too damn short to waste a single moment.'

'I'm sure you're right.'

He tried to kiss her. 'I love you!'

'But I don't love you,' she replied, backing away. 'Goodnight, Frank.'

He grasped her shoulders clumsily and managed to plant a kiss on her cheek. When she got free, he put his foot in the door and there was a brief tussle. His balance wasn't very good, and she managed to push him away and slam the door in his face. He continued to knock for ten minutes, and at last went back to his taxi and drove away.

'Sharpening your claws, darling?' Chiara asked. 'Your first rejected suitor.'

'I don't want any more, thank you,' Felicity replied. She was somewhat shaken by the force of Frank's disappointment.

She found a little bedsit in north London and moved out, giving Oliver and Chiara their privacy. In the few weeks that she had seen Oliver and Chiara together, she had gathered a much better understanding of their relationship. Oliver would not marry Chiara because he felt that doing so would impose unfair restrictions on her. He would grow old and she would be tied to an infirm husband. He wanted her to be free to leave and make a new life for herself as he aged. He did not seem to grasp that Chiara would never love another man, and would find it impossible to leave him – at whatever age – for anyone else.

There were so many misguided people in the world, Felicity thought, looking for love and not finding it, or not recognizing it when they did find it. It was always a gamble, rather like taking a bath, she thought. Sometimes the boiler burst into a promising blaze, but the ensuing water was lukewarm (which had been her own experience) and sometimes scalding floods issued from an unpromising start. The metaphor was a banal one, but she felt it held some truth.

She and Chiara were on much better terms. Chiara seemed to take comfort in her presence, rather than finding her an irritant. They became close again in a way they hadn't been for years. And Felicity herself was changing. Her hair had grown to a respectable length. She looked normal. It had been a hot summer and her pallor was overlaid with gold now. She felt stronger, more confident. She dashed across busy streets, answered back confidently when questioned, and earned the grudging praise of McTaggart. She was growing accustomed to being whistled at by soldiers, to defending her place in queues, to wearing a uniform and being part of the war effort.

September came. She completed her course at the War Office and was given a pair of stripes to sew on her uniform and the right to call herself a lance corporal. She was now on permanent posting to Codes and Ciphers.

'You've done very well, young leddy,' McTaggart told her approvingly. 'I wish all my young leddies had your brains and your application.' Chiara took her to Prunier to celebrate on champagne and oysters.

She was now ready for her first real posting. She was summoned to Colonel Parker's office again, and this time found him in a more warlike mood. His pipe was clenched jauntily in his teeth. A map of North Africa was unrolled on his desk. A service revolver lay on it, as well as a compass and a pair of binoculars. What these theatrical props meant, Felicity could not guess.

'How would you like to see the Pyramids?' he asked her.

She was astonished. 'I'm not sure, sir.'

'Not sure? I expected something more positive than that.'

'I mean – do I have a choice?'

'If you want to serve your country, no. You don't have a choice. There's a vacancy at the Cipher Office in Cairo. It must be filled. Are you up to the job? That's the question.'

'I think I am,' she said uncertainly.

'Then you'll be leaving for Egypt within the month.'

'Within the month?'

He cut her off. 'You've made the right decision, Lance Corporal. You'd better start preparing.' He had a sheaf of forms for her to sign. As she filled them in, she tried to form a mental picture of her future. Egypt! She had not expected anything of that sort. The news from that quarter was hardly good. It was all over the news. Rommel had pushed the Allied lines back almost to Alexandria. The British army had retreated to Cairo in a disorderly panic. The city was now threatened by Germans to the west and Italians to the south. The horrible prospect of being captured, and what the Germans might do to her, overlay more pleasant visions of mysterious, warm locations where palm trees waved.

She went out, dazed. But as the shock wore off, excitement kindled in her. To get away from London, the Blitz, rationing; to avoid the coming English winter; to be in an exotic city in an exotic land; all that was much. The only heartbreak would come in saying goodbye to Chiara, her newly regained sister.

Chiara, however, was delighted. 'Oh, darling! I'm so glad you're getting out of London. And I'm very proud of you. You'll be doing important work!'

'I don't know about that. He stuck the forms under my nose and I just signed. I wish I hadn't, now. I feel as though I'm running away from everything.'

Chiara grew serious. 'Our generation hardly knows what happiness is,' she said. 'Everything's been messed up for us. Even when the war is over, there'll be years of gloom to follow. Take this in both hands, darling. It's a gift from the gods.'

6.
CHIARA

London, Autumn, 1942

Chiara's happiness could not have been more complete. Not only had Oliver unexpectedly returned to England, having been given a desk job in Whitehall, but Isobel had returned from America! Moreover, she had made peace with Felicity after many years of estrangement, and in a few weeks, Felicity would be in sunny Egypt, where she was sure to grow up and lose the strangeness and awkwardness which made her so hard to deal with. Now that Oliver had returned to England, Felicity had tactfully moved out of Chiara's flat in Tisbury Mansions, and found a bedsit in Islington. It was tiny, but as Felicity said, it was only for a few weeks before she left for Egypt. This had given Chiara and Oliver their much-needed seclusion. All in all, Chiara felt, as the three sisters settled at a gilded table in the Palm Court at the Ritz, things could not have worked out better.

Outwardly, Isobel was just the same as ever: supremely confident, bossy and beautiful. But Chiara saw changes in her. She was tougher than she had been. Her indifference to the opinion of others, always notable, was hardening into selfishness, a way of looking at the world which put her own wishes first and expressed itself in a cynicism which was occasionally shocking.

'This war is a racket,' she said to Chiara. 'Look at them. All making a fortune and spending it on whores.'

Chiara and Felicity followed Isobel's heavy-lidded gaze. The couples at the tables around them fell into a pattern, older men wearing suits or the uniforms of senior officers, together with women barely into their twenties. Behind the fronds of the palms, grey heads were inclining closely towards platinum tresses. This season, blonde was in.

'I'm sure some of them are fathers and daughters,' Felicity said innocently.

'Only you would say that,' Isobel retorted. 'The war was dreamed up by these people. Bankers and generals and factory owners. The longer it lasts, the happier they are. They're cashing in every way they know. And as a bonus, all the young men are away fighting, giving them a clear field with the fillies half their age. The same thing's happening in Germany, of course. No difference.'

Chiara felt uncomfortable. For one thing, her own relationship with Oliver corresponded to the scenario Isobel depicted, if only superficially. She was, after all, half Oliver's age. For another, Isobel was talking too loudly. She was too loud in every way. Her lecture tour of the United States, which had raised tens of thousands of dollars from ordinary Americans for the British war effort, had obviously also been profitable on a personal level. She had taken a flat in De Vere Gardens, a smart address in Kensington, and was managing to clothe herself magnificently. In this year of austerity and self-denial, Isobel was resplendent in a flouncy polka-dot dress and a smart hat – while Chiara had been careful to wear one of the mouse-coloured and unadorned suits approved by the Utility Clothing scheme (two pockets, four buttons, straight skirt – together with plain and sturdy shoes. Felicity, who had come from the War Office, was proudly wearing her khaki uniform.

Isobel fitted a cigarette into her ebony holder and lit it. At thirty-one, she was a striking woman who caught the eye of every man in the room. Many people knew who she was, but even if they didn't, they stared. Isobel remained arrogantly indifferent to the stares. The set of her chin stated plainly that she simply didn't care who looked at her or what they thought of her. She went through life as she pleased, encountering good times or bad ones with equal defiance.

'I think the war's about more than profit,' Chiara said, 'but let's not argue, darling. It's wonderful to see you again.'

'Likewise.' Isobel flashed her a brilliant smile. 'Even in those dreary clothes. Tell me how you winkled Felicity out of the nunnery, you clever thing.'

'I didn't do any winkling. She winkled herself.'

'And how did you manage that?' Isobel asked Felicity. 'I thought it was a life sentence.'

'It wasn't all that difficult,' Felicity said. 'I applied to have my vows annulled. It had to be referred to Rome, and it just took months, that's all. But nobody tried to talk me out of it. I was rather insulted, really.'

'Extraordinary child.' Isobel exhaled a plume of smoke at the ceiling. 'And are you cured?'

Felicity smiled. 'I'm cured of being a nun, I think.'

'She got herself a job in a canteen as soon as she was out,' Chiara put in, 'and started running around with an American airman.'

'You're joking.'

'I'm not. She changed from a nun to a Modern Woman literally overnight.'

'Amazing. Did you lose your virginity to this man?' Isobel asked Felicity.

'You can't ask that sort of question, Izzy,' Felicity said. 'I'm not fourteen any more.'

'Well, I certainly hope you widened your experience,' Isobel said. 'And I do hope Egypt's going to be good for you.'

'So do I.'

'You'll have to pick up a sheikh or two.'

'I'll do my best.' Two waiters arrived with a silver cake stand of dainty sandwiches and cakes. Tea was reverently poured into bone china cups. 'This is like old times,' Felicity said wistfully.

'Not really.' Isobel stubbed out her cigarette. 'Nothing will ever be the same again.'

'Don't you think so? I keep dreaming that when this hateful war is over, we'll go back to the beauty and peace we had.'

'Bluebirds over the white cliffs of Dover? Lilacs in the spring again? No chance of that. Too much has changed. We've buggered up the old world. It can't be rebuilt.'

'It makes me sad to hear you say that.'

'Why?' Isobel retorted. 'The old world wasn't a paradise, darling. It was a dreary, hypocritical hell. At least the veneer is off, now. We can see the ugly truth for what it is.'

Chiara was struck by the bitterness of Isobel's tone. 'I didn't know you were so disillusioned.'

'I lived for years with nothing,' Isobel said, helping herself to smoked salmon sandwiches. 'All that stood between me and the world was my face. Having a little beauty saved me from the gutter.'

'I think you're exaggerating about the gutter,' Chiara said, following suit. 'but you're certainly lovely. I don't think I've ever seen you looking so well.'

'You're not so bad yourselves. Being in love obviously suits you, Chiara.'

Chiara smiled. 'I'm happy.'

'So you should be. You've found what we're all looking for. You're very lucky. Neither Felicity nor I have done that, yet.'

Chiara knew it was true, but shied away from congratulating herself on her good fortune. It was tempting fate. Isobel inspected her sandwich critically, then summoned the waiter. 'I don't know what this is,' she told him, 'but it's not salmon.'

The elderly waiter was shocked. 'It's the finest Loch Fyne smoked salmon, madam.'

'Nonsense,' Isobel said in a clear voice which carried around the room. 'It's a disgrace. Take it away and bring us something decent.'

The man scuttled to obey. Chiara and Felicity surrendered their salmon sandwiches very reluctantly – they had been the most delicious things they'd eaten in months. 'I was enjoying those.'

'As a matter of fact,' Isobel said, 'I'm going to stand for Parliament.'

Felicity gasped. 'Oh Isobel! Really?'

'For Labour, of course.'

Chiara raised her eyebrows. 'Labour? You're hardly a Socialist, dear.'

'I'm not anything,' Isobel said dryly. 'But I can spout claptrap with the best of them.'

'That's very cynical.'

'Backing the winning horse isn't cynical, it's sane. People are sick of the Tories and their wars. Labour's time has come, and the time of women in politics has come, too.'

Chiara tried to hide her scepticism. 'But aren't you a little – well, *notorious* – for political life?'

'What could be better than notoriety?'

'In politics it's generally considered rather a handicap. You're divorced – and your book, you know. A lot of people were shocked. You've got rather a reputation.'

'A reputation is exactly what's wanted. Especially where the Labour Party is concerned. And they want women, too. I've already spoken to Clem Attlee. He's very interested.'

'Good heavens, Isobel,' Felicity said. 'What about your Nazi connections?'

'I severed those very publicly. They kicked me out of Germany. I covered the Spanish Civil War for the Left, remember? I was at the fall of Barcelona. Once the coalition is over, I tell you, Britain will vote Labour. And I intend them to vote for me. They don't mind me not having been born in some dreary Northern town with rickets.'

The waiter had reappeared with some new sandwiches, wafers of white bread covered with glistening leaves of pink salmon. 'With the chef's compliments, madam,' he said, 'the very finest we have, from Uist. Brought down from the Outer Hebrides especially for the chef .'

Isobel sampled one, 'Somewhat better. It'll have to do.' The man disappeared gratefully. 'Don't look like that,' she said to Chiara. 'If I pay for something, I want the best. Doesn't everybody?'

Chiara couldn't help laughing. 'I think you want rather more, darling.' Suddenly, she caught sight of Oliver's tall, distinguished figure walking towards their table. He'd promised to join them if he could get away from the office, though she hadn't expected he would be able to make it. She greeted him joyfully.

'I can't stay long,' he said, kissing her. He greeted Isobel and Felicity courteously and sat with them. He was wearing an immaculate grey suit with a white carnation in his buttonhole. Oliver and Isobel had already met two or three times. They treated each other with cool politeness, but Chiara knew they didn't really like each other. They were too different, Oliver old-school and bound by duty, Isobel rebellious and self-centred. Chiara longed for them to be on better terms, but knew it would never happen. Somewhat to her dismay, Isobel continued to talk about her plans to become a Labour MP. Amusing as Isobel's vanity and materialism had been a moment ago, in Oliver's presence Chiara was embarrassed.

As Isobel rattled on, extolling her own political savoir-faire, talking about 'Clem Attlee' and 'old Ernie Bevin', Chiara couldn't help glancing at Oliver's face. His expression was outwardly urbane, but she knew him well enough to detect scornful amusement in the curl of his lip and the flare of his nostrils.

'I don't think you're going to be able to eat smoked salmon at the Ritz when you're a Socialist candidate,' Oliver suggested when Isobel's flow paused for a moment. 'Or wear Paris clothes.'

'Why ever not?' Isobel retorted. 'That's what the working classes aspire to, don't you know that? Anyway, I'm going to be a new kind of Labour MP. People are sick of the old brigade in fusty frock coats. They're sick of austerity, hypocrisy and keeping a stiff upper lip. Your generation have given them enough of that, Oliver.'

'Indeed,' he murmured.

'Indeed. People want glamour. They want scandal, excitement. I'll give it to 'em, by golly. They'll love me. Especially the women. The men, too.'

'I'm sure you're right,' he said, with the ghost of a smile. 'Although with your penchant for extremes, I'm surprised you didn't choose the Communist Party.'

'Oh, I would never do that. I like to be on the side that's going to win.'

'Is that why you were on Hitler's side before the war?'

'Exactly.'

'I hope you'll be a little less honest when you're on the stump.'

She dabbed the corners of her lipsticked mouth with her napkin. 'At least I can say I've tried both sides. Most people get into one party or another because they inherit their parents' boring attitudes. I've made my own mind up.'

'And you're sure now that Hitler is going to lose?' Oliver asked gently.

'Oh, yes. Now that America is in the war, it's a foregone conclusion. It's an astonishing country. There's such an abundance of everything, especially energy. When you go there, you see the impossibility of fighting them. At first I felt very strange there, but Americans have a way of making you feel at home.' She took another sandwich. 'Of course, they're going to be top dogs when the war ends. They'll run the show and the rest of us will be in their shadow. We won't be able to keep our empire. It'll probably be given to the Americans to pay off our debts. Britain will be a third-rate power.'

Oliver considered her, his chin on his fist. 'Why don't you move to America, then?'

'*Au contraire.* I'm staying. There are lots of opportunities on a sinking ship.'

'You sound like a pickpocket,' Felicity commented.

'That's what I'm reduced to. I'm alone in this world. I have to make my way somehow. If I have to pick a pocket now and then, so be it.'

'Well, I wish you the best of luck in your new career,' he said. 'I'm sure you'll do brilliantly.'

'So am I.' She gave him a wicked smile. 'And now you have something new to put in that file you keep on me at MI5.'

'Isobel!' Chiara said, glancing at Oliver. It was not the first time Isobel had twitted Oliver with the supposed file that was kept on her – whereas Chiara herself hardly dared refer to Oliver's job at MI5, regarding it as a sacrosanct subject, never to be mentioned, especially not in jest.

But he did not seem fazed. 'Well, at least I can now have it moved from the Fascist-sympathizer section to the red-menace section.'

Isobel laughed merrily. 'So you finally admit you have a file on me!'

'I admit no such thing.'

She leaned forward, dark eyes sparkling. 'Is it very thick? What colour is it? Crimson, I hope! What's in it? Do tell!'

He remained deadpan. 'If you had a file, I would be unlikely to tell you anything about it. But in this case, *entre nous*, I hope you'll accept my assurance that there is no such file.'

'I don't believe you,' Isobel scoffed.

'Why not? Is your vanity piqued?'

'Let's say that my credulity is stretched.'

'Do you imagine hordes of analysts logging your every move?' he enquired dryly.

'No, but I imagine a couple of dirty old men regularly going through my underwear.'

'Isobel,' Felicity protested, 'you're not being respectful.'

She raised her immaculate eyebrows at Felicity. 'Respectful? He isn't our father, darling, though he's old enough to be. You respect him if you want to, though for my own part I never found a man I could respect once I'd slept with him.'

Some devil had got into Isobel today, and Chiara felt her cheeks flush. 'There probably *is* a file on you, after the reckless way you've behaved. And it may interest you to know that while you were gal-livanting around Europe, Oliver was trying to rescue you. He even went to Barcelona to try and find you.'

'That was very gallant of him,' Isobel replied coolly, 'but I didn't require to be found or rescued. I managed quite well all on my own.'

'You're impossible,' Chiara said, annoyed.

'Six impossible things before breakfast,' Isobel replied. 'That was what the Red Queen prescribed, wasn't it?'

'I think it was the White Queen,' Oliver said mildly, 'but it doesn't matter.' He showed no sign that he was provoked in any way by Isobel, but Chiara knew he was probably annoyed. 'Having feasted my eyes on your loveliness, my dears, I must, alas, get back to my desk. But before I do, I have an invitation to issue. I'm going to open my place in the country next weekend. It's been shut for most of the war, and it's time the old place saw some life again. I'd like you all to spend a few days with me – if you don't mind a little discomfort and boredom, that is.'

'Discomfort and boredom have been the tenor of my days,' Isobel replied, before Chiara could say anything. 'A little more won't hurt.'

'I'm glad to see you so stoical.'

'I won't be able to come,' Felicity said sadly. 'I'm doing a special course next weekend. To get me ready for Cairo.'

'Very sorry to hear that. But you and Isobel will come, won't you, Chiara?'

'Of course.' He'd said nothing to her about opening Court-field Park, his place in Oxfordshire. As he had just said, it had been closed up since the start of the war. She been there with him twice, but most of the rooms had been closed, the furniture draped. They had stayed in one bedroom. She'd seen almost nothing of the place. She'd regarded it as one of the many parts of his life where she did not have full admittance.

'Good.' He rose. 'I'll make all the arrangements, then.'

When Oliver had left, Chiara rounded on her sister. 'What got into you?' she demanded angrily.

Felicity was similarly annoyed. 'How could you talk to him like that?'

Isobel yawned. 'Darlings, he's such a stuffed shirt. One simply longs to stick a pin in him.' She put on an imitation of Oliver's clipped voice. '"I'm opening my little place in the Shires next week-end." Sometimes I wonder how you stay awake with him.'

'You know nothing about him,' Chiara said shortly. 'Just because he's polite to you, you think he's a stuffed shirt. He's been fighting the Germans face-to-face for three years. As for staying awake, I know how lucky I am that he's still alive and unhurt. If the Gestapo had captured him—' She shuddered, unable to finish.

'There, darling,' Isobel said contritely, blowing Chiara a kiss, 'I'm sorry I misbehaved with your White Knight. He doesn't take it seriously, I can see that. At least he has a sense of humour.'

Chiara was not mollified. 'Promise me you won't speak to him like that again.'

'I can't promise to be an angel. I know you love him, but men like your Oliver Courtfield tend to bring out the worst in me. Smug, fatherly, patronizing bastards who always know better than the little woman. I've suffered more at their hands than at anybody else's.'

'Oliver isn't like that,' Felicity said. 'He's been so kind to me, I won't hear a word against him!'

'Whatever you say. I'll bite my tongue. Now, what about these petits fours?'

❦

The next week was a busy one at the Censor's Office, starting early on Monday morning with an interview with a belligerent Australian journalist, whose piece Chiara had heavily cut.

'This is a shambles,' the man said, shaking the newspaper in Chiara's face. 'The public have a right to know what's going on!'

The autumn of 1942 was producing a stream of bad news from every theatre of war. The Minister of Information, Chiara's ultimate boss, had deemed that the public should not hear too much more, lest morale be affected. 'This is a war of nerves,' he had told the censors. 'If we don't keep ours, we're beaten before we start.'

Reporting which cast a pessimistic light on the outcome of the conflict, or which hinted that the struggle naught availed, or which was overtly critical of Allied decisions, tactics or leadership, was accordingly to be suppressed. So were opinions which were strongly party-political in nature and which tended to widen class divisions.

All this Chiara endeavoured to explain to the reporter, who (as he repeatedly informed her) had been doing his job since she was in pinafores. 'It's not what you said, Mr Harris, it's the way you said it. We can't have Fleet Street spreading despondency and alarm among the civilian population. We need optimism.'

'Yes, no bloody bananas, eh? That's not journalism. Isn't this a war between the free nations and the kind of nations who muzzle their newspapers?'

'Yes, but—'

'What the hell are we fighting for, then?' Harris demanded. 'If you lot behave like the bloody Nazis, there's no bloody point, is there?'

'Mr Harris, for this country to endure the war, and more than that, to support it, our citizens have to feel that there *is* a bloody point. We can't allow you or anyone else to take that away. Britain's enthusiasm for the war would swiftly fade if we published photographs of the dead on our front pages every day—'

'Don't you lecture me about the dead, Miss Redcliffe!'

' – or articles explaining how our generals are failing to win battles—'

'I fought at Gallipoli!'

' – or pieces which tell us, as yours did, that we are defenceless against the Luftwaffe, which incidentally is not even true—'

'I was doing this job when you were in pinafores!'

' – and I can assure you—'

'You're no better than bloody Goebbels!'

' – that if you present such articles again, they will be dealt with in exactly the same manner. Good day, Mr Harris!'

Mr Harris did not take the hint, and remained in her office long enough to give her the benefit of his opinion on the government, the Ministry of Information and her own incompetence. He was red-faced and sweating, and when he finally left, she had to open the window to clear the air in her office, though it was a crisp autumn morning. Yes, no bloody bananas, indeed.

On Tuesday evening, to her delight, she arrived back at Tisbury Mansions to find that Oliver was there. He had a key, and had let himself in. She had seen little of him in the past week. He looked tired. 'You should have told me you were coming,' she protested. 'I would have made something special. I've only got soup!'

'Soup is perfect,' he replied, 'soup and you.' She put it on the stove, gave him a glass of the Lagavulin whisky he liked and massaged his shoulders. 'I heard about your interview with Andrew Harris,' he said.

'He was very insistent that I was no better than Josef Goebbels.'

'Oh, he was just being kind. You're much worse.'

'I do my best.'

'He's a veteran of the last lot, and thinks we betrayed the Anzacs at Gallipoli. He believes he's entitled to say what he pleases in print. There are lots more like him. We're going to have a tough job controlling the press from now on.'

'Perhaps he's right. Perhaps we are no better than the Nazis.'

'If that were true, he would be in a concentration camp. We have to restrict them. There's no choice. It's total war, you know that. Don't let people like that upset you.'

She went behind him and kneaded the tense muscles of his shoulders. 'I was so embarrassed when Isobel was going on and on about standing for Parliament. She's really so brilliant, but sometimes she does a very good impersonation of a congenital idiot. I'm sorry she was rude to you. I don't know what you must think of her.'

Oliver laughed. 'I think that you and she are very different. There's no need to be embarrassed, darling. Your sister Isobel does things her own way.'

'Do you think she actually has a chance of getting into Parliament?' she asked curiously.

'If she's prepared to work hard, I don't see why not. She has character enough.'

'But she doesn't believe in anything. You heard her.'

'She believes in herself. That's what matters.'

After their light supper, she clambered onto the sofa to get the silver candelabra out of the top shelf of the cupboard. It had belonged to her grandmother, and she always lit it when they made love. She lit the candles and took them into her bedroom, placing them at the foot of her bed. The soft glow filled the room. Oliver followed her. He took her in his arms. 'Chiara,' he said quietly. 'My darling.' He kissed her forehead, then her eyelids, then her mouth. His lips were warm. She found that she was shaking.

She'd had little sexual experience before Oliver, despite her many suitors, but she could not imagine that a better lover existed. He understood her body perfectly, in some ways better than she herself did, for he had taught her to find delight in parts of herself that she had never before considered pleasurable. He could enrapture her for what seemed like hours on end, always knowing what to do, always in control. The only disappointment was that she seemed unable to give him the same ecstasy. He would not abandon himself to her in the way she abandoned herself to him. Perhaps, she suspected, he found her unskilled, or perhaps he simply had to be in charge. Transfigured by the pleasure he gave her, it was easy to ignore that small frustration.

Sprawled on a throne of pillows, she floated as he ministered to her desires with his mouth and hands. Time with Oliver was so precious and so rare, even now that he was back in England. Time without him was to be endured, nothing more. But it was not life.

When he was certain she was satiated, he entered her at last. She held him tight as he moved in her and finally let himself go. Afterwards, she lay in his arms, her head pillowed on his chest.

'Are you really happy with me?' she asked.

'Of course. What makes you ask such a strange question?'

'I don't know. I seem able to give you so little.'

'My darling, I assure you that you give me a great deal.'

'I don't just mean in bed. I mean outside, too. Sometimes I feel I play such a small part in your life that you could forget me altogether.'

Oliver kissed her brow. 'You are always in my heart, Chiara. Don't let such silly thoughts come into your mind.'

'I can't help it. The months you were in France were terrible. I hardly slept all that time. Not knowing if you were alive or dead, whether you'd been captured—'

'Hush. I'm too wily an old bird to be captured. I was always safe.'

'I don't believe you. I know you were in dreadful danger. I don't think I could go through that again.'

'You won't have to, I promise. I'm officially off active service. No more to go a-roving, by the light of the silvery moon.'

'I long for this war to be over.'

He stroked her hair. 'So do I. And when the war is over . . .'

'When it is?' she prompted, for he had stopped speaking.

'When it is,' he continued, 'life will be beautiful again.'

'Isobel says nothing will ever be the same.'

The candles burned down. He was silent for a long while, then checked his watch. 'I have to go. Forgive me, darling.'

She stayed in bed, feeling sad, and watched his tall, lean figure as he dressed. There was never enough time together, and it always ended too soon. 'Are you going home?' she asked.

'No, back to Whitehall to brief Winston. He works all night, so we must, too.'

She didn't reply. It was the first time she'd been given a glimpse of how senior Oliver had become, and how close he was to the men who ran the war.

After he'd left, she lay awake for a long time, thinking of that unfinished sentence, *And when the war is over . . .* What had he been going to say? She was sure it was not the platitude he'd finally uttered. Was it something about her, about them, about their future together? What *was* going to happen after the war? Would he finally bring her fully into his life? Would he marry her? Or would he – given that the war, in some strange way, held them together – dispense with her entirely?

That was a thought which terrified her. She had so little of him. To have none at all would devastate her. She believed that he loved her. He was so tender with her. But he had always kept her at a distance, and she feared that he always would.

❧

As he'd promised, Oliver 'made all the arrangements' for Courtfield Park. His Jaguar arrived for her on Saturday morning. Isobel was already in it. It was driven by a uniformed chauffeur who spoke little, even in answer to questions – Oliver seemed to favour silent retainers. It was very cold, an early snow having fallen.

'This place will be freezing,' Isobel predicted disdainfully, 'and damp into the bargain. I can't think why I agreed to come.' She was in a bad mood, and evidently had no idea of the honour which was being done to her, which Chiara didn't bother trying to explain.

They drove through the monotonous suburbs of West London, sandwiched between endless convoys of rumbling army lorries. Once out of the city, however, the claustrophobic sense of tension which hung over the capital, heightened by the barrage balloons, the bomb sites and the inescapable military presence, dissipated steadily. When they left the arterial roads, the countryside was revealed in delicate traceries, trimmed and inlaid with white. What had once been so lush was now pared to its bare essentials of unadorned form. Tranquillity settled on them like balm. There was little traffic on the lanes to spoil the peace.

Oliver's part of Oxfordshire, as he'd said, was not far from their part of Gloucestershire. It was familiar country to her, almost like coming home. Chiara felt the fields and woods calling to her, and asked whether Isobel felt the same thing.

'I hate the country,' Isobel replied tersely. 'Roberto wanted me to sell the house before the war began. I should have listened to him. It'll be a rat's nest by now.'

Courtfield Park was near Chipping Norton, a small market town in the Cotswolds. They entered the estate through stone gates. The road to the house led through ploughed fields which were sprinkled with snow now, but which she knew would be busy in the summer. The park itself was large, evidently landscaped in some golden era, with a lake and great trees which had now reached their maturity. Chiara saw red deer lift their heads to gaze at the car. The lake was swathed with thin sheets of ice. Isobel shuddered. 'Frozen,' she said. 'I told you.'

The house came into view, a square structure of fawn stone with mullioned windows, set against a rise, with a backdrop of dark woods. It was not so much beautiful in itself as perfectly matched to its setting, with a feeling of rightness and serenity. They pulled up in front of the house, where three other smart cars were already parked. Oliver himself came down the steps to meet them. He was

wearing rather faded tweeds, a different picture from his immaculate London attire. He took Chiara's hand and smiled into her eyes.
'Welcome.' He greeted Isobel warmly. 'I expect you want to go to
your rooms first. I'll take you up.' The hallway was dominated by
an Adam fireplace above which a large oil painting of three fleshy
nudes glowed. 'Claimed to be Lely,' he said in answer to Isobel's
enquiry. 'The Three English Graces. My mother calls it The Three
English Arses.' Chiara could hear conversation and laughter in
another part of the house, and felt a twinge of apprehension.

Oliver led them up the stairs to their rooms, which were at
opposite ends of a long corridor. Her own was papered in pink
damask, with two large windows looking out over the lake, where
wildfowl were now clustering in the ice-free stretches. Her bed was a
four-poster hung with white linen. The logs in the grate had not yet
been lit, but the room was warm. Chiara was taken aback. 'Aren't
we sharing a bedroom?'

'Not with house guests here. That wouldn't be quite the done
thing,' he replied gently, kissing her. 'But I'll come to you tonight,
when everyone's asleep. That will be even more exciting than sharing a bedroom.'

She made a face at him. He left her to settle in. A lady's maid
appeared to help her unpack.

'Oh, there's quite a small party, Miss,' she said in answer to
Chiara's enquiry about who was in the house. 'There's Mrs de
Robillard, of course, she's down from London. And there's General
Granville and his wife and their daughter, Bryony. He was in the
last War with Mr Courtfield, they're old friends. What lovely under-
wear you have, Miss. *That's* not Utility.'

'It's Belgian, pre-war. Getting rather old now, unfortunately.
Who else is here?'

'There's Sir James Altringham and his wife, Lady Mary. He's
the cabinet minister, you know. And their two boys, though you

won't see much of them, they're never off a horse. So that's ten altogether, including your sister and yourself.'

It sounded far more the sort of company that Isobel would enjoy, and Chiara's heart sank. Isobel was at her best with politicians and such people. She knew how to talk. Chiara didn't, and feared she would probably reveal herself as a fool within five minutes. There was nothing for it, however, but face the music. She brushed her hair, checked her make-up and went downstairs to meet the company.

The guests had assembled in a large drawing room where a fire was burning. Isobel had come down before her, and Chiara could hear her voice. For a moment she was lost as she entered the room. There seemed to be far more than ten people present, though perhaps that was just nervousness. It did not help her nerves to see Oliver's mother walking briskly towards her.

'Ah, child.' As before, Chiara was struck by the whiteness and smoothness of Cécile de Robillard's skin, much of which was revealed in a black dress which showed off her legs and bust in a very un-English fashion. 'Did you have a perfectly dreadful drive down here, slithering and sliding on the ice?'

'Oh no, the driver was very careful, though he hardly said a word. Your son seems to prefer the quiet ones.'

'He has their tongues cut out,' Cécile replied. 'Speaking of which, your charming sister has been entertaining us all with her stories. Come and see if you can outdo her.'

With her arm firmly imprisoned by Cécile, Chiara was led over and introduced to the other guests. Oliver was not present. At first acquaintance, the Altringhams and the Granvilles were indistinguishable, self-confident, middle-aged couples at ease with the power they wielded and at home in this house. They studied Chiara with undisguised interest, if not with any great warmth. No doubt they had been curious for months about Oliver's liaison. The young people, who were more or less her own age, were friendly enough, but she felt tongue-tied and shy.

'I knew your father in the Great War. He was a fine officer,' General Granville said in his clipped way, 'and a good man. We could do with some of that generation now.'

Chiara murmured something appreciative. Her eyes were drawn to the full-length portrait over the mantelpiece, depicting a young woman in the clothes of the Twenties, holding a basket of roses.

'Oliver's wife, Margaret,' Cécile said, following Chiara's gaze.

'What a beautiful painting.'

'She was a beautiful woman. Younger than you when she died, *chérie*.'

'They got married after the Great War,' Mrs Granville informed Chiara. 'A real love match. Oliver and she were inseparable. It was a terrible tragedy.'

'How did she die?' Chiara asked.

'She had a weak heart.'

Chiara stared at the lovely face. The expression was serene, the mouth smiling. There was no foreboding of early death in that face. The painting was an emblem of youth and happiness. 'She's so elegant.'

'Oh, yes. She knew how to dress.' There was the faintest, pointed emphasis on that *she*. Chiara became aware that she was being scrutinized, especially by the two older women, who were examining her hands, clothes and shoes without any affectation of concealment. 'I must say,' Mrs Granville went on, looking Chiara up and down, 'the fashions of those days were a great deal more feminine than the sort of thing you young women wear today.'

'Well, that's not really fair,' Chiara smiled. 'We're all in Utility Clothing, you know.'

'I don't see how being dowdy helps the war effort,' Mrs Granville retorted. It seemed like a personal attack, and Chiara

felt her cheeks flush. 'Your sister seems to have more of an idea.'
The questions began. It was swiftly ascertained that she worked at the
Censor's Office and was twenty-seven years old.

'I told you to remain twenty-three forever,' Cécile said. 'You
didn't take my advice.'

'I'm afraid not,' Chiara replied, 'I let the years pass.'

'Very careless of you,' Cécile scolded her, 'you should have listened to me.' Her green eyes always seemed icy cold to Chiara, her
banter uncomfortable.

'What school did you go to?' Mrs Granville enquired.

'My sisters and I went to St Helena's.'

'I don't think I've heard of that particular institution,' Mrs
Granville said with a frown.

'It's a convent school in Sussex.'

'The Redcliffes are Romans,' her husband put in significantly.

'Ah. Jolly good.' Her expression said otherwise. 'Irish family?'

'Not that I know of,' Chiara replied, 'just eccentric.'

'Chiara may still be a Catholic, but I gave up superstitions a
long time ago,' Isobel said with a laugh.

'I don't think I'm anything any more,' Chiara said.

'Fascinating,' Lady Mary Altringham drawled. '*Not anything
any more*. There it is in a nutshell.'

'There what is in a nutshell?' Chiara enquired, feeling she was
being attacked again.

'Your lot don't play by any rules.'

Chiara felt herself colour. 'It seems to me that my life is full of
rules, which I disobey at my peril.'

'You young women generally do as you please nowadays,'
Lady Mary retorted, 'and I doubt whether any of you are the better
for it.'

Mrs Altringham glanced at her daughter Bryony, who was very
plain and overweight, hugging a cushion to her bosom on the sofa

as though trying to conceal her bulk. 'Thankfully, not all of them are like that.'

Chiara grew hotter still. They were clearly twitting her for being Oliver's paramour. Why wasn't Oliver here to defend her from these harridans? She felt like retorting that her own friends and relations were no more delighted by the alliance than the Granville or Altringham factions.

The grilling was mercifully brief. It was Isobel who held the floor, and the eyes soon turned back to her. To Chiara's dismay, she had once again brought up the subject of her political career. Chiara stood awkwardly with a cup of tea as Isobel held forth, effortlessly commanding the attention of all present.

'But why the Labour Party?' Lady Mary demanded with a frown.

'It's the party of the future,' Isobel replied authoritatively.

'I seem to recall reading a pronouncement of yours to that effect about the Nazis,' Lady Mary said dryly. 'Quite recently, too.'

Isobel was unembarrassed. 'I was mistaken about Hitler, not about Fascism. As a political system, National Socialism was near-flawless. The flaws that couldn't be predicted were the human ones – the aggression of the world towards Germany, and the ambition of the German leaders. The basic ideas are of benefit to all humanity.'

'Really,' someone said ironically.

'Oh yes. And if you remove the Nationalism from National Socialism, you're left with Socialism. It's the same idea. The greatest good of the greatest number. After the war, the Socialists are going to dominate politics all over Europe. Including here.'

'And you're going to be in the vanguard?'

'If it's humanly possible.' She laughed. 'They're going to be in charge of people like Us. Wouldn't you rather see a few people like Us on their benches? Or do you want to be at the mercy of the *sans-culottes*?'

Chiara glanced around at their faces. Were they impressed by Isobel? Or did they see her as a pretentious egoist?

'Do you ride?' one of the Altringham boys asked Chiara. He was a tall young man named Simon, about the same age as she was, to judge by appearances.

'I haven't ridden for years,' she replied, 'but I do enjoy it.'

'My brother and Bryony and I are going for a hack shortly on Oliver's horses.' He glanced at her obliquely from deep blue eyes. 'Would you care to join us?'

'I haven't brought any suitable clothes, I'm afraid.'

'Oh, there are bound to be some odds and ends lying about in the house. We can make you warm, if not stylish.' His voice dropped even further. 'Might be more amusing than listening to politics all day.'

She looked at him more closely. He had his father's long nose, but made crooked by some old injury; he was a presentable young man with a good mouth, arresting eyes and a pleasant voice. His brother Adrian was younger, a quiet boy of around nineteen, with similar features, barring the broken nose. Bryony Granville was unmistakeably horsy, robust and red-cheeked. They were all looking at her expectantly. It would certainly be nicer to be out with people of her own age rather than listen to Isobel boast all day. 'That's very kind of you,' she said. 'All right.'

'Let's *carpe* the jolly old *diem*, then.'

The four of them made excuses and slipped out. Chiara was aware of Cécile's sharp eyes following her as she departed. In the hall they met Oliver. Chiara had something of the sensation of meeting her old headmistress whilst bunking class. But he was very affable.

'There's a hacking jacket that should fit you,' he said, 'as well as some jodhpurs and boots.' He went with them to the tack room. The jacket turned out to be an ancient Barbour that smelled pungently of horse and musty wax. However, as he'd predicted, it did fit her, and luckily the other clothes were less unsavoury.

The horses, rather shaggy in their winter coats, seemed reluctant to be saddled and taken out of their warm stable. But she and the three other young people were soon riding away from the house towards the open land. The frosty air bit her cheeks and made her eyes water, but it was good to be out of doors.

'I say, your sister can talk a blue streak.' Bryony was riding her horse at Chiara's side. She wiped her nose, which was running with the cold. 'Wish I had that gift.'

'Do you?' Chiara said dryly. 'I'm not so sure I do.'

'She has everybody eating out of her hand. The best I can do is try to blend into the wallpaper.'

'That's usually my ambition, too. Isn't Simon in the army?'

'He's about to do his final exams at medical school in Oxford. He's very clever. He'll be a doctor by the summer, and he'll probably be snapped up by the army. Adrian's just been called up. This is his last week in civvies.'

They had reached a field which looked inviting. 'Shall we canter?' Simon Altringham called. They set off at a slow canter, picking up the pace until Chiara felt like laughing aloud at the pleasure of it. The sky above was cloudy, with blue patches, a true English sky, like the Constable she had given to Oliver.

The ground rose. They soon reached the brow of the hill. The landscape stretched out before them, open and soft. They broke into a gallop and spread out, Bryony and Adrian taking one way, towards the stream, she and Simon taking another, towards the woods.

The ride over the uneven ground was exhilarating, though the muscles of her thighs were soon aching with the unaccustomed exertion. It had been years since she'd ridden a horse. At the edge of the woods they changed gait into a walk again. The horses were steaming and Chiara was panting. Simon rode his horse close up against hers. She smiled at him. He leaned out of the saddle, hooked one arm around her neck and kissed her resoundingly on the lips. He was so forceful that she almost slipped out of the saddle

'What the hell are you playing at?' she exclaimed.

'You look so beautiful. I couldn't help myself.'

'You can't just kiss any woman you choose,' she snapped.

'It was an understandable impulse.'

'You're a very impertinent young man.'

'I'm the same age as you,' he pointed out calmly.

'I have a good mind to tell Oliver.'

'Don't do that. I won't try it again, don't worry.' They had entered the woods now, and were following a winding track, so she could hardly gallop away from him as she would have preferred to do. 'Speaking of Oliver, how did you meet him?'

'That has nothing to do with you.'

'It's a fair question.'

She glared at him. 'What's your implication? That because I'm Oliver's lover, I'm supposed to be available to the offspring of his friends?'

'I didn't mean that at all. It was a simple enquiry. Everybody's very curious about you, I'm sure you can understand that.'

'And you've been instructed to pump me for information.'

'Not at all.'

'Where does this path lead?' she asked coldly.

'Back to the house. We'll meet Adrian and Bryony there.' He glanced at her. 'Actually, I thought you'd be glad to be out of the limelight. You're taking a simple kiss far too seriously.'

'Kisses are not simple.'

'To me they are. At least, that one was.'

She maintained an icy silence all the way back to the house. Bryony and Adrian had not arrived yet. A young stable boy was on hand to help them unsaddle their horses and rub them down. Chiara wondered whether the short ride had been worth the vexation she'd suffered.

Carrying his saddle towards the rack, Simon paused and turned to her. 'Look, I've said I'm sorry. I don't want to get off on the wrong foot with you.'

'It's a bit late for that.'

'You looked very tense and unhappy in the drawing room. I could see you weren't enjoying any of it. After that gallop, you were like another woman. Radiant. I kissed you because of that, not because I was trying to seduce you. I was very sorry to see the unhappy look come back. It's not what I intended.' He went to put his saddle on the rack. He was broad-shouldered and lithe. She put her own tack away thoughtfully.

'All right,' she said at last, 'I forgive you. But don't do it again.'

'I won't.' He smiled. 'Unless you ask me to.'

☙

Chiara was hungry, and the lunch, rabbit stew with parsnips and other vegetables from the estate, was very welcome. The dining room was beautifully panelled, the table set with heavy Georgian silver. The centrepiece of the table was an arrangement of helle-bores, Oliver's favourite flower. The blooms were so dark as to be a true black. She recalled their first meal together, at Boodle's. That seemed a very long time ago now.

This was a magnificent house for entertaining, she thought, and it was sad that it was shut up so much of the time. Perhaps it was one of the things Oliver had deferred until 'when the war is over'. Oliver sat at the head of the table, his mother at the other end. Chiara tried to see herself as the mistress here, occupying an honoured place in Oliver's life, rather than the tangential one she now held. A pang of longing went through her. She wanted that so much that she had to stop herself from thinking about it.

After lunch, at Oliver's suggestion, they went for a walk because, as he said, 'It will rain later, and we'll regret not going out.' The sky had indeed become dark and lowering, a cold wind blowing across the water. The ten of them straggled along the shore of the lake in three groups, Isobel with Cécile, the Altringhams and the Granvilles, Chiara with Oliver, the younger people some way behind them.

He took her arm. 'You're very quiet, my darling girl. I've never known you so subdued.'

'This isn't altogether a happy experience for me, Oliver.'

'Why not?'

'Well, for one thing, I don't think your friends like me very much. They treat me as if I didn't belong here. The old hags were perfectly horrible to me in the drawing room while you were away. That's why I was desperate to get out.'

'They're plain-spoken people, but I hardly think they dislike you.'

'They do dislike me. And I don't blame them, Oliver.' She shot him a hot glance. 'I'm an impostor. You shouldn't have brought me here. I'm not your wife. I'm not anything. I don't have any status at all. They think it's shameful that I'm being presented to them.'

'You have Isobel to chaperone you,' he said mildly.

'Isobel! What kind of chaperone is she? She's making a complete fool of herself with all her boasting.'

'Actually, I think they're rather taken by her,' he said with a laugh.

'You didn't see their faces back there.'

'I think you're being oversensitive. They're entertained by her. They were very eager to meet you both.'

'Is that why you arranged this weekend?' Chiara demanded. 'To satisfy their curiosity?'

'I thought it was time you started to meet some of my friends.' He stooped and picked up a stick to throw for the spaniels that had accompanied them. The dogs rushed off in excitement. 'I'm not ashamed of you. Why should you be ashamed of yourself?'

'I'm not ashamed. I dislike being told I'm an immoral tramp by some boot-faced old bat. And under your roof, too.'

'Did they really say that?'

'Yes.'

'You once told me that you refused to have your life ruled by what your Aunt Patsy thought, or anyone else.'

'That seems a long time ago. I was twenty-three then. I'm twenty-seven now. And life's not such a lark any more. I'm starting to wonder what's going to become of us, Oliver. You and me, I mean.' The dogs came rushing back, two of them attached to the same stick. She wrested it away from them and threw it again. 'Am I going to spend the rest of my life in this state of limbo?'

'Chiara—'

Now that it was all coming out, she refused to stop the flow. 'I've waited for you during three years of war, wondering every moment if you were in a torture cell or in front of a firing squad. That wasn't funny. I think I've proved that I love you and that I'm true to you.'

'Of course you have.'

'How many more years, Oliver? Isn't it time you proved you're true to me?'

'You're twenty-seven, but I'll be forty-nine this year,' he said quietly.

'You don't need to rehearse that argument,' she said impatiently. 'I know it well. I love you as you are, and as you will be. I'm prepared to accept the difference in our ages. It makes no difference to me. Why should it make any difference to you?'

'It simply does.'

'So I can never expect to be your wife?'

'I told you before we ever became lovers that I was not a marrying man,' he said, his voice growing even quieter.

'And I accepted that,' she rejoined, 'because I was young and didn't know any better. But I don't accept it any more.' The dogs were scampering around them with the stick, barking for attention. Simon Altringham came up to them, yanked the stick away from the dogs and ran off up the path with the stick held high, the dogs leaping up at him, hysterical with the fun. 'He kissed me this morning,' Chiara said, watching Simon's frolics.

'Who kissed you?'

'Simon Altringham.'

Oliver frowned. 'Why did you allow that?'

'He took me by surprise. We'd just finished a gallop. He came up beside me and kissed me on the lips. I gave him hell, but it was too late by then, of course.'

Oliver followed her gaze towards Simon's tall, athletic figure. 'Is that supposed to make me jealous?'

'No, Oliver,' she said shortly. 'It's supposed to make you understand that my position here is untenable. He would never have dared be so insolent to me if I was your wife. As it is, everyone knows I'm only your mistress, and they treat me accordingly. His parents look down on me and talk to me as though I'm a tart, and he thinks he can sample the wares any time he chooses.'

Oliver gave her the ghost of a smile. 'Knowing Simon, I think he would have done the same even if you were my wife. I'm sure he didn't mean anything by it.'

'You're back in England now,' she said forcefully. 'There's no danger of you being captured by the Germans any more. You're going to be around. There's no reason for us not to be married.'

'Except that I don't want to be married,' he said calmly.

His tone was such that Chiara felt a dagger pierce her heart. She tried to catch her breath. 'Oliver!'

'I'm not telling you anything new,' he said unemotionally. 'I explained this from the start. It's not fair of you to bring it up here, now, in this manner, as though I've deceived you in some way. I haven't. I have been as clear as crystal with you.'

'It's been three years.' She heard the pleading in her own voice. 'Haven't your feelings for me deepened in any way at all?'

'That is not the point. The reasons for my not wanting to marry you were valid three years ago and they are just as valid now.'

'Yes, your reasons – that you don't want me to be tied to you when you grow old. When exactly will you grow old, Oliver? At sixty-five? Seventy? Can I expect to get my marching orders then? Is there a set date at which you'll tell me it's all over? How old will I be when you discard me? And what am I supposed to do when you do discard me? Just forget about you and go off to live out the rest of my life as though you and I never met?'

'Chiara, darling, don't do this.'

She was crying now, the tears burning cold on her flushed cheeks. 'Don't you see that it's absurd, Oliver! It's cruel and stupid and absurd. I love you, and unless you have no feelings for me, we can't go on like this!'

'Enough!' he said sharply. 'Stop. I made you no promises. I explicitly told you my conditions, and you accepted them.'

Shaking with emotion and the cold, Chiara found a handkerchief in her pocket and tried to staunch her tears. 'I was a fool.'

'The arrangement we have is the best possible solution.'

'For *you*. You can come and sleep with me any time you choose, and disappear again.'

The angrier he got, the colder he became. 'I don't see it like that.'

'But that's exactly what happens. It's just sex, Oliver. People who love each other share their lives. They live together, get married. Have children.'

'Children!' he echoed, exasperated.

'Yes, children! I want children! And I want them while I'm still young enough to have them!'

'If you want children,' he shot back, 'go to him.' He pointed to the distant figure of Simon Altringham.

She was too upset to continue arguing. She turned on her heel and walked back to the house. Bryony and Adrian stared at her as she strode past them, but said nothing.

She was thinking of all the warnings she'd been given when she'd first fallen in love with Oliver Courtfield, warnings she'd scorned and dismissed. They'd all tried to tell her, and she'd laughed at them all, because she'd known better. She'd thought she could change Oliver, that she would not be like all the others. What a fool she had been. She had given him three years of her life and she would never get them back. She was trapped now; she knew that she loved him far too much to leave him.

By the time they all returned from the walk, she'd got herself under control again, though the mirror told her that she was puffy-eyed and blotchy. It had started to rain. It was already dark at four in the afternoon, and the house now seemed gloomy, its rooms full of shadows.

Tea was served in the drawing room. The young people set up a Monopoly board next to the fire and played with frequent explosions of laughter and exclamations of triumph or dismay. Chiara declined an invitation to join them. Nor did she get close to the older couples, who were discussing politics with Isobel over buttered scones. She avoided meeting Oliver's eyes, though he was once again affable and urbane. She supposed he had been through these scenes many times in his life.

Cécile came to sit beside her with a glass of wine in her hand. She alone was drinking alcohol instead of tea. 'One of the few good things about being in this house,' she said. 'My late husband and his father between them laid down a good cellar.'

'Don't you like being here?' Chiara asked.

'Why do you think I left?' Cécile retorted. 'I hate this house. It's a prison.' She drank, savouring the wine. 'I see your eyes. You would like to be mistress here. Forget it. These are Dead Sea fruits. Your youth and your joy would crumble into dust here. Be thankful for your escape.'

'I'm tired of the life I have, Cécile. I want to be settled.'

'Is that what you are fighting with Oliver about? Did I not warn you that he will never trust a woman?'

'Yes, you warned me.'

'*Chérie*, marriage is a prison too, the worst kind, and the bitterest of the Dead Sea fruits. Ask your sister. I tell you again, you should thank God that Oliver is not *un homme de se marier*. It is a lucky escape for you.'

'And yet I want nothing more,' Chiara said sadly. It was strange to be confiding in Cécile, a person whom she did not trust, but there was nobody else. 'Other people seem to enjoy it.'

'They endure it. And at least Oliver is *amoureux*. Most marriages do not even have that.'

'It's as though he has a wall around his heart,' Chiara mourned, 'and I can't get through it.'

Cécile gave a grunt of exasperation. 'You have more to worry about than that,' she said irritably. 'I've got no patience with you, child.'

She went off, and Chiara was left friendless.

There were two extra guests at supper, a couple named Hilliard who were neighbours of Oliver's. The wife, Alice, was placed opposite Chiara at the table. She was in her forties, a willowy brunette with a sweet face which was made melancholy by the candlelight. Almost the first thing she told Chiara was that she'd never had children.

'My fault, I'm sure,' she said, 'though every cloud has a silver lining, doesn't it? The war, I mean. To have sons now . . .' Her voice tailed off and she looked down at her plate.

'I would like to have children, too,' Chiara said quietly.

Alice looked up brightly. 'Would you? I have dogs, of course, red setters.'

'They must be beautiful,' Chiara said, though privately she thought they were a rather foolish breed.

'They're a great joy. At least they help alleviate the boredom. Life in the country is endless boredom sometimes. And with the winter coming on . . .' She sighed. 'I do so envy you living in London, bombs and all.'

'I could do without the bombs. Perhaps we should swap places for a week at a time.'

'Oh yes, that would be fun, wouldn't it! Except you'd have Miles to deal with, and I'd have . . .' Her voice tailed off once again. She looked confused and embarrassed.

At the other end of the table, it was Isobel who was once again the centre of attention. Admittedly, she looked magnificent, the glow of the candles hiding any signs of her age. She was wearing a splendid evening gown, in striking contrast to the rather dowdy clothes of the other women. Dressing *à la mode* had always been her way of sticking two fingers up at the world. She was also wearing, Chiara noted, the emerald necklace and earrings which Felicity had given her when she'd entered the convent. By rights, Chiara thought, Isobel should give the jewellery back to Felicity now that she was out of the nunnery, but Chiara doubted there would be ever be any such initiative on Isobel's part. And Felicity was still too unworldly to be concerned with such things. So as usual, Isobel came out ahead.

Isobel was holding forth now in her usual authoritative way, supremely confident that everyone wanted to hear her opinions on everything under the sun. Chiara caught the ironic expression on Oliver's face, but he was too courteous to try to suppress Isobel at his dinner table.

'Your sister's very beautiful,' Alice Hilliard said confidentially. 'And so clever. You must be awfully proud of her.'

'Oh, we are indeed,' Chiara said, but Alice did not seem to pick up the dry note in her voice.

'Her book was absolutely thrilling. I couldn't put it down.'

'Of course the war is a racket,' Isobel was announcing in her vibrant voice. 'It's an immensely profitable business for the people who started it.'

This time she seemed to have gone too far for the Granvilles and the Altringhams, who responded furiously. It was Lady Mary's voice which rose above the chorus of outrage. ' – don't know how you can say such a terrible thing when our people are being slaughtered by the Germans and our cities are being pounded into rubble nightly!'

'Oh, it's a dreadful crime,' Isobel said collectedly, indifferent to the reaction she was provoking. 'But as the profits eclipse mere smash-and-grab, so too the injuries to life and property are vast. That's the way it works. A vicious thug knocks an old lady on the head for her handbag. A vicious government murders and steals from millions.'

'That may be true of the Nazis,' General Granville said loudly, 'but I'm damned if it's true of us!'

Isobel shrugged, maddeningly cool. 'What about the men who make the uniforms? The men who build the tanks and the bombers and the battleships? And all the rest, politicians and soldiers and the Establishment as a whole? Aren't you all cashing in, one way or another? It all means money for someone. The more work, the more money.'

'Is this the kind of thing you intend to say to your prospective constituents?' Oliver asked quietly. The distaste on his face was clear now.

'Yes, of course,' Isobel retorted. 'It's what they know to be the truth.'

'It's a damned lie,' the general thundered. 'And the working classes will never believe a word of it. They're too honest.'

'I fear that they will believe it,' Oliver said, even more quietly, looking at Isobel speculatively.

'But it's poisonous rubbish,' Lady Mary protested.

'It will have a very powerful impact,' Oliver replied. 'The Conservatives will have little hope against arguments like that.'

'No hope at all,' Isobel said serenely. 'It's very simple. Just a question of capital and labour. Slaughtering workers makes capitalists rich. We've had two great wars in a single generation. The workers will never vote Conservative again.' She sipped her wine. 'This is a wonderful burgundy.'

'It is a Nuits-Saint-Georges *premier grand cru*,' Cécile said. 'I congratulate you on having the palate to appreciate it.'

'One would have to be an ignoramus not to appreciate this. It's nectar.'

Cécile smiled her silky smile. 'Nectar of the gods, indeed.'

Sir James didn't care about the wine. 'I've never heard such nonsense,' he harrumphed, glaring around the table. 'What about patriotism? What about loyalty?'

'Those are concepts, my dear Sir James, which are going to have to be redefined.' Isobel smiled sweetly. 'If there's anything that the war has taught the working man, it's that patriotism will get him killed, and that he should be loyal only to himself.'

'I find that very sad,' Lady Mary said in a quiet voice. 'I thought that the war had taught us other lessons. To overcome class divisions, to end gluttony and waste, to work together.'

'That's the sort of notion my sister tries to disseminate to the press,' Isobel said, smiling down the table, 'Isn't it, Chiara? Charming but naïve.'

There was more outrage, but such was Isobel's charisma and beauty that within five minutes they were all eating out of her hand again, as Bryony had put it. Oliver alone remained cool, his eyes watchful as he continued to observe Isobel. Chiara recalled his joke at the Ritz about moving her MI5 file to the Left Wing section. He didn't take her nonsense seriously, did he? It would not be pleasant to have Oliver and Isobel as enemies. But she feared that was inevitable.

Isobel's theatrical behaviour at least kept the attention off her, but it was another unhappy occasion for Chiara. She spent the evening largely silent, ignored by all except Alice Hilliard, who seemed to content to have someone to talk to about her red setters.

At midnight the guests went up to their beds carrying glasses of warm Ovaltine or cups of tea from the kitchen, according to taste. Chiara bade Oliver an indifferent goodnight and went to her own room. She undressed and made preparations for bed. The logs in the grate had been lit, and there was a smoky, sweet smell in the room. She had forgotten how quiet the countryside was. Once a fox yapped, but otherwise the night was silent as the grave. She got into bed, wondering whether Oliver would come to her, as he had promised when she arrived. She suspected he wouldn't. All round, it had been a horrible day.

His touch woke her. She had inadvertently fallen deeply asleep, and she rolled over groggily. Hours had passed. 'Oliver? Where have you been? What time is it?'

'Shhh.' He slid into bed beside her and kissed her, his hand moving down between her thighs.

'Don't!' she protested, 'I want to sleep.'

He coaxed her into letting him have his way, but she was resentful and uncooperative. She lay stiffly, enduring rather than enjoying his attentions, her eyes shut. It was the first time, since they had become lovers, that she felt completely separate from him in their lovemaking. There was no union of souls, only a series of sensations, some pleasurable, some not.

When they had finished, she lay in his arms as she always did, and felt the tears sliding down her cheek. Oliver did not seem to notice. They did not speak. She drifted into sleep again, and when she awoke to the grey light of the morning reaching around the curtains, she was alone.

She belted her dressing gown around her waist and went down the silent corridor to Isobel's room. She tapped, but there was no answer, so she went in. Isobel was fast asleep in a pile of rumpled bed linen and scattered pillows, one pale arm hanging down.

'Do you want to come down to breakfast with me?' Chiara asked gently, touching Isobel's tumbled hair.

'Go away,' Isobel mumbled, clearly very grumpy. Chiara went downstairs alone.

❦

It was a misty, gloomy day. There was in the house a silent atmosphere of Sunday morning dullness and dreary duty. The breakfast room, with its heavy drapes, was dim. Apart from Isobel, the whole party had assembled for toast and marmalade before going to church. Their lovemaking had hardly been a reconciliation, and when she met Oliver at the breakfast table, Chiara was cool with him.

'You don't have to come to church, of course,' he said, pouring tea for her.

'I'm perfectly happy to tag along. I don't think I'll burst into flames or anything like that.'

'Where's Isobel?'

'Still in bed.'

'Typical,' someone muttered.

They went in several cars, the Altringham brothers leading the way in their sporty two-seater, Oliver bringing up the rear sedately in his Jaguar, with Cécile beside him and Chiara in the back seat.

Chiara had never been a person for sulks and moods. Walking up the path, past the lichen-speckled gravestones which sagged in the soft grass, she took Oliver's arm. 'I'm sorry I made a scene yesterday. You're right, it wasn't fair of me to spring that on you. I apologize.'

He patted her hand. 'Thank you.'

Roses were still blooming pink and white in the churchyard, though autumnal mist hung in the trees. The church itself was built of Cotswold stone, once golden, now grey with age. Chiara sat beside Oliver in the family pew. She took no part in the service, but absorbed the atmosphere of the church, the vivid stained glass, the murky flags of other wars, the high nave that resounded with the voices of the congregation.

Oliver led the responses in a loud, clear voice. He was very much at home in this setting, Chiara thought, where his roots went deep. She glanced at Cécile who, like herself, was sitting silent, her eyelids lowered. No wonder she had hated this life and had escaped it as soon as she could. She was an alien here and couldn't possibly feel anything but boredom and loneliness. That Oliver had grown up without a mother's love, she felt, had left a deep mark on him. The death of his wife had set the seal on his refusal to consider remarriage. He hadn't had very good examples of the institution to base his life on. All round, it was a tragedy.

The vicar delivered a sermon almost an hour long, which seemed to be mostly about his personal plan to end British military weakness. He went into great detail, and Chiara felt her eyes constantly closing, but Oliver listened as attentively as though to a great general.

The drive home after the service was slow, through a world that had been swallowed by the mist. Cows and hedgerows loomed out of the mist like primeval monsters, vanishing again swiftly in the billowing wake left by the cars.

When they got back to the house, Isobel had finally arisen, and was languidly breakfasting with the Sunday papers, wearing her dressing gown. The gown was loosely belted and revealed the creamy cleavage of her bust. The women muttered indignantly at her not having dressed yet, but Chiara noticed that the men couldn't take their eyes off her, including the Altringham boys, who eagerly claimed the seats on either side of her.

A wartime breakfast of country fare was on the sideboard. While Chiara helped herself to grilled field mushrooms and cold woodcock, a debate began over what to do with the rest of the morning. They were all leaving in the afternoon. The weather was still bad, and the older couples preferred to stay indoors, but the younger members of the party protested.

'What about going to White Horse Hill?' Simon said. 'It's only thirty miles away from here.'

'In this fog?' his father scoffed. 'You won't see a thing. Besides, you've been a hundred times.'

'The fog might clear,' Chiara said. The idea of staying in this gloomy house all day was repugnant to her. 'I haven't been there for years. I'd like to go.'

Isobel stretched languidly, exposing even more of her generous bosom to the attentive gaze of the males. 'Count me out. Tramping around the hills in the mist lost its charm for me years ago. I'm going back to bed.'

'And I must also excuse myself,' Oliver smiled, 'though not on such slothful grounds. There are a multitude of tasks I need to do around the place.'

After discussion, it was decided that Chiara, Bryony and the Altringham boys would go in the Altringhams' majestic Bentley. Lunch would be postponed to give them time for their jaunt, and they promised to be back by three.

Courtfield Park was one of the highest points in the county, and as they drove down into the Vale the mist thinned out somewhat. Chiara was sitting in the front seat beside Simon, Bryony and Adrian giggling behind them over some silly joke.

'Are you still angry with me?' he asked her, wiping condensation off the windscreen with his handkerchief.

'Not any more. Do I seem angry?'

'You've had a face like thunder since yesterday.'

'Ah. You're not the one to blame.'

'Glad to hear it. Your sister's awfully jolly, isn't she?'

'If you say so.'

'I do say so. I admire her. She doesn't give a damn about anything. I like people like that.'

'You feel an affinity, do you?' she said dryly.

'I do, as a matter of fact. She doesn't take life too seriously. That's a very good attitude.'

'Can we not talk about her?' Chiara said irritably.

'All right, let's talk about you.'

'I'd rather not, thanks, all the same.'

He shot her an amused glance. 'Last time I asked, you bit my head off, but I'll risk it again: How did you meet Oliver?'

'Initially, by chance,' she replied. 'But it turned out that he knew my father well, so . . .'

'So one thing led to another?'

'One thing led to another,' she agreed. 'Why are you so nosey?'

'Oh, I've known Oliver since I was a child.'

'And?'

'I'm just curious.'

'I believe that's characteristic of medical students. You're obviously bursting to give me a load of good advice, Simon. I advise you to keep it very brief.'

'All right,' Simon said, 'I'll be brief. You're young and he's old.'

'Your medical studies have certainly paid off,' she replied ironically. 'Thank you so much for the diagnosis.'

'You should be with someone of your own age,' he said.

'You're no longer being brief.'

'And you should be with someone you can rely on.'

'Can't I rely on Oliver?' she asked. 'You're not very loyal to your old family friend.'

'I know him very well,' Simon replied. 'He's a great man but he's hardly a domesticated one.'

Chiara laughed sharply. 'And you are domesticated?'

'I'm not proposing myself as a replacement.'

'Then what is this all in aid of?'

He shrugged. 'I've got an inkling what you two have been arguing about. I just want to tell you that it's not a blind bit of use. And the longer you wait, the harder it's going to be.'

She did not reply. They passed through the tiny village of Uffington and drove up the winding, crumbling road to White

Horse Hill. The mist was heavy here, and chances of seeing the horse itself from the road were slim.

'I hope we can find the damned thing,' Simon muttered, rolling down the window and peering through the mist.

'We're almost there,' Chiara said. As children, she and her sisters had tramped this rather eerie landscape with their parents, hunting out the ancient burial mounds and stone circles which were hidden among the hills. What would those vanished people have made of this war, she wondered, with its terrible machines which could rain destruction from the skies, killing thousands as easily as a man crushes an anthill with his heel? 'You can park here,' she said.

'I can't see anything. Are you sure?'

'Quite sure.'

It was cold and wet in the mist. They huddled into their coats. Chiara tied her scarf around her hair. Sheep were dotted across the hillside, tearing at the coarse grass; it was the only sound to be heard in an empty world. They walked along the drooping barbed-wire fence, where the tractors hadn't reached and the thistles had grown head-high through the summer. Simon was next to her, Bryony and Adrian amusing themselves by loudly reciting *The Charge of the Light Brigade* behind them.

'You're the opposite of your sister,' Simon said. 'You take everything much too seriously.'

'I used to be considered a madcap,' she said gloomily. 'I think the war's getting me down.'

'You need to pack up your troubles in your old kit bag,' he advised, 'and smile, smile, smile.'

'That was one of my father's songs,' she said, made even more despondent.

'Cannon to right of them,' Bryony and Adrian were chanting in the rear, 'cannon to left of them, cannon in front of them, volleyed and thundered!'

'Well, I'm almost a doctor,' Simon said, 'and my prescription is that you have a little fun. Don't spend your life with old fogeys. Go out. You must have lots of amusing pals in London.'

'I used to. They've fallen by the wayside, or been called up.' The truth was, she reflected, that in the past three years, she had deliberately shed almost all of her friends, avoiding them and turning down their invitations, so she could have every moment free for Oliver. They had persisted for a while, complaining. Then they had given up, one by one. The last to go had been poor Charlie Grosvenor, now tramping the forests of Burma with Orde Wingate. Of the gay whirl she had once enjoyed, nothing was left.

'What do you do in the evenings?' Simon asked. 'Sit at home, waiting for Oliver to show up?'

'Something like that.'

'And most of the time, he doesn't show up, I suppose?'

Chiara shrugged irritably. 'He's an important man. I can't expect to monopolize his time.'

'Still, it can't be much of a life. And working in the Censor's Office sounds awfully dreary. Look, next time I'm in London, I'll get in touch. We'll go out for dinner somewhere that has black-market champagne, and then trip the light fantastic in a night club. Put the roses back in your cheeks.'

'You don't give up, do you?'

He laid a hand on his heart. 'I'm a medical man. My intentions are purely therapeutic.'

'Yes, I can hear the milk of human kindness sloshing around inside you.'

'You're not married,' he said. 'It wouldn't be improper. What harm could we do?'

'Came through the jaws of death,' the other two chorused, 'back from the mouth of hell, all that was left of them, left of six hundred!'

The hilltop was bleak and bare. 'We're here,' Chiara said quietly. The huge figure of a galloping horse, carved into the chalk of the hillside, was now visible, the changing patterns of the mist revealing its outlines in glimpses. They all stood staring at it for a while.

'You'd need to be in a balloon to see it properly,' Bryony remarked. 'Did Bronze Age people have wings?'

'God knows,' Chiara said. 'Perhaps they were very tall.'

'Well, we came, we saw and we froze,' Bryony said. 'I'm starving, now. Let's go back for lunch.' She and Adrian set off back down the hill, still reciting Tennyson. Chiara and Simon lingered, staring at the chalk troughs that receded into the mist.

'I don't want you to be hurt,' Simon said.

'You're very concerned about my welfare,' Chiara said absently.

'I feel I owe it to you.'

'Why?'

'For one thing, you and I are the same age. They're a different generation. They like to tell us how wonderful they are, but they're mostly mental cases. The last war did that to them. We'll probably be the same, once this war has done with us. For another, I'm a family friend, insofar as Oliver has a family. I knew your predecessors, and I saw what happened to them.'

'Were there very many?' she asked, trying to sound light.

'There were quite a few.'

Chiara recalled a long-ago evening at Boulestin. 'Was a woman named Monica Langford one of them?'

'Yes. Your immediate precursor.'

'I see.'

'It's not a pretty story. She was married.'

'And did you know Oliver's wife?'

'I was a boy when she died, but I remember her well. She was a lovely woman.'

'I suppose none of us can match up to her,' she said dully.

'I don't think that's the problem,' Simon replied. 'People talk as though she was the great love of his life. But the fact is, he wasn't a good husband to her.'

'What do you mean?'

'What do you think I mean?'

In the silence that followed, they could hear Adrian and Bryony calling them from the car. 'Hurry up, you two! We're freezing!'

'We'd better go,' Chiara said, wanting to leave the place and subject of conversation.

They turned and set off into the mist.

∞

She returned to work on Monday to find her desk piled high with submissions. The war had reached a critical stage, and the journalists of Britain were writing furiously. The front pages of the newspapers were black with headline ink. The apparently inexorable German advance into Russia was finally faltering and coming to a halt. People said that now it was the turn of General Winter, that the coming Russian winter would ravage Hitler's armies the way it had ravaged Napoleon's a hundred and thirty years earlier. At Guadalcanal in the Pacific, the U.S. Navy had inflicted a heavy defeat on the Japanese. But for every victory there was added danger, it seemed. The might of Germany threatened on all sides.

In North Africa, a pitched battle was being fought around El Alamein. A large number of Allied tanks and troops were surrounded by Rommel's brilliantly directed forces. If they were destroyed or captured, the German path to Alexandria and then Cairo would be wide open. And Felicity was going to Cairo.

By contrast, Chiara's own work at the Censor's Office was often uninspiring. She was required to read everything submitted to her in great detail, and often it was difficult to assess the potential impact on the public. It was frequently not clear what would spread despondency and alarm, and was to be rewritten or suppressed, and what was a sober assessment of fact which was safe for public consumption.

The accusation that she was 'no better than Goebbels', which was frequently thrown at her by journalists and editors, always stung. Preventing the truth from being told was not an agreeable occupation. She had to remind herself that she was a part of the greater war effort, and that just as killing people was not an agreeable occupation, but necessary for victory, hers was a duty which had to be performed for the greater good.

The wail of the air-raid sirens sent them all down to the basement shelter at mid-afternoon, but the raid was apparently short, or it was a false alarm, for half an hour later, the All Clear sounded.

She left work with a sense of relief. Her office was in the monolithic Senate House in Bloomsbury, a new block which towered over the British Museum. It was the rush hour, and she decided that it was preferable to walk the two miles or so back to Tisbury Mansions, rather than fight for a place on the crowded buses. It would help clear her head of the day's business too, and give her time to think. The evening was cold and clear, and she walked briskly along the busy pavements.

The weekend in Oxfordshire had been a miserable experience. Many things haunted her memory: the delicate painting of Margaret Courtfield over the mantelpiece, things Cécile had said, the way Oliver had listened so courteously to a country vicar's dull sermon. If the weekend at Courtfield Park had been of any value at all, it had given her a deeper insight into Oliver's character, and how he had been formed.

At first, Simon's words had depressed her, but now she felt angry with him. Three years of her life had been devoted to Oliver.

Why should she give up now? Just because Simon Altringham, who wanted to get into her bed, told her to? That was absurd. What did he know about their relationship? The important thing was to understand Oliver and to be sympathetic to his needs.

He had always told her that marriage was out of the question. He fled from commitment. Of course, he never wanted to experience again the hurt he'd suffered in youth. That was understandable. But she could change that. He'd told her that if he fell in love, commitment would follow. Well, she was not like the others. She was young, unmarried, full of energy. Her youth and her innocence were the very things he needed most. None of the others could offer that. None of the others could heal him the way she could.

Above all things, he needed love. She could give it in abundance. And she would give it all the days of his life, unstintingly and unceasingly.

By now he loved her deeply, she was completely certain of that. She'd had assurances of his love in so many ways. He had opened his heart to her. After the horrors of war he'd been through, he'd come back to her and to no one else. For three years, she had been his beloved, and no one else. She would be different, she *was* different. They loved one another, and nothing else mattered. What was required was not retreat, but courage. They were committed to each other, and she simply had to make him understand that fact.

As she crossed Shaftesbury Avenue, she heard the clangour of fire engines and saw the familiar black clouds of burning buildings drifting over the Park, half a mile or so ahead of her. So there had been a raid, after all. Her heart sank. She hoped the bombs had not fallen too close to her flat. She quickened her pace.

By the time she reached Mayfair, she knew that the bombs had indeed fallen very close. One had landed in Hyde Park, and blown all the branches off a hundred trees, leaving them stark. She broke into a run, her heart pounding, everything starting to blur around her. Smoke billowed into her face, burning her eyes. It couldn't be. It just couldn't. For three years a magic spell had protected her. It couldn't be broken now.

Crowds of helpers and onlookers blocked her own street. She pushed through the mass of people, her heart pounding. The sight that met her eyes was shattering. Half of the little street had gone. It had turned into a landslide of rubble. Two fire engines were pumping water onto a pile of brick and blazing timber that had once been, she realized, the little church on the corner. Firemen were helping dazed survivors, wrapped in blankets, through the dust and smoke. One fireman carried a child, whose body was dreadfully limp.

Of Tisbury Mansions, nothing remained. There didn't even seem to be much rubble, just a gaping hole through which the next street could be seen. What had been an elegant Victorian structure had vanished into thin air, as though it had been made of paper. Gripped by a feeling of unreality, she trudged through the debris towards what until today had been her home.

'You can't go up there, Miss.' A grimy fireman took her arm firmly and stopped her. 'There might be unexploded bombs.'

'I live there,' Chiara said numbly, pointing. 'Tisbury Mansions.'

'I'm very sorry to hear it,' he said. 'Direct hit. Was there anybody living with you? Anybody who might have been at home? Kids, relations?'

She shook her head. 'Nobody.'

'Good. There ain't nothing left. It was just one bomber. No warning at all. Came up the Thames on his tod. Probably headed up north, got separated from his formation and decided to drop his load and scarper. Bad luck.'

'What am I going to do?' Chiara asked, like a child. 'Everything I had was in there. My whole life.'

'You sure there wasn't nobody at home?'

'I'm sure.'

He took off his helmet and wiped his sweating brow. 'There you are, then. You can start again. Possessions is nothing. It's people what count.' He shook her gently, seeing that she was in shock. 'Miss! Wake up! You need to get to the WVS.' He pointed. 'They'll give you a nice cup of tea to settle you down, and then take care of everything else you need. You got somewhere to go tonight?'

'My sister.'

'Good. Get a cup of tea and then go to her. All right?'

She nodded. None of this was real. It was all a dream, a dream from which she would shortly awaken and find the world right again. All she could find in the meantime were the trite words of a little girl. 'All right. Thanks ever so.'

'Come back tomorrow, lovey. You can look for your things, but I don't think there'll be much left.' He hurried back to his work.

She turned and walked back down the street. She looked up at the useless fleets of barrage balloons that hadn't saved her home. She was no longer a woman of substance. So much of her had been tied up in that flat – her money, her possessions, the paintings she'd invested in. Isobel would have to put her up. She would have to start from nothing. She didn't have a stick of furniture nor a rag of clothing. She was thinking of the flowerpots on her windowsill. The photographs of her parents. All her things. The cutlery and the crockery and the linen and the paintings and the clocks and the books and the clothes and the silver candlesticks –

A terrible thought struck her, so terrible that she stopped in her tracks. Oliver. He had a key to the flat. On occasions, he came to see her at this hour. What if he had done so today? What if he had been in the flat when the bombs had fallen?

Firemen were still working in the rubble, and they wouldn't let her in the street.

She felt as though her body had turned to water. There was a telephone box in Albion Street. It was still working, but there was a queue of people outside it, some of them neighbours from the street. Everyone needed the phone. Among them was Alf, the elderly porter from Tisbury Mansions. She took his arm.

'Alf! Did Mr Courtfield come to my flat this evening?'

'I didn't see him,' he said vacantly. He was evidently in shock, slack-faced and rheumy-eyed. 'I went out to take some letters for the last collection, and then I stopped to get some fags at Riley's. I was in the shop when the bomb landed. If it wasn't for the letters, it'd be curtains for me.'

'You're sure you didn't see him?' she pressed urgently.

'He could have come while I was gone. I was out for half an hour.'

'Damn,' she said under her breath.

'They got us at last,' he said. 'Bloody bastards.'

It was dark now, the hooded headlights of a few cars creeping along through the blackout. At last it was her turn to use the telephone. She dialled Oliver's office with trembling fingers.

'Mr Courtfield left the office at four,' the secretary told her. 'No, I haven't heard from him since.'

She replaced the receiver, her lungs empty, and stood there like a fool until the people outside began shouting and banging on the door. She emerged from the booth, trying to order her thoughts. Isobel's flat was in De Vere Gardens, across the Park. She could make more calls from there.

She set off at across the Park, trying to block the horrible images from coming into her mind. Oliver had spent years behind enemy lines, under their very noses. It was impossible that they could have killed him like this, at a distance of hundreds of miles, casually, by accident. Impossible, too, that their love should have been the cause of his death, that he should have been waiting for her when the bombs fell. Nevertheless, she started to run.

The trees loomed out of the darkness. The Park was empty, and nowadays frequented by thugs after dark, but it was the quickest route to Kensington. She was panting, the air icy in her lungs. She reached Kensington High Street and made for Isobel's. She would find out where Oliver was. He would be safe. There was no other possibility.

Isobel's building was a grand, neoclassical structure with a marble-pillared portico. Chiara rang the bell and the door almost immediately clicked open. The flat was on the fourth floor. She took the lift, a gilt-and-mahogany birdcage which ascended with unhurried dignity. It didn't matter, as the Cockney fireman had said. If Oliver was all right, nothing else in the world mattered. She would exchange it all for him.

She knocked on Isobel's door. It swung open to reveal Isobel, smiling warmly, already wearing a glamorous black peignoir though it was early evening. Isobel's smile vanished when she saw Chiara.

'What are you doing here?' she asked sharply.

'I've been bombed out,' Chiara said. She spread her hands. 'All I've got are the clothes I'm standing in.'

'Oh, Chiara. Damn it. Are you hurt?'

'No. I was at work. But I've got to find Oliver.'

'What do you mean?' Isobel demanded.

'He might have been in the flat. He sometimes lets himself in and waits for me. I need to use your telephone. I need to find him.'

Isobel shook her head brusquely. 'You can't stay here.'

'Why ever not?'

'I'm expecting someone. You have to go, Chiara.'

'This isn't a joke.' She stared at Isobel in incomprehension. 'Don't you understand? Tisbury Mansions is gone. Everything's gone. It's just a hole in the ground. Oliver might have been there!'

'He wasn't.'

'How do you know that?'

Chiara stepped forward but Isobel pushed her back, grim-faced. 'Go away. Come back in an hour. Everything will be all right then.'

'What's wrong with you?' Chiara asked. 'You're not listening to me!'

'I am listening to you,' Isobel replied impatiently, 'but you're not listening to me. Please, Chiara—'

They were interrupted by the arrival of a tall figure in the doorway. It was Oliver. Chiara flew to him with a sob and flung her arms around him. 'Oh Oliver! Thank God!' She found release in tears. 'I thought you were dead!' She clung to his broad chest. Oliver's arms did not close around her. He stood stiffly, unresponsive. She drew back and looked up at his face. 'Oliver, what's wrong?' He was staring not at her, but at Isobel. His expression was strained.

Chiara looked around. Slowly, painfully, she began to take in the details she had missed until now. The bottle of champagne in the ice bucket. The two glasses, side by side on the silver tray. The lights turned down in the apartment. Isobel's sheer silk peignoir, through which her naked body glowed. And more than all this, their silence and the expressions on their faces.

She faltered as though she had been shot through the heart. She heard herself laugh. 'This isn't what it looks like, is it?'

'I'm afraid it is,' Oliver said gently.

She swayed. 'Oh, I see. How silly of me. I thought you hated one another.'

'You had to find out,' Isobel said. 'We were going to tell you. I'm sorry it had to be today.' She pulled her peignoir closer around herself. 'She's been bombed out,' she said to Oliver. 'She's lost everything.'

'I'm very sorry, Chiara,' Oliver said gravely. 'We'll do everything we can to help, of course.'

'I was afraid you might have been in my flat. I see I needn't have worried.' Chiara tried to control her trembling. 'I'm sure I sound like someone in a play, but may I ask how long this has been going on?' Neither of them answered. She nodded, determined to hold herself together, at least until she got out. The important thing was not to break down in front of them. Something terrible had happened, after all, and there was nothing she could do about it. 'I don't want to interrupt your evening. Goodnight.'

They called after her as she hurried down the stairs, but neither of them tried to follow her. She stumbled several times, her knees giving way beneath her. The stair carpet was peacock blue but the stairs beneath it were mustard-streaked marble. It was a poorly chosen colour combination, she thought, very poorly chosen.

She emerged into the cold, dark night.

∽

It had been raining heavily for the past fortnight. The world seemed drowned to Chiara. Even these hurrying crowds wore blind, white, drowned faces. It was an ill-omened thought. The *Albion* loomed over the quayside, trails of rust striping her black and red flanks. Rows of faces peered out of her portholes, some incurious, some laughing or weeping or waving hankies.

Chiara was carrying Felicity's passport and papers for safety – Felicity herself was trembling with alternating grief and excitement. The immigration officer was impatient.

'Which one of you is sailing?' he demanded irritably.

'She is,' Chiara said, indicating Felicity. 'But I want to go on board with her to see her settled in. She's my sister.'

'You've only got half an hour,' he warned. The officer stamped Felicity's documents, gave Chiara a deck pass, and waved them through. Lugging Felicity's two heavy suitcases, they joined the bustle of people shoving up and down the gangplanks. Hawsers were being reeled in, steam was billowing from the *Albion's* funnel. The deck thrummed underfoot.

The purser signed Felicity on board and showed them the gangway to the lower decks, where the cabins were. The *Albion* had done long service as a mail boat on the East Africa run, and had now been recommissioned in her dotage to carry military personnel. Most of the passengers were in uniform of one sort or another. She smelled of diesel and stale seawater. Chiara led the way down determinedly, following the numbers and letters stencilled on the bulkheads. Felicity seemed dazed among the noise and the crowds. As it turned out, she was going to be sharing her poky cabin with three other young women, who were unpacking their things. None of them looked very happy, and one, whose name was Sydney, was crying her eyes out. They made introductions. The other two were called Dora-Ann and Jennifer. All were, like Felicity, bound for Cairo, and were already squabbling over the upper bunks, which were thought to be more desirable. Chiara heaved Felicity's suitcases onto one of the uncontested lower bunks. It was opposite a porthole, which Chiara opened, letting damp, cold air into the cabin, which was stifling with scent and tears.

'You'll be better off down here, anyway,' she told Felicity in an undertone, as Sydney sobbed loudly. 'A lot cooler when the weather gets hot, and not so far to fall if it gets rough.'

'I'll unpack later,' Felicity said. 'Let's go up on deck and spend the last bit of time together.'

'All right.'

They clambered back up the companionways. A light rain had started to fall, but that didn't keep passengers from thronging the rails, waving to the hundreds of people on the quayside. A young woman at the rail was screaming, 'Mummy! Daddy!' to her family down on the quay. Nobody here knew when or where they would see their loved ones again. The journey was an immense one, since the Mediterranean route would take the ship through enemy waters. Instead, the *Albion* would have to go all the way around Africa and through the Red Sea to Aden. When Chiara thought of the dangers that faced this rusty old boat, her heart failed her – submarines, the Luftwaffe, the storms and shoals and rocks along the way, all of these could take Felicity from her, and Felicity was her only remaining sister.

'Are you going to be all right?' Felicity asked, linking her arm through Chiara's.

'I was just going to ask the same about you,' Chiara replied with a wry smile.

'I'm getting away from it all,' Felicity replied practically. 'You have to stay here and face it.'

Chiara was silent for a while, thinking of all the things she had to stay and face. 'I'll get through it,' she said at last.

'I know you will. But I'm so very sorry, darling.'

'It's my own fault.'

'How can it be your fault!'

'I made scenes. Especially during that awful weekend at Court-field Park. I drove Oliver into Isobel's arms.'

'That's ridiculous,' Felicity retorted. 'Don't blame yourself for their disgusting behaviour. It's simply unforgivable. I'll never speak to Isobel again as long as I live!'

'I don't want that.'

'Never,' Felicity repeated with emphasis. 'And nor will you.' Chiara didn't want to think about it now, but Felicity was going on. 'Bloody, bloody Isobel! She can't bear to see any of us happy! She destroys everything we have. She did the same to me.'

'It's all over now. I'm all right. *This life's a dream, an empty show*,' Chiara said, quoting from the sampler that had hung in their childhood playroom. Felicity joined in, and they chanted together,

'But the bright world to which I go, Hath joys substantial and sincere; When shall I wake and find me there?'

'If I was a man, I'd never choose anybody over you,' Felicity said. 'Oliver must have lost his mind.'

It was not a subject Chiara wanted to pursue. 'I hope your cabin-mates are going to be fun. You've got a long voyage ahead of you.'

'You should get out of London. Maybe out of England altogether. Get yourself posted abroad, like me.'

'Thanks, but no, thanks. I'm going to stay and see it through.'

'Bombs and all?'

'Bombs and all.'

An officer strode down the deck with a loud hailer, bawling, 'All shore crew and non-passengers to leave the ship in five minutes. Five minutes!'

To underline his command, the ship's horn unleashed a huge, prolonged blast of sound which made Chiara and Felicity put their hands over their ears. The deck began to bustle even more frantically as people hugged and wept and jostled. The old iron ship gave a shudder, like a dog awakening, and there were shrieks of dismay from those who still had to get off.

'Promise you'll write,' Chiara shouted over the hubbub. 'Every week!'

'I promise!'

They embraced tightly. The sun emerged from the rain clouds for a moment, low and dim, sending a slanting light across the milling crowds, illuminating the flabby underbellies of the barrage balloons that hung over the docks. Departures and arrivals were hasty affairs these days; there was always the danger of an air raid at any moment. Felicity was slim and fragile in Chiara's arms, little more than a girl. For the first time, she confronted the awful reality of losing this sister whom she loved so much, of not being able to hold her or look into her face for months, perhaps years. How bleak that prospect was! She felt bereaved, alone, wounded to her soul.

Suddenly, someone else was trying to get between them. To her dismay, Chiara saw that it was Isobel, who had arrived at the last moment, wearing a large felt hat and carrying a bottle of whisky with a ribbon round the neck, as though going to a party.

'I know you didn't want me here,' Isobel said, 'but I couldn't stay away. I had to see you both.'

'Go away!' Felicity's face was turning very red. Her mouth was screwed up, and she seemed to be trying to push Isobel violently away for a moment; but Isobel resisted fiercely. They grappled, the way they had done as children. Chiara had a flashing memory of their nursery fights, tearful and vicious, which Isobel always won. And as she had the thought, Felicity crumpled, and suddenly they were all hugging each other and crying bitterly. Chiara felt emotions pierce her heart like thorns – rage, desolation, tenderness.

'I didn't mean to hurt anybody,' Isobel said through her tears. 'Of course I didn't!'

'Well you have,' Felicity blurted out, holding her hanky to her eyes. 'You've ruined everything!'

'I haven't. It's for the best. It'll all be all right. You'll see.'

'Rubbish! You're a monster.'

'I'm not. It wasn't meant to happen.'

'It never is. But it always does! You can't bear to see either of us happy. You have to take away whatever we've got. You think it's your bloody right! Well, you're going to be punished for it. Look what you've done to Chiara. God will punish you. Just wait and see.'

'Oh, please spare me that guff. It's just the way of the world.' Isobel turned to Chiara, who so far had not said a word. 'It's not true,' she repeated, as though imploring Chiara to believe her. 'It wasn't deliberate. It just happened! Darling, you have to talk to me and Oliver.'

Chiara just shook her head. 'Goodbye, Fee,' she said in a low voice.

'Take this.' Isobel thrust the whisky into Felicity's arms. Chiara saw that it was Lagavulin, no doubt from Oliver's private store. Isobel's lipstick had left a vivid red smear on Felicity's cheek. 'If you don't want it, you can swap it for something you do want.'

People were streaming to the gangplank now. 'Come along ladies,' the purser shouted, 'we're casting off. Buy a ticket or go ashore.'

The press of people pulled them apart. Felicity was left forlorn, her face wet with tears, as Chiara and Isobel were borne away from her. They didn't speak to one another as they left the boat. Isobel was ahead of Chiara in the crowd. Chiara had a sudden, raging urge to pull the large felt hat off Isobel's head and throw it into the dirty water of the bay. She resisted.

They joined the multitude on the quay and looked up, squinting against the gusts of rain. The rails of the *Albion* above them were so crowded that they could barely make out Felicity, waving her hanky over somebody's shoulder.

'I hope she's going to be all right,' Isobel said. She was no longer crying. She gave Chiara a shrewd look as she repaired her makeup. 'How long are you going to keep up the great stone face, Chiara? You have to come to terms with us, you know.'

Chiara made no reply. She'd promised herself never to engage with Isobel or Oliver, but to maintain a complete separation from them. To indulge in reproaches or recriminations would destroy what little peace and dignity she had left.

She'd been warned. They had all tried to warn her. They had all told her so. She hadn't listened. How could she? She'd been so much in love. And only the burned child truly understands the fire.

She'd spent years in the pursuit of folly. Isobel and Oliver weren't like that. They were powerful personalities, used to having their own way in everything. Neither was ever going to admit any fault. They thought they were above the rest, and to a great extent, they were – cleverer, stronger. She didn't wish them any ill. It was just a pity for others who got caught up in their chariot wheels.

The past weeks had been terrible. A vale of tears. She was only starting to emerge from that darkness. Chiara thought of the women from Oliver's past she had occasionally glimpsed while they'd been together. Was she going to become one of those haunted wraiths? She wouldn't allow that. She had to be strong. She would gather her forces.

The sun slipped down, tinting the docks in paintbox colours. Half the buildings around them had been blitzed. The orange sky glowed through empty windows. Chiara glanced up at the clouds. German planes could burst through the clouds at any moment, as they had done so many times before, scattering death. But the lurid sky remained peaceful.

With a succession of deafening blasts on her siren, the *Albion* cast off. A busy tug nosed her out of her berth and nudged her down the river towards the open sea. Chiara watched the ship recede in the gathering darkness. It became a silhouette, dim and fading. Beyond the river mouth, the rough sea waited to carry Felicity to an unknown future.

She was aware of something departing from herself, too. She was not sure what it was. There were no words to describe it yet. But a part of herself that was innocent, trusting, young, was sailing away with Felicity. And she knew that it would never return. An era of her life had ended. Another was now beginning.

She had loved and lost. But she hadn't lost herself. She still had her gifts, her strength, her integrity. And with those, she could go far.

She could no longer make out the *Albion*. She turned and walked away. 'Chiara!' she heard Isobel call behind her. 'Wait!'

Chiara found herself crying, though she'd vowed not to give way. She wiped her eyes.

'Chiara!' Isobel was still calling her name, but Chiara didn't look back. She walked away quickly, determinedly, towards her own destiny.

ACKNOWLEDGMENTS

My heartfelt thanks go to the people who licked the manuscript into shape, especially Emilie Marneur, Jenny Parrott, Catja Pafort, David Haviland, Frances Smythe and Jenny Morton Potts.